INVERSIONS

M V MELCER

Storm
PUBLISHING

Ebook ISBN: 978-1-80508-366-5
Paperback ISBN: 978-1-80508-368-9

Cover design: Phil Dannels Design
Cover images: Phil Dannels Design

Published by Storm Publishing.
For further information, visit:
www.stormpublishing.co

ALSO BY M V MELCER

The Guardian Cycle

Refractions

To Jan, for giving me my dream

NOTE TO READER

Dear Reader,

Inversions follows up from the events of *Refractions*. I believe the books are best appreciated if read in order, however, they can be read separately. As a reminder, I have provided a summary in the **Appendix**. Beware, the Appendix contains spoilers for *Refractions*, so if you have both books, start with the first!

M V Melcer

PROLOGUE

Video message
From: Nathalie Hart, Rescue Ship The Samaritan, *Bethesda*
To: Jason Nevsky, Canada, Earth
Sent: 15 July 2348
Received: 13 December 2354
Play message

Jason! My little boy! Is this really you? I'm looking at all the
pictures you've sent, months and years flashing between every
image, and I just can't stop crying with joy. You're a man now!
Your smile's so much like your father's, but your eyes are your
mother's. I can see both of them in you now. They'd have been
so proud... Oh, damn, forgive the tears. It's only been a few
months for me. Barely a blink. I can still feel your tiny hand in
mine that day when Feidi was burning, and I was going away. I
thought you'd never forgive me. I'm so sorry, Jason. I should
have stayed; I should have been there for you. I just... I wasn't
quite myself in the days after your parents died.

But enough of the past. It's the present that matters, and the future. You're older than me now, can you believe it? That's what thirty-five years in cold-sleep will do! I had a five-year-old nephew when I left—and now you have a daughter about that age. Anna Nathalie! You named her after us, too, after my sister and me. Thank you. And there, I'm crying again. But these are happy tears, believe me. I hope she grows up to be as happy and proud of you as I am. I hope to see you both when I return. One long sleep for me. Another thirty-five years for you.

I wish this was all I needed to share with you, Jason. Just the joy of seeing you alive and happy. But you must have heard our report by now, the truth about what happened here on Bethesda. How the Yun Ju factions used the first human colony in deep space as a field test for a new Mind-Link, a technology they designed to control our minds, our very thoughts and desires. I'm sure that's what everyone's talking about, speculating about those responsible and demanding that they be brought to justice. It must happen, yes—but I fear that the rest of our message will be lost in the fervour. This is why I have to tell you, why I have to beg you to remember.

The people behind the conspiracy, they call themselves Destiny —a Yun Ju faction so secretive that even most in the orbitals don't know about its existence. I doubt they'll ever be found. Destiny have planned for this; they will hide and divert attention till public interest has waned and the matter forgotten. They will remain concealed till the time is ripe for their return. I do not dare to think what they will try next.

But that's not all I need you to remember, not even the most important. See, I believe Destiny were right—not in their methods, of course not—but in the reasons why the mind control device was conceived. Destiny thought it was the only way to save our world from collapse. And here's the truth, Jason, the fact no one wants to face: we are on the brink. Earth has never adapted to the changed climate; we've never recovered from the scarcity wars and the plague. We told ourselves that we have, that the worst was behind us, and we squandered the few resources we had left. We focused on trade wars and national rivalries instead of working together. But time's running out. The tipping point is approaching—unless we find a way to stop it.

Mind-Link was designed to compel people to live more sustainable lives, to focus on their communities, the common good. That's what Destiny believed, why they sent one of their own—the man who called himself the Guardian—to give his life to protect the secret. They had to be stopped because such mind-control technology can't be allowed to exist. No one, no individual or a faction can wield such power and never let it be misused. That's why we sent the message, why we warned you about it.

But the tragic truth is, without it, there's nothing stopping humanity from descending into total war once food runs out. And it will, sooner than anyone wants to admit. I'm scared, Jason. Scared for you, for your family, for the world I'll find when I return. I hope we—you—will find your way through it.

I wish I had some words of wisdom, some useful advice to share. I'm sorry to leave you with this, to abandon you to fend for yourself once again. But you need to know the truth so you can fight for a better future. I know you're a fighter, Jason, you have it in your blood. A fighter like your father, and your mother. Like me, even, for what little I've been able to do. Don't let the worst happen, Jason. It's up to you now. Save yourself, and save them all.

I love you, kiddo. Always will.

End message

ONE

JASON

Jason taps his wrist-pad, then points its little camera at the map projected above the meeting table: squares and rectangles of farmland surrounding a pitiful patch of green. Apparently, even the wrist-pad's tiny machine brain understands the situation better than the gathered heads of Brazil's new government. It fires a new projection, bright enough to overwrite their suggestions. The green patch is now twenty times as large, reaching almost to the edges of the map, the entirety of the Pará region.

The people around him groan; a few swear loudly. Jason's used to that. They represent the food industry and the farmers; they've been appointed to fight for their interests. Recreating the rainforest contradicts all their election pledges.

'This is the absolute minimum of land we need to achieve the necessary biodiversity,' he says. 'Anything less and we might as well not bother.'

A sharp-faced woman leans over the table. Souza, the Science and Education Minister, if he remembers correctly. 'Our estimations suggest we could start with a much smaller patch—'

'Which would promptly die. Sure, we could plant some trees. Drop in some animals for decoration. But that's not a rainforest, and certainly not one that can be hoped to survive and expand.' Jason pauses. The faces around him are angry and defiant—yet the way they keep staring at the projection and not at him tells him they know he's right. Their experts have told them the same. It's just reality that refuses to conform to expectations.

'We can't do this,' the eagle-nosed Agriculture Minister says. 'We can't afford to lose so much farmland.'

'We've got no choice.'

Several people start to protest but they all fall silent as Manuel Queirós, the President himself, weighs in.

'Yes, we do, Mr Nevsky. It is still our country, our land. Our decision.'

Jason stifles a sigh. He hoped it wouldn't come to that, but it always inevitably does. 'Your land is not an island, Mr President. Destruction of the Amazon was one of the factors that put us here. And now you rely on the aid my organisation provides —just as much as the rest of the world relies on you to try to fix the damage we've caused.'

Their eyes meet. Queirós understands the warning in Jason's words, and so do all the others: past the ecological Armageddon, no country can be self-sufficient. The Food Alliance decides on the best locations for each crop, and all the members share in the harvest. Provided they do their share and follow the Alliance's orders.

'Mr Nevsky, do you realise how many people will starve if we do what you say?' President Queirós says flatly.

'And how many will if we don't?'

'We don't know that. We don't know the future. But we know the children alive today, the children who will die while we waste land resources on someone's hobby project.'

Jason's fingers curl into a fist. 'That's exactly the kind of thinking that brought us into this situation, Mr President. Thinking about now and hoping the future will take care of itself. It won't. It will only get worse. The tipping point—'

Manuel Queirós taps the table. 'Spare me the propaganda at least. I realise you're beholden to your family's gospel, but that one false prophet has caused the world as much damage as the climate disaster.'

Jason winces. He's used to insults, but few cut as deep. Twenty years ago, his aunt's message from Bethesda gave Earth a wake-up call. The second ecological tipping point was closer than they'd let themselves believe. For a moment, the world stopped squabbling. The leaders got together to figure out the plan: pool resources, optimise what was left, regulate and rebuild. Jason, already an expert in sustainability, was a natural choice to head the newly appointed Food Alliance. Over the nineteen years since its creation, he's given all his waking hours to keeping the world fed even as the fleeting unity that created his job fractured, and the world fell back into conflict and antagonism.

But it seems the more successful he's been at preventing a disaster, the less people like Queirós believe it was ever a risk.

'You are free to go it alone. The membership in the Food Alliance is entirely voluntary,' Jason says coldly. It's a gamble, one he's played too many times. A day will come when someone calls his bluff. Not today.

He waits another moment, but nobody in the room seems to breathe. Jason shuts down his pad and slides it into his shoulder bag. 'I'll be expecting the report on your progress on the rainforest revival. Your officials have received full details of what that entails.'

He pushes up from his chair and heads to the exit, his footsteps echoing in the deadly silence he leaves in his wake. Something splatters; someone has spat on the floor behind him. Jason almost smiles. He's learned to take that as good news—such hate means they've resigned themselves to cooperation. That *is* better than the alternative. Not for him, nor for any of them, for sure. But for the world. For the future.

Government security deposits him into the same armoured vehicle that brought him here from the airport. The windows turn opaque, but that makes no difference: everybody in the city knows who's come to visit. Angry crowds fill the streets, spitting, shouting, and throwing excrement at the speeding car. Jason still remembers the good old days when they'd be throwing rotten vegetables, but no food remains uneaten long enough to rot anymore.

He forces his attention to the meeting notes, then flips to the briefing for his next destination, his mind refusing to focus. He looks up as the vehicle slows down. A siren blares in the distance. Hoarse, amplified voices order the protesters to disperse. He speaks no Portuguese, but the police calls sound the same in all the languages he's heard. That's why he's here, why he insists on attending these meetings in person—so no one can tell him he doesn't understand, that he hasn't seen the worst. He makes himself look, staring through the frosted windows at the hungry faces, the scrawny children with large eyes and swollen bellies, the work-worn arms clutching stones and then hurling them at his car. At him. Then the spray of a water cannon hides them behind a frothing curtain and the convoy moves on again.

Jason's lip cracks between his clenched teeth, the taste of blood on his tongue. He wipes his mouth, then his eyes. He didn't make them hungry, he tells himself for the millionth time. If he feeds them now, hundreds of others somewhere else will starve. It doesn't matter how much it hurts. He can't save them all. He can only keep fighting, for as long as he's alive.

. . .

The silver blimp-jet waits behind a heavy cordon of armed police drones. It's a sleek, arrow-shaped machine, half airship, half hydrogen-powered jet, the most fuel-efficient thing ever created. Jason's aide, Aya Nakamura, waits at the door. One look at Jason and she doesn't ask how the meeting went.

Usually, his two aides would have accompanied him to the meeting, but Otto's heart problems have finally forced the man to retire. The inter-governmental panel that oversees the Alliance took forever to approve Otto's replacement, and then even longer to issue travel permits—meaning the new aide only joined them this very morning. Aya stayed behind to bring the man up to speed, as much as could be done in those few hours.

Jason climbs up the stairs to the aircraft, then turns right into the open area they use as their field office. To the left are the tiny cabins where they can sleep and rest between destinations. Jason could definitely use a break, but now's not the time.

'Are we clear to depart?'

Aya nods. 'Uri's confirmed the routing and the permits.'

'Tell him we're ready.'

Aya moves to the front, to what once would have been called the cockpit back when flying machines still required human pilots. Now it's just another workstation, one occupied by the blimp's four-person logistics and security team. He can see Uri's bulk as the man nods in confirmation of Aya's message. A moment later, the whining of the engines grows louder, then softens again as the frequencies exceed the range of human hearing. The floor vibrates, and the ground behind the windows slides down and out of Jason's sight. If only he could forget as easily.

He circles the round projection table in the middle of the floor and slides into the seat opposite his new aide. Khalil Ahmed seems about thirty, lean if rather short, with olive skin, thick dark hair and tar-black eyes.

'How did the meeting go?' Khalil asks.

Jason tries not to cringe. Instead, he reaches for the coffee jug. He takes a cup, then glances at Khalil, but the man shakes his head.

'Too much already.'

Jason fills his cup and takes a sip. 'Your CV says you worked in population trends. Are you a statistician?'

'Double masters, in statistics and environmental management. Undergraduate in anthropology, but I decided it was too much theory. Fascinating, but not for when the world is on fire, if you know what I mean.'

Jason sniffs. 'You can say so.' He taps the top of the table to call up the display. 'I guess you've heard about our purpose in Brazil?'

'Yes, Aya's briefed me on the issues. How did the government respond?'

Jason leans back. He tries to keep his voice steady. 'What do you think?'

'Well, the data's very clear on what needs to be done, so—' Khalil pauses at Jason's loud snort. 'They didn't agree?'

Jason points to the window but keeps his eyes on the man. 'There—you can see the protesters from here. Just not how skinny and desperate they are. Or how much they despise us.'

Khalil freezes, half-turned to the window. He was going to look, but now he's afraid, the reality of their position sinking in. The sooner, the better, Jason thinks, even though a part of him regrets destroying the man's naivety.

'You've never travelled, have you.' It's not a question. Few people can, nowadays, and the restrictions are only getting tighter. He's often wondered if travel would make a difference, if people could meet and see with their own eyes how the others live—or try to. But maybe it'd make things even worse. There's so much hatred now, so much blame.

'I was born in Quetta. Then I got the apprenticeship with

the Alliance.' Khalil looks at his hands. 'Pretty much stayed on the campus since then. My work was strictly on data.'

'I'm afraid reality's slightly less... forgiving.'

'So, what's going to happen here? Can they refuse?'

'They can, but they won't,' Aya says, sliding into the third chair, a cup of coffee in her hand. 'They can't afford to. If they drop out of the Alliance, they'll lose access to the anti-phage treatment. They won't get seeds modified for their acid soil or any new tech we get from the Yun Ju. We provide them with what they need to survive.'

Jason nods. 'Have you shown Khalil the map?'

'I thought you'd rather do it yourself.'

Fair enough—he's the one who created it, gradually, over the last two decades. Jason types the familiar set of commands to call up the master-map. The pixels float up and congeal into the image of the old Earth, the one still familiar through the centuries of maps. It rotates slowly, just long enough for the viewer to realise what they are about to see. The land changes first: the green of the Amazon turning muddy brown, the Sahara bursting out in a yellow flood, the forests of central Africa wilting into red deserts. The oceans go next: swelling, swallowing, turning swathes of land into archipelagos of scattered islands. Grey smudges mark land ravaged by the rotting phage that crawled out of the thawed permafrost. Annotated bursts play out the history of plague and famine, the scarcity wars, and the new peace.

Khalil glances up at Jason, slightly puzzled at the history lesson. Jason raises his hand: *Wait.* Over the years, he's discovered that the message has the intended impact only with this introduction. The map changes again: every strip of fertile soil tagged for optimal corps, supply lines criss-crossing the globe: wheat, soya, rice, fruits, and legumes, ocean-floating plantations, and fish farms. The threads multiply and tangle, each supply and barter chain marked for volume and complexity. The end result looks like a tangled mess of wires or what remains of a ball of yarn after it's been played with by a dozen kittens.

Khalil leans forward, his lips puckered in concentration as his eyes try to follow the trails then get lost in the snarl. He nods appreciatively. 'Impressive work. I mean, I knew it in principle, but never all together like this.'

Jason and Aya exchange glances. The complexity is part of the message, yes. But not the most important one.

Jason touches another button. 'The green and lime lines are where we have surplus, yellow where we're meeting demand. The redder it gets, the closer we are to shortages.'

As he speaks, the supply lines start to glow: first the few green ones, then the limes, and yellows. Finally, the oranges spill out, wrapping the globe in a tight tangle until it looks like a glowing lump of coal.

The apple in his throat jerks as Khalil swallows. It takes him a moment to speak. 'Is this...?'

'The tipping point,' Aya says. 'We're at it.'

'But I thought...' Khalil trails off. He shakes his head. 'What now?'

Jason doesn't meet his gaze. He wants to sound hopeful, but his voice comes out heavy. 'We can hold at this level for a couple of years. If our plans succeed, we'll start crawling back from the brink. If not...' He touches another button. 'Any deviation tips us over the edge. This is what another wave of the rotting phage will do. Or population growth a quarter of a per cent higher than predicted. Or a bad hurricane season.'

On the projection, the orange lines turn flashing red. Like blood or flames, Jason thinks, he can never decide which. It means the same, in the end. Famine, the third Horseman. War will come next, the final Horseman to complete the Apocalypse.

Khalil pulls his gaze away from the projection, his lips pale. 'Do... do people know this?'

'We keep the governments informed. Not that it makes much difference. Those who believe us get voted out, and those who don't... At best, they say we're too pessimistic. At worst they accuse us of fear mongering to keep ourselves in power.' Jason sniffs at that last word. *Power.* To do the dirty work the rest of the world can hate them for.

They fall silent, their eyes on the flaming globe.

Out of the corner of his eye, Jason sees Khalil's jaw harden. He's understood. This is why they fight, why they cannot give in, not even an inch. Because the world is burning and they are the only ones without elections to win, voters to appease, and donors to please. The only ones who can face the truth of those flaming lines on the globe rotating in front of them.

The only ones who can keep Earth from starving.

TWO

LIZ

'Elizabeth Lake, proceed to the interview room.'

She's been waiting for the call, and still the soft, inflectionless voice makes her shiver. Liz gets up, resisting the urge to wipe her palms on her trousers. She's alone in the white hallway, but those tiny dimples in the ceiling may be cameras. Every move she makes might matter, every gesture.

She draws a sharp breath and moves to the frosted glass door. This is it. Her future will be decided in the next ten minutes. Everything she's worked for concentrated into these final moments with the selection committee.

The door slides open before her, letting out the previous candidate: dark hair and golden-brown skin, his face only vaguely familiar. He avoids her glance, his lips pursed into a tight line. Not a good sign.

Liz looks away, fighting to keep her focus. He might have failed, but that means nothing for her chances. She keeps her head high as she enters the high-ceilinged room, its walls pearly white except for the double-arrowhead logo of the Aspire Academy opposite the door. A C-shaped table of milky glass faces a lonely chair at its focus. Five people watch her from behind the table. The heads of the engineering and astronomy departments sit together at one end, Dr Ende, her thesis advisor, on the other. Somewhat separate and in the middle are Dean Solik and a thin-faced man she doesn't recognise. His name doesn't matter, though; one look at his clothes tells her all she needs to know: a long, tailored jacket of steel-blue silk worn over matching shirt and trousers, soft, embroidered shoes not meant for treading on stone ground. This man is from the Yun Ju, descended from orbit to interview the graduates desperate to join him there.

It takes all her self-control to keep her knees from folding under her as Liz crosses the short distance and lowers herself into the chair. The Yun Ju man smiles thinly, his gaze apprising, probing, searching for faults under her skin. A drop of sweat slides down her back. Everything she's worked for will depend on his word. Her entire future.

Dean Solik taps the projection in the glass surface of the table. 'Elizabeth Lake, double doctorate from heliophysics and magnetospherics. Interesting combination. Looking at your marks, though, maybe you should have gone for depth instead of breadth?'

Liz winces. The double speciality was supposed to be an advantage, not a liability.

'Ms Lake's grades are above satisfactory,' Dr Ende says.

'We don't care for satisfactory,' Solik says, and the Yun Ju man next to him nods. 'We're only interested in exceptional.'

Liz's mind's reeling. She's in the top five per cent of the student cohort in both profiles. Not enough. The entire point of the Academy is to find the best of the best, those good enough for the elite jobs in orbit. Top one per cent, at most. She was never going to make that—she's smart, but not brilliant, and at thirty-two, her mind is no longer as nimble as it used to be. Her gamble was choosing the double speciality. Has she made a wrong bet?

The thin-faced man from the Yun Ju stretches his lips in another half-smile. 'We are indeed only interested in exceptional. Are you exceptional, Ms Lake?'

Liz bites her lip. She's not done yet. It's been a gamble, and she'd be damned if she folded before playing her hand. 'Yes, I very much am. Not because I'm another one-per-center. The Academy churns those out every year. But none of them can help you the way I can. You need me.'

The Yun Ju man leans back, one brow inching its way up his forehead. But when he speaks, he doesn't sound surprised. 'Is that so?'

Liz pulls a slow breath, her voice settling into something close to confidence. 'My previous career has taught me that there are few problems a single speciality can solve. The solutions often hide in the interstices. That's why I chose my fields. Heliophysics, to forecast the types and the severity of solar events. Magnetospherics, to study the interactions between the storms and the radiation belts. We're at solar maximum; sooner or later, it's bound to destabilise the belts. That's why you've invited me to this interview. Because you need me.'

She holds the man's gaze. He tilts his head. His smile falters, then reappears like a snake slithering over his face.

'You make some good points, Ms Lake. But tell me, which is it for you: are you hoping to build a future in the Yun Ju, or are you simply trying to get away from your father?'

A gasp escapes her lips before she can stop it. He knows. They know. Of course they do, the Yun Ju security was bound to find out. They've seen through her even after she's gone through the legal nightmare of changing her name twice just so she could disappear.

All the others are studying her now, examining her like she's the last tiger left in a closing zoo. Only Dean Solik shows no surprise. How long has he known? Is he the one who warned the Yun Ju or... It doesn't matter. They know now. She tried to run, but she's back in that same old trap.

Until Liz joined the Academy, she existed only as Jason Nevsky's daughter, her entire life defined by the hate his name stirred. She was fifteen the last time her family went out without a security detail, seventeen the last time they travelled without spit or excrement flung at their car. They retreated into the safety of a guarded compound soon after, but even there she was still *his* daughter. She tried to run, first when she went to college on the other side of the country, then her first job out on the ocean solar farms—but there were only so many Nevskys in Canada. Even after she changed her name, the truth caught up with her eventually. She was always going to be Anna Nathalie Nevsky. There was no place she could hide, at least not on Earth.

That was when she heard about the Academy.

It took all her savings to push through the second name change. Then came the five years of studying—twelve hours a day, every day. So many doubts. So many times she pushed herself beyond exhaustion. Only to find herself now back where she'd started.

It's a small kindness that neither Dean Solik nor the Yun Ju man speak her old name. At least she won't have to face the moment when the others' curiosity turns to disgust and hate. Dr Ende has been kind to her. Will her teacher regret that now, when she finds out who she helped?

Liz's fingers curl into fists. Fuck it. She's worked too hard. This will not end in yet another defeat because of *him*.

She lifts her head and stares at the Yun Ju man, who still hasn't given her the courtesy of a name. 'I'm not my father. If you know anything about me, then you know that I hate every-thing he stands for. That's why I'm here, why I've changed my name, why I want a new start as my own person. Yes, I'm running away. And so is everybody else. This planet is dying;

Yun Ju is a dream we all chase. I just have one extra reason to want to leave. You can say it makes me even more motivated. Your other candidates may consider a return. I don't have that option.'

The man nods. His gaze loses focus, his lips twitching as he subvocalises a conversation. He's talking to someone he can see on his lenses. Ranath Eyre, the funder and the owner of the Academy? She's the one Liz has been hoping to impress. She holds her breath, her lungs bursting with air and anxiety.

The man nods imperceptibly, then his gaze refocuses. 'Congratulations, Ms Lake. We've approved a temporary apprenticeship. You'll have six months to prove that you really are as indispensable as you claim.'

Liz pulls herself up, her limbs shaking. She nods a stiff goodbye and heads to the door. She wants to laugh, or to dance, or to just scream with all the pent-up fears and anguish of the last two decades. She's done it—*she* has done it, the first thing in her life her father hasn't managed to ruin. She is free. At last.

The cab pushes through the third checkpoint, sliding past the armoured fence and the silver-nozzled turrets tracking its every move. Liz is all too aware how easily they could vaporise the car and everyone in it. She wipes her hands on her trousers, trying to calm her breathing. She's never seen such tight defences. Even the Food Alliance compound looked like a pillow fort in comparison. But this is the Kilimanjaro Space Elevator, and this is the Feidi. Here, rioting is a daily occurrence. The enclave itself is a shadow of what she remembers from her mother's tales of a thriving metropolis around the world's first space elevator. The decline started with those first riots, back when her grandfather was killed, and Great-Aunt Nathalie escaped justice into space. The Chinese government lost interest in the rest of the enclave soon after. The fact that the city still exists is testament to the ingenuity of the Kenyans who refuse to abandon it, even when so much of equatorial Africa has turned into a wasteland.

Liz glances at the silent faces of the other interns, their postures stiff with apprehension. Twenty of them made it past that interview committee, twenty out of three hundred Academy graduates.

And she's one of them.

She allows herself a small smile before a chill settles in again: they are twenty now—but only ten will be allowed to stay. The rest will return here, to join the other graduates in dead-end engineering jobs in one of Sahara's manufactories. Not her. She will make it, somehow. She must.

The cab pulls into a glass-walled terminal—or rather, what used to be glass-walled but is now covered with dirty, yellowed plastic. They file out, the conversation picking up the farther they are from the walls and the guns. The last check is fully automatic: silver booths open to admit them one by one, their scanners blinking. Liz presents her wrist, and the machine reads the data on the chip implanted under her skin. The pa-pian, as they still call it here, the word yet another relic of the Chinese influence.

The machine chirps—and for a moment Liz wonders if it will scream in alarm at discovering her true identity. Her old name must still be somewhere in the system. But her papers are fine, her name changes perfectly legal, and for the machine, that's all that matters.

The light blinks green, and she is through, following the others down a long corridor towards the elevator. The place is spotlessly clean, but that's all that can be said about it: low light barely illuminates the grey walls and the charcoal flooring. She's momentarily puzzled by this plainness when the sight of electronic connections interspersed over the floor catches her eye. Projectors. The interior uses holographic decor, but it's off now. All the important people must have already boarded, and whoever is running the place decided their group was not worth the effort. Liz chuckles. The best day of her life, and she doesn't even get a hologram.

'What?' someone asks—Kene, a petite Black woman with skin-short hair.

Liz starts to answer as they round the corner. The elevator bulkhead door stands open just ten metres ahead, two bored technicians leaning on the wall beside it. But the words die on her lips as six figures emerge from the shadows, their silver suits glistening like drops of mercury. Sky Sharks. The Yun Ju security.

Liz tenses, her gaze sliding from the mirrored visors to the stubby nozzles of the Sharks' weapons. She tries not to think of her grandfather, of the Sharks who gunned down him and dozens of unarmed civilians as he tried to save his wife and baby.

You've got nothing to be afraid of, she tells herself. That was sixty years ago. And who knows what really happened that day —her father's not exactly a reliable source.

Something touches her side. Kene slides closer, her eyes wide. Of course: she's Kenyan; she grew up on the same tales of the Feidi riots.

'Routine checks,' Liz says. Her voice sounds hoarse. 'That's all it is.'

Kene pulls her gaze away from the Sharks and nods, desperate rather than reassured.

The Sharks watch them, human-shaped statues made of silver. Liz's skin tingles. Is it just nerves—or some invisible scan? If it is, then the technology is beyond anything she's ever seen. This shouldn't be possible.

Just as her mouth falls open in a question, the right-most Shark steps forward. 'The security scan is completed. You can now get your six-month residence permits.'

The Sharks split into pairs, one holding a sniffer, the other a narrow tube of a hypodermic. One by one, their arms are scanned, their DNA sampled and recorded. Somehow Liz is next, her arm ready. The injector pierces her skin, the pain gone before it even registers. Her residence permit. She has six months to make it count.

Because she's sure as hell not coming back here.

THREE

RANATH

Ranath scans the blocks of figures floating above the conference table in the centre of her office. The blocks are numbered and colour-coded, each representing one of her Renewal Corporation's assemblers' manufactories. The output looks in line with expectation, maybe slightly better, so this can't be why Sandip Bagrah, the newly appointed head of operations, has asked to see her in person.

Ranath raises an eyebrow, and Min Woo, her ever-vigilant assistant, clears his throat.

Bagrah gets the hint. 'What I wanted you to see, Zhu Eyre—'

'My name is Ranath. I suggest you keep that in mind, or you won't remain my head of operations.'

She holds Bagrah's gaze just long enough to let him believe she means it. She's made it clear to everyone that she doesn't like being called by her last name. Insisting on it means Bagrah is either ignorant or obtuse, neither a good sign, especially in a head of operations. She wouldn't immediately fire him for this, but her patience is not infinite.

Bagrah flushes, which she finds kind of endearing given he

is about twice her size. Tall, broad and in good shape, judging by the muscular lines of his shoulders. 'Ranath, of course. My apologies. There's something I thought you should see.'

He wiggles his fingers, and the numbers on the display melt and reassemble into an image of the spiky cubes of orbital manufactories, each as large as her entire station. To one side, chunks of broken asteroids float in a loose cloud trailing beyond the field of the projection. Miner bots crawl over the rocks like black-bodied insects. These are the lowest-grade drones, just smart enough to break the rocks apart and separate the contents by chemical element. Huge suction pipes feed the raw materials into the manufactory cubes. There, Renewal's highly guarded proprietary technology turns the space dust into the intelligent, autonomous assemblers the corporation is famous for.

Bagrah points to something at the edge of the picture. Another space rock, a stray asteroid or a piece of debris, hurtles towards the manufactories, tumbling unnaturally fast. Ranath taps the projection, calling up the trajectory and the time code. Heading right for cube number three—late last night. Which means nothing bad came of it, or she'd have already heard.

Bagrah catches her glance. 'Intercepted and destroyed, though we've had some minor damage from the debris. Not the first such attack—but this one's different. The way that rock moved, its trajectory—it was just too obvious this wasn't an accident. Whoever sent it our way wanted us to know that.'

'A message,' Min Woo says. 'Did you manage to trace it?'

'Not precisely, but enough to know it came from the Belt.'

Ranath stares at the tumbling rock for a moment longer. 'The miners, then. Tarkovsky's people. The assemblers are taking their jobs so they're throwing their shoes at them. Ironic, in a way.'

Bagrah glances at Min Woo, confused, but Ranath's not about to explain what *sabotage* actually means. In their line of business, one should know one's history.

Min Woo circles the table, his eyes on the tumbling rock now frozen with the rest of the projection. 'If it's the miners, this is probably the opening salvo. Their union has just called for a general meeting. They're getting desperate.'

Ranath nods. She knew this was going to happen. Sooner or later, they were bound to take some kind of action. This is just exquisitely bad timing. Ark construction has reached a critical phase; she doesn't want to draw any attention to herself or the extra stock the manufactories have been preparing. She can't let any hint of her plan slip before she's ready.

She swipes her arm over the table, dismissing the projection. 'Thank you, Bagrah. Keep me informed—and get whatever extra security you need.'

'I will.' An odd smile appears on Bagrah's lips. He hesitates, then makes up his mind. 'It's Sandip. If I'm to stay your head of operations...'

Ranath laughs. Perfection. And such good timing. 'Touché! Point for you. I don't suppose you enjoy fencing?'

'Fencing? You mean...'

'The "sport".' Min Woo's lip curls in mock disapproval. 'The kind where it's all right to stab people in the back.'

'In that case, I think I prefer not getting stabbed.'

'Let me know if you change your mind.' Ranath tilts her head towards Min Woo. 'It's so hard to find worthy opponents.'

Min Woo sniffs, but that's the extent of his comment. He walks Sandip to the exit, passing Ester, Ranath's other assistant, on her way in. Ester holds the door open as the two men leave and a service drone carrying a lunch tray slides inside. She waves it on towards the meeting table. The projection has vanished by now, the surface as smooth as a slab of granite.

Ranath signals the walls to enter the personal mode. The grey surfaces brighten, and the entire one side of her office transforms into a bay 'window' overlooking a forest clearing, complete with the rustle of leaves and a distant birdsong. The ventilation system sprays in a dose of some fresh scent. Pine, she thinks, but she can't be sure. She's never seen a full-sized tree. Too big for the gardens, especially on New Hope.

'Are the miners going to be trouble?' Ester asks. She's guessed Sandip's news or watched the projection on her screen.

'As expected—except probably bigger trouble and sooner than I anticipated.'

'What do you mean?'

'This is too bold, even for Tarkovsky's unions. They are desperate, but they're not stupid. Sending such an open message gives us a chance to track it back—and if we can prove the miners did it, the Yun Ju Council will make them pay. It'd cost them more than the jobs they are losing to us.'

Ester folds her arms. 'You think they've had help?'

'Encouragement. From someone who promised to shield them from the Council.'

'Someone influential, then.'

'Influential, and crude enough to resort to throwing rocks.'

'Richardson?' Ester asks.

'Possibly. Our friends on Liberty would sleep much better if we lost half of the manufacturing cubes.'

Ranath picks up a bowl from the lunch selection. A soup of some sort—dhal? It tastes like dhal, except it's purple. The latest of the nutrition engineers' experiments, and far from the most successful. Still, they're in space, and it's their job to try out anything they can sustainably grow.

Ester leans on the chair next to her. 'How are you planning to respond?'

'If that's how he's reacting now, Richardson will have a fit when we release the upgrade. If it's really him... I think I'm going to wait and see what he does. He makes mistakes when he's angry.'

'And the miners?'

Ranath sighs. 'We might actually have to hire them.'

Ester tilts her head, her brows rising. 'For Ark?'

'Yes. One aspect of it, something that won't let them figure out the extend of the project...' Ranath puts the bowl away and sends an instruction to her system to never serve her the purple dhal-wannabe again. On Ark, they will be able to grow real food. They'll be safe from radiation and rock-throwing neighbours. That's her legacy: a new, permanent home for humanity's best, far away from orbital uncertainties. 'Anyway, you haven't come here to bring me lunch, have you?'

'No. Li Qiang's invitation has arrived. And... it's odd.'

'In what way?'

It's Li Qiang's turn to host the quarterly reception, a tradition that started when the stations first moved to private hands. Some bright soul decided it was a good idea to get everyone together, so they won't forget how much they share, how they are all a big happy Yun Ju family. Ridiculous, in retrospect, but the tradition stuck. Probably because no one here would miss the opportunity to spy on the neighbours.

'There's an addition. Have a look.'

Ester wiggles her fingers, sending the file directly to Ranath's lenses. The image appears in front of her—a formal invitation with the Sunrise Group's crest in the header. The print is a perfect imitation of traditional calligraphy, each Hanzi character beautifully drawn. She scans the message, but the text is standard enough—until she gets to the very end and the slightly less perfectly calligraphed annotation: *Looking forward to seeing you again, Zhu Ranath. Everybody will be there.*

Her brows knit as she stares at the addition. 'You're right. This *is* odd.'

'Any idea what he means?'

The annotation is a message, for sure. Li Qiang has never bothered with anything beyond the standard invitation; his 'standard' is elaborate enough. So, why now? And what's the point of adding *everybody will be there*? That's the entire point of the damn reception.

Unless others have been invited as well, those beyond the usual group.

Ranath picks up her coffee (this, too, is an engineered variety, but this time they got it right) and strolls to the old wooden desk in the corner of her office, a gift from her grandmother. Ranath doesn't have much sentiment for antiques, but this piece is an exception. Apparently, it was made from the last tree from the Amazonian rainforest. Now it serves as testament to human stupidity, and a warning to always focus on the long term.

She waves her arm over the desk, waking up the holographic horary. It's not as old as the desk, but it still takes it a good five seconds to congeal into the projection: a blue Earth in the centre and the glowing marbles of the stations zooming around it. Yu Huan and Liberty are the largest, both displayed in imperial yellow. They were the flagship stations, back when China created the Yun Ju. Now they've gone private, just like the rest. Yu Huan is the home of Li Qiang's Sunrise Group; Liberty is just Liberty—the Americans renamed their station when they bought it. The other big players are Harmony at Xin Ju station and Endeavour at Yun Shi. Ranath's Renewal Corporation here on New Hope is a distant fifth. She likes it this way; it lets her do what she wants without too much scrutiny. But if her suspicions are right, this is about to change. The others may have realised how much power she's accumulated. Li Qiang must know—nothing slips past that man. Harmony's in the middle of a power transition, but that doesn't mean they're not paying attention. And Richardson? Liberty's boss is so full of himself he basically floats. He's so secure in his number one spot, he might just burst if he's ever threatened.

Everybody will be there. Ranath looks at the spinning marbles. There are also the growth platforms, the storage depots, and the minor outposts owned or allied with the bigger players. The An Ju station is still out there, but it's a ghost now, with only the maintenance crews overlooking the husks of the colony ships, grounded for good after the Bethesda debacle. There's also Shui Lian and Tian Gong, Ranath's old home. Both are shared by minor businesses, a religious cult, and a security and logistics co-op. Is that what Li Qiang's saying? That he's invited the co-ops as well? There's about a dozen of them renting space across the stations. And if the co-ops will be there, then so will be the unions. Including the miners.

Ranath smiles appreciatively. This invitation—it's Li Qiang's way of letting her know he's been paying attention. Not only that: the miners throwing rocks at her wouldn't be worth his scrutiny if he believed only the miners were involved. Which confirms her suspicion that someone has been spurring them on—and that it's not Li Qiang or he wouldn't be inviting them to the party.

'It's Richardson,' she says aloud. 'He's going after us. The question is how much he knows, and how hard he is going to hit.' She turns to Ester. 'Get me the details of all his latest acquisitions. And as much of Liberty's financial records as you can dig up without getting in trouble.'

Allan Duarte comes to see her at the end of the day. The Aspire Academy liaison enters her office almost silently, his shoes too soft to make a sound. Thin-faced and lean, Duarte has a sharp nose and narrow lips that keep twitching as if he's always on the verge of a comment. He dresses impeccably in silks of various shades of blue—today it's teal, from the pale aqua of his shirt to almost-black velvet shoes.

He dips his head in a greeting. 'Good evening, Ranath. The graduates are on their way to the station. I've prepared a dossier for you, as usual.'

'Thank you.' Ranath rubs her temples and heaves an exaggerated sigh. She could just send him away, tell him she's too busy to think about the graduates at the moment. It wouldn't even be a lie. At least, not all of it. She's been thinking about one graduate—and probably more than she's willing to admit, even to herself.

She motions to the wall sensors, and the sunlit forest retreats into the background. Twenty life-sized images appear, upper body only, a row of legless torsos floating along the side of the office. They stare ahead, some serious, some smiling, all trying to look more confident than they are.

'All handpicked specialities, as per the department heads' requirements,' Duarte says as they walk past the images. 'And your pick as well...'

They stop in front of the eighth picture. A woman, early thirties, with tightly pressed lips and an angry, defiant spark in her eyes. Deep frown lines cut between her brows. Ranath has seen her face before—first when they found out her real name and just recently at the selection interview. Elizabeth Lake—or rather, Anna Nathalie Nevsky. Jason Nevsky's daughter, the grandniece of Nathalie Hart, her namesake. The goddamned Hero of Bethesda herself, the woman who uncovered Destiny's Mind-Link plot and killed the man they sent to protect it.

Ranath pulls in a slow breath, forcing her body under control. Mind over matter, always.

'Am I correct that you want to keep her identity hidden?' Duarte asks.

'It's her choice. I don't see a reason to intervene.'

Duarte's lip twitches. 'Don't you think she may be a security risk?'

Ranath sniffs. 'Have you looked into her background? She's spent her life trying to escape her legacy. Besides, why would Nevsky send his daughter to spy on us?'

'I'll keep my eye on her still. If you agree.'

'Keep your eye on them all, Duarte. None are part of us until the final selection.'

'Of course.'

She makes to walk on, then pauses. 'I think I'm going to give her to Lars immediately.'

'He's not going to like it.'

'She's got the right specialities. He can fire her if she's not up to it.'

'He's still not going to like it.'

'So?'

'Just an observation.' Duarte gives her his twisty smile. 'I'll schedule your introductions after the onboarding week, as usual.'

'Please do.'

Duarte nods and retreats, his footsteps perfectly silent. Ranath remains motionless till the door closes behind him, then turns back to the image.

Anna Nathalie Nevsky.

In a few days she'll be here, walking the same floors, breathing the same air—and on Ranath's own invitation.

Ranath probes her feelings—but no, she doesn't hate the younger woman. Anna Nathalie had no part in the past. In a way, it cost them both the same. They both lost their mothers too early. Their fathers, too, lost to their causes, even if Anna Nathalie's is still alive.

Such similarities. They could be friends, if Ranath were half her age and just starting out. If she could forget that the woman's family caused the destruction of her own.

She shuts off the display. Some secrets cut too deep—and this is one she must keep hidden, even from Ester and Min Woo.

No one must ever find out.

FOUR

JASON

'The Siberian Archipelago, or the New Russ, as they like to call it now,' Aya says, keying in the projection to bring up the map.

They're back in the blimp-jet's main office, having breakfast —or possibly dinner. After the few hours of sleep following the Brazil meetings, Jason can't decide what time it is for his body. In front of him, the display congeals into the map of the Archipelago: about a hundred islands separated by winding tongues of water. Once, this was clearly part of one land, the old coastline defeated by the encroaching ocean.

'They sprang out of nowhere at the end of the last century, when the water levels stabilised,' Aya continues. 'They had a hell of a fight with the phage after the permafrost retreated, but once they got rid of it, this suddenly became fertile land.'

She touches another button, and a colour-coded overlay appears, highlighting the areas of agriculture and farming, with flashing figures showing yield for each major crop. Greyed-out splotches mark industry and urban centres.

'It would all be good news, especially as it's now a favourable climate zone for the most demanded crops. Unfortunately, the locals took the change of fortune for some kind of a message from the Heavens and developed a nasty strain of a messianic complex. They believe themselves to be the chosen ones, spared by God for some higher purpose. And now they seem to have found it.'

Two figures appear floating above the map: both blue-eyed, bearded men, one dressed in the robes of an orthodox bishop, and the other wearing a maroon jacket over a traditional Russian shirt with red embroidery on the front.

'Patriarch Ivan Volkov, the ideological father of the movement.' Aya pauses long enough to glare at the image. 'And his twin brother, Alexy Volkov, the country's president.'

'Wait. I remember a warning on the trends report...' Khalil calls up the population figures, then winces at the flaming red +7%. 'Is this for real?'

'Yep.'

'Geez. That's doubling the population every decade. What are they thinking?'

Jason snorts. 'According to Patriarch Volkov, they are 'reseeding Earth with the worthy.' Which means those of Russ stock, preferably, but they'll settle for other shades of white.'

Khalil rolls his eyes. 'Some things never die...'

'Nope,' Aya says. 'And now that they've been fairly successful, the ideology is catching up with the nationalists on the mainland. Some are already calling for dissolution of the Food Alliance.'

'Can they survive on their own?'

'They have enough fertile land, so they don't need modified seeds or any other help in that respect. But they don't have manufacturing—or at least they shouldn't have.'

Redistributing agriculture and manufacturing to the most suitable regions was Jason's cleverest move, his biggest achievement back when the Alliance still had widespread support: they would grow food wherever the soil was fertile and relocate industry and manufacturing to the dried-out deserts. Everybody agreed it made sense—but even so, centuries of mistrust among the nations would have probably destroyed the project if not for his deal with the Yun Ju. The orbitals wanted a single trading partner, so they offered Jason an exclusive contract: Earth-grown food and rare minerals in exchange for advanced tech for the newly created industrial centres, most of them in central Africa.

Jason drums his fingers on the table, his eyes on the map. The Archipelago is an agricultural zone, the land too good to be wasted on factories. Those greyed-out splotches could be food-processing centres, canning and freezing produce before shipment. Could be.

'There's also some doubt about their yields,' Aya says. 'Between the greenhouses and the orchards, it's getting increasingly hard to track. Almost like they are trying to hide something.'

'They may be massaging the data,' Jason says. 'Hiding the truth from us or from their own population. Or both. Anyway, we have to find out what's going on to get the best angle.'

'The best angle?' Khalil asks.

'To lean on them. Because these two can't be allowed to continue.'

'Can we, I don't know... endorse the opposition—' Khalil breaks off as Jason and Aya start laughing. 'Bad idea?'

'I can't think of a better way of ruining their chances,' Jason says. 'Never underestimate how much people hate us.'

'What, then?'

Jason shrugs. He's not proud of his methods, but he's long past caring. 'We bribe who we can. Though I doubt it will help; there's no candidate who could realistically oppose them.'

He pauses, staring at the floating figures of the Archipelago's twin fathers. Ironically, he's almost grateful to the pair for concocting such a perfect mix of white supremacy and eugenics. For once he can feel good about trying to undermine

democratically elected leaders. 'Keep your eyes open, both of
you. Find me something useful. I'm going to see if there's
anything I can offer the President to rein in his brother's
messianic ambitions.'

They land on the biggest of the islands and the Archipelago's
capital, Rooka, the Russian word for a *hand*. The reason for the
name becomes obvious as they approach: an almost circular hill
stretches out into the Siberian Sea in seven finger-like peninsu-
las. Merely ten years ago these used to be fields—now the whole
island is a thriving city. Clearly, Patriarch Volkov's plan is
working.

Aya and Khalil depart with a delegation of low-ranking
staffers and a heavy security unit. Jason gets an armoured
limousine all to himself, his escorts in similar vehicles in front
and behind his. It's hard to tell if the guards are there to protect
or restrain him, but that ambiguity follows him everywhere he
goes. At least here there are no starving crowds lining the
streets.

Three security agents escort him down long, marble-floored
corridors of the Spring Palace, the brand-new presidential residence. Only one wing has been constructed so far, a promise of
the grandeur to come. Gold-framed images line the walls,
stylised paintings of local vistas interspersed with portraits of
the country's two blue-eyed statesmen, usually encircled by
similarly blue-eyed, rose-cheeked children. The agents leave
him at the doors of the state chamber, all whites and golds and
domed with a cupola, like a church. Alexy Volkov sits behind a
desk the size of a small room. He looks up, then rises slowly
with the practised reluctance of a busy man pulled away from
his duties.

Jason keeps his expression neutral, though this time the task
is harder than usual. He's got little patience for megalomaniacs

—and even less for those using the global crisis to fuel their twisted ambitions. But it *is* a crisis, and it is his responsibility to manage it, no matter his personal feelings.

'Privet, Gospodin Stepanovitch.' Volkov extends his hand to greet him. His smile is probing, testing Jason's reaction—to the language and to the otchestvo, the patronymic referring to his Russian father.

'Thank you for seeing me, Mr President,' Jason answers in English. He is a Canadian citizen, like his mother and his Aunt Nathalie.

They shake hands, Volkov's grip as hard as his gaze. At least he switches to English now.

'But of course. Though I must say, you surprise me with this sudden inspection. May I ask why?'

They remain standing, no hint from Volkov to act like the gracious host his words proclaim him.

There was a time when Jason would have considered punching the man—not done it, of course, just let himself exercise the thought—but even that little joy is now beyond his reach. He smiles instead. 'Inspection? I wouldn't call it that. But we do need to talk. And I'm sure you can guess the subject.'

Volkov chuckles. 'Impressed by our population growth?'

'"Impressed" is not exactly how I'd describe it.'

'Why not? My people are thriving. No hunger here—not what you can say about the other places you visit.'

The memories of Brazil's hungry children flood his mind. Jason pushes them away. 'And how long can you keep them this way?'

Volkov starts to answer but changes his mind. He gestures to a side door. 'Let's walk. Some fresh air will do us both good.'

Jason follows him out to an enclosed garden. The scent hits him first: almond and orange trees in full bloom, the fragrance intoxicating. Small birds hop between the branches, chirping excitedly. Barely a cloud in the blue square of sky above. A little paradise, for the President's personal use.

Jason pulls in a breath and savours it like the best wine. How long since he's taken a walk among the trees? Years. Maybe decades. The realisation pinches his chest tight. It hurts to be here, hurts to see what's possible. What could be his, if he became like Volkov. Is that why the man has brought him here?

The President walks in silence. In the bright light of the day, he looks weary, the crow's feet around his eyes and the deep folds framing his mouth carved by frowns and scowls rather than laughter. Probably in his late fifties, Jason decides, about a decade his junior.

'We've been blessed,' Volkov says eventually. 'Look at this land. The phage almost destroyed it—yet we quashed it.'

'You got lucky. And you're in the part of the globe where the climate made things better, not worse.'

'You call it luck, we call it destiny.'

'I know you do. It's a comfortable way of looking at things. It makes it seem like you deserve your fate—and the others theirs.'

'I know you disagree. And I'm not going to waste your time or mine trying to argue. So, let's cut to the point: you want me to infringe on my people's reproductive rights. I'm not going to do that.'

Volkov barely glances at him as he speaks, his tone confident, and his demeanour almost bored. This gives Jason pause: he's used to arguing, used to hate or threats—those are the reactions of people who still respect his power, who understand that they won't survive without the Alliance's help. This is not what he senses from Volkov.

'Your people are only doing what your brother tells them to. You can change his message. Admit that this rate of growth is unsustainable, that the global resources can't support—'

'And here's the problem, Stepanovitch.'

The otchestvo again, but Jason manages not to wince.

'This is where you and your Alliance have gone wrong. Destroying communities because you want our fertile land to feed the entire world. It can't. Call it fate, call it luck, call it whatever you want, but parts of the globe are beyond salvation. The sooner you admit it, the sooner we can move on and start rebuilding.'

'And watch the rest of the world die while you do it?'

'My duty is to my own people. Let nature take its course. It's precisely not listening to nature that brought us here.'

Jason grits his teeth. He can't afford indignation, can't alienate the man because he needs Volkov and his rich soil. His arguments won't make a difference anyway, nor will calling for compassion, or solidarity, or justice. And yet he must compel Volkov to adhere to his quota, to deliver his share of food stocks and keep the population down to the targets. 'You agreed to do your part when you signed the charter, Mr President. As a member of the Alliance—'

Volkov waves his hand. 'I didn't sign it. My predecessor did, before he knew better.'

Jason stops. 'Are you telling me you want to leave? Because if you do, then you'd be advised to remember all the things you are getting from us: the machinery, the raw materials, the technology. If you leave, you're on your own.'

Volkov gives him a twisted smile. He keeps walking, and Jason has no choice but to follow.

'I'm not the only one,' Volkov says when Jason catches up with him. 'Others would join me. I could trade with them.'

Jason tries to keep his face still. This is what he feared, the kind of sedition that could bring the end of the Alliance and push Earth over the brink. Is that what those greyed-out splotches on the map signify? Is Volkov creating manufacturing capacity in preparation for a secession? They can't pull it off. That's the safety catch in the deal: they grow food in one region with machines built somewhere else using technology and research provided by the Yun Ju exclusively to the Alliance.

He forces confidence into his voice. 'That's a dead end, Mr President, you must realise that. Only food producers could possibly consider leaving—but none of you have much industry nor the expertise to create it. Within months you'll run out of spare parts.'

'We can build factories. We have land, and we can reclaim more. And if we...' Volkov breaks off. He frowns, displeased, as if he said too much. 'I tell you what—I'll stay in the Alliance and deliver our quota down to the last potato. And I'll even talk to my brother to... encourage restraint. But I want something in return.'

They both stop now, facing each other under a fragrant orange tree. Volkov smooths his beard, his eyes as blue as the sky but infinitely colder. Jason has that shaky feeling that something momentous is about to happen, something he's desperately unprepared for.

'I want assemblers. They have all that amazing technology up in orbit, but we get nothing but scraps. I need to reclaim more land, build more homes, more farms. It's all possible, with the right machinery. You give me assemblers, and I won't take us or our allies out of your Alliance. How's that for a deal?'

Assemblers. The one orbital invention even Jason struggles to get despite his pact with the Yun Ju. He stifles a gasp as the pieces fall together. Anyone else would be asking for harvesters or pollinator drones; these are always the first priority. Volkov requesting assemblers means he's not worried about the basic tech—because he's already getting more than his share.

He's been trading directly with the stations.

How? The Alliance's deal is supposed to be exclusive, that's the core of the agreement Jason has negotiated. Food the orbital hydroponic platforms can't grow and the rare minerals the asteroids can't reliably provide in exchange for high-level technology.

Not manufacturing, that can easily be done in the African industrial parks, but the know-how, the research, the advances—everything the Yun Ju has had to master to survive in orbit. The result is a perfect symbiosis: technology beyond anything Earth can produce at a cost of feeding an equivalent of a small city.

But this symbiosis can only endure if all the trade goes through the Alliance. If Volkov is suppling anyone directly, then he can also receive the technology, build his own factories, and manufacture anything he wants. The Archipelago will truly be independent—and it's a matter of time before the other food producers will follow. There will be no incentive for them to share their crops, nothing of value the Alliance can offer. Compassion or justice certainly aren't going to do it. The Alliance will fall apart, and the death toll will count in billions.

Volkov's watching him, his hands behind his back, the red embroidery on his shirt moving in rhythm with his deep breaths. He must know what conclusions Jason has drawn from his words, but there's nothing in his demeanour to signal shame or regret. Or apprehension at what Jason might do with that knowledge. That last realisation makes Jason shiver. Whoever Volkov's trading with must be powerful enough not to fear Jason's intervention.

'The assemblers are a precious technology,' Jason says, if only to play for time. 'In short supply even in the Yun Ju.'

Volkov tuts. 'That's what they tell *us*. Who knows if that's even true?'

'I'll see what I can do. But I've only managed to get them a handful of times, and even then on a short lease.'

'Then you need to negotiate better. Hold off the shipments, and they'll come begging!' Volkov laughs, his beard shaking and droplets of his saliva floating in the fragrant air.

'I'm afraid it's slightly more complicated...' Jason looks away. He's not going to remind him where his pollinators come from, or the anti-phage treatment that healed his land. Or how a single, well-targeted asteroid could obliterate his entire Archipelago. The Yun Ju are demanding bedfellows; the symbiosis can last only as long as both sides find it useful. 'I'll do what I can, Mr President.'

Aya and Khalil listen to Jason's report with grim faces. They are back in the blimp-jet, the craft itself a gift from the Alliance's Yun Ju partners. Neither is surprised that Volkov would double-cross them, that's perfectly in character. But if one of the orbital players has broken ranks, more may follow.

'Any clues on who he's trading with?' Jason asks.

'Not that I could tell from my tour of the potato fields...' Aya says.

Khalil shakes his head. 'No, but I think I know what they are selling.'

'What?'

'Apples, pears, cherries—tree-grown fruit. A real pain to cultivate in orbit, so it makes sense they'd want it.'

Aya's brows knit in surprise. 'How did you find out?'

'I got the chatty guide—and I managed to snap an image when he was showing off their record yields.' Khalil taps the projection button, and the figures materialise above the meeting table. 'Their output is way higher than what the reports say—so either they're stocking up or selling it on.'

Aya's still frowning, but now Jason scowls at Khalil as well. 'You snapped an image?'

Khalil taps behind his ear and grins. 'They never scanned us for automation...'

Jason glares. He doesn't trust the automation, not even the new one, despite the safety claims. They said the same things about the old Mind-Link, until Bethesda. Until Destiny used it to turn five thousand happy colonists into bloodthirsty monsters who slaughtered each other down to the very last child. That device was meant for them, for all the humans on Earth, to be moulded to the will of whoever controlled the implants. It chills him to think what might have happened if Aunt Nathalie hadn't uncovered the plot.

'Totally external,' Khalil says, picking up on Jason's disapproval. 'Wearable lenses and a receiver hub. I wouldn't allow a single wire inside my skull.'

Jason nods, unconvinced. 'Fine, but get our techs to scan it after each visit. I don't want anyone planting something on you.'

'Will do,' Khalil says.

Jason returns to the image floating above the table: an electronic ledger, columns of colour-coded numbers. His aide is right, Volkov's orchards are putting out twenty per cent over their official figures. 'We've got to track the shipments. They're getting it to the elevators and up to orbit somehow—if we find out how, we might be able to trace the buyers. Aya, you check planet-side links; Khalil, try the elevators. Kilimanjaro will be my guess; it's easier to find shady dealers in the Feidi. But check the Atlantic and the Singapore sites as well.'

His aides rise, each heading to their own workstation. Jason remains at the table, staring at the floating figures. Unless they find a way to stop this, all the nightmares he's fought over the last two decades will come true. This is too big for his Earth-bound team; they must follow the chain from both ends. He needs help from higher places—his partners up in the Yun Ju. And there's probably only one person with enough power to prevent a disaster.

Jason taps on his wrist band and requests a meeting with Nevil Richardson.

FIVE

LIZ

The elevator slows down for its first transit point at eight thousand kilometres above the surface. Liz rubs her eyes. She's barely managed to snooze over the thirty-six-hour journey. The nausea doesn't help, and her stomach laments the loss of gravity with loud grumbling and incessant burps. By now they have all acquired a greenish hue; from Hiroko's porcelain paleness to Kene's deep brown, all complexions finding their own way to sickly green.

Liz folds her reading pad and drops it into her shoulder bag. The other graduates are packing, too, their glances darting to the altitude marker above the cramped, windowless cabin they shared on the way up. Nobody speaks, their postures tense, like runners waiting for the starter gun. In six months, ten of them will be back in the elevator, making the return trip. The realisation returns with a sudden chill, the truth of it somehow more real now that her destination is finally so close. Liz shakes it away. She's come this far, she can manage the last stretch.

When the arrival gong finally chimes, Alejandro is the first out, fumbling with his travel bag as he attempts to assume a dignified posture in zero-g. He's been trying to position himself as the group leader from the moment they left: always the first to speak and the last to finish. Liz doesn't mind. On the contrary, let him take the point, make all the mistakes he's bound to make in this new land. Her plan is to keep her head low until she knows how everything works here. She doesn't need the glory—or the spotlight. She just needs a place in the top ten.

They glide out of the cabin, following a handful of other travellers disembarking at this transit point. Most of the passengers will remain on board as the elevator continues up to Yu Huan and farther still to Liberty, all the stations nested together in the relative safety between the two Van Allen belts. Everyone but their group are Yun Ju natives, the fact made obvious not just by their outfits but by the way they appear relaxed while Liz still tries to figure out which way is up. The other graduates aren't faring any better, bumping into walls or each other, increasingly frustrated. A small luggage drone rolls by, and Liz latches on to it, using the momentum to make her legs point in the same direction as the natives. At least now she looks like she belongs. Besides, there has to be a reason why the locals have assumed the same orientation, even while free floating.

She understands why a moment later, as they arrive in front of another bulkhead door: the only way to stop is by holding on to the handholds protruding from the ceiling. Liz grabs one with her right hand—just in time to reach out with her left and catch Kene, who's tumbling headlong towards the waiting passengers, a panicked look in her eyes.

'Thanks!' Kene gasps. 'Not the way I wished to meet the zhu-yuan!'

Zhu-yuan—Liz is not sure what the name means, but it reminds her of the way her mother spoke, the odd mix of Mandarin and English of people who grew up in the Feidi. The memory feels thorny, like it came at the wrong time, when she should be looking forward, not back. Or maybe it's because she wishes her mother could see her here, proud and happy, a soon-to-be citizen of the orbit. Her mother left the day after Liz's eighteenth birthday, returning home to the Feidi, or maybe just getting as far away from her husband as she could. Liz never saw her again—she planned to join her after she left college, but then her mother died in a stupid accident and Liz was left with the regrets.

'You all right?' Kene asks, picking up on her discomfort.

'Yes. Sure.' Liz blinks. 'Just that damn nausea!'

'Tell me about it.' Kene squeezes the hand she's still holding. 'Not long now. The shuttle's here.'

Liz follows her gaze to the bulkhead. Soft yellow letters have appeared above, spelling *acquiring connection* in English and Mandarin. The elevator doesn't stop on its way; the shuttles link up at each transit point and whisk the passengers to their destinations. The stations' orbital trajectories pass at a considerable distance from the shaft, zooming past at relative speeds of hundreds of kilometres per hour.

Connection established blinks in green a moment later, and the door slides open. The waiting passengers propel themselves towards the gangway with subtle flicks of their wrists against the handholds. Alejandro is the first to follow, holding to the grips to control his speed.

'Wait there.' A figure emerges from inside the gangway, gliding against the current: a man, probably, early thirties, pale-skinned, with short blond hair and a silver jacket bearing the Academy's double arrowhead logo. He nods to the passengers as he passes, then pulls himself to a stop in front of Alejandro.

'The Academy group? I'm Jacques Perez, your guide and liaison.' His English carries the slightly staccato accent of the orbitals. He gives them a wide smile. 'Wait for the others to board. That's the only way you'll avoid bumping into every single one of them on your way. Trust me, I've been there.'

Next to Liz, Kene nods. Definitely a good idea.

It doesn't take long for the dozen or so passengers to disappear inside. Jacques waits another twenty seconds before waving them on. Liz follows close behind him as they slide into a dark, soft-walled tube that suddenly makes her think of a birth canal. She keeps her eyes on the red glowing arrows marking the way, even though she can't tell if they are in the floor or in the ceiling. When she looks ahead again, she's entering the shuttle, crossing the airlock into a wide cabin. The floor is too dark to see, but the walls seem to shimmer, pearly white from this angle but then turning translucent as soon as she glides inside.

Liz gasps. The others stop moving, only the momentum carrying them forward. She looks down—or what has suddenly become *down*—at the place where they've come from, far beyond the shuttle's transparent walls. It's sunrise, or sunset, the furnace of the Sun half-hidden behind the dark globe of Earth. Above, the Milky Way sparkles too bright to be real. Can stars really be so intense?

'Go on in.' Jacques gestures towards a semi-circle of seats at the back of the shuttle. 'Over there.'

The other passengers watch them glide past, some impatient, others amused. Liz pushes herself into the padded seat, and the armrests twist to hold her in place. The airlock seals as soon as they're all secured, the chairs sending some automated message to the guiding systems. The shuttle trembles, tiny flashes just below the edge of the windows betraying the location of the engines.

'This won't be long. New Hope's right over there.' Jacques points to a bright light rushing against the background of stars. 'Still, we have a few minutes to ourselves.'

Liz glances at the passengers in front, realising she can't hear them anymore. Something like a curtain cuts the shuttle in two, almost invisible, except for a slight bending of light as if from high heat. A privacy bubble. She's never seen one in action; she's only ever heard about the technology from her father. Obviously, the Yun Ju is where he got it from.

She lifts her brows in feigned awe. Jacques meets her gaze. His smile is knowing, too knowing... No, she's being paranoid.

'Any questions? Now's the time!' Jacques says, his grin back on.

Where to start? Liz glances at the others, their expressions similarly uncertain. Any question they ask may reveal their fears—and vulnerabilities. This is a competition, with their futures as the prize.

'When will we meet Eyre?' Alejandro starts.

'Is it true that she makes the final call?' Fatima adds.

'In a way, yes. The Academy is Zhu Ranath's private enterprise, so she can choose who she wants to keep. She usually goes along with the recommendations, though.'

'Usually?'

'She might have... other considerations. Ones she's not inclined to share with mere mortals.' Jacques laughs; the rest of them just stare.

'So, when will we meet her?' Alejandro repeats.

'In due time. And if I were you, I'd make sure not to meet her too soon.'

'What do you mean?'

Jacques doesn't answer. Instead, he juts his chin towards the window. 'Isn't she pretty?'

Liz presses her head to the glass. The bright spark they've been chasing has resolved itself into a toroid, flat and dark, with a thin strip of blue light along the middle. Long prongs extend outwards from the torus, each ending in a flat, star-shaped structure: the mag-shield generators, enveloping the station in its own magnetic field to protect it from solar events and space radiation. On the inside, she can just about glimpse the tall silhouette of the central axis: a scaffold encrusted with bulges of service installations, docks, and storage areas, all of them implied from the way they obscure the star field behind rather than seen directly.

'Welcome to New Hope,' Jacques announces. 'It was the first American station in the Yun Ju, but has since moved into private hands, like most of the others. The current owner is the Renewal Corporation, presently administered by Zhu Ranath Eyre.'

Liz pulls her gaze away from the view to cast him a sideways glance. Does he think this is news?

Jacques responds with a cunning smile. 'So far these were just words for you, pages from the Academy's prospectus. I know; I was an intern only eight years ago.'

Now he's got her attention. 'You came through the Academy?'

'Yes. So believe me when I tell you: you'd better start paying attention. Because these two sentences I just gave you were *packed* with information.'

'What information?' Alejandro asks. 'And if it's so important, then why not just tell us?'

'I've told you everything you need to know.'

Hiroko groans. 'I'm a medical engineer, not a code breaker.'

The others look equally puzzled. Liz turns to the window, studying the approaching station. Jacques is trying to teach them something—what? What *did* he tell them? That stations change hands, bought and sold to the highest bidder. New Hope was sold or rented before, and it might be again.

Her residence permit—is it bound to the station? The whole of the Yun Ju? Or just to the temporary job contract she has with Renewal? She's never asked; never even realised she should have.

What else did he say? *The current owner is the Renewal Corporation, presently administered by Zhu Ranath Eyre.*

Presently administered.

There's something transitory about this phrase, something

about to be broken. Is Eyre on her way out? If yes, then what will happen to them? The Aspire Academy is Eyre's pet project, everybody knows that. And so, are they beholden to her somehow? What if she falls out of grace, moves to a different station, or different corporation? Is she even allowed to do that?

Liz feels dizzy again, her nausea returning with a dull throb in her stomach. She pulls in a steadying breath. *Easy.* She has six months to figure things out.

Behind her, the others resume their chatter. Liz catches Jacques's glance. He smiles, pleased, and points up.

The shuttle has just dipped under the habitat ring, a dark behemoth hanging in the sky. From this close, she can make out the fronds of the cooler fins, the thick-lipped mouths of shuttle docks, and pinpricks of what look like windows. Flashing lights outline the emergency airlocks, icy blue and the opposite of reassuring. At twenty-two metres thick, the ring manages to look both immense and fragile. A hypersonic asteroid the size of her fist could shatter it into a dust cloud. A freak solar storm could fry the machinery that sustains the life inside. How long can they cheat fate?

'The stations have been going for almost two centuries,' Jacques says, as if reading her mind. 'Half of all our resources go to safety. Nothing's guaranteed, of course, but nothing ever is.'

The shuttle glides past the inner edge of the torus and along the spokes that connect it to the axis. Thrusters engage, and the craft veers sideways, matching the ring's rotation. Liz's limbs become heavy, her legs settling on what is now definitely the *floor*. A garland of soft flashing lights appears directly ahead. They slide into the open mouth of the dock, the mooring clamps closing around them like hungry jaws.

'Welcome home,' Jacques says.

He leads the way, the airlock light blinking green as he passes. One by one they follow, through the airlock scanner and into the warm yellow lights of the corridor.

When Liz reaches Jacques, she stops. 'If you could go back in time—is there something you wish you'd known then?'

Jacques frowns, considering, then makes up his mind. 'Yes. To never let myself forget I was in space.'

Liz must look unimpressed because he continues, 'You think you know what it means. You don't. You know the fact, but you haven't yet internalised the implications. *Everything's* different here. Not just the tech, that's the easiest part. It's what you take for granted that will catch you off guard.'

'Like what?' Kene asks, sidling in beside her.

Jacques chews his lip. 'Say, back at home, your nationality was everything: the chip you got implanted on the day you were born would determine where you could live and work. Here, it's meaningless. Nobody cares which patch of land your progenitors came from. Once you're part of the Yun Ju, that's the only "nationality" that matters. This is the new "us" and' —he points in the vague direction of Earth—'and "them".'

He moves on, waving for them to follow. Liz stands motionless for another moment, feeling the reality shift around her. Jacques is right: she thought she knew it and yet she's never felt it in her bones. She truly *is* in a different world now. She's not sure she likes this new definition of 'us' and 'them.' Or if she dislikes it, either.

SIX

RANATH

Apparently, antiquity is back in fashion—or at least a gold-enhanced version of ancient Greece. Ranath tries not roll her eyes as she watches the smart fabric of her jacket transform into the design Ester has picked for her. The material has acquired an opalescent sheen, and now a thick golden thread weaves looping meanders into a labyrinthine pattern. The result is pleasing enough, so she lets it be. She's never understood the idea of fashion, but she does understand the purpose of armour, and sometimes, they are the same thing. Ranath suspects she will be the centre of attention at today's reception, and she must dress for the occasion.

Her garment is still finishing its metamorphosis as the shuttle slides into one of Yu Huan station's voluminous docks. Ester and Min Woo are at her sides. Both are wearing gold: Min Woo in high-waisted trousers and a bolero jacket in cream white with a golden shimmer, and Ester in a sky-blue gown embroidered with gold butterflies. Come to think of it, Ranath could swear the butterflies were not there a moment ago.

An usher balloon waits for them to disembark, spraying gold sparkles that melt and vanish as they land on her clothes.

Ranath follows it down stucco-covered corridors, along golden garlands imitating laurel leaves, and past white columns similarly adorned in golden vines. As they reach the reception rooms, the balloon spins one last time before somersaulting away. Soft music seeps from the walls, something appropriately ancient. Low-ranking officials with watchful eyes and gaudy garments part before her, the hum of their voices resuming in Ranath's wake. Ester and Min Woo peel off with the softest of nods. Their task is to mingle with the other staffers and sift for useful intel, while Ranath tackles the big players inside the main hall.

Server drones swoop towards her as she enters. She picks up a heavy chalice of something that smells too sweet to be good and looks around. The interior decor hits the precise spot between class and kitsch. She should have expected nothing less; Li Qiang's taste has always been immaculate. Seven columns support a glass platform where a troupe of live musicians labour over antique instruments. Underneath, projection screens divide the space into semi-private areas, each with its own simulated vista of ancient ruins, Sun-baked hills, olive trees swaying in gentle breezes, or wine-dark seascapes. Sound dampeners subdue the babble of conversations to a soft murmur, the voices—and the words—unintelligible.

Ranath wiggles her fingers, and her skin-tight gauntlet instructs her lenses to enter the support mode. The people counter flashes 235. More than usual—and she can't be the last to arrive. She has interpreted Li Qiang's message correctly—everybody's been invited. Another tap of her fingers signals the lenses to locate the host. Her perception narrows into sharp focus, everything but the man's distant figure blurred grey. He's turning towards her, his mouth stretching into a smile of recognition. Alerted to her arrival, no doubt.

'Zhu Ranath! There you are at last.' Li Qiang's voice finds her across the room—a trick of sound channelling.

Ranath slides into the crowd, making her way towards him. She can't see him as she answers but he'll surely hear her just as well. 'Well, you chose the time for when our stations are on the exact opposite side of the planet...'

Qiang laughs. 'The charms of orbital mechanics. We'd be in sync if you chose to share orbit...'

Li Qiang appears in front of her a moment later: bare-chested, in a full-length open robe and tailored trousers, both of exquisite white silk with gossamer lines of gold embroidery. His jet-black hair is longer than usual, ruffled in a way of someone reckless and spontaneous. Oh, appearances... The man doesn't blink without a plan. But then, who is she to complain?

Li Qiang's entourage, a dozen strong, shuffle reverently behind him. Their names pop up in Ranath's field of vision at the slightest inclination of her head in their direction. Two remain unassigned for a good second before her system manages to identify them. Acquisitions and expansion secretaries, both new in their posts. Interesting.

'Welcome!' Qiang greets her with his perfect smile. His chest glistens as he leans in for an air kiss, his perfume leathery and musky.

Ranath gestures to the surroundings. 'Greece?'

'I thought I'd try something exotic... And I must say, the style fits you perfectly... It's like I've picked it just for you...'

His grin stays on, but his voice has a steely ring that tells her Li Qiang's got a plan for this evening. The note in the invitation was only the first move.

Qiang's gaze shifts in the direction of the entrance. 'Oh, Zhu Owande has arrived. You must excuse me—the host's duties... Do help yourself to the food. I'm told the vine leaves are something of a delicacy. An acquired taste, if you ask me, but I hope you like them.'

Li Qiang saunters off, and Ranath feels herself nod. He would only abandon her to greet someone like Nebu Owande, the zhu of a minor co-op, if he wanted Ranath to know she's here. Another confirmation that all the independents have been invited—and that will include the miners.

She hesitates. Qiang has alerted her to the situation but never said who issued the invitations. It's his party, but the guest list is open to all the faction heads. They all know the miners hate her and her assemblers. Which means that this is an ambush, and the miners are the weapon. Someone wants a confrontation, out here, in public. But she can still beat them to the punch.

She throws the chalice to a passing drone and exchanges it for a glass of water. The system transcribes the taps of her fingers into a message to Ester and Min Woo: *Get me a private meeting with Tarkovsky, of the miners' union. He's somewhere here, I'm sure. Be discreet.*

She strolls farther into the hall, redrawing her mental map of the ever-changing rivalries and alliances. The heads of the Big Family co-op stand clustered around Renata Fujikawa, the de-facto leader of Harmony since both her mothers retired last year. Ranath will have to catch her later; Harmony has just placed the biggest assembler order in Renewal's history. Vagish Lee from Endeavour is just entering, Li Qiang moving in to greet him. No sign of Richardson yet.

The factions used to be loose lobby groups allied behind a world view or a doctrine about the future of the Yun Ju or even all of humanity. These ties grew stronger, the businesses merging and the leaders inbreeding, morphing into little orbital kingdoms—a process that solidified once the stations moved into private hands. Ranath snapped up New Hope the moment it became available. It'd been the New American Union's only venture in the Yun Ju, before they gave up on trying to compete with China. It's only about a third of the size of Yu Huan or Liberty, a minor start-up nobody has paid much attention to. Until now.

Any news on Tarkovsky

He's just arriving, Ester says in her ear. *I'll try to intercept him.*

Ranath busies herself exchanging greetings with Nebu Owande, alone now that Li Qiang has moved on to other guests. Owande's logistics co-op maintains the space elevators, but they also house the Sky Sharks, the orbital security team, and that fact may one day come in useful. Owande proves unexpectedly funny, especially recounting the tribulations of sharing a station with the Sun cultists. Apparently, they insist on moving the whole structure to higher orbit. Closer to enlightenment—and the not-quite-heavenly fires of the upper Van Allen belt.

Ten minutes later a map appears on Ranath's lenses.

I suggest you hurry, Ester says. *I can't keep him here very long.*

Tarkovsky looks like he considered dressing up for the occasion but gave up halfway. His blue shirt bears traces of gold embroidery, but on top of it he wears a functional, almost casual brown jacket of some cheap composite material. A statement, Ranath guesses. He's white, likely past sixty and looks it, too, his hair streaked with grey and his short beard almost silver.

He waits for Ranath in a private room, far enough from the main hall to ensure nobody will walk in on them—though she's certain Li Qiang will know about the meeting soon enough, if he doesn't already. There's some furniture here, sofas and low tables, but they remain standing, the man's hate so thick he could use it as a skin lotion.

He scowls at her from under untrimmed eyebrows. 'Now you want to talk? You've put most of my people out of work.'

Ranath wavers for another instant—but really, this is her only option. She has to get the miners on her side before they cause any serious trouble.

She gives the man a broad smile. 'True. And I did that on purpose.'

Tarkovsky winces. He expected excuses, not candour.

Ranath continues before he can regain his composure. 'I need you somewhere else. I could say I'm sorry to have to force your cooperation, but let's just say I didn't have much room to manoeuvre.'

Emotions run though Tarkovsky's face as clear as if he calls them out: distrust, curiosity, apprehension. Some disdain, too, but he's too aware of his place in the food chain to let pride dictate his moves.

'I will hire all those who've lost their jobs,' Ranath says. 'At double your current pay, and with guaranteed input on the project parameters to ensure your safety.'

His eyes light up. He bargained hard for that in the union charter, so it was bound to get his attention. He pushes his hands into his pockets. 'What's the catch, then?'

'The catch is that you stop throwing rocks at me.'

Tarkovsky doesn't respond, but a sparkle in his eye confirms he's glad his stunt has proven effective. 'Is that all?'

'Almost. The job...' Ranath pauses. How much to tell him? He must know enough to believe her offer, but not enough to put the project in danger. 'It will take you far away from home.'

He cocks an eyebrow. It's common knowledge that most miners are either single or travel with their families.

'More than you're used to. Say, Saturn?'

Tarkovsky nods. The recent prospecting on Saturn's moons brought some interesting results, so this makes sense to him. He's wrong, but not in a way that would make a difference to his people. She doesn't need him to mine the moons. She needs him to help build her Ark.

'Can't you get your precious assemblers to do that for you?' he asks.

A predictable jab, but only human. She might as well let

him relish the moment. 'There are some jobs only humans can do. The Belt is a known quantity now. Out there, it's a different matter.'

Tarkovsky bobs his head, hesitating. He may have made Richardson a promise, some deal he'll now need to cancel. Ranath's offer is too good to pass, and they both know it.

'I suppose you want me to keep it quiet, too?'

'Good guess. But I realise you need guarantees. My assistant has a draft contract waiting for you. All current co-op members hired, double salaries. We can negotiate the smaller details later.'

A ping in her ear confirms her aides have received the message, both of them having listened to the conversation. Min Woo will now be frantically assembling the contract from the outline Ester has prepared.

Tarkovsky grins like he's won a lottery. He's probably already rehearsing the speech he'll give to the members, with details of the tough negotiations he pushed through. Good for him. They both get what they want, and Richardson loses an ally.

Ranath reaches out her hand. 'Do we have a deal?'

He gives it a hard shake, then hurries out behind Ester as if afraid Ranath may change her mind.

Ranath reaches for a champagne glass as she returns to the main hall. She deserves it—besides, it projects just the right image. Richardson must be here by now, waiting for his moment. He's waited too long.

She's about to instruct her system to locate him when the heads around her turn and the voices hush. Nevil Richardson strides across the tiled floor: a tall white man with blond hair gathered in a loose braid, his back straight and his jaw set. He wears a long jacket tied at the waist with a sash belt, matching trousers and shoes, all in pearl-blue with golden print, but in contrast to the Greek theme, his pattern is the Liberty's fleur-de-lis. His wife is a step behind, dressed in a body-hugging golden dress and a nano-thin cloak that make her look like a goddess.

'Zhu Eyre.' Richardson grins, waiting for Ranath to react to the use of her last name.

Ranath lifts her glass, a perfectly controlled smile on her lips. 'Hello, Nevil.'

Richardson sniffs. 'I'd like to say it's a pleasure to see you, but you know I hate lying.'

He speaks in English with a heavy American accent, Liberty's native tongue. English is the Yun Ju's second language, after Mandarin. Most people speak both, yet it's an established courtesy to speak the language of the host—and here it's Li Qiang and his Sunrise Group.

'I'm sorry to hear that,' Ranath answers in Mandarin. 'Do tell me why, though. I mean, other than the usual.'

'Oh, this is far from the usual.'

'Really? Do tell?'

He continues in English and she in Mandarin, the mismatch clearly increasing his discomfort. Ranath is half American after all, if such things mattered in the Yun Ju. He sucks in a breath, a lopsided smile on his lips. Around them, everyone's fallen into tense silence, even those at the edge of her vision no longer pretending to mind their own business.

'I'll never understand how we could have let you manoeuvre yourself into a monopoly in assemblers. A gross oversight, that's for sure. And highly skilful acquisition planning.' Richardson tips his head towards her.

The compliment is genuine, she's sure. He'd have loved to have done it himself if he'd thought of it first. 'Well, thank you.'

'But you're not finished, are you?' Richardson moves closer, only a step away now. 'Controlling the production isn't enough?'

Ranath waits, a cautious smile fixed on her lips. She needs to learn how much he knows before letting any reaction betray her intentions.

Richardson pauses. He's waiting, too, both of them locked in a stalemate of unfolding tactics. Ranath holds his gaze. She probably has a decade on him, and she will make it count.

Richardson huffs—a minor surrender. He looks around, speaking to the gathered audience as much as to her. 'The patents. You've been buying out the patents for all the assemblers' sub-systems. Effectively blocking anyone from setting up production.'

He knows more than she expected. Time for a counterattack.

'My lease rates are generous in the extreme, as your agro companies will confirm. They, on the other hand, have been hiking food prices every quarter. Not only do you control the trade with Earth, you're also taking over the food business here. Sun-Grow is yours now, right? And Hydro-Farm?'

Around her, whispers rise like the hum of an engine spooling up for take-off. This is news to at least some of the others, and they are not pleased. Good.

'So, if we're really going to talk monopolies, I dare say we should start with yours. Food supply is far more critical to the rest of us.'

The corners of Richardson's mouth twitch. 'I only manage the food trade for the Council. And without your assemblers, very soon none of us will be able to build new platforms.'

It's a weak response, especially after Ranath mentioned her lease rates. He feels it, too, because he follows with the next punch. 'You should know, I'm not the only one unhappy with your assemblers. I hear they've been putting people out of work. Just something to consider in case of, you know, any industrial action.'

Ranath takes a sip of her champagne. 'Is that so?'

Richardson frowns at her lack of concern. He glances around, searching the crowd for someone—the union boss ready to voice his misgivings. His fingers tap against his thigh. Messaging his aides, no doubt. Asking about Tarkovsky and learning that his trump card has already departed—after a meeting with Ranath.

Richardson tenses. His cheeks flash pink, then pale, his entire posture a study in barely controlled anger. 'I see...'

He draws a breath, struggling for focus. Then his frown eases and he leans towards her, his teeth bared in a wolfish grin. 'You're a skilful player, I give you that. But don't forget one thing: we're not the same, you and me. There's a difference between us no amount of cunning will let you cross. People trust Liberty. We've been up here from the beginning. You're a newcomer with a shady reputation. You've done well to rebrand your business after Bethesda, but our memory's better than that.' He gestures to the people around them, his grin widening. 'If I asked everyone here to choose in whose hands they'd rather put their lives, do you think anyone would vote for you?'

It's Ranath's turn to stiffen, a cold wave sweeping up her back. Around her, heads nod in agreement, some tentative, others not at all.

She puts on a relaxed smile, one she's practised so well it doesn't even feel forced. 'How about letting everyone keep their lives in their own hands? Because that's my preferred option.'

'Is that why you've been buying the patents?'

'Self-defence, what can I say? Being left at your mercy didn't quite appeal.'

'The feeling's mutual.'

He gives her another grin, then saunters away. Conversations resume in his wake, the music and the voices rising in excited crescendo.

She's won the first round—but everything she knows about Richardson tells her that such public defeat will only make him more determined. He'll be watching her every move, ready to pounce at the tiniest error. She was a target before, now she's made herself the bull's-eye.

'That was fun to watch.' Li Qiang's voice sounds in her ear.

Ranath glances around. On the other side of the room, Qiang leans on a Grecian column, watching her with an amused expression. 'Well played, Zhu Ranath. Though you must realise he won't let you forget this.'

'Is that why you did it? To get him off your back?'

Qiang laughs. 'Did what? But also, would you rather I hadn't?'

Ranath shakes her head. She'd always choose to be a step ahead, even if it makes the game tougher. Of course, Qiang's setting his own gambit, one that may prove even more dangerous than Richardson's. But at least now she's prepared.

A drone appears next to her carrying a single glass of champagne.

'You know, we and Liberty have been running the show for over a century. I have a feeling things are about to get much more interesting.'

Ranath lifts the glass, their eyes locked across the room. 'I'll drink to that.'

SEVEN

JASON

The next three stops cover the same issue: half-submerged nations with their remaining planting ground devastated by another outbreak of the rotting phage. The Yun Ju is sending the new generation of phage remedies, but it's too late to save this year's harvest. The forecast is dire; in some regions, food riots have already brought people out to the streets. The first shipments from the Alliance emergency reserves have arrived at local distribution centres, only to be met by activists armed with slogans and flame throwers trying to burn them. Apparently, they blame the crop failure not on the phage but on the red rice they've been forced to grow.

The new variety was developed specifically for these regions at a considerable cost to the Alliance. It should be a godsend: it tastes almost identical to regular rice and gives reliable yields even in the saltwater contaminated soil. But somehow, the rumour spread that it would make people infertile, alter their DNA, and corrupt their fields, all part of some extended conspiracy in which the Alliance wanted to take over their land. Half of the farmers burned the seeds, the rest refused to harvest the rice. And when the phage struck, it seemed to confirm their worst fears.

Jason's outreach team has spent weeks trying to educate the activists, with little effect. Before the famine, the protests were a mere annoyance; now they are life-threatening. Jason visits each government site in turn, but the leaders he helped get elected only spread their arms and shake their heads. They are doing their utmost, they say, but they can't change people's minds. Until, of course, he produces the bribes they've been waiting for. Then the riot police come out, the protesters vanish, and the aid deliveries resume. Jason departs in another excrement-showered armoured car, driving past hungry-eyed children and snaking food lines, wondering if it's those same leaders who spread disinformation just so they can collect the bribes. The thought makes him sick, but there's nothing else he can do. He never knows what happens to the protesters after he leaves, and if they ever get back to farming their fields with any kind of rice. The blimp-jet moves on, while Jason spends another sleepless night reminding himself that whatever happens to them must be better than the rest of the nation starving to death. Probably.

Jason finishes a hurried breakfast alone, his people already—or still—at work. He checks his messages. Richardson has finally responded to the meeting request, four days late. Apparently, they're dealing with an emergency following the latest Sun storm, but Jason's not sure how much he can believe the excuse. The delay has made him suspicious, even though he can't think of a reason why Richardson might be involved with Volkov's swindle. Liberty's business is orbital trade, especially in food-stuffs hard to obtain in the Yun Ju. They make a killing distrib-uting these to the stations. Richardson wouldn't risk his most lucrative deal for a discount on Volkov's apples. It has to be someone else, sniffing an opportunity—or trying to undermine

Liberty's position. But then, Jason reminds himself, who really knows what's going through their minds? The orbital elites play by a different rulebook.

Below them, orange sand gives way to the greys of the city-spanning industrial complex: the Sub-Saharan Research Institute and the manufactories of New Lagos. The Institute's new dean has requested a call, but since their route passed close to the area, Jason's decided to pay her a visit instead. It helps to know who he's dealing with, especially now, when Volkov and his ilk may be trying to make friends in the manufacturing circles.

Jason enters the main room as the blimp-jet settles on the edge of the landing strip. Outside the window, hot air turns the landscape into a shimmering mirage. The air conditioning unit revs up, fighting the heat.

'Did she mention why she wanted to talk?' Jason asks for probably the third time. He's having trouble staying focused, his mind stuck in a loop between Volkov, Richardson, and the sunburned faces of protesters haunting his dreams.

'Maybe just an introduction?' Aya lifts her head from the screen where she's tracking Volkov's shipments across the globe. She rubs her eyes, her skin grey and without lustre. Khalil is asleep with his head on the table.

They're scheduled for a break after this stop, way overdue. He really should give his people more time off. The fact that he hates returning to his empty house doesn't mean that they do.

'Get some rest, the two of you. You're wearing yourselves too thin.'

Aya looks like she's about to mention a pot and a kettle, but he picks up his pad and heads for the blimp's door before she gets the chance.

The car waiting for him outside is a regular passenger taxi, light green with the sheen of solar-glass. No armoured vehicles here, no police escort or hungry protesters. This is the receiving end of the global food chain—in turn only made possible due to the machines produced here. And probably the only place in the world where nobody hates him.

Dean Tejumola Abiola's office consists of chairs, screens, and a single picture hanging askew on the wall opposite the entrance: Earth, as it used to be, with the Sahara's sands still contained in their north-African basin. The room is empty as Jason arrives; the dean herself appears behind him an instant later: a full figure, round face, ebony-dark skin, the cracked lips of someone who chews on her stylus. A frown cuts her forehead, vanishing the moment she passes the door.

'Mr Nevsky, I appreciate you coming to see me in person. Have a seat.'

An assistant rolls in a small table carrying glasses and a couple of metal jugs wet with condensation. The choice is water or iced coffee, and they both choose the latter.

Jason takes a large sip, the liquid more bitter than how he usually takes it but at least that will keep him awake. Lack of sleep has been creeping up on him. It really is time for a break.

'What is it that you wanted to talk about?'

Abiola's frown returns. 'I need your help. Not just me—the other research institutes have the same issue.'

'Which is?'

'The Yun Ju. They are stealing our best people.'

Jason freezes with the glass halfway to his lips. The Yun Ju took his daughter, too. Except they didn't steal her—she ran away, from him. The ice cubes rattle as his hand shakes. How is she now? Until she left Earth, he could still keep track of her, even from a distance. He could be there if she ever needed him, if she ever changed her mind... Now she's out of reach. His only child. Will he ever see her again?

He puts on a smile. 'You mean, the Aspire Academy?'

Abiola waves her arm. 'No, they're good for us. They only

take a fraction of the people they train. No, it's whoever steals our current scientists, and their research.'

'What do you mean?'

'Like just now: my bio-engineering team lead. He had very promising results in his recent study. And now he's gone, together with the team's research data—and after he erased all the backups. The last I heard he was heading to Kenya.'

Abiola pauses, as if waiting for him to make the connection between Kenya and the Feidi space elevator. Except—something doesn't add up here. The Yun Ju could certainly headhunt a brilliant scientist, but they are never coy about it. And why would they have him erase the research data?

'What was he working on?'

'Orchard yields. Fruit abundance vs size.'

Jason stifles a curse. That's just something Volkov would pay for.

'And it's not the first time it's happened. The brightest minds we train, somehow they always get a better offer in the Yun Ju. It's like...'Abiola trails off. Her eyes narrow in hesitation. 'Like they don't want us to succeed.'

Jason laughs—a bit too loudly, his nerves frayed. 'Now that's a bit of an exaggeration!'

'Is it?' Abiola waves her arm towards the grey blocks outside. 'This entire industrial complex—all we do is assemble standard kits. And only the mechanical parts; the actual brains of the machines arrive from the Yun Ju ready-made—and sealed. We're not even allowed to look inside.'

Damn. He's touched a sore spot. Now she's angry and will push him where he doesn't want to go. 'The Yun Ju are very careful about—'

'Yeah, their industrial secrets, I know. I can even understand that part. But we are a *research* institute. Yet every year our funding's cut, our equipment requests delayed or denied. Our best people disappear for better jobs in the Yun Ju. And not just here—all the research facilities say the same thing.' Abiola leans forward, cutting the distance between them. 'The Yun Ju aren't just protecting their expertise, Mr Nevsky. They're stopping us from developing ours.'

Abiola pulls away, defiant. What she's said could cost her her job, and she knows it. He could get her fired. He would, if he thought it would help. The last thing he needs is a flock of disgruntled scientists undermining the Alliance while Volkov and his pack are circling. Oh, the irony.

Jason rises. The chairs are too confining, the lack of a table between them leaving him too exposed. He walks to a narrow window overlooking the grey cubes of labs and a maze of concrete paths. Distant figures of scientists scuttle over the concrete. He draws a deep breath. He's tired, so tired. But he won't give up, not now, not ever.

What to tell her? She's too smart for a lie, too principled for a bribe. But he can't let the suspicion spread or it will burn them from the inside. She has to understand what's at stake. 'The Yun Ju... They are scared of us becoming independent. Their food supply is too vulnerable, and they rely on us for the rare minerals. They need us, and they're terrified of being at our mercy. If they feel we are catching up, about to become self-sufficient, they will find a way to stop that from happening. How long do you think we'd survive without the pollinator drones, or the engineered seeds?'

'Then why don't we make them ourselves? If we could do real research—'

'And how quickly could you do that? How many people would die in a single year without pollinators?'

'If the Yun Ju need our food, then they'll have to listen.'

'They can survive longer than we can. Believe me, I've run the numbers. I could also tell you how they have a whole belt of asteroids to throw at us to ensure we listen—but we don't need to go into the extreme scenarios. The truth is, this arrangement benefits all of us. Especially you.'

'How so?'

'Without the Yun Ju it's just you against the food growers. We have little fertile land, and already those who own it want to keep it to themselves. The only thing that's stopping them is the lack of manufacturing, because we, the Alliance, don't let them have it. Now, if you could do all the research, if you could make the seeds and the drones, how long do you think you could keep it secret? How long before somebody sold it out to the highest bidder? Before the food growers didn't need you anymore? If you're counting on human solidarity, then I have bad news for you.'

Abiola bites her lip. Her face has grown paler, the colour of the Sahara's sand at dusk. She lifts her glass towards her mouth, but the movement dies halfway. 'Do you think... it's the growers who've been stealing our research? Not the Yun Ju?'

Jason returns to his chair, but doesn't sit, only leans against it. 'I don't know. I'm going to try to find out, that I can promise.'

The woman doesn't seem to hear him anymore. He wonders what futures she's envisioning, and if they are as bleak as those he's seen in his nightmares.

'We're fucked, aren't we?' she says after a while.

'We keep fighting. The Alliance—'

'Please. No promises. We've heard those before.'

'You're right. I'm sorry.' Jason waits another moment, but it seems everything's been said. 'Send me any information about your missing scientist. We'll try to track him.'

The air shimmers as the privacy bubble seals around Jason. The tech is another gift from the Yun Ju, just like most of the equipment the Alliance uses. This is a deal that benefits them all, he reminds himself, no matter how sour the words taste. The art is to keep the exchange going, to always keep the balance tipped slightly in Earth's favour. Jason retains his own security team, though; he's not naive enough to trust anybody but his own people. They're just behind the bubble's opaque walls, monitoring every transmission without actually hearing a word of the conversation.

Nevil Richardson materialises out of thin air on the other side of the table, only the slight paleness of the image betraying the man is not really there. He's wearing his usual soft aqua-coloured shirt and a darker jacket, his long white hair loose over his broad shoulders. Dyed white, surely, since Richardson doesn't look more than forty—though who knows what cosmetic tech they have in orbit.

Richardson spreads his arms apologetically. 'I'm so sorry for delaying our meeting. We've had such bad luck with the last solar storm; it knocked out three of our mag-shield generators. It was all hands on deck getting them repaired before we got fried up here!'

His laughter rolls and gurgles like something practised in front of a mirror. Jason forces a grin and hopes it looks amused rather than desperate.

'Anyway, we're here now,' Richardson continues. 'So, what was so urgent?'

Jason studies the other man's face, analysing every twitch of his mouth. 'I've paid a visit to the Siberian Archipelago.'

The corners of Richardson's mouth quiver.

'Had a chat with President Volkov there. I assume you've heard about his brother's preaching?'

Richardson frowns. 'Now that you mention it, the name does sound familiar. I have no details, though. We've got our share of self-important buffoons up here in orbit!'

He laughs again—slightly too loudly, his expression too eager while his eyes remain cold.

Jason bobs his head in agreement. 'I'm sure you do. They grow on the most barren land. Probably even in vacuum.'

Richardson stabs a manicured finger at Jason. 'You've got that right. Anyway, what's our friend's... Volkov, his name was? What's he up to?'

'Many things that I'll not bore you with—but one in our common interest. He's backdoor trading with someone—or someones—on the stations.'

'What?!' Richardson leans forward, all rage. 'That's... I want to say that's impossible, but of course, you must have proof or you wouldn't be saying this...'

His brow rises in a question, his gaze probing, hungry for information. He wants Jason to reveal his sources, to divulge how much he knows. Interesting.

'I'm afraid I'm quite certain this is the case.' Jason sighs. 'Though as yet no idea on how he's getting around the barriers. Or who his partners are.'

Richardson drums his fingers on the table. His jaw is working as he considers the answer. 'It's got to be one of the elevators. Kilimanjaro would be my guess.'

'That's what we're thinking, yes,' Jason says. 'We'll crack the Earth side of the operation sooner or later. But once the cargo leaves the surface, it's out of our reach. Quite literally.'

'So it is.' Richardson nods. A deep line cuts his forehead above the knotted brow. 'It will be tricky to trace, even for me. Cargo manifests are confidential. And there's so much traffic between the transit docks and the stations, it's impossible to track—especially since half of the time we're on the opposite side of the planet.'

'Will it help if we find out what he's selling?'

Richardson winces as if the idea hasn't occurred to him. 'What? Yes, yes, of course. It'd greatly help. I mean, they must be selling it on at the stations, so if we suddenly have an overabundance of, I don't know, peanuts, then we'll need to talk to the peanut merchants, right?'

'Absolutely.'

'Leave it with me,' Richardson says, rising. 'I'll get to the bottom of this. But send me everything you've got—and I mean, everything. This will take some fine detective work, so the more information I have, the better.'

'Absolutely,' Jason repeats. He keeps his grateful smile plastered on as Richardson bows a curt farewell and stomps out into digital fog. Only when the last pixels of the man are gone, does he let his smile fall. The conversation hasn't gone exactly as he expected. But Richardson wasn't born to be an actor—and now Jason will have to find out why the one man he expected to be on his side has been lying.

EIGHT

LIZ

Their week-long orientation starts the morning after their arrival. Liz, Kene, and Vithakan, a skinny Tamil man she's barely heard utter a word, are supposed to meet someone called Angela for an 'Introduction to Shielding' session. They've been issued new uniforms, with just the Academy's logo in the place usually taken by their national flags. This feels odd, wrong in a way that really drives home how much these used to define them. Ridiculous, in retrospect, even if her 'retrospect' is only two days old. Here, in the Yun Ju, it matters only what you can contribute, not where you've come from.

Liz pulls on the new clothes: sturdy trousers and a fitted jacket made for crawling into tight equipment spaces and resisting minor electrical shocks, then examines her allocated wrist band. It's chunkier and heavier than any she's used before, like something you'd see in old vids. Pulled out from storage for the rookies, she decides. Probably the machine's last stint before the recycler.

She scrolls through the menus on her way to the common room, the shared area in the mini 'compound' that is the graduate quarters: a complex of tiny private bedrooms centred around a communal space with sections for study and rest. The wrist band's interface seems designed to confuse, but at least the messages are easy to access. There's the confirmation of the briefing with Angela, but also a new item in her agenda, starting in... ten minutes?

'I'm meeting a J. Lars at Research Central?' Liz glances at the others. 'Anyone else?'

Kene and Vithakan sit at a high, round table in the dining area, remnants of breakfast scattered before them.

'Nothing for me,' Kene says. 'Just Angela, as before.'

Alejandro retrieves a coffee from the machine in the corner, then plops himself at a neighbouring table. 'The name sounds familiar. I think he's the head of one of the sections...' His eyes narrow with suspicion. 'Why would *you* be seeing him?'

A chill runs down Liz's back. Why indeed? What's different about her—other than the one thing she'd rather nobody knew?

'It may be good news,' Kene tries.

'Well, they wouldn't bring you all the way up here to fire you now!' Vithakan laughs.

He's trying to be encouraging, but he doesn't know the truth. What if the news about her identity has leaked out? If the people here decided they wanted nothing to do with her? It's happened before—why should now be different?

Liz bites her lip. 'I guess I'd better be going, then.'

'We'll see you later with Angela,' Kene calls behind her.

Liz doesn't stop to tell her how much she hopes there really is a 'later.'

Once outside the door, she taps her wrist band for details of her appointment. It gives her the time and the room number, but no instructions how to get there. Damn, now she'll either be late or have to ask the way at each junction. For a small station, New Hope is still kilometres of winding passages, and three different levels. How do people find anything here?

Pink is for science, she remembers Jacques saying as he led them to their quarters last night. By then her nausea had given way to a throbbing headache and she barely paid him any attention. But he must have been talking about the floor markings, the thin strips of colour just where the walls meet the soft decking. There are five lines here, blue for engineering and green for medical, as far as she can recall. Red and black, too, but she doesn't remember what those mean. The fifth one is pink, but without any indication whether she should turn left or right.

She turns left on a hunch, and because she vaguely remembers Jacques pointing to the 'quarters section' farther to the right. For once she's lucky—the pink line grows marginally thicker at the next junction, and then even thicker after that, until she reaches a door in translucent pink with black letters announcing *Research Central*. Behind it, pink carpeted corridors branch out into a maze of glass-walled offices and open spaces with computer terminals, only half of them occupied. Liz checks the time: one minute late. Shit.

She pops her head into the nearest office. 'Er, J. Lars?'

The three people inside stare at her as if she's an alien. Finally, one decides to speak. 'The big office. On the corner to the right.'

Liz rushes on, then pauses for five seconds to calm her breathing. Three minutes late. Damn.

J. Lars is a log of a man: tall and broad, with wavy blond hair that begs for a cut, thick brows and the bluest eyes she has ever seen. He glances up as she enters, then returns to his work. She waits, wondering if there's been some kind of mix-up, when the man finally looks at her again.

'Elizabeth Lake, I presume?'

'Yes. I got a message that—'

'You have been brought to my attention.'

Liz swallows. Is this good news or bad? And who exactly has brought her to his attention?

'I read your thesis,' the man continues. 'It was decent.'

Is that a compliment or a put down? Damn, why can't this man just talk? 'You wanted to see me?'

'Yes. Well. Ranath's taken an interest in you, for obvious reasons. She wants you in my group. I'm not convinced. You're too new here. But she's the boss, so we'll give it a try.'

Liz nods. Her throat has gone dry, and her knees threaten to cave in under her. Ranath knows who she is—of course she does, that's how the Academy found out. And now for some reason Ranath puts her here, with the man who hates the idea. Why? They didn't have to offer her the job if they didn't want her. Unless they plan to humiliate her? Get at her father somehow?

She thought she'd escaped his shadow. She might have just fallen deeper under it.

She stifles the urge to turn on her heel and run back where she came from, back to the elevator and her old misery. No. Fuck them. She's not done yet.

Liz lifts her chin. 'What do you want me to do?'

Lars doesn't look at her as he gestures to his screen. 'I've sent you some assignments. Send them back as soon as you're done. Then we'll talk again.'

She waits another moment, but the man pays her no more attention. *Well, fuck you, too.* She turns and heads out, hoping to find her way in the maze of colour-coded corridors, now suddenly blurry through the moisture in her eyes.

Her eyes are dry by the time she returns to the graduate quarters. Liz itches to ask if by now the others have also received messages from their new bosses, but she knows it's just wishful thinking. Nobody but her will be getting special treatment. They are here to prove themselves, not pay for their family's sins.

She puts on a defiant smile as Kene and Vithakan appear in the door. They cast her curious glances, but luckily, their guide arrives before they can ask them.

'Hello there!' Angela is a tall, athletic woman, with dark brown skin and a shaved head. Her smile has a mischievous edge, like she's about to let you in on a secret. 'I'm one of the solar defence engineers, otherwise known as the most important people on the station. And you must be my lucky three?'

Angela grins as they nod, then waves them on. 'We'll start with the equipment tour. I hope you've had a solid breakfast, because it's going to be a long day.'

She marches them down a long corridor that seems to run the length of the station's ring. Smaller passages break off to the left and right. The walls are mostly white, or bluish now in the cold light of the day hours. In the evening the light will shift to yellow and orange, aiding their circadian rhythms.

Liz slows as a drone approaches from the opposite direction—disc-shaped but with a small cupola in the centre, like a UFO from an old movie. There's enough space for it to pass overhead, but the thing seems to be heading straight at her, the angry buzzing of its propellers jumping up an octave. She glances at Angela, but their guide is checking something on her wrist band, oblivious. Kene and Vithakan shift to the sides, leaving Liz to take point. Damn. The last thing she needs now is a game of chicken with a flying saucer. Liz waits another instant, then sidesteps to her right—just as the drone swerves in exactly the same direction. The machine beeps, its engines revving as it dashes towards the ceiling. It misses her by inches, its lights flashing in something very close to indignation.

Angela bursts out laughing. 'Oh, just ignore them. They're annoyingly obtuse, but they'll get out of your way.'

'Thanks,' Liz mutters, trying not to swear.

'They do ping you to confirm they see you.' Angela does a

double take, as if remembering something. 'I hope you're planning to get yourself wired. It'll make your life much easier.'

Right. Of course. That's why nobody here asks for directions, why her wrist band is an ancient model, why the people in Lars's office looked at her so strange—because they get all the information they need right onto their lenses.

Kene shakes her head, unconvinced. They all grew up on horror stories from Bethesda and the mind-control devices tested there.

'It's perfectly safe. Just look around if you want proof. Everyone here's got some sort of a wire. Opt for external if you're that scared.' Angela almost rolls her eyes.

'That's what they said last time,' Kene says.

'Oh, come on. The technology is completely different. The old Mind-Link scare—that was ages ago, and who knows if any of it really happened.'

Liz stares. She may resent what her great-aunt's doomsday messages have done to her family, but she's never doubted the truth of what happened on Bethesda. She's heard the reports too many times, seen them analysed and dissected. It happened. The Mind-Link, Destiny, the Guardian...

A sudden chill climbs up her spine. The Guardian, the man Destiny sent to destroy Aunt Nathalie's ship to protect their secret—he was American. New Hope used to be an American station. The Guardian may have been here, walking down this very corridor as he planned his murders. The thought makes her dizzy—but it's like visiting ancient ruins, a place of historical significance, nothing more. It was so long ago, decades before she was even born. Something her father would dwell on—Liz has a future to look forward to.

Angela is talking again, her voice bright and confident. She turns into a side corridor and opens the door to a vast, empty room. Black pinpricks of holo-projectors cover all the surfaces, the air still carrying the lingering smell of ozone. 'I hope you weren't expecting a spacewalk!'

'At this point, I've cancelled all expectations,' Vithakan says.

Angela laughs—but it's a warm, friendly laugh, supportive rather than derisive. 'I guess it could be overwhelming. I mean, I wouldn't know, I've never been ground-side.'

'Never?'

'Nope. Born and raised here.'

They peer at her as if she's suddenly grown gills or scales. But no, she's human. They shouldn't be surprised; most people now in orbit were born here. And yet, the idea takes Liz's breath away. To have always been so comfortable, so far away from the riots and the hunger... This really is a different world.

'Ready?' Angela asks.

Beams of light erupt all around them, connecting into shapes, translucent at first, then weaving into perfect 3D objects. An instant later, only the soft hum of the projectors and the faint scent of ozone betray that the generators now standing before them are holograms. The three graduates exchange glances. Liz has never seen projections with such lifelike fidelity.

Angela walks to the nearest machine. She cuts through it with a sweeping gesture of her arm, and the holo splits into a cross-section. Detailed schematics appear above it, hovering in mid-air in colour-coded layers of circuits and coils.

'Ninth generation mag-shield inducer,' she says. 'Looks familiar?'

Not in a million years. This doesn't resemble anything Liz has seen at the Academy.

'You said ninth generation?' she asks, and Angela nods. 'The prototypes we had—what we thought were prototypes— were the fifth generation.'

Angela scrunches her mouth, displeased. 'Hmm. They told me you were trained on outdated technology, but not obsolescent...' She scowls, apparently at a loss of what to do next, then makes up her mind. 'No point taking you through the changes. Let's go back to the first principles, and how they are used in the current tech.'

Liz swallows, her throat dry and the floor soft under her feet. What's the use of her skills if everything she has studied is years—decades—out of date? How can she even hope to solve Lars's assignments, let alone do well enough to impress him?

'Why?' she manages to ask. 'Why have we been trained on outdated technology?'

Angela's face brightens. 'I've asked the same question. But think about it: you are the select few. Most of the graduates will remain on Earth. They need to be able to work with the technology that's actually there.'

The answer seems logical and yet it makes Liz dizzy by its implications. It's not a surprise that the stations are so far ahead —she's always known that to be the case, even if she never realised the size of the gap. But there's something disturbing in the fact that even the Academy wouldn't give them a glimpse of the current research, wouldn't let them see what was possible. She has no time to dwell on it, though, as Angela sweeps the projection away.

'First principles, then,' she says as graphs and equations materialise in front of them.

They hardly talk on the way back, overwhelmed and exhausted. Liz's head feels like it's now a home to a deranged woodpecker, pounding its way out through her temples. They worked through lunch, because for Angela food was apparently optional. She'd probably still be going if Vithakan's loudly grumbling stomach didn't remind her that, unlike the holograms they studied, they were, in fact, creatures of flesh.

They find most of the others already back in their shared

quarters, some crowded around the meal dispenser, others crumpled on the sofas, eyes closed. And yet, everyone manages to look up as Liz enters, their questioning glances confirming she's the only one who's already met her future boss. Judging by the way they shift around her, they probably believe it's a good sign—or at least they are hedging their bets in case it is. For all they know, she might have got a promotion. Liz wants to laugh, but she's too tired even for that. And her evening is only just starting—Lars's 'assignments' arrived soon after she left his office, but she hasn't had a chance to look at them yet.

She picks up whatever the food machine has spat out without giving it a glance. It's food, and she needs it. The second thing she needs is an empty workstation—and she has all of them to choose from. She selects a spot farthest from the crowd and syncs up her wrist band. Lars's message pops up on the screen. Fifteen attachments. She closes her eyes for a moment, stifling a gasp or a groan, then returns to the dining area for a big mug of coffee. She might as well not plan on sleeping, because there's no chance in hell she'll get this finished before the morning.

NINE

RANATH

The newscast plays on Ranath's bedroom wall: a report from Singapore, the site of Earth's second largest space elevator. Angry crowds surround the elevator base, kept away by cordons of local police. Inside the perimeter, private security contractors hold the line with tasers and water cannons. Deeper still, guarding the critical elements of the structure, are Yun Ju's own agents: the Sky Sharks, armed to the teeth with all the weapons they need to keep the elevator safe.

Apparently, the locals have attempted to stop a food shipment. Understandable, if misguided. She can't blame the hungry masses for forgetting that what they get in return is invaluable for the planet's agriculture: seeds engineered for the toughest conditions, pollinator drones without which no orchard would bear fruit. All that for feeding less than the numbers now gathered there, shouting their protests. By the last count, little over twenty thousand people now live in orbit. Less than half of their food still comes from the planet. But the people now storming the elevator are too desperate to think straight—and that makes them dangerous.

Ranath zooms in on the projection and queries the system

for details. The numbers are higher than the last time, almost double. For now, they are still individuals drawn together by anger at the supposed injustice—but there's enough of them to have put the elevator security on high alert. How long till they decide to organise, or get their hands on some weapons? Officially, the old ground-to-orbit missiles have been destroyed, but who knows how thorough that destruction has been? Even one surviving warhead could easily take down a station. Five guided missiles, like those used in the scarcity wars, and there will be nothing left of the Yun Ju.

An exasperated groan escapes her lips. This is what she's been trying to get the others to see for a decade: that they can't survive here, so close to the planet and so dependent on its resources. No one on the Council will listen. Richardson claims he's got it 'under control,' and the others believe him, too focused on building their fat little kingdoms to pay attention. Even Li Qiang doesn't acknowledge the threat. He's building new agro platforms so he doesn't have to rely on Liberty, but it's not Liberty who's the real danger to them all. It's those hungry millions who will one day demand their share.

She waves the projection away. The others can do what they want; she's not going to wait for the barbarians to tear down the gates. Her father lost his life trying to save humanity from its self-inflicted hell—that's sacrifice enough for one family. They've had their chance. And she's not going to stick around to watch them self-immolate.

Ranath checks the time. By now, she should be finishing her morning stretches, but the news has soured her mood. She shouldn't let herself get emotional. She has a plan—her Ark—and the resources to make it happen. She just needs to keep Richardson from getting in the way.

The server drone glides into the room with her breakfast tray. Ranath glances at the offerings, noticing a gilded envelope next to the coffee cup: the paper embossed with the Sunrise

Group's golden insignia, but her name spelled out in blood-red ink in Li Qiang's lavish handwriting. She picks it up, a grin pouring onto her face. Alone in her bedroom, she can allow herself a moment of delight. It is exactly what she expects: a challenge to a duel. They've been joking about it for years after discovering they were both aficionados of the ancient sport of fencing, the zero-g version. This is perfection—not just the prospect of the bout, but the timing. Li Qiang wants to talk— and she'll be very happy to oblige.

Ranath heads to her office, the server drone following behind like a flying puppy. Min Woo's ping flashes on her lenses. She blinks twice to accept the call and her aide appears next to her, the circles under his eyes betraying a sleepless night.

'We've finalised the miners' contract.' Min Woo clears his throat, his voice gruff. 'It's in your files.'

'Good. Anything I should note?'

'Not really. We've killed the costliest demands but gave in on all the small stuff, so they are happy. Medical provisions and pensions, nothing beyond what we were willing to offer in the first place. Tarkovsky's already signed his part.'

Ranath sniffs. Amazing what amount of goodwill you can get by giving people what they actually want. She'd have included medical coverage even if they hadn't asked for it—the cost is negligible if you know how to negotiate, and a healthy workforce costs less in the long term. Not to mention being more productive and loyal.

'They are asking about departure arrangements,' Min Woo says. 'We can delay them for a couple of weeks, but more than that is asking for trouble.'

Right. Everybody will expect them to set off as soon as the contract is signed. Waiting makes no financial sense, so any delay will get attention. But Ranath's not ready yet—and she can't let the details of her plan slip before the deeds are signed and the rock is hers forever.

She paces to the meeting table and calls up the projection: a tiny moon, barely the size of an Earth city, one of dozens swirling around Saturn. Her assemblers are there already, concealed under the surface as they excavate and construct the first layer of what this moon will become: a shell-world of concentric levels, each a habitat capable of housing and feeding thousands. Enough to ensure a healthy gene pool. The scientists, the artists, the creators, and the philosophers—the best of humanity given a second chance. Her secret Ark.

But if her plans leak before she's ready, the others will stop her. The competition inside the Yun Ju is fierce, every player guarding their place not just for prestige and profit but as a matter of survival. They are a finely tuned network of power and output, production and consumption, all centred on the resources received from Earth. No one is allowed to get too strong lest they tip the balance in their favour. Her assembler monopoly has already sent disgruntled ripples—but a new base would be another matter entirely. They will never see it as a new chance for humanity—they will see only what they want to see, a new outpost for Renewal with all the resources of Saturn at her disposal.

It will make her a threat significant enough for the rest of the Yun Ju to pull together in order to stop her. They will find a way, especially with the Council dragging their feet ratifying her purchase.

'We have to stall,' Ranath says. 'Once the miners reach Saturn, they'll figure out the truth. The news will spill; we won't be able to contain it.'

Min Woo reaches for a cup—she can't tell what it is, but his tired expression suggests it's probably coffee. 'I agree, but this deal has forced our hand. If we wait, people will start asking questions.'

Ranath returns to the breakfast tray the drone has left on her desk: sliced peaches, apples, and pears on a bed of soya yoghurt. They source soya locally now, but the fruit must have come up from the planet, right past the rioting mobs. They will have real trees on Ark, one day. Not at first, maybe not in her lifetime, but it's never been about her.

'We need to find an excuse,' she says slowly.

'We could start mining,' Min Woo says. 'Check out the most promising moons. We may actually find useful raw materials.'

Ranath nods. The others—Richardson, Li Qiang, and everyone else—they will be watching her every move, but if she plays into their expectations, their own biases will blind them. And then she knows. As always, truth makes the best lies. 'The miners will need a base.'

Min Woo tilts his head expectantly. 'Other than a ship?'

The obvious move would be to rent one of the mothballed colony ships to transport the miners and set up a base. Three of those are sitting idle after the populace lost enthusiasm for colonisation when the news from Bethesda arrived. No one has had the heart to scrap them, out of some sense of duty to the colonists still out there. They've been re-purposed, though, their cold-sleep pods now an emergency back up in case any station needed to evacuate.

'We could skip all that work to remove the cryo-pods and create living space... Once the miners are there—'

Min Woo's eyes brighten. 'They can build themselves a base.'

'A shallow one, the outermost shell level. Far away from where the assemblers are now working.'

They are both smiling now, satisfied. They will tell the miners to build themselves a home. Paid by Renewal, of course, and on a minor moon Ranath already happens to own. No one will think twice about a mining base. No one will consider the base to be the real plan.

'A good excuse to ask for the sale process to be expedited,' Ranath says.

'I'll put in a request,' Min Woo says. 'And ask Tarkovsky to back it.'

Ranath nods. Of course, she'll still have to decide how to handle the miners once that first base is completed. She may find them suitable jobs, mining other moons for all the minerals Ark will need to become self-sufficient. Some might even qualify to join them; she's already found a trove of geniuses in the most underprivileged corners of the planet. Anyway, she has months before this becomes a problem. No need to worry about it now.

The rest of the day flashes by in meetings: first with the engineers, checking the progress of the Ark works. They agree on a plan that will get the miners started—a miniature base that will later form the kernel of the outmost shell of the habitat. Sandip Bagrah returns with news that the attacks on the manufacturing cubes have miraculously stopped. Ranath takes her time with him, feeling the man out. He's not part of the insider group who knows about Ark, even though the newest line of assemblers his factories produce was designed precisely to carry out the construction. Officially, they are meant for building agro platforms—and the bots are really good at that, too, which is why Renewal makes such good money on them. Sandip could be an asset, but he's new in his role and this is not the time for wrong choices. She asks Ester to put a tracker on him instead. If the monitoring AI finds nothing to challenge his loyalty, they will have another chat in a week or two.

Duarte sends a message to schedule the meeting with the graduates, something they usually do at the end of their first week. Ranath hates breaking the routine—it sends the wrong message about the state of her business—but she hates the prospect of meeting the graduates—of meeting *her*—even more. She composes a message asking to postpone, then changes her mind. She's never let her emotions get the better of her, and starting now is unacceptable. Besides, the Nevsky woman is here on Ranath's own invitation.

She confirms the meeting with Duarte, then allows herself the indulgence of answering Li Qiang's duel challenge: she wastes half an hour procuring actual paper, a functioning fountain pen, and ink (blood red, of course), then sends Ester to find a wax seal for good measure. The woman glares at Ranath with an expression very close to panic, probably considering calling on the medics as well. Oh hell, sometimes even Ranath needs to let herself go. She *is* human, despite doing her best to make everyone forget that.

She's scanning the local news—Richardson's talks with Harmony about a joint medical venture and Nebu Owande from the Tian Gong co-op renewing their license for inter-orbital transport—when the distinctive sound of a high-pitched ping makes her sit up straight. Only one source uses that sound —and only once a year, on the same date for the last two decades. Ranath peers at the icon that has popped up on her screen. They are not due to talk for another five months. What happened?

She touches the icon to acknowledge the summons. A countdown clock flashes on the screen, then disappears. She has three minutes.

Ranath returns to her personal quarters, her residence adjacent to the offices. She walks to her meditation room, locks the door, and sets her house filters to private and secure. Her palms are moist, like they belong to someone else. She stands in the middle of the room, waiting.

Three minutes after she activated the icon, the air in front of her shimmers. The image is only a projection on her lenses, but the illusion is perfect. Two figures coalesce before her, shapes made of light. The faces are clear enough to read their expressions but not enough to betray their identity.

The apparitions bow slightly. 'Greetings, Caretaker.'

Ranath returns the gesture. 'Greetings, Caretakers.'

The ritual is ridiculous. The others know her name; she is the public face of Renewal while they revel in obscurity. But then, she agreed to play the part when she took the job two decades ago. This is how she became Zhu Ranath.

'Is there a problem?' she asks.

'We have detected an unusual number of attacks on your data. Someone very persistent is trying to access Renewal's accounts.'

'Do you know who?'

'No. Until the situation becomes critical, we cannot risk revealing ourselves by trying to investigate. This is up to you, Ranath.'

Damn. It has to be Liberty, who else? Richardson's flailing, and the others would be more discreet. Does Li Qiang's sudden invitation play into it somehow? Hacking attacks are not unusual—but they have never before alerted the Caretakers.

'What's different this time?' she asks.

'The nature of the attacks has changed.'

'Are they more sophisticated?'

'Not by much,' the right figure says. 'But this time they are not just probing your investments. They are digging into the past.'

Ranath winces. The past. The one secret that can destroy everything she's worked for. Take Ark from her when she's so close.

'We've done all we could to obscure the sources of our founding capital,' the right figure says. 'But we won't know if we've done enough.'

'Another question is, why would anyone start looking into it now...?' The left figure pauses, its brows furrowed accusingly. 'You must have done something to provoke them.'

They wait, scowling at her with something between suspicion and impatience.

'They're threatened by my progress,' Ranath says.

'Is that all?'

Ranath doesn't answer. Five years ago, she told them that the Yun Ju wasn't safe, that they needed to look for a better place, abandon this failed version of humanity and start again, build a new future with the brightest minds. She showed them the plans for Ark.

They didn't listen. They dismissed the idea and barred her from using Renewal's funds on the project. She's continued regardless, in secret.

The left figure steps towards her, the pinpricks of its eyes focused on hers. 'I've been looking into your personal investments, Zhu Ranath. You've done well for yourself. You seem to be branching out. All those purchases, the stock buybacks... I'm beginning to doubt the sincerity of your commitment.'

Ranath glares. How dare they? She's given her life to the mission while they grow comfortable in their cushioned hideaways, refusing to face the truth. 'My loyalty remains unchanged.'

'Don't forget who you are, Ranath Eyre,' the right figure says. 'You are useful, and you *have* done well. We'd rather keep things as they are—but Renewal will never be yours. And we can always get a new zhu.'

The apparitions vanish, the light of their pixels fading from her lenses.

Ranath sucks in air through her nostrils until her chest hurts and her diaphragm spasms. She wants to scream, but such comforts are for lesser minds. She pulls in a breath and presses her hands to her thighs. *Hold yourself together. You're Ranath. Zhu Ranath. Focus.*

Somebody is after her. Richardson, most likely, digging for proof for his innuendos after he called her a newcomer at the reception. And now his attacks have alerted the Caretakers. They must know about the miners, about Saturn. If they find out she's ignored their ruling on Ark, they will stop her. She's a zhu, not Renewal's owner. Without the faction's resources, her own funds won't be enough.

She pulls in another deep breath, then exhales slowly, her eyes closed in concentration. Nothing's lost yet. This was a warning—but also a signal to safeguard her plans. Whoever has been digging into her past—Richardson or whoever else—she will find them, and she will annihilate them before they can do any real damage. She won't let anyone destroy Ark.

TEN

JASON

They set off back to the Alliance base in Northern Canada the same night. Jason has promised everyone a break, and they deserve it. The world is not going to fall apart in the next few days—or at least not any more than it already has. The promise of a holiday seems to have given everyone more energy, because by the time Jason emerges for breakfast, Khalil and Aya are already leaning over the display, excited.

Aya waves him over. 'Good news: we might have a lead on Volkov's shipments. Khalil called the Feidi Sentry office. I thought they were defunct, but evidently not!'

Jason almost smacks himself on the forehead. He should have thought about that. The Sentry was set up in the aftermath of the Feidi riots, when medical supplies were diverted from local hospitals to the highest bidders in the Yun Ju. The very supplies that could have saved his mother's life. The Sentry's charter gave it emergency access to the cargo manifests of all the goods passing through the Feidi—but sixty years on, it's never been invoked. By now, most people have forgotten the Sentry ever existed. He should have remembered it, though.

'They only have an automated responder, but I kept ping-ing,' Khalil says. His eyes are bloodshot with lack of sleep, but his voice rings with energy. 'Finally, I got lucky, and it passed me to a real person. Though it took a while to persuade them that this was indeed an emergency that required the Sentry powers.'

'Did you tell them about Volkov?'

'No, I assumed it wasn't something we wanted to share widely. I told them we had an issue with a shipping company—subcontracting without agreement, incurring extra cost to the Alliance, and some such.'

Jason nods. Khalil is learning fast. Only a pity that his first new skill is the art of lying. 'Did they buy it?'

'I was lucky Mr Hassan there seemed to have a good day. Or a need to feel important. Anyway, he not only sent me the records for the entire year, he also promised nobody would know we had them.' Khalil grins. 'I'm not sure if he was covering his back or ours, but I'll take it!'

'We've only just started looking at it,' Aya says. 'But if Volkov's shipments are going through the Feidi, then they'll be here.'

'Excellent.' Jason gestures to the data rolling across the table in rows of tiny figures. 'Aya, you get started on this. I want to see if Khalil's luck will hold on our other problem.'

Aya cocks an eyebrow, then nods, her attention already shifting back to the data.

Jason waves Khalil over to the coffee machine and pours them both a cup.

'By 'our other problem' I assume you mean Dean Abiola's absconded scientist?' Khalil asks.

'Yes. Doctor Ekene Kanye, if I remember correctly. My bet is that he's heading to Volkov with the stolen research, but...' Jason pauses as Khalil frowns. 'What? You don't think he's gone to Volkov?'

'No, you're probably right, this does smell like Volkov. It just... never mind. Do you have an idea how to find him?'

'Abiola thinks he's gone to the Yun Ju. Whether she's right or wrong, it could make our work faster if we excluded that possibility. Do you think you can persuade Mr Hassan to help us with the passenger listings?'

'Ha!' Khalil grins, already turning towards the comms room. 'Let me try, before he gets off shift.'

Jason glances between Khalil's retreating back and the numbers flickering on Aya's screen, then retreats to his desk to check the dailies. Another phage outbreak in Jaipur. More flooding in Bangladesh. He closes his eyes, remembering the protesters that lined the streets there on his last visit. Their anger turning into fear as the riot police appeared. He shakes his head, pulling himself to the present. He can't help them. But he can stop people like Volkov making things worse. And Richardson, whatever he's after.

There's still no news from Khalil when Aya pings him twenty minutes later. He finds her with Lucia and Ken in the security team's narrow cabin. The three of them huddle around a holo showing what looks like a pile of children's blocks.

'The data's badly indexed, but we've managed to extract all the shipments labelled as 'food.' Most of them we can trace to our licensed traders. Except for those.' Aya swipes her arm over the holo. The colours fade, leaving only a handful of red blocks. 'Apples. Plums. Walnuts. All tree-grown fruit. Sold by companies that have since vanished from the register.'

'They will have left a trace somewhere,' Lucia says. 'We'll find them.'

Jason nods. 'Good. That's half of it. How about the recipients?'

'That's trickier,' Ken says. 'All we have are tracking codes, but no key to what they mean. We think they are going to Shui Lian station, though.'

Jason and Aya exchange glances. He's shared his suspicions about Richardson with his two aides but not with the wider team. Shui Lian is a small, unaffiliated station with business links to all the big Yun Ju players. Pretty much a dead end.

'Damn,' he starts to say when Khalil pops his head inside the security cabin, hair ruffled and his brows furrowed.

'Er... Can I borrow you two for a moment?'

'How's your luck holding?' Aya asks when she and Jason follow Khalil outside. 'Because I seem to have lost mine.'

'Not so good. Turns out, the Sentry doesn't have access to the passenger information. Still, I've got something—I'm not sure what, but I want to run it past you.'

They stop at the display table, now showing a holo of a brown-skinned man with grey hair and a matching goatee.

'Doctor Ekene Kanye, Abiola's missing scientist,' Khalil says. 'He reminded me of something, but I wasn't sure what—until I remembered this person.'

Another holo appears next to Kanye: a round-faced, Asian man with thin, shoulder-length hair and gold-rimmed glasses. 'Professor Cheng Wei, disappeared from the Northern China University, apparently to our friends at the Siberian Archipelago.'

Jason recalls it now: the Chinese government threatening sanctions, demanding the return of their scholar and the proprietary research the man had apparently stolen. It happened at the same time as a wave of food riots in Argentina, which took all of his attention back then. Bad mistake. 'So, Volkov's building a research base.'

Khalil screws his mouth, unconvinced. 'It would seem so with Kanye and his fruit research. But Cheng Wei worked on coral reef restoration. Honestly, I don't see how this fits the picture, either for Volkov or for the Yun Ju.'

Jason chews the inside of his cheek. He's missing something

here. Coral reefs? And what would Volkov gain from antagonising China?

'This gave me the idea to search for other missing scientists,' Khalil says. 'This one disappeared only three days ago.'

Another figure appears above the table, female-presenting, with wiry, weathered features, green eyes, and a thin, stubborn mouth.

'Professor Teressa Hike, a bio-geneticist from the Australian Science Institute. The same story: stolen data and the Institute insisting she got a job in the Yun Ju. But this time I was lucky: she chose the Atlantic elevator, and we have enough contacts there to get the passenger manifest.'

Khalil brings up a tightly printed list, focusing on Hike's name and the date she left Earth.

'Okay, I don't get it.' Aya sounds as puzzled as Jason feels. 'Why would the Yun Ju headhunt a bio-geneticist? They are decades ahead of whatever research she'd been running.'

She's right; this doesn't make sense. And why destroy the data? No scientist works alone; Hike's colleagues would be able to recreate the research sooner or later. All this achieved was turning the academic institutions against the Yun Ju.

Jason looks at the woman's weathered face. A green headband holds back her ash-blonde hair, matching her jade necklace. That necklace... A string of jade beads with a large, silver-embossed piece in the middle. A statement piece, made to be remembered. He's seen it before. Where?

'Wait.' Aya leans into the holo, mirroring his movement. 'Isn't that...?'

She calls up a keyboard and types a search command. Flat images appear on the surface a moment later: 'genetic purity' info-blasts denouncing red rice as a tool of genetic warfare, corruption of mind and soil. Aya sifts through the images till she finds the photo of the anonymous expert behind the claims: a wiry woman with a striking jade necklace.

Teressa Hike, the scientist in the holo.

'Fucking hell,' Khalil swears, probably for the first time ever. Jason can't blame him.

'Could be a fake,' Aya says.

Jason shakes his head. Digital clones never last long before the originals denounce them. For propagandists, generating a fictional expert is far easier than impersonating a real one.

'No denouncement on record,' Khalil says, clearly following the same train of thought. He types frantically, searching for more images, more records. 'We're in luck. Look what I found.'

The images disappear, replaced by a slow-motion video: the woman, Hike, surrounded by cheering supporters; in the background, a police cordon guarding a cavalcade of armoured cars. Jason's car, from his visit to Bangladesh. The rice protests. Just days ago.

The image zooms in on Hike's figure, spider lines of identification software wrapping her in a tight cocoon.

'The security feed from our own drones,' Khalil says. 'Positive ident. It's her.'

The woman responsible for the protests. For a moment all Jason can see are the hungry faces of the children lining the streets, their hands out for whatever the government PR goons would throw them. The phage took most of their food. And then people like Hike destroyed everything else.

He walks away from the table, forcing his mind to focus as he refills his cup with coffee. What's going on? Nothing about what he's just seen adds up. How can someone run a disinformation campaign against the Yun Ju-designed rice, and then get a clear pass to orbit? Unless whoever invited her didn't know about her other hobby. But why invite her? Why steal any scientists at all?

He takes a sip of his coffee, watching Aya and Khalil exchange hypotheses. Something else bothers him, though he can't put his finger on what it is. Too many discoveries piling up in the last few days, too many new turns. That Richardson might be in cahoots with Volkov is unlikely, but not entirely unexpected—the profit might be too tempting, even if he's risking a blowback from both the Alliance and the Yun Ju Council. But the scientists don't fit anywhere in this picture. There's no profit to be gained. And unlikely that Richardson might be involved; to the best of Jason's knowledge, Harmony and Endeavour run the biggest research centres.

So maybe this has nothing to do with the Yun Ju, but it's either a coincidence or something else entirely. What? Jason can't say, but he's learned to trust his intuition and right now it's screaming for caution. Too many coincidences, too many lucky discoveries in just a few days.

The jet-blimp's PA announces its descent to the landing pad in the Alliance compound, and for the first time in years Jason is glad to be back. He needs a break to chew over the revelations, figure out the source of this nagging feeling in his stomach. The search can wait a few days—and maybe at the end of this long weekend, he will know what it is that they are really seeking.

Jason pauses with his hand on the door. This is always the hardest moment: arriving at his empty apartment, the echo of his lonely footsteps reverberating on the tiled floor. He makes himself enter. His eyes slide past the walls lined with smiling pictures as dust motes dance in the last rays of the setting Sun prying through the window blinds. He drops his travel case, grateful for the familiar whirling sound of the house drone sliding out of its docking slot to retrieve his luggage. The lights come on softly as he crosses the hall. His brain does the counting almost without his will: thirteen years, nine months, and ten days since Maia left. The day after Anna Nathalie's eighteenth birthday, he found his wife standing in this very hallway, her raincoat on, a small suitcase by her feet. She didn't say much, didn't need to repeat what she'd said so many times before: that he was losing perspective, losing himself, turning into a shyster and a spin doctor for warlords and dictators. He reached out his hand and her lips cracked in a sad smile—but she turned and walked away. He can hear her footsteps still, slow at first, then accelerating as she rushed to her new life without him.

He planned to visit her in Feidi, hoped... He never made it. He was too busy fighting one Alliance crisis after another, until the day she died, killed in a pointless traffic accident.

Would she still be alive if she hadn't left? If he hadn't chased her away? Anna Nathalie seems to think so, yet another reason for why she hates him.

He should move; the duplex apartment is much too big for one person. Annalie is never coming back. She will get her permanent contract and remain in the Yun Ju, and he might as well stop hoping to see her again. He should gather the courage and clear out her and Maia's dusty closets, pack the clothes still hanging there like an accusation. Or he could send in the house-keeping drones if he lacked the nerve. Yes, that's what he should do. Soon. Tomorrow maybe. Or next week.

He walks to the kitchen and studies the contents of the fridge. Pictures of the meals scroll up the smooth surface, enlarging whenever he points to one with his finger. They all look the same—or rather, he can't make himself care, it's just food, nutrients his body needs. He used to enjoy eating out, a long time ago, in the long-gone life before the news from Bethesda. Maia and he would go... He shakes his head, hoping to banish the memories. There's a reason he hates coming back here, the dusty air sticky with memories even after all those years. Damn, only three days of this 'break' and then he can be on the road again. And he might drop into the office tomorrow anyway.

Jason jabs his finger at one of the meals: red rice risotto with some greens, good enough. A five-minute counter appears as the fridge transfers his selection to the fast cooker. Time enough to kick off his shoes and grab a drink.

He makes his way to a cabinet on the other side of the kitchen, and only now notices a gift-wrapped package waiting there. He smiles as he unwraps the whisky bottle, a rare product from one of the few remaining distilleries in the Scottish highlands. A perfectly timed gift. There's only one person who could have sent it: Otto, his former aide.

Jason presses the message button attached to the package and Otto's smiling face appears on the wall display. 'Happy birthday! I wish I could join you to celebrate—and try some of that whisky—but I've moved off campus. Back to my hometown, actually. Time to enjoy life while I still can!'

Otto stands on a deck somewhere, pine tips swaying in the wind behind him. His hair seems whiter and his eyes bluer than when Jason last saw him—but then he realises that it's just Otto's tan creating the contrast. For a man forced to retire because of heart problems, Otto looks like a picture of health.

'I bet you thought I'd forget—but have I ever in those nineteen years? Anyway, how's my replacement doing? Khalil's one of the most perceptive people I've ever met. That's why I recommended him; he can see connections like no one else.'

Jason pauses with his hand on the cork. He didn't realise Otto recommended Khalil—he'd assumed it was just the Alliance's bureaucratic machine spitting out their newest protege, another political compromise between the funding nations. All the more reason to be grateful to his former aide— Khalil does seem like an excellent choice.

A ping from the fridge announces that his meal is ready— but it will have to wait till Jason's had a taste of the whisky. He pours a finger into a curved glass, just enough to slosh it around and inhale the smoky aroma. Perfection.

'Come visit me one day. The mountains are beautiful here,' Otto's image continues. 'Now that I've been out for a few weeks... I'd forgotten how it felt to be alive, you know?' He shakes his head, almost embarrassed. 'It's time to move on, for me, and maybe for you, too. Catch what's left of our lives. Who knows how long we still have? Anyway, think about it. Happy birthday, my friend.'

The message winks out, and Jason raises his glass to the blank wall. 'Cheers.'

He's glad that Otto's fine, that the man can find it in himself to enjoy life again. The idea that it's even possible warms him from the inside as much as the whisky he's just swallowed. He might even visit him one day. Maybe.

Jason carries his meal and his whisky glass to the kitchen table and slumps into a chair. The niggling feeling that he's missing something returns like a shadow of something he almost saw. He sips the whisky, thinking of Otto again, and of Khalil. The young man really is incredibly perceptive. Back at the Siberian Archipelago, it was Khalil who gave them the first good lead about Volkov's fruit trade. And then yesterday he came up with the idea of checking with the Feidi Trade Sentry—something Jason should have thought of if he hadn't been so unnerved by the rice riots, his conversation with Dean Abiola, and then his suspicions about Richardson. Is that what's bothering him? The guilt of forgetting the institution linked to his parents' deaths?

He finishes his food, pausing to examine the last forkful of his risotto—the grains are more orange than red, the colour of Saharan sand. The taste is fine, though he's never been a foodie. Tastes better than hunger, that's for sure. His back protests as he bends to drop the empty meal bowl into the recycler. He refills the whisky glass, then, after a moment's hesitation, stashes the bottle under his arm, pours himself a glass of water to placate his conscience, and carries it all to the living room.

He waves the lights off, vanquishing the photographs and the collection of dusty knickknacks into the evening shadows. Outside the window, only half of the residential buildings of the Alliance's once mighty compound remain lit. Farther out, the headquarters still glitter with office lights, but even these are fainter now, interspersed with whole levels of shuttered darkness. 'Streamlining the operations,' the board calls it. 'Respecting the wishes of the governments who fund us.' Bullshit. Putting our heads back in the sand, more likely.

He pours another finger's worth of the whisky and savours it, still standing, his eyes half-closed as he rocks on his feet. The scratchy feeling returns, like something snagging at the corners of his mind. It's not about the Sentry office or about his parents. It's about his team and what they found out yesterday. Abiola's missing man leading them to Hike, the disinformation-spreading scientist. Such a lucky coincidence. Like Volkov's chatty guide letting Khalil take a snapshot of their output. Like Mr Hassan, with all his helpful information.

Jason puts down his glass, his hand shaking. That's it, the snag that's been bothering him: all those lucky coincidences. Khalil getting just the information they needed, when they needed it. So perceptive. So lucky.

He hobbles back to the kitchen. In the bright light, his suspicions seem like a fevered dream. Coincidences do happen. Because the alternative is that he has an infiltrator on his team.

He reaches for the wrapper that came with his birthday gift. If Otto recommended Khalil, then he must have known him. Jason squeezes the message button to request a call back—then swears for not remembering to check the time. How late—or early—is it at Otto's place?

His former aide's face appears on his kitchen wall before Jason's clumsy fingers can reach the disconnect. Otto's hair is ruffled, but he's dressed and the light around him has the blue hue of early morning. 'Jason?'

'Sorry, I didn't consider the hour. Still thinking you're next door, you know?' Jason tries to laugh but stops at the hint of guilt in his aide's face. 'Did I wake you? I... just may have had too much of my birthday present...'

'Ha ha, no, I've been up already. Never thought I'd enjoy mornings, but here... it's just different.' Otto cracks a smile, but something in it feels off.

'How's your heart coping?' Jason asks.

Otto scratches the back of his head, his gaze not quite meeting Jason's. 'Damn, I don't know how to say this... My heart's fine. They gave me a wrong diagnosis. It got stuck in the system, so they kept treating me for a condition I didn't have. No idea how that happened. It only got flagged once they transferred my files here. Turns out, all I needed was a minor procedure!'

'That's great news,' Jason manages to say. He grabs the edge of the table to keep himself from shaking. Yet another coincidence. A lucky opening for Khalil to fill.

'I should have told you. I'm sorry.'

'Come on. After all these years, you deserve your retirement.'

Otto gives a grateful nod. 'How's Khalil? Living up to my standards?'

'Oh, he's great. Very perceptive, as you said.' Jason reaches for his glass but realises he left it in the other room. Damn. He could use a prop for his trembling hands. 'How did you find him anyway?'

'He was my neighbour, down the hall. That's what you get living in the compound; everyone's in some branch of the Alliance. We started chatting. He was so astute, always asking the right questions. I thought he was wasted in statistics, so I asked if he wanted to join the team.'

Jason nods. Astute indeed. And always at the right place by some strike of luck.

Otto's smile fades, probably mirroring Jason's strained expression. 'I'll come back, if you need me?'

There's not much conviction in his voice.

'Don't even think about it.' Jason puts on a grin. 'At least one of us should have a life... Just wanted to thank you for the bottle. I've been enjoying this one!'

He breaks the connection while he can still keep his smile plastered on. He's shaking with anger and pain, his insides turning into concrete. He's got an infiltrator on his team. A traitor. Working for whom? Volkov? One of the other governments or conspiracy groups who want to destroy the Alliance?

He heads for the door. He knows where Otto used to live, and there are just two apartments on that floor. He'll find his neighbour. This time Khalil won't be so lucky.

ELEVEN

LIZ

Over the last three days, Liz has slept maybe eight hours total. Lars's initial assignment took most of the first two nights. She hoped for a break afterwards, but a new task arrived on her wrist band moments after she sent her report. It's all been the same: pages and pages of raw sensor data that she's expected to turn into an accurate forecast of solar activity. This is exactly what she hoped to work on—but at normal hours, and in a lab with powerful computers and state of the art programming. Instead, all she has is the workstation next to the food dispenser. The only saving grace is that she's brought with her the program she wrote for her thesis, and that it could be prompted to work with Lars's data. She figures he's testing her on archival info—checking how her predictions line up with reality. If she had more time, she could probably identify the events herself, but at this point keeping her eyes open takes all she has.

She squints at her latest report just as the other graduates emerge for breakfast.

Kene groans as she sees her. 'You're still at it? Girl, you need some rest!'

Liz tries to sniff, but even that takes too much energy. She looks up as a mug of coffee and a bowl of breakfast-mix appear in front of her.

'Thank you.' Liz presses send and wonders how long it will take for the next batch of data to arrive. Five seconds later, her wrist band vibrates. The bastard must have it automated, new assignment sent the moment the last one is received.

Kene pushes the bowl towards her. 'Eat. And have a chat with Jacques. This whole thing...'

She doesn't finish. By now the others seem to have decided Liz's extra work isn't any kind of favour but a test she needs to pass—one that none of them are required to take. Most glance at her with a mix of pity and compassion, though some relief, too, at having a competitor drop out of the race. Because she clearly looks like she can't do this much longer.

Liz checks the time. Two hours till the next session with Angela, enough for a shower and maybe an hour's snooze?

'Good morning!' Jacques calls from the entrance, disgustingly chirpy.

Damn. She's forgotten about the mid-week debrief. Liz sinks deeper into the seat, defeated. Three more days and the onboarding week is over. She can survive three more days. Whatever the next stage brings, it will have to be easier, or she might as well pack up and go home.

Jacques saunters into the breakfast area and picks up a coffee. His smile falters at the sight of her, but then he returns to the others, grinning again like it's the best day of his life. 'Question time! Whatever you were too embarrassed to ask your guides, now's the time. Come on, let me hear it.'

'Do people really use the cold-sleep pods?' Hiroko asks.

'What cold-sleep pods?' Kene asks.

Hiroko spreads her arms wide. 'There's a whole section with just the pods. *Hundreds* of them. And most apparently occupied.'

The others stare in disbelief, their eyes on Jacques.

'They're meant for emergencies,' he says. 'A major malfunction, or damage to the life support systems. Or if there's a supply crisis. The pods can keep people safe till it's over.'

'A supply crisis?' Alejandro asks. 'Like what?'

'Food mostly. We're getting more independent, but a bad Sun storm can take out several agro platforms. Or a phage infection.'

'Has that ever happened?'

'Why not store supplies?'

'Don't we get food from Earth?'

Jacques raises his hands to stop the questions. 'Yes, it has happened, and yes, we have emergency food stores. And we do get food from Earth, but we can't let ourselves be entirely dependent, or they may use it as a weapon.'

Liz has been drifting to sleep, but her eyes pop open at this last sentence. Food used as a weapon? By Earth? The notion seems ridiculous at first, but—what did Jacques say that first day? *Never forget you're in space.* She's never considered Earth having any power against the Yun Ju. The shift in perspective is dizzying.

The others are talking again, only a few thoughtful faces betraying similar confusion.

'But why would the pods be occupied now? Are we in crisis?'

'Some people are just getting their beauty sleep.' Jacques laughs, but it's clear he's the only one in on the joke. 'Cryo-sleep does something to the senescent cells in your body. The effect is something like... maybe not rejuvenation, but delayed ageing. A lot of wealthy seniors take turns in the pods. But it's not the only reason. Some use cold-sleep as a business strategy. You invest, set things in motion, and then leave it to a caretaker till it's ready for you to emerge and reap the benefits.'

Liz tries to imagine a mindset that would make someone lock themself up in a freezer for however long it took their business to make a profit. No way, ever. To consider that a sensible strategy... This is a strange world indeed.

She lets her thoughts drift away, her eyes closing again, when Kene's raised voice snaps her back.

'They are so far ahead! Like, not just decades but centuries!'

'Correction: not *they*. Us,' Jacques says. 'The sooner you start thinking about yourselves this way, the sooner the others will consider you as such.'

'Not all of us,' Alejandro says.

Jacques shrugs, as if to say that those who won't make the cut don't count anyway.

Kene keeps shaking her head. 'Still. Why is none of this technology on Earth? We—they—need it.'

'All the equipment is available for purchase,' Jacques says softly. What he doesn't add is obvious: few, if anyone, on Earth can afford the price.

'You may want to know that there are plans to make the essential technology more affordable,' Jacques continues, his smile returning. 'We're now in talks with the Food Alliance about—'

'Geez, not those fuckers!' somebody swears.

Other voices join in, angry and accusing. Liz stares ahead, frozen, trying very hard not to react. Until she feels someone's gaze on her.

Alejandro. He's looking right at her, ignoring the others. Their eyes meet and he holds her gaze, his lip curving ever so slightly.

He knows.

How? He works in data security, she realises. Of course he's gone digging. Probably on that first day, when she got Lars's summons.

He knows.

Liz's fingers curl around the edge of her chair. What is he going to do with that knowledge?

The fact that he hasn't exposed her yet means he's either waiting for the best moment or he's hedging his bets. Most of the others think her extra tasks are a sign of her failings, but Alejandro's likely to be more cautious. He won't strike until he's sure.

Once he is, he will pounce for the kill.

Another night, another set of data from Lars. Each batch Liz gets is different, each requiring a new approach and its own distinct set of algorithms to process. Kene brings her food; the others fall silent when they see her. Only Alejandro approaches, sometimes standing silently behind her back to glance at her screen. She still tenses at the sight of him, but she must have run out of adrenaline because even that threat feels too distant to be real.

Liz rubs her eyes, the numbers on the screen greying into a mush. Done. She should double-check the results, but at this point she's more likely to just mess things up. She presses send and waits five seconds for her wrist band to vibrate again. She laughs, too loudly, too unhinged. The others cringe, shifting away from her like she's cursed. Maybe she is. Maybe she was born like that, her family's bane fraying the thread of her fate.

Or maybe not. Maybe she's letting it destroy her.

She's on her feet before the thought crystallises in her head, stomping out of the door and tracing the pink floor markers down to Research Central, towards Lars's glass-walled office. The place is almost empty at this hour and she's beginning to wonder if Lars is even there or if she'll just get to scream at his empty chair—when a shadow falls across his open door: the man himself, settling behind his desk with a steaming cup in his hand.

She stops just inside his office, her anger fighting her exhaustion for the right to go first. 'Why are you doing this?'

Lars doesn't answer, his brows rising as he studies her with surprise or amusement.

'If you want me to fail, then just fire me now. Or do you need an excuse to offer Ranath? Or is it to get back at...' She can't bring herself to say her father's name. There's still a chance he doesn't know, that it's all just internal politics, a game between the man and his boss.

Lars turns to his screen. Her mouth starts to open in reproach when he shifts the data to a wall display—he's looking at the results she's just sent. His chin tips with something resembling approval, then he turns to face her.

'I told you to send your work when you were finished. I didn't give you a deadline.'

Liz huffs. 'Right. If you wanted to give me time, then why not wait till after the onboarding? Like with all the other graduates? Why single me out?'

'You are right. This was a test.' Lars takes a long sip of his coffee. A small smile dances on his lips. 'And you are right that —well, I didn't exactly want to get you fired, but I wanted to show Ranath she made a mistake assigning you to my group.'

He pauses. There's more he wants to say, his jaw working, but he ends up with a shrug. 'Anyway. I'm beginning to think you may have potential. Not convinced yet, no. But enough to give it a try.'

Liz opens her mouth. Is this approval? Has she passed the test? Is she... hired?

She stares at Lars, but he's closed his eyes like it's time for a mid-morning nap.

'No, you're not hired yet. It's not my decision, and I'm a long way from making my mind up anyway,' he says when he opens his eyes again. 'I've cleared you with Angela; the rest of your onboarding can wait. Use the rest of the day to get lenses fitted, you'll need them. Come back tomorrow, after you've had some rest.'

Lars returns to his screen. Liz waits another breath, but his posture makes it clear he's done talking. She leaves, the sound of her heartbeat thudding in her ears. She feels herself grin. *Not hired yet*—but definitely a hell of a lot closer.

Liz's wrist band alarm snaps her out of dreamless slumber six hours later. She feels like she could sleep another six, or sixteen, but she's due for her appointment with the info-tech team. The prospect makes her uncomfortable; she's absorbed too many horror stories of mind-controlling devices all through her childhood. But her system will be external, she reminds herself, chasing away her father's disapproval before it can wedge itself in her mind. The tech they use here goes deeper than anything he'd accept. It's not just contacts and ear buds— her lenses will be attached to her corneas and the comm system embedded into her ears. Still, no wire will reach her brain. And she's already seen how much more effective it could make her.

She rushes out of her tiny bedroom, belatedly registering the cacophony of agitated voices in the common room—the sound cuts to sudden silence as she enters. Nineteen pairs of eyes turn to her, the expressions ranging from impressed to resentful or jealous.

I'm not hired yet, she wants to tell them, but her wrist band chimes again in urgent appeal. She's late, and they gave her the last appointment of the day. If she misses her slot, she won't get her lenses in time for tomorrow. Lars doesn't strike her like someone who'd accept oversleeping as a valid excuse.

Liz starts for the door just as Kene moves towards her. 'Angela said you're—'

'Sorry, I've got to run.' Liz gives her her warmest smile. Of all the graduates, Kene is the only one she doesn't want to disappoint. The woman has become the closest thing to a friend Liz has had in years. 'I'll tell you everything when I'm back. Promise!'

The rumble of conversation resumes as soon as she passes the door. They're trying to figure out what her not-yet-promotion means for their prospects. There will be plenty of questions once she's back.

Liz rushes down the side passage, trying to remember which colour of the floor markers she should follow. The medical? The engineering? If she had her lenses already, they would show her the way. It has to be the medical, she decides. She's not some broken drone in need of repair. At least, not yet...

She makes it only a few metres down the main corridor when another set of footsteps closes in on her, heavy, determined feet hurrying to catch up.

Another moment and Alejandro is with her, slowing to match her pace. One side of his face contorts into a simper. 'Daddy pulled some strings?'

Liz stops. She'd prefer to ignore him or pretend she doesn't know what he means, but that would only make him more persistent. She makes herself shrug. 'My father doesn't even know I'm here. And if he—'

'Bullshit. The damn Alliance tracks all the passes; they know exactly where everyone is. You can't cross a border without them knowing. Can't even look at the elevators without alerting the security.'

Liz rolls her eyes. This is all nonsense, the exaggerated notions people have about the Alliance's power. The Alliance has no control of the borders, and only as much information about the elevators as the Yun Ju is willing to share. She knows, because she asked her father about it back when she was dreaming up her escape. Trying to explain this to Alejandro is pointless, though; he is one of those who always knows better. She's met his type before, in college and all the jobs she tried. Without fail, they attributed all her achievements to her father's help, the idea that she could accomplish anything on her own simply unimaginable.

'What do you want?' she asks.

'I want the same favour. He gets me hired and in exchange I keep my mouth shut about how he sends his daughter off to safety while the rest of the planet starve under his rules.'

Liz stifles a groan. 'He didn't send me here. I escaped. Why do you think I've changed my name?'

Alejandro snorts. 'I would, if I had yours.'

'Why would I put myself through the Academy if I could just ask for 'a favour?' And what makes you think he'd have any sway with the Yun Ju?'

Alejandro just stares at her, unwavering.

'I'm telling you the truth. This whole thing, it's some internal feud between Lars and Ranath. Nothing to do—'

'Come on. Of all the graduates, it just happens to be about you?'

Liz shakes her head, but stops short of an answer as her wrist band buzzes again. If she misses her appointment, this will be the end of her, with or without Alejandro's help. 'I've got to go.'

'Getting yourself wired?'

How does he know? Doesn't matter. She hurries away, but Alejandro follows, matching her pace. Ahead, the corridor forks, rows of identical semi-transparent doors stretching in both directions. Liz glances from left to right, unsure.

Alejandro juts his head to the left. 'This way.'

'How do you know?'

'I came here yesterday. Asked about the procedure...' This sounds like a question, like he wants her advice.

'It can't do any harm if it's external. You can switch it off at any time.'

'I know that. I just didn't want to spend my own money. If

they ask you to do it, they pay for it. But I guess, since I'll be getting the job soon...'

Now Liz just laughs. 'I told you the truth. I can't help you.'

He holds her gaze, challenging. 'I gave you a choice—'

'I can't do it. He can't do it, even if I asked him.'

'Have it your way, then.' Alejandro glares at her for another moment, then stomps away, his anger like an aura around him.

Liz wants to chase after him, beg him to keep her secret. Lie that she will do what he asks. Promise to—

'Elizabeth Lake?'

The voice makes her wince. A slender figure wrapped in a green medical suit scowls at her from three doors ahead.

'I'm late. I'm so sorry.'

'Well, come on in, before we pack up for the day.'

The procedure takes less than an hour. Liz dozes through most of it, half-sedated, while tiny machines crawl inside her ears and under her eyelids. Distantly, she realises that she should probably howl in horror, but whatever the medic has sprayed into her airways makes everything seem fine. The doctors talk all the time, but their words blend into the ambient noise of the room, the humming of the instruments and the buzz of the ventilators. She's measured and calibrated in nanometre detail; the lenses and the hearing implant printed to her exact specifications. The process makes her feel drunk, which is just what she needs, or she might start crying or screaming about her father's ghost haunting her however far she tries to run from him.

What will Alejandro do? She can't tell, and for the brief reprieve the sedative gives her, she actually doesn't care.

'All right, you're good,' the medic announces.

A puff of something foul enters her nostrils, and her focus turns sharp again.

'Start slowly, it may be disorienting at first. Just concentrate on what you want the system to do. It's quite intuitive.'

Liz blinks, the pressure of the lenses barely perceptible against her corneas. Something in her ear tickles, and she can feel the feather-light receiver just behind the earlobe. She slides down from the chair, turning her head slowly to take in the view. Nothing happens, until her eyes linger on something. As she watches the medic, *Alex Keir (they), senior interface technician,* appears in small letters above their head. She examines the data pad in Alex's hand: *Connection established. Send message?* The door: *Minor Medical Procedures section.*

Whoa.

Can you hear me? the medic says in her ear.

'Yes, I hear—'

Don't speak. Sub-vocalize.

She tries, not quite sure what she's supposed to be doing. She speaks inside her mouth only, her lips moving without a sound. *Like this? I don't know how—*

'Perfect. Focus on the send icon to select the person you want to speak to. There are thousands of other options, but don't try them all till you're ready.' Alex laughs. 'Any questions?'

Liz swallows. The question seems embarrassing, but she must know. 'How... how do I turn it off?'

Alex tries very hard not to roll their eyes, but a sigh escapes their lips anyway. 'It's safe. You really don't need to worry. But'—Alex raises both arms in surrender—'for your peace of mind, the off switch is there. A five-second press, and everything powers down.'

They guide her finger to a bulge on the tiny emitter at the back of her earlobe. 'Got it?'

'Yes. Thank you.'

'Let me know if you ever use it. That will be one for the

history books.' Alex winks. 'Now, can you get back on your own or are you too dizzy?'

She's not dizzy—at least she wasn't until the mention of getting back to her quarters and facing the others.

'I'm fine,' she says, and tries to smile.

Finding her way back is a breeze: all she has to do is request the directions and follow the arrows floating in the air before her. Actually making the way is another matter. Liz slows as she turns the last corner, then stops outside the door, her heart pounding. She can hear the others, their voices muted but frantic, speaking over each other in emotional bursts. He's told them.

Liz rubs her eyes, then wonders if she's just damaged her lenses. It's hard to make herself care. She pulls in a breath. There's no escaping her fate, not now, not ever. She might as well stop running.

She pushes the door and walks inside.

Hate fills the space like fog. It spills out of their eyes, drips to the floor in thick, acrid pools. It burns her skin red with shame. Nobody speaks as she crosses the room to the drinks dispenser. She should tell them something... What? They won't believe her any more than Alejandro has.

She turns at the sound of footsteps. The others are leaving, shuffling off to their bedrooms with mouths screwed and brows creased. Only two remain—Alejandro, his arms crossed as he savours her distress, and Kene, her eyes red and her cheeks moist.

'Are you really his daughter? Nevsky's?'

Liz wants to lie but it's too late, the truth is out and lies will only bring more pain. 'I... I am. But it's not what Alejandro told you...'

She doesn't finish, as Kene runs out of the room, her door slamming behind her.

TWELVE
RANATH

Li Qiang arrives a day later—duels, after all, are an important affair. Officially, they should be meeting on 'neutral ground,' but they both agree that Ranath's purpose-built salle will do just fine. Qiang insists that he can't wait to see the space and that it really is his time to visit—a clear enough message that he wants to talk on her turf. Interesting. Is there someone in his entourage he doesn't trust?

He arrives late in the afternoon, docking at Ranath's personal shuttle port. His attire is still vaguely Greek: tight navy trousers and a cream, buttonless shirt tied with a gold sash. A filigree chain mimicking a knot hangs around his neck, the ends disappearing down his chest.

He grins when he sees her. 'Oh, my honoured opponent. Thank you for accepting my challenge.'

He speaks in English, of course, his manners impeccable.

'The pleasure is mine. Or will be, after you're crushed in defeat.'

Qiang laughs. 'I'm glad to find you in good spirits. I might even be tempted to lose, just to keep it this way.'

'I see you've prepared your excuses.' Ranath raises her brow at the sight of a porter drone trailing behind him with two large bags. 'Though you needn't have brought medical supplies. We may be a small station, but we have the basics.'

He laughs again. If she didn't know better, she'd think he were genuinely cheerful. But the zhu of the Sunrise Group doesn't come to visit unless he's got a damn good reason.

Ranath points towards the corridor. 'Shall we? Or would you prefer to start with some refreshments?'

'Duty always first.'

'Wonderful.'

He follows her the short route down to the nearest spoke, watchful eyes scanning every inch of the station even though he's seen the place before. Checking for changes or just a habit he can't shake. New Hope's less than a third of the size of Yu Huan, the decor favouring efficiency over extravagance. The inner section of the habitat they are now crossing is the most ostentatious, with wide corridors and large rooms designed to impress. This was the New American Union's first venture in the Yun Ju, and they were trying very hard to live up to the challenge. Ranath—Renewal—bought the place when the stations started to move into private hands fifteen years ago. Got a good price for it, too, though she's got Richardson's father to thank for that. He and Fujikawa senior started the independence movement, if you can call it that, after they created the Habitat Ownership Act. The Act declared that once a space-borne structure exceeded a certain number of inhabitants, the residents acquired full governance over their habitat, with continuous lease paid to the original owners. Then they informed those owners that they could ratify the Act and collect the rent, or the stations would secede anyway, without paying. By then, most of the Earth governments had already been affiliated with one Yun Ju faction or another, so they did what politicians do best: pretended it had always been the plan. The Americans sold off their assets outright; the Chinese government chose the pretence of claiming they still had a say. They sold Yu Huan and Liberty, but kept some of the smaller stations under permanent lease.

A service car—nothing fancy but comfortable enough—carries them up the spoke into the station's axis. It's always an odd feeling—getting lighter, but somehow askew, with the 'gravity' pushing sideways as the rotation becomes noticeable. And then it's gone, and they are floating, restrained only by the seatbelts. Qiang pushes himself up, the movement too powerful and he has to wedge his foot under the chair before he drifts off to the ceiling. Ranath has expected as much; few of the yun-ying spend much time in zero-g nowadays. She, on the other hand, has passed most of her teens hiding away in the axis, trying to forget who she was and decide who she was going to be. Who would have expected this could one day come in handy?

She pretends not to notice as she gracefully glides out of the car, past the cargo bays and into a tubular corridor lined with soft red tiles. An iris-like hatch blocks the way ahead; on the opposite sides, two narrow, tapered doors look like silver slits in the red fabric. The sides retract as they approach, revealing identical dressing rooms, complete with a selection of armour and blades.

'Your choice of weapon?' Qiang says, his voice momentarily missing its confident edge.

They both prefer épée—but Qiang is more than a head taller, so his reach means Ranath's only good chance of scoring is if she chooses foil and uses the priority rule to her advantage. He knows that.

She smiles. 'Épée. This is one game I play for the pleasure of the encounter, not the glory of winning.'

'I thought you valued contest above all else.'

'And I thought you only cared about winning.'

'Maybe we can both learn something today?'

'That's what I'm hoping for.'

She leaves Qiang by the door on the right and glides to the dressing room opposite. Most of the items in her kit are perfect replicas of the gear used when fencing was still an Olympic sport—when they still had the Olympics. Except for the chest protector, of course—that contraption should never see the light of day again—and the magnetised shoes. She pulls on the plastron, the socks, and the breeches, then zips up the jacket. Her glove and mask wait on the shelf by the door, and above them her selection of blades.

Outside, Qiang looks stunning in his white outfit, traditional and yet somehow modern in the way it's tailored to his slim figure, thin silver lines following the curves of his muscles. She may have a crush on him, Ranath realises, and almost laughs out loud. Wouldn't that be hilarious?

She leads the way to the salle, turning just in time to see him gasp. They are inside a silver sphere, ten metres in diameter, empty except for a ball-shaped referee drone hovering in the middle. The light seems to seep out of the air itself, radiating from millimetre-thick light fibres imbedded into the metal surface.

Qiang bows his head in a small salute. 'You've done the impossible, Zhu Ranath. I find myself impressed.'

'I'm glad. Shall we?'

He follows her inside, their magnetised shoes clinking against the floor. The attraction is just strong enough to keep them from floating away. The door seals behind them, making the sphere complete. The referee drone flashes green and red, signalling readiness.

They check their blades, pull the masks on, then salute. Ranath can barely keep the grin off her face. She can't remember the last time she did something purely for fun. She might as well enjoy it.

'En garde!' the drone chirps.

Qiang bursts out laughing. 'You made it speak French!'

'En garde!' the drone repeats, forcing them to attention. 'Prêts? Allez!'

Ranath slides forward, then back, testing his responses. Qiang follows, the tip of his blade maintaining the distance. His posture is perfect and so is his footwork. A worthy opponent, at last. She moves in—a feint attack, one they both know isn't the real thing. Qiang parries lightly, then counterattacks, but it's still just a test. They dance, testing each other's patience, sliding back and forth on the featureless surface. This piste has no beginning and no end. There's only them, the clank of their footsteps, and the swish of their breaths.

Qiang gives up first—his shoulders tense for an instant before he attacks. Two quick steps and he lunges, his arm extending as he thrusts towards her. He's fast, too fast: her parry slides off his forte and the tip of his weapon hits her shoulder.

'Touche!'

'Nice one,' she says, and it's the truth. He's good—younger and fitter, too. But this game is about more than just skill.

'En garde! Prêts? Allez!'

She lets Qiang score another point. He's getting comfortable now, secure in his superiority. Good.

'En garde! Prêts? Allez!'

They repeat the dance. He's careful, though, doesn't take anything for granted. Ranath focuses on his movements, the grip loose in her hand, her breathing and the tip of his blade her only focus. He moves in—another feint, luring her to counterattack. She obliges, pushing herself into a lunge—except instead of going forward she jumps, somersaulting in zero-g till her feet hit the wall above. She kicks off, blade first, landing behind Qiang with her point pressed against his back.

'Touche!'

Qiang pulls off his mask. 'What the hell?' He's laughing, though, his eyes bright and exhilarated. 'How did you do that?'

'I may have mentioned that zero-g pistes were special.'

'I'm beginning to see that...'

Ranath gets the next point by jumping above his lunge and scoring a flick on his back, and the next one, too, this time side-stepping his attack and forcing him to turn so fast his shoes lose grip and he floats up, defenceless.

'I can see now how you do it,' he says as they face off again.

'Fence?'

'That, too.'

'Do tell.'

He smiles, the curve of his lips barely visible behind the mask. 'Let everyone think you're exactly what they expect. Make them feel they have the upper hand, till they no longer pay attention.'

'Pay attention to what exactly?'

'To what you're really doing. Like sending the miners to Saturn.'

He lunges, no—it's a flèche, fast as lightning, soaring in zero-g. Ranath rotates—not fast enough, his blade bending as it snags on her arm.

'Touche!'

A fast learner. She should have expected no less.

Ranath makes her tone light. 'Richardson may have forced my hand—but don't tell me you weren't thinking about mining there. The prospecting reports—'

'Are a good pretext, I agree. But you've been busy buying rocks there even before there was any good news.'

Another attack, but this time she's ready. The game has changed now, the questions more dangerous than the weapons. Ranath leaps away, too awkwardly to score her own hit but at least not losing a point.

'We diversify, all of us,' she says. 'Sunrise used to be all shielding and power generators. Now it will be hard to find an industry you don't have your fingers in—or are you going to tell me otherwise?'

'No, but my manoeuvres are straightforward—'

Ranath laughs.

'I didn't say they were simple. Or predictable. God, I hope not. But they are everything you'd expect someone in my position to do. It all adds up.'

'And so it does for me. I think what you're missing is the scale.' Ranath lunges, a poor attack and easily defended. 'I'm small fry compared to you or Liberty. To survive, I need different tactics.'

Qiang pulls off his mask. This time his face is serious. 'And yet... isn't this exactly what you expect me to think?'

Ranath takes off her mask and runs her fingers through her hair before meeting his gaze. 'Why are you here, Zhu Li?'

He takes a moment to consider his answer. 'Richardson came to see me. He's furious.'

'At me?'

'Worse. At himself—for failing to see how you manoeuvred yourself into dominance with assemblers.'

Ranath shrugs. Richardson has got only himself to blame, for focusing on the Alliance and the games he plays on Earth. 'He's still got the food trade. That will always trump my assemblers.'

'Not really. The Alliance trade falls under the Yun Ju Council, so he's got little scope to manoeuvre. If he denies anyone our share of food, we'll take Liberty apart with our bare hands. It's a precedence no one would tolerate.'

'I'm sure food isn't his only focus. Or that the deal with the Alliance won't stop him from seeking other options.' That's a gambit—Ranath has no idea if Richardson's cheating on the Alliance, but knowing the man, that's a very likely option.

'Maybe. Probably. But that doesn't change the fact that he now sees *you* as a threat.' Qiang points his blade at her as he says that.

'I guess he had a proposal for you?'

'He says that he can stop you once and for good. That he's close to proving that...' Qiang doesn't finish, studying her reaction.

Ranath's lips twitch. Damn, such lack of control. Qiang's bound to have noticed.

She's guessed right that's what Richardson's after. He's looking for evidence of Renewal's origin, the source of its founding capital. Li Qiang must realise what that means. He's old enough to remember how Renewal started—apparently out of nowhere and only days before the news from Bethesda arrived. How no trace of Destiny, the clandestine creators of the mind-controlling devices, was ever found. Few in the Yun Ju ever mention the matter, the unspoken agreement maintained in the knowledge that Destiny had members in all the factions. But if Richardson finds proof, something to link Renewal to that old secret, the others will jump at the opportunity to clear their names. The end will be swift: the matter brought to judgement, maybe even to Earth courts, Renewal's assets impounded, the station taken over. If she's lucky, Ranath may be able to deny personal involvement, but it would be the end of her business, and her plans. The end of Ark.

She busies herself pulling off her glove and pushing it into the mask, her mind racing through options. She won't insult Qiang by pretending she doesn't know what he means—but acknowledging that she does is not an option, either. He's here because she's useful to him; the moment that changes, he'll join Richardson or whoever else will help him achieve his goals. The Yun Ju zhus don't have friends.

'What did you tell him?' she asks eventually.

Qiang's face is perfectly placid. Machiavelli's Prince couldn't do better. 'That I needed time to think.'

'Choosing your enemy?'

'Something like that.'

Ranath nods. Li Qiang's been using her as a distraction for

Liberty. With Renewal out of the picture, he'll be Richardson's main target.

Qiang wipes his forehead. He seems tired, but the gesture is slightly too theatrical to be genuine. 'Richardson is a bully, but he's useful. And easy to manipulate. All you need to come second in the profit ratings. As long as he can call himself a winner, he'll eat out of your hand.'

Ranath waits, a well-worn smile on her lips. They're coming to the point now. Her future will be played in his next words.

'Richardson may be telling the truth about you. It was all a long time ago, though. I'm not sure I care—at least not as much as I care for here and now. But if what you're doing up there by Saturn... If that has anything to do with that old game...'

He holds her gaze. What to tell him? A reassurance won't do, he won't trust it. She needs to give him something he can believe. What?

Ranath chuckles—and Qiang winces, unprepared.

'What?'

'This is ridiculous. I'm searching for a good lie to give you because the truth is so banal you'll think I'm lying...' She shakes her head. 'When did we get ourselves so entangled that lies are more believable than the truth?'

Qiang huffs. 'Hasn't it always been that way? But why don't you try me—with the truth?'

Ranath paces around him. Qiang matches her steps, the two of them facing each other, sparring without blades.

'Richardson will want to destroy me if he finds out—but since that's what he's trying to do anyway...' She pauses, her hesitation perfectly believable as she searches for the right words for her lie. 'You are correct that I'm not interested in Titan—at least not for the rare minerals everybody else craves. What I'm after is much simpler. I want independence—from Liberty, and from Earth. I want to grow my own food.'

'You've got two platforms—'

'I might have five and it wouldn't be enough. Not when bad luck or a phage infection can wipe them out inside of a week. You know what I'm talking about.'

Qiang nods reluctantly. He lost one of his platforms to a stray asteroid impact two years ago.

'I want more space. Something that resembles actual soil. A place not reliant on the elevators or the good will of my neighbours—no offence.'

'Why not Mars then? Or the Moon?'

'Because I can't own Mars or the Moon. I *can* buy an asteroid. And frankly, I prefer to be far from Earth. Less chance of contamination—or sabotage.'

Qiang's expression doesn't betray if he believes her. She was vocal about the issues of food dependence in the past, so that at least is consistent. It *is* a move someone in her position would make. Is it enough to quell his doubts, to reassure him that food is the only thing she's after?

Qiang's gaze is flitting. The muscles in his neck twitch, his shoulders tight as he pokes the steel floor with his blade. Not enough.

'And yes, there's the other thing, too.' Ranath sounds resigned as she makes her confession. 'I knew I wouldn't be able to hide it forever. You probably guessed...'

Qiang tilts his head. 'Why don't you tell me?'

'I want raw materials to expand the station. We're growing and... well, they say size doesn't matter, but it does. And let's just say my ambitions are bigger than my current means.'

Qiang grins. She has him now, because this is exactly what he expected—exactly what he'd do in her place.

'Is that why you're recruiting all the engineers? With your Academy?'

She smiles in response, like he's caught her stealing candy.

'I can't say I blame you.' He unzips his jacket, the duel—and the conversation—over.

'Wait. Now that you know... Don't tell me you're just going to leave me to it.'

Qiang grins. 'Of course not. You are too clever and too cunning to be allowed to grow much bigger. But I won't let Richardson destroy you. At least, not right away.'

He presses the tip of his blade against her chest, jokingly but strong enough to make the idiot drone shout 'Touche!' His lip curls in a cruel delight that she's seen before but never from the receiving end.

She may have just swapped a stupid enemy for a smart one. But it's not like she's had a choice.

Ranath shifts, letting his blade slide away. 'How are you planning to control him?'

'I've got my ways. You'll have to trust me on this.'

'I assume there's a price?'

Qiang gives her a lopsided smile. 'As much as I'd like to say I'm only doing it for our wonderful friendship... I'm in need of a rather large quantity of your assemblers. Construction grade.'

Ranath nods. This makes sense. More growth platforms probably, to reduce his dependence on Liberty. Except there has to be a catch or he'd just order them like everyone else. 'How many?'

'Four thousand.'

Ranath manages not to gasp. That's more than she plans to send to Saturn. Four times more than the Harmony order, the biggest deal in Renewal's history. More than you'd need to build an entire station. Unless... Unless you wanted to do it fast, before your competitors could notice or do anything about it. Then you'd need four thousand.

She holds his gaze. Qiang doesn't flinch, his smile growing a sharper edge. So, that's his game. He'll get a whole new outpost, either industrial or agro, with full mag-shield protection. It will make Sunrise self-sufficient, as close to independent as anyone in orbit can ever get. A league of Qiang's own, with Richardson a distant second. The others will catch up, of course, but not before he's cemented his position. It's going to be interesting times in the Yun Ju, indeed. She might even enjoy watching the fallout. And it would certainly keep everyone's attention away from her—except... She'd have to give Qiang all of her assemblers. Including those she'd been holding for Ark.

She paces again, but this time Li Qiang doesn't follow, still as the Sun at the centre of her solar system.

'I will need some time to ramp up the production—'

'You've done that already. I can't see inside your cubes, but their heat output tells me you've been busy for months. Preparing for your Saturn mission?'

Ranath stops. It's a new feeling to be outplayed, and she's sure she doesn't ever want to experience it again. She steps towards him, craning her neck to meet his eyes. 'Yes. And I'm not going to give it up for you.'

'I don't see how you have a choice.'

He's right. She's got nothing on him—the worst she can do is reveal his plans to the others, which might block his expansion but won't hurt his current position. And if he lets Richardson go after her, she will lose everything.

'I can offer the assemblers to Liberty.' Ranath pauses for a tiny moment, enough to see Qiang's jaw tighten. 'I'd rather not, though. But it won't be much of a deal if I have to give up everything.'

'For the sake of your safety.'

'At the cost of my future.'

'A counteroffer, then?'

'Two thousand bots.'

'I thought you were serious.' Qiang starts for the exit. The petals of the iris door unfold before him, shining like silver blades. He slows down, though, giving her a chance to catch up.

Ranath makes her tone final. 'Three thousand. Anything more and I lose more than I gain.'

Qiang nods, his barbed smile returning. 'Only for you, Zhu Ranath. And our wonderful friendship.'

Ranath slips inside the meditation room and locks the door behind her. It's perfectly quiet, only the whisper of a distant wind rustling in the tips of the simulated pine trees in the wall projection. The space is almost empty: a soft mat in the middle, a reclining chair and an old chest, another of her grandmother's antiques, pushed into the far corner.

She slides to the chair, slow and hesitant. A slit in the red velvet seat hides a small metal case, unremarkable, except for the levels of encryption it takes to unlock. Inside sits a single data pad, probably the best protected gadget in the solar system, and certainly the most expensive. There's only this one copy of the data it stores, the content too sensitive to entrust to even her most devoted security: a spare identity Ranath has cultivated for an emergency, and a couple of old videos. Only two people have ever watched them, and the other one—her mother—has been dead for decades.

The screen comes to life so slowly that for a moment Ranath wonders if the recording has finally given up the ghost. But no—it is a ghost keeper, and it remains faithful to its duty. The icons appear, only two, for the two messages the pad contains. Her finger trembles as she touches the first one. The description pops up, the details etched into her memory:

Video message
From: undisclosed, rescue ship The Samaritan
To: Ranath Eyre, Tian Gong station, Earth
Sent: 5 May 2330
Received: 3 June 2333
Play message

A man smiles at her from the screen: late thirties, a hand-some face with bold, regular features, blue eyes and thick blond hair that looks like he's just run his fingers through it. He looks at the camera, his smile eager and yet somehow uncertain, as if he was forcing the cheer. His chin trembles, and the smile crumbles for a moment, but then returns after he pulls in a deep breath.

'Hi there. Ranath. Such a pretty name. I just saw your mother's message. All the pictures she sent. Such a beautiful baby. Three years old now! And reading already.' He trails off. His shoulders heave, but he keeps his smile on. 'I'm just realising you'll be nine by the time you even get this message. I'm sorry I can't send more. I only woke up this one time before our destination, and only for a few minutes. So I have to tell you everything now and hope you'll make sense of it later.

'I love you, kiddo. I've never even met you and I love you more than anything. I'm glad your mother decided not to wait. I left my seed in case... If she didn't want to or couldn't go into cold-sleep...' He shakes his head, the gesture almost shy. 'She's probably explained it all already, or she will, when you're old enough to understand. Trust her, please. Your mother is an inspiring person. I love her—almost as much as I love you.'

Her father smiles, and for an instant he looks truly happy, as if forgetting the light years and the decades separating them. But then his brows crease again. 'I've got to go now, sweetie. This isn't much for the only message you'll get for another twenty years. What I'm doing here is important. I volunteered for the good of humanity—but now I know who I'm really doing this for. Be well, my child. Be strong.'

The image blinks out. Ranath stares at the ghosts of the pixels fading into darkness. She sucks in air, her hand shaking as she touches the second icon. She needs to see it. She needs to remember why she must fight.

Video message
From: undisclosed, rescue ship The Samaritan
To: Ranath Eyre, Tian Gong station, Earth
Sent: 3 July 2348
Received: 1 December 2354
Play message

The man on the screen hasn't aged more than a few days, and yet he hardly looks like the same person: his handsome face has grown pale and gaunt, his cheeks unshaven, his hair a mass of tangles. He rubs his eyes, bloodshot and rimmed with dark circles. He tries to smile, but his lips seem too stiff.

'Hi there. This is only my second message, and if things go as I think they will, it'll be my last. I'm sorry, honey. I'm so sorry. I'm sorry I wasn't there for you when you were growing up, when you needed a father. I'm sorry I wasn't there when your mother died. And now I'm gone as well. I'm sorry to leave you alone. I'm sorry to never have had the chance to hold you, to kiss your head and tell you how much I love you.'

He seems to gasp. His shoulders quiver and the recording stops, as if to spare her the sight. Or to give him time to collect himself. The words cut too deep. They cut into her, too, every syllable like a shard of glass under her skin.

When the image returns, he's smiling again, determined as much as he seems desperate. He wants to smile, she thinks, smile for her and for himself, wants to feel good about the world he leaves her. 'Ranath, darling. You know the truth from your mother—why I became the Guardian and the reasons behind my mission. But now there will be another truth, that told by those who have won this battle. Theirs is the version the world will hear and embrace. It will paint me as the villain, and my mission as the act of unspeakable evil. You know better—but don't let anyone hear you protest. Don't let them make you a scapegoat for my crimes.

'Your mother was wise to conceal your identity, to give you only her name. Don't ever reveal that you're my child. But remember the truth: I volunteered for this mission because there was nobody else. Because humanity is worth saving, even if it means going against the will of the masses. They can't save themselves; they've tried and failed too many times to count. I won't give up—and I hope you won't, either.

'Destiny will go into hiding now, as we've planned. A few will remain, the caretakers of a new business they will set up to restore the funds. We will try again, somehow, some day. I hope you live to see that day.'

He pauses, his expression broken, lost somewhere between encouragement and resolve. He glances to the side, his eyes narrowing, as if expecting someone to interrupt. When he speaks again, he sounds hurried, breathless. 'Goodbye, Ranath. Goodbye, my daughter. I wish... too much to say. I'm out of words and out of time. Goodbye. I love you.'

The image vanishes, the last glimpse of the father she never met. Ranath presses the pad to her chest. Her shoulders heave.

'Lights out!'

Darkness cocoons her, blind and indifferent. Better. Her chin trembles, tears sliding down her cheeks, down her neck, onto her arms still curled around the pad.

'I love you, too, Dad. And I will never, ever give up.'

THIRTEEN

JASON

It's started to rain. Fat drops hit Jason's face, the rain too warm to cool his fever. The Alliance compound is dead still at this hour, only the luminescent strips on the sidewalk guiding his way. He stops once, hesitating, but the memory of Khalil's 'luck' spurs him on. Too many coincidences and only one explanation. Khalil is an infiltrator. A traitor posing as a friend. How much damage has he done already? On whose orders?

Jason crosses the half mile to Otto's apartment building in a frenzied run, the tails of his shirt flapping in the wind, his shoes soaking up water. He leaves wet footprints in the entrance hall, then on the fake wood of the elevator floor. The levels slide down behind the glass door. He reeks of whisky and sweat, he realises, but doesn't care. His mind is a jumble of angry questions, none fully formed. Jason tries to quiet his breathing. He's a politician; he should be setting up his moves, choosing the best tactics. All he wants to do is scream. This cuts too deep, hurts too much. A blade slicing through his very soul.

He crosses the hall to Khalil's door. No call pads here, no doorbells. Any visitor would ping to announce themselves, but that doesn't feel right. Nothing feels right. Jason raps at the door. What time is it? Must be past midnight. Khalil could be in bed or calling the compound security. Let him.

Jason knocks again, louder. There's silence, then steps, the sound of someone stopping on the other side. A moment of hesitation, then the door swings open.

'Jas...' Khalil trails off. He stares at Jason, eyes widening, his breath catching in his throat. He sways, as if hit by a blow of wind.

'Who are you working for?' The words roll out of Jason's mouth like pebbles. He bites his lip so he won't start shouting.

Khalil stands frozen, his hand on the door frame, his expression vacant. Seconds pass. Finally, he stirs, his gaze focusing on Jason again. 'My kid's asleep. Can we talk in Otto's old place? I've got the key.'

Khalil has a child? Not that it makes a difference.

Jason nods. They walk in silence the twenty steps to the door on the opposite side of the hall. Khalil swipes his wrist band over the sensor, and the locks click open. For an instant, Jason wonders if it's safe—but this is the compound, purpose-built to protect the Alliance workers. Security cameras would have tracked him into the building. Low-level systems would be monitoring their wrist bands even in this empty apartment. He steps inside, his wet shoes sinking into the carpet. Dim yellow night lights come on as they enter. The last of Otto's furniture remains inside: a coat rack, a dusty display cabinet, the ghosts of picture frames clinging to the walls.

Jason turns as Khalil closes the door behind them. 'Who are you working for?'

Khalil leans on the wall and folds his arms across his chest. He's barefoot, in a blue sweatshirt and cotton pyjama pants. 'We're on the same side, Jason.'

'Who—are—you—working—for?'

'Have you figured out what connects them? The missing scientists?'

Jason lunges. He grabs Khalil's shirt and pulls him up to his face. Jason's a head taller, even though the young man is thirty years his junior and could probably knock him out with one punch. Jason doesn't care. He's given his life to this mission, lost everything and everyone. He must know.

Khalil doesn't struggle, though. His eyes meet Jason's, their breaths mixed in the odour of whisky, sleep, and rage. 'You came here because you want answers. I will give you the answers—but to understand them, you have to answer my questions.'

Jason should call security and be done with it. But what proof does he have? And even if he can get him arrested, then Khalil will be out of his hands, and the truth further from his grasp. He might learn more if he plays the man's game for a short while.

He releases his grip but doesn't step away, their chests almost touching. 'Start by telling me who you're working for.'

'We call ourselves the Watch. It used to be Watchmen, but English is so stupid with the gendering of the word, so...' Khalil shrugs.

'Is it Volkov? Or—'

'My turn now.'

'Fucking hell, Khalil, answer me!'

'I will, as I promised.' Khalil stands perfectly still, like a tamer facing a wild beast. 'Have you figured out what connects the missing scientists?'

'No. Have you?' Shit, Jason's lost a question. Never mind, they have the whole night, and this *is* useful information.

'Yes, I have. You will, too, if you consider who gains from their departure, and who loses.'

Damn charades. Khalil's just trying to distract him. Back to the point. 'Who leads the Watch? Give me names, not codewords.'

'Not a single person. We have a strategy group with rotating membership. I don't know who's in it at the moment—'

'That's bull—'

'But I *can* tell you who I report to. Their name is Sandy Wang.'

Jason reaches for his wrist band—but no, there's probably a hundred Sandy Wangs out there. And none of them will have 'traitor' in their job description.

'What...' Jason trails off as Khalil raises his hand.

'My turn. So: who benefits? And who loses?'

'That's two questions.' Jason sucks in a breath, fighting impatience. But Khalil clearly has a point he wants Jason to reach, and it just might shed more light on what the Watch is really after.

He shifts three steps away, leaning against the empty cabinet on the opposite side of the hallway. 'Okay. The scientists benefit. They get new lives in orbit or wherever else they've defected to. And their sponsors—Volkov with Kanye and Cheng, and whoever in the Yun Ju arranged Hike's visa.'

Khalil frowns in frustration, and despite the predicament Jason can't help but share the feeling. They'd already rejected these very answers back on the blimp because they don't make sense. Who'd sponsor Hike after the 'genetic purity' lies she spread? Why would Volkov make an enemy of China about coral reef research they'd likely trade him anyway?

Who loses, then? China won't miss one scientist—but the relations between them and Volkov are now badly damaged. Both sides are the losers here, as far as Jason can see.

The second case is trickier. The destroyed research can be redone, that's not the biggest loss. For Abiola and the other science institutes, the real problem is in the Yun Ju stealing their people—and the Alliance apparently refusing to stop it. In fact, the research heads might have chosen Abiola to sound him out on the matter before going public with their complaints.

This is it—the answer Khalil wants, and one that makes Jason shiver. If Abiola and the others do go public, if they accuse the Alliance of collaborating with the orbitals to hinder their efforts to make Earth independent—that will destroy what's left of people's trust. And with Volkov and his allies already lobbying for their share of orbital trade, this could be the end of the Alliance.

And no one would be left to stop them from tumbling into the abyss.

'*We* lose,' Jason croaks. His throat feels like sandpaper. 'The Alliance. Is this what you want me to see? A warning, from a traitor?'

Khalil winces. His lips part as if he wants to protest, but he presses them together, his chin forward.

Jason draws a steadying breath as he considers his next question. He must stay focused, must remember why he's come here. Asking for names got him nowhere, so he needs a different tactic. 'What's your goal? What were you trying to do on my team?'

'My job was to find out what the Yun Ju had on you. How they manage to manipulate you.'

Jason laughs. 'What? And have you found out?'

'I think I have. Though it's not what I hoped. I expected a large pay-off, a promise of a luxury spot on one of the stations, a future for you and your daughter...'

'Leave her out of this,' Jason snaps. 'She's got nothing to do with my work.'

'Yes, I believe so.' Khalil nods. 'You are a tougher case, though. They didn't just bribe you. They made you believe.'

'Oh, come on! That's your point?' Jason rubs his face, disappointed now more than angry. 'So you and your Watch are now going to enlighten me on how the Yun Ju are bad and that we'd be better off without them? I *know* that. They are nothing but a bunch of self-serving arseholes too rich for their own good. But

that makes them predictable: all they care about is themselves
and their profits. That's how *we* use them to get what we want.'

'Then why is Richardson trading with Volkov?'

'We don't know who—'

'It's him. He's using an intermediary, but Richardson set it
all up. We've been tracking him for a while now.'

That's how Khalil knew about the fruit. Can he also explain
why? 'Richardson wouldn't undermine his entire business for
some extra apples.'

'What does he risk, though? Who loses if the news comes
out?'

A question out of turn, but this time Jason doesn't mind.
Who does lose? The Alliance would lodge a protest about
Richardson or the Yun Ju breaking the terms of their agreement,
but in reality, they can do nothing about it. And the louder they
protest, the clearer it becomes to everyone else that they don't
actually need the Alliance to conduct the trade.

Jason's stomach tightens. He feels sick, from the whisky and
the bitter reality poking its head from the facts.

Someone in the Yun Ju has turned on the Alliance. But
why? He's been walking the tightrope, always trying to make
the Yun Ju feel they had the upper hand. Making sure Earth
was as dependent on the orbitals as they were dependent on
Earth.

Jason swallows. He's come here to expose a traitor, but the
traitor has turned the tables on him.

'Why would they want to undermine us? We already do
what they want. Mostly.' The last word sounds like consolation,
something even Jason doesn't believe.

'It's not about the Alliance.' Khalil's voice has softened, as if
to counter the weight of what he's about to say. 'We're just a
tool, one of many. As you said, all they care about is themselves.
They want to be safe, and they see us as a threat to that safety.'

Right. He may have underestimated how many in the Yun

Ju believe Earth's independence would jeopardise their existence—that they kept some old weapons hidden away somewhere, ready for the final strike. He's assured them a hundred times that anything capable of reaching orbit was long gone. It seems no matter how low he bows, they still consider him a threat. And the best way to mitigate it is to ensure Earth's divided, always fighting, always too focused on their squabbles to live up to their potential.

Jason pushes off the cabinet he's been leaning against and crosses the hall deeper into Otto's empty apartment. The living room windows overlook a tiny park, empty swings swaying in the wind. Anna Nathalie used to play here, so long ago. He can almost see Maia standing there, laughing as she pushes the swing higher and higher. Now there are only shadows.

What now? None of Khalil's revelations are news, not really. It's just uglier than Jason has allowed himself to realise. And it doesn't change anything. They still need the Yun Ju, or it will be people like Volkov who will win. Reseed the planet with their own, over the graves of everyone else.

'I'm afraid that's not all,' Khalil says.

'Of course not. You still haven't told me anything I don't already know.'

'What you think you know.' Khalil stands beside him, the sharp note in his voice compelling Jason to face him. 'You think you can go on playing politics, kidding yourself that you're choosing the lesser evil. Tell that to the protesters killed in Bangladesh right when you were dining with the dictator, the very one whose coup you supported with your donations.'

Jason winces. He sees them in his nightmares every night, a sea of angry faces screaming in defiance of the food that was going to save them from hunger. They were arrested... and killed?

'How do you know they died?'

'Because I asked. Ten dead, twenty injured, more beaten up and tortured. And that's Bangladesh alone.'

'And how many would starve if we didn't do it?! If we caved in and rejected the red rice?' Jason shouts the questions, his nails digging into the balls of his hands.

'They died because of us—and because they believed the lies the Yun Ju paid people like Hike to spread.'

'You don't know that. You're basing everything on one crooked—'

'I *do* know. She wasn't the only one they paid, either. And the rice rumours, that's not even the worst that they've done— that they keep doing.'

'Prove it! Prove any of it!' Jason spits out the words, everything inside him squashed into a tight ball of rage.

Khalil takes a step back, as if repelled by the anguish in Jason's voice.

'Prove it. Or I'm calling security.'

Khalil bites his lip, his brows furrowed, the muscles in his face twitching as if under the weight of a decision. Finally, he nods. 'I will. If I can still get a link here...'

He presses his wrist band. A light in the ceiling blinks to confirm a connection. Khalil twists away from Jason, tapping in a complex code. The wall to the right shimmers in blue, the glow intensifying as the connection goes live.

A figure appears on the screen, Asian features, black hair with long bangs that fall over the eyes. The blurred background makes Jason think of a storeroom. 'What the fuck, Khalil? This is not a secure line.'

'Nevsky knows who I am.'

'Damn. How? Never mind, let's get you out of there. Is your family safe?'

'They're safe. Sandy, listen—'

'Okay, let me...' Sandy—Sandy Wang, presumably—reaches

to their ear, their mouth moving rapidly though no sound comes through the speakers.

'Sandy, stop. He's here. With me.'

Sandy's hand drops. 'The fuck?'

Khalil juts his head towards him, and Jason steps out of the shadows.

Sandy recoils, mouth half-open, wide eyes studying Jason as if he's a demon summoned in some dark seance. 'Fuuuuuuck...'

At any other time Jason would comment on how much nuance they managed to wrench out of that one word—all he manages now is to keep his back straight and his head high. He will know the truth, and he will prove them wrong. Show them that his strategy is the only thing keeping Earth from disaster.

'He's not what we thought,' Khalil says. 'He... I think we can trust him.'

Sandy tuts. 'He's a politician; it's his job to make you trust him. How do you think he's survived those twenty years? You have just exposed all of us for your hunch.'

Khalil starts to answer, but Jason has had enough. 'It's done. I'm here. He's called you because I've challenged him to prove his claims. Starting with Hike being on Yun Ju's payroll.'

Sandy shifts their gaze between Jason and Khalil, hesitating.

'If this is indeed the case, then the Alliance needs to take action. And you may be spared the consequences if you cooperate...' Jason trails off as Sandy starts to laugh.

'Is he for real?'

Khalil nods, but his face remains as serious as Jason's. 'He's here, Sandy. You're not taking any more risk talking to him. We may not get another chance.'

This time Jason doesn't comment as Sandy studies his face for another moment.

Finally, they bob their head. 'I need the others on it, then. Give me a minute.'

The image fades into a mosaic of shifting colours. Jason and Khalil stand motionless, facing the wall, not meeting each other's eyes. Jason counts the seconds, his hands balled into fists. He shouldn't be afraid of what he's about to see. These are just traitors trying to feed him lies. He will prove them wrong easily enough.

When the connection returns, four grey silhouettes float in the air behind Sandy, icons rather than actual human figures.

'I hope you don't expect introductions,' Sandy says. 'And not everybody agrees this is a good idea, but since Khalil and I are both blown now, we'll give it a try. So, let's start with Hike.'

The image splits: half of it drifts to one side, the other rapidly filling with photos and data files rimmed with green to show they're ready for download. Jason steps closer to the screen and sifts through the offerings. The images first: Hike speaking at rallies, in a church, a string of undefined locations with blacked-out windows, always surrounded by rapt audiences as she shows them pictures of... Jason pulls out an image to magnify it, then recoils. Deformed babies. Solemn doctors examining corpses, pointing to scans of heads without brains. Jason stifles a gasp. Is this what she's been claiming as the effects of the modified rice? The images were unrelated or fabricated, of course, but someone was spreading those lies and it could well have been Hike.

He moves to the next digital pile: a clip of Hike booed out of a science conference, a headline announcing a retracted research paper. Then a data bundle: money moving between anonymous accounts, each transaction traced through a familiar tangle of sale-return-reimbursement he recognises from the tricks his corrupted politicians use to disguise the bribes. It would take his data team hours to verify any of it. Still, the data's offered for download, so he loads it all to his wrist band, then checks the names at the ends of the money chains. Hike and three other individuals on the recipient side. On the other, a corporation he's never heard of, located on the Shui Lian station.

He turns to Khalil. 'That's where Volkov's shipments are going, right? At least according to what *you* got from your Mr Hassan.'

Khalil nods. 'The data's real. You can verify everything with Aya and the rest of the team.'

For an instant, Jason wonders if he can trust any of them now. But that's a worry for later.

'I will have it checked, of course. But you were going to prove your claims to me.' Jason points to the screen. 'All this is just a delaying tactic.'

'I'm sorry.' Sandy's head appears over the image. 'Next time we'll ask the Yun Ju Council to sign the transfers personally.'

Jason shrugs. 'You made the accusations. You were so sure, I assumed you had something evident.'

He's almost relieved—almost, because the amount of data now on his wrist band couldn't be something they've generated just for this call. It felt real—and if the rest of the Watch are as smart as Khalil... Jason pushes the thought away. No, they're all traitors, that's all they are.

'Show him the maps,' a gruff voice says. Probably one of the greyed-out listeners.

Sandy scrunches their mouth, but a moment later the collage of Hike's files is replaced by two identical maps: white continents over a grey background and the national borders drawn in black.

'These are the countries that have reached agricultural self-sufficiency.' As Sandy speaks, green dots appear on the left map, their size corresponding to their output. A moment later, red dots appear on the right, their distribution mirroring those on the left. 'And these are the recent outbreaks of the rotting phage.'

Jason examines the maps—the details look familiar enough to have been based on the Alliance's public data. 'And?'

'Amazing similarity, wouldn't you say?' the gruff voice asks.

'I'd be surprised if they weren't, since they're linked. The more we use the land, the more vulnerable it is to attack. You'd know that if you read the research.'

'Whose research?'

Damn. Jason wants to swear out loud. Most of the research comes from the Yun Ju. A few Alliance-funded studies are still running—in Australia and China as far as he can remember—but money's been getting tight, and since the Yun Ju shared their data there was no need...

He clears his throat. 'What are you trying to tell me? Because if you think the phage is some Yun Ju plot, then you may want to remember that they found the cure—and gave us the formula. For free. That's the only reason we can contain the outbreaks so quickly nowadays. It's nothing like what it—'

'Of course they did!' Sandy throws their hands in the air. 'They need us to farm and mine and however else they want to use us. They don't want to kill us. They just want us on our knees, ready to do their bidding.'

'The phage had been gone for close to a century,' the gruff voice says. 'If you recall your aunt's message, she talked about all the environmental issues but never once mentioned the phage.'

'What does she—'

'And then, the first outbreak happened just days before her message arrived. Almost as if someone had warned the Yun Ju that the Mind-Link plan was about to fail.'

The Guardian—Destiny's envoy on the Bethesda mission. Everybody believed he'd sent a warning message that drove his co-conspirators into hiding. Destiny had planned to use Mind-Link to control humanity—Earth-bound humanity. It would make sense they'd concoct another plan if the first one had failed.

Jason pushes his hands into his pockets. Destiny wanted to force people to live more sustainable lives, to prevent the ecological disaster. But that was sixty years ago. Who knew who ran the faction now, and how their objectives had changed? That was why Aunt Nathalie chose to send her message—because no one should be allowed to hold that much power. It seems she was right.

But no, this is nonsense. He's letting himself be manipulated, and without a shred of proof. It's time to put an end to this game.

Jason starts to turn when his gaze snags on the northern edge of the map. The Siberian Archipelago, its contours clear, unaffected by the phage. What was it that Volkov told him? *We've been blessed.* Blessed indeed. By friends in the Yun Ju?

He wants to keep on turning, to dismiss the sudden pang of suspicion—it's nothing new after all, he's known about the outbreaks and the Archipelago... He can't. If there's even the slightest chance...

He walks closer to the map, ignoring the studious glances that follow his every move. Jason reaches out and, as if reading his mind, a green hand icon appears on the screen, giving him access. He examines the Archipelago, then shifts the map down, tracing the recent outbreaks. The dates—they seem familiar. But no, he's never been to these places. On that day he was travelling, enroute from...

His hand trembles. He swallows, then again, his throat too dry for speech. 'Show me... my movements. You must be tracking me.'

Nobody answers, but a moment later the image blinks. The map returns, this time only the one showing the phage outbreaks. Blue dots appear, each marked with an N and a date. His trips, over the last three years.

'Show me the routing.'

Jason stares at the image, his body weightless, all senses gone leaving only his sight. His eyes shift from one dot to the next, tracing the route, checking the date, and it's always the same: the outbreak starting days after he passed overhead.

He is spreading the phage.

Jason doesn't dare to breathe. He's standing at the edge of something, teetering, feeling the next inhalation will push him over the edge.

He is spreading the *phage*.

His hearing returns, elevated voices arguing, calling, insisting.

'How did we miss it?'

'Impossible. He never landed there!'

'Then how do you explain this?'

'There must be something—'

'The blimp,' Jason says, and everyone falls silent. 'A gift from the Yun Ju. They send people down every six months to service it. Proprietary technology, you know?'

He starts to laugh. He's been cruising the world in a phage-spraying machine. Doing what they told him. Bowing and smiling and thinking he was saving the world.

He rubs his eyes, laughing and crying, his chest heaving uncontrollably. How many has he killed? Hundreds? Thousands? It only cost him his whole life. His wife's life. His daughter.

A hand lands on his shoulder. Someone says something, but Jason doesn't care. He is grief and he is pain and he is fury. He thrusts his fist into his mouth and screams.

When he opens his eyes again, eons seem to have passed. He looks at Khalil, then at Sandy, then at the grey icons still watching him from the screen.

Jason pulls in a slow breath. He has only one question now. 'How do we destroy them?'

FOURTEEN

LIZ

Liz gets up early the next morning, determined to set out before the other graduates leave their bedrooms. She listens with her ear to the door to make sure she won't run into anyone. If they choose to hate her for something she can't change, then she wants nothing to do with them. Still, it doesn't mean she has to endure their scowls.

She tiptoes down the narrow corridor between the bedrooms, then through the common area and out of the door, casting a longing glance at the coffee machine in the breakfast nook. She'll locate another one somewhere nearby—now that she's got the lenses, finding her way around should be a breeze.

Out of habit, she follows the pink-line route towards Research Central. The illumination is just changing into day mode, the purple note of dawn brightening into bluish white that feels almost identical to a bright Canadian morning. Almost. Enough to make her body demand its daily dose of caffeine. She should probably eat something, too.

She types 'breakfa' into her wrist band, and before she even finishes the word, the options appear in her field of vision. Each has a name and a location tag, starting from an inner-ring banquet hall, to restaurants and cafes on the middle level, and multiple 'refreshment areas' with food and drink dispensers just like the one in their quarters. More details appear whenever her gaze rests on one of the options, from menu listings to pictures of the interior, those in turn expanding into immersive 3D views, the reality around her fading into a grey outline. Liz stares, stunned equally by the vividness of the projection and the realisation of how much of the station is out there for her to explore. There are gardens here, restaurants, and theatres, all full of light and energy that makes her heart pump faster. There's even an art gallery on the inner level, right beside the flower-motif banquet hall that looks like a place where Ranath herself might dine. Liz blinks and the vision fades, leaving her alone in the middle of an empty corridor. She gasps, then chuckles, her elation returning after the weeks—years—of hiding and struggle. This is her home now. She's made it. She won't let anyone take it from her.

She considers the nearest restaurant—a cafeteria, really, with long tables and a breakfast buffet (already at thirty per cent capacity, according to her lenses)—but changes her mind. The restaurants can wait till after she's secured her job and can sit among the others as an equal. Instead, she locates the nearest refreshment area, and then heads to Research Central armed with a coffee cup and a snack bar, like a soldier marching to battle.

She finds the place deserted at this early hour. Lars's office door is open, but the man doesn't seem to be around. Instead, his message pops up on her lenses as she approaches, probably programmed to detect her arrival. 'Away in a meeting. Essa is waiting for you—he'll be your supervisor in this period.' All right, then.

She requests directions to 'Essa', momentarily wondering

what she'll do if there's more than one person with that name. Whether there's only one or the system somehow knows what she wants, the now-familiar green arrows appear in front of her, showing the way down a narrow corridor that she hasn't noticed before. At the other end, the passage opens on another cluster of offices or labs, a smaller version of the main section. Most have walls made of projection glass, transparent when not in use. Unlike the front area, these labs are bustling with people, the walls glowing with graphs and numbers and the air ringing with agitated voices. This doesn't feel like the beginning of a working day—more like a change of shifts in a twenty-four-hour operation. Liz gasps. These are not ordinary science labs. These are the monitoring stations studying live solar data, tracking space junk and rogue asteroids to ensure the Yun Ju—or at least New Hope—is secure. And she is going to work right at the heart of it.

Liz speeds up, the energy of the place seeping into her. She tries not to show her disappointment as the arrows lead her past the busy observation rooms to an office in the far corner. One day she'll get to work with real data—she still has to prove herself to Lars and this Essa person.

The door is open, so she walks inside. No projection glass here, just four large monitors lining the wall opposite the entrance. Three work surfaces form a triangle around a holo emitter in the middle of the room. Two desks and several chairs huddle on the right.

'Hello. You must be Elizabeth,' a voice says in her ear, the sound transmitted directly by her new implant.

One of the chairs moves, and only now does she notice a thin person strapped into it, the chair—the *wheelchair*—holding their legs and arms inside soft guards almost like part of their clothing. *Essa Nguyen (he), Research*, appears on her lenses.

Essa rolls towards her without any visible instruction from

his body. His hands lay motionless inside the arm guards, his head cocooned in a puffed-up collar. His face is perfectly still, only his eyes shifting to meet her gaze. There's little muscle on his body, his face gaunt and his shoulder bones poking from under his shirt. His eyes are bright, though, watching her as she watches him.

'You didn't expect to see a disabled person in the Yun Ju?' the voice says in her head. 'Even our medicine has its limits.'

Heat rises to her face. She's staring, she realises, but it's not because of his disability. She's worked with wheelchair users before—but none of them could speak into her head, could move with just their minds. Essa must have Mind-Link, the wires implanted directly into his brain. Like those people on Bethesda.

'No, it's not—' She glances down, embarrassed. 'I'm sorry. I—'

'Oh, it's the Mind-Link?'

Liz nods.

'I keep forgetting how it freaks out the grounders. Yep, I have full Mind-Link, the newest version. The tech was never the problem; it was the assholes with messianic complex who tried to abuse it. Though we probably shouldn't be saying that aloud on this station...'

Essa laughs, the sound perfectly natural even as the person in front of her remains immobile. This is the miracle of Yun Ju technology, Liz realises—the Mind-Link that allows Essa to live and interact as he chooses. Another thing her father was wrong about. He wouldn't even try the lenses, all because of a failed conspiracy from half a century ago.

Essa's chair turns towards the holo emitter in the centre of the room. 'Come. I've got more interesting stuff to show you.'

The holo surface lights up as he approaches. A moment later, the burning orb of the Sun materialises in the air above the emitter. Around the star float the tiny sparks of the suntries, the hundred-strong squadron of Sun-sentry satellites that provide the monitoring data. Liz has seen the schematics back at the Academy, but this is the reality. She focuses on one of the suntries and a close-up image of the satellite appears on her lenses, accompanied by its specs and status data.

'Live feed,' Essa says. 'Try it.'

A menu appears—on her lenses or on the holo itself, Liz can't quite tell, her full attention on the list of options in front of her. She starts with infra-red, watching ruddy blotches of the chromosphere appear on the orange exterior. In UV, the surface darkens and violent bursts of superheated plasma ravage the corona. She adds the magnetic field, and the Sun turns into a ball of yarn, thin lines curling over the surface and out past the suntries, beyond the frame of the image. Liz returns to visual range and zooms in on the bubbling violence of the corona, erupting plasma flares stretching out like hungry arms. She leans in, giddy with excitement. This is the Sun, live—well, live minus the eight minutes it takes the signal from the suntries to reach them.

'It's damn amazing, isn't it?' Essa says, his voice eager. 'Sometimes I just sit here and stare at it. But then I remember...'

The projection zooms out. In the centre, the Sun shrinks, no longer an orb but a spark of piercing brightness. The scorched marble of Mercury slides into view, followed by cloud-covered Venus and the blue droplet of Earth. Pinpricks of light mark the positions of the stations. So tiny. So exposed.

'This is a simulation of a level three event,' Essa says. 'Coronal mass ejection and radiation storm.'

Lines of magnetic fields erupt from the Sun. Yellow bands of solar wind stretch out all the way to Jupiter's orbit, trailing the magnetic lines. A limb of a solar flare rises on the Sun's surface, sending out another wave of radiation and relativistic particles. The image zooms in as auroras light up the Earth's atmosphere, the planet's magnetic field shielding it and the near-Earth objects from the worst of the onslaught. No such luck for the stations. They've got no atmosphere, no natural magnetic field. Thin blue lines mark the output of the mag-shield generators—barely enough to deflect the bombardment.

'That's the generators working on full power. They can deflect a level three event for a couple of hours. We can get a stronger field but for a shorter time. With a level five event we'll only last for a few minutes.' Essa swivels his chair to face her. 'If our forecast is wrong, if we fire up too early or at a wrong power setting, all our systems will get fried. And that's... not optimal for our survival probabilities.'

Liz shivers. Her eyes return to the projection, where the sand-grain-sized stations are now all flashing urgent red. She reminds herself that this is a simulation, that they are safe, that level four events are rare...

Not rare enough. The Sun has entered an active period, and the storms are now more frequent and more intense. That's why she decided to study heliophysics, why she thought it'd make her useful in the Yun Ju. Yet until now, that knowledge felt abstract, like the figures in her thesis. Momentary vertigo engulfs her; she is both here and there, on that tiny dot of a station suspended in endless vacuum. What happens when the generators fail? How long can the station's machinery keep going before its electronic brain gives up and the life support systems fail?

Never forget you're in space... Jacques' words ring back in her ears. Her research was going to get her hired—now it seems it may have to keep her alive.

'Right. Enough fun for now.' Essa sounds amused, as if scaring the life out of her is the highlight of his day. He swivels towards the monitors on the back wall. 'Now, let's look at your work.'

Rows of figures appear on the leftmost screen, each batch marked with a number. A glance at the headings confirms that these are data Lars had her analyse. Her forecasts appear next: timed graphs of solar activity she predicted.

Liz licks her lips. An hour ago, this would have only been a matter of personal pride. Not anymore. 'How did I do?'

Essa doesn't answer—but a new set of graphs appears next to hers.

Liz approaches the screens, her frown deepening as she compares the two sets. There's significant overlap there, for sure —but the differences... Her solar wind intensity is off by an order of magnitude. The timings of the flares are off by hours. The lines of magnetic field intensity...

She drops her head. 'Damn. I thought I was closer.'

'You did pretty good with the sample you had,' Essa says. 'My guess is, plugging the entire data set into your model would halve the discrepancies. Still, that's not what got us interested.'

Liz swings towards him, but he's facing the screens and she can't see his eyes. 'What, then?'

'Look.'

A third set of graphs has appeared between her predictions and the actual, recorded data. The new graphs are much closer to reality—not a perfect match but a significant improvement on any of her efforts.

'Is that your forecast?' she asks.

'My team's. Now, watch this.'

On the screen, the graphs split, the aggregate result broken into the component parameters. Most of the lines from her model disappear—the variables where her results diverge too widely from actual data. It hurts to see her work proven so wrong, but really, Essa has had years and an entire team, probably even the rest of the Yun Ju, to help him perfect his model. And they clearly haven't been sharing their progress with the Academy. No surprise there. Only three of her lines remain— yet among them is the most important one, the heart of her model and the years of her study: the predictions of the radiation belts response to the storms. As she watches, the lines shift over to Essa's results, replacing the variables from his model's prediction. The graph merges back into the aggregate, and the new plot travels over to the final figure, the one showing the actual records in glowing red. The lines settle—and Liz gasps, her disappointment turning to triumph. It's almost a perfect match.

'We've been struggling with the rebound effect on the Van Allen belts. You seem to have cracked something we've missed.' Essa swings his chair to face her. She grins, and somehow, she knows he's grinning, too, even though his face remains blank.

'Combine the two models, and we have a winner,' he says. 'Everyone gets to sleep better—and you get a job offer.'

Liz turns back to the screen. It's not going to be easy, she can tell it from the way the two models push against each other at the boundaries. But she can do it. Hell, she can most definitely do it.

Over the next three days, Liz tears through her forecasts, dissecting every place where the modelling went wrong, comparing her assumptions to those of Essa's team and feeding her results back to them. She loses herself in the project, in the feeling of being wanted and useful, judged only on the merits of her work. She arrives early and returns to the graduate quarters only after the others have gone to bed. She doesn't miss their company, doesn't miss the friendships that failed at the first test. If anyone on Essa's team knows her identity, they have never alluded to it in any way.

Even the cat seems to like her. The orange tabby, appropriately named Mr Sunshine, once belonged to someone on the Shield team but became the office cat once his owner realised they spent more time in the lab than in their quarters. Mr Sunshine makes his rounds at the beginning of every shift, demanding pets and treats—the latter now following a strict roster after the tabby made himself sick with the treats he cunningly procured from every single person.

Jacques pings her twice with invitations to join his debrief sessions; each time she tells him she's too busy. He can't force her to attend; he's just a guide, not someone with any power over her future. She can't ignore his latest ping, though, a message announcing the end of the onboarding week and their first meeting with Ranath.

Liz groans, then wonders at the sudden weight in her stomach. Back at the Academy, she couldn't wait to meet the founder, to score a chance to impress the woman. She's not so sure anymore. Ranath's feud—or whatever it was—with Lars resulted in the 'test' he put her through. She's passed, so far, but it could have as easily gone the other way and she'd be packing her bags now, her one chance at a new life falling casualty to the station's politics. She can't tell if it had any connection to her identity—either way, she'd rather postpone the meeting till she had something irrefutable to prove her worth. Ever since joining the team, she's been quietly feeding live solar data into her ever-improving algorithm. If she could catch a minor storm that the official model missed, that would be her ticket.

She checks the readouts just in case, but there's no last-minute miracle.

I've got to leave early today. The graduate parade, she sends to Essa.

'Sorry,' his voice says in her ear.

Liz huffs. 'Thanks.'

'You'll be fine. It's just an intro meeting. I've heard she's been busy, so she'll probably keep it short. Just don't make the mistake of trying to suck up to her. She'll eat you alive if you do.'

Interesting. 'Anything else I should know?'

Essa falls silent for a moment. 'She's smart, and she appreciates intellect. You can argue with her—but you'd better have your facts right or you're mincemeat.'

'That doesn't sound too bad.'

'No. It's just...' He hesitates. 'Don't quote me on that, but there's something odd about her. She seems to look right through you, like some god-damned mind reader. I mean, I've got the best poker face ever and I couldn't lie to her the one time I tried.'

Liz bites her tongue before she asks what it was about. She might, one day, after she gets to know him better. 'Thank you.'

She makes it back to the graduate quarters with ten minutes to spare, time enough to change into a clean shirt. Jacques' message didn't mention dress code, so hopefully that will be enough. And it's not like she's packed a ballgown anyway.

Most of the others are in the common room as she enters. The conversation stops in mid-word; all heads turn towards her. She doesn't meet their stares as she scurries past, her eyes on the corridor leading to her bedroom.

'Just in time,' Jacques calls, his voice strained. Have they told him how her father bribed her way past more deserving candidates? Probably.

'I'll be a minute.'

Another figure emerges from the corridor just as Liz heads inside. Kene.

She stops, her eyes wide and hesitant, her mouth opening—with what? More scorn or anger? Liz doesn't wait to hear it. She swerves around Kene, hurrying to her bedroom. There's a sound behind her, maybe footsteps or a word, but Liz slams the door just in time. They can hate all they want. She won't let them hurt her.

She takes off her shirt and throws it into the cleaner end of the wardrobe. A spare shirt and jacket hang ready on the other end. She pulls them on, then smooths her hair in the mirror. Ready. Or as ready as she can be.

She waits with her back against the door till the babble of voices grows louder, followed by the sound of eager footsteps.

'Let's go!' Jacques calls. 'Liz? We're leaving.'

'Coming!'

She trails behind the others, keeping just close enough so it doesn't look like a statement. A few times, Kene glances back at her, but Liz pretends not to notice. Alejandro scowls, but luckily, he doesn't say anything. Hiroko and Vithakan seem to want to make eye contact when they stop to wait for the elevator, but the last thing Liz wants now is to lose her temper and appear before Ranath shaken and in tears.

'There we go,' Jacques says as the door slides open. He steps aside as they file inside, then walks in behind them. He tilts his head slightly, projecting his command towards the ceiling, 'Level one.'

The others seem to hold their breaths. It's unlikely any of them has ever ventured into the inner sanctum.

Most orbitals share a donut structure, with a rotating, multi-level habitat ring connected to the central axis like a spinning top. A small station, New Hope's habitat has only three levels: the outer shell, most exposed to radiation and other space-borne hazards, holds everything that doesn't require human presence —the machinery, supply stores, basic hydroponics, and, of course, the mag-shield generators. The middle ring houses the working and living guts of the station: the labs, the businesses, the popular eateries and entertainment areas. This is where most of the station's three thousand inhabitants live and work. The final, inner ring is the domain of Ranath and her like: the top managers of Renewal or the owners of the smaller corporations renting the space here. In theory, all the levels are open to residents, but so far Liz hasn't noticed much mingling. From what she glimpsed the day she tested her lenses, the inner-ring facilities come with a price tag that doesn't encourage visiting.

Her assumption is confirmed the moment the elevator door

opens again and they step onto a stone-grey surface that looks like granite but feels like moss under her feet. Tiny islands of greenery seem to float on the grey floor: each maybe two square metres, tightly packed with bushes, tall grasses, and dwarf trees. They stretch out as far as Liz can see, much farther than the width of the habitat's ring. A holographic illusion, of course, executed to perfection. The impression is that of a park, a space wide open, and inviting—the very opposite to the constraints of a mid-sized station.

They have arrived at the centre of a spacious hall, the elevator shaft encased in a mirrored tube that makes it meld into the surroundings. A faint fragrance permeates the air, a hint of flowers hidden among the bushes—it, too, most likely artificial, but indistinguishable from the real thing. Even the light has a different quality here, not brighter, but more day-like, as if the Sun was about to emerge from behind a soft cloud. This feels like Earth. Smells like Earth, too, like those gardens in the Alliance compound she remembers from her childhood. No wind, though, or rain.

'This way,' Jacques says.

His tone's subdued, his movements guarded as he casts reverent glances at the people crossing the hall. The locals move in twos or threes, meandering among the green islands, unhurried but purposeful. Most wear light, pastel colours and shimmering, dichroic fabrics that look like they cost more than all the graduate wages combined.

They follow Jacques to the right, where the green islands converge into strips that line the sides of a wide corridor. Smaller passages cut away at acute angles, the floor changing colour to sandy yellows and sage greens. They continue down the promenade for another minute, arriving at a double door open wide to receive them. Inside is a vast room that must be a museum or a gallery: sculptures and art installations take up half of the space, the rest given to a grand piano. Large graphic pieces, paintings or drawings, hang on the walls.

Jacques gestures to the exhibits. 'The Create Academy graduate showcase.'

'Who?' Liz asks.

'If you'd attended the briefings, you'd know that the Aspire Academy is not the only source of talent we sponsor. We need the artists as much as we need scientists and engineers. One can't do without the other...' Jacques trails off, his back tensing as his eyes fix on something behind her.

Two figures approach from the door. The thin-faced, exquisitely dressed man she recognises from her Academy interview—Allan Duarte, as she now knows. Next to him is a short woman wearing a red jacket over a black bodysuit. Her short hair is raven black and her lips a hue of red that matches her jacket. The outfit would look striking in a different context, but it appears subdued in contrast to the clothes Liz has seen on display in the inner level. Even Duarte seems like a peacock in comparison, the one to pay attention to in this duo. And yet he trails half a step behind, his hands behind his back, silent and deferential to the small figure striding beside him.

Ranath lifts her head, her gaze sweeping over them, taking everyone in as it passes. Liz shivers. There's power in those burning black eyes, the force of unyielding certainty, a fortress secure in its defences.

Wordlessly, the graduates arrange themselves into a line that the woman can march along, like a general surveying her troops. Jacques stands at the head, a smile plastered to a face that has turned clammy and pale. Ranath gives him a curt nod as she passes. Jacques jerks his head in a nervous bow, then seems to breathe with relief at not getting any more attention.

Ranath stops—and another wordless transformation turns their line into a curve with the small woman at its focus. How does she do that?

'Welcome,' Ranath says. 'Thank you for accepting my internship offer and joining us here on New Hope. I know you believe it to be an honour—and it is, very much so. But choosing to leave everything and everyone behind couldn't have been easy. For this I am grateful, because this station needs the best minds to make it what it can be. I need you as much as you need me.'

Ranath tilts her head as she smiles, and suddenly she looks like a long-lost friend, someone you want to trust, to please, to be found deserving. Liz trembles. Her father used to look at her like that. When he was still her best friend and her hero, when she could trust his every word. A long time ago.

Liz swallows as Ranath shifts her gaze along their line, slowly this time, meeting each pair of eyes for long enough to register personal contact. When she looks at Liz, the corners of her lips quiver in recognition, the motion barely perceptible and easily dismissed if Liz didn't know exactly what it meant: Ranath knows who she is—whose daughter she is. And yet she's allowed her to be here. Is Liz only a pawn in her games? In her feud with Lars, or something bigger still, something Liz has no way of grasping?

She keeps her face still as she returns the woman's gaze—but Ranath's eyes have already slid past to the next graduate and the next. There's something metallic about her, something sharp and unbendable that's both frightening and reassuring. The comfort of never doubting oneself, always knowing your place and your worth. What does that even feel like?

'You've now finished your onboarding week and are beginning to understand what life here is really like,' Ranath continues. Her voice is calm and resonant, perfectly pitched for the size of the room and her audience. 'The real test is still ahead of you, though. If you haven't yet, you will now be assigned to your new teams. How you work with them—and with each other— will determine your future here. We're not testing your skills now, not anymore. You've proven your worth or you wouldn't be here. But what you still have to prove is your character, your usefulness to us, to this station. This goes beyond mere technical skills. I need people I can trust with my life, because that's exactly what I'll be doing if I keep you here.'

A ripple passes through the line. Of course. There's little difference in the level of their academic skills. All twenty of them have already passed the toughest exams. It's not enough.

Ranath pauses, letting her words sink in. A small smile curves her mouth as she takes them in again, assessing each graduate with those burning black eyes. What does she see when she looks at Liz?

On instinct, Liz straightens and pushes her chin out, as if making herself look bigger could help her measure up to Ranath's standards.

'Think about it,' the woman says. 'Consider who of your colleagues you'd choose to rely on in a crisis. Who *you* would trust with your life. Think about why and why not, and let that insight guide you. You have six months. Keep your minds open. Learn. I've seen what you are—show me what you can be.'

Ranath dips her head in a slow goodbye. She turns to leave, and in the small instant before her back is turned to them, her gaze snags on Liz again, then pulls back as if scalded. Liz winces —but no, this has to be an illusion. Ranath has invited her here, in full knowledge of her identity. An illusion, a trick of the light misinterpreted by her troubled mind.

Duarte remains with them, relaxed now and somehow taller, a bit player given his chance in the spotlight.

'The best advice you can get, so I suggest you consider it well.' He bobs his head as he studies their anxious faces. 'But in the meantime, we have a welcome treat for you. All the restaurants and entertainment areas are free to you tonight—yes, including the inner ring. Explore what the station has to offer— and then make us believe you are the one who deserves to get it.'

He nods, and then it's Duarte's turn to leave, and they are alone again in the strange room filled with art Liz doesn't understand. Nobody speaks, and then everybody speaks at once, the voices loud and excited.

'Well, I'm glad this part's over.' Jacques grins, relieved. 'Now, drinks or food? I know the best places.'

The others don't pay him much attention, consumed by their own discussion.

'How exactly are they going to measure the results?'

'Can you even measure character?'

'Or trust?'

'At least that gets rid of one competitor...' Alejandro's voice cuts above the others, muting them into uneasy silence. 'Because I sure as hell wouldn't trust *her* with my life.'

They are all staring at her now, vindicated rather than angry, as if a great justice has been done. Liz sways in a flash of fever, her heart thumping, cold sweat beading on her forehead. They are wrong—because it's going to be Ranath's decision in the end, the very woman her father supposedly bribed to get Liz here. Ranath will know the truth. Nothing else matters.

She stares at the others, her vision clouding with helpless fury. Tears, too, but she's had practice in holding them back. Somebody moves, a small figure emerging from the group. Kene. Hiroko and Vithakan are behind her, shaking their heads uneasily.

'We've never heard your side of the story, Liz,' Kene says.

Alejandro laughs. 'Really? She told you who she is. What else do you want to know?'

Kene hesitates.

'We know her name,' Vithakan says, 'but that's not a proof that her father helped her.'

Kene joins in, nodding—but Liz has had enough. If her future is a matter of trust, then there is nothing she can do to persuade the others to trust her. Nor her to trust them—not after how they turned on her. But that doesn't matter; the decision isn't theirs. It's Ranath's and Lars's and Essa's. She can't tell if she can make them trust *her*, but she already knows they trust her mind.

She turns on her heel, rushing back to the safety of the lab.

'You're not coming with us?' Jacques asks behind her, and she laughs.

FIFTEEN

RANATH

Ranath rushes down the promenade, keeping her expression preoccupied but not anxious, just busy enough to deter anyone from approaching her but not so as to send them into panic. She slows down when she's sure Duarte won't try to catch up with her. She can't stand the man on a good day, and today is not a good day. She draws a deep breath, trying to calm her pounding heart. It was a mistake to get that Nevsky woman up here. What was she even thinking? That she could have her revenge, a vendetta against a man who was but a child when his aunt had abandoned him? Neither Nevsky nor his daughter had any part in her own father's death. And now she can't even send her back, because little Miss Nevsky proved to be smarter than the lot and actually useful to the station. Elizabeth Lake, Ranath reminds herself, lest she let herself slip in front of the others. Apparently, the graduates already know Lake's identity, thanks to a particularly industrious security engineer in the group. That little weasel has made himself the first person to be sent packing. Ranath doesn't need backstabbers on her team.

She clenches her fists, her frustration turning to anger for letting her emotions get the better of her. Her father is dead, gone before she could meet him. She is the Guardian now, the guardian of his legacy and his mission. That has to be her only focus.

She crosses the reception hall with its infuriating maze of green islands, some previous designer's brilliant idea to create an Earth-like feeling. Illusions work solely when made for others, not for oneself. Pretending they were still as good as on Earth only got them deeper into this mess. Humanity's one chance was to start again—on her Ark. Yet between Richardson's attacks, Li Qiang's blackmail, and the Caretakers watching over her shoulder, the project now looks shakier than ever. But she'd be damned if she let the others win. She is Zhu Ranath. She's survived worse. Once, she used to hide in the axis, terrified of anyone discovering her identity. She's become what she is by will alone, by her devotion to her father's idea of a better future for humanity. She won't let them defeat her now.

Ranath composes herself as she approaches the headquarters—the chunk of the inner ring that encompasses her private rooms and her and her aide's offices. She draws in another calming breath and arranges her face into the expression of relaxed focus—determined but in control. Always in control.

Inside her office, Min Woo and Sandip Bagrah stand around the projection table showing figures and graphs she can't recognise from a distance. They fall silent as she enters, but their postures betray an agitated discussion.

Ranath nods a greeting and heads straight to the table. 'Sorry to keep you waiting. Have you got the data I requested?'

'Yes, yes, of course. Current production and stock levels for all the cubes. Including the scheduled deliveries that have now been halted.' Sandip shoots a doubting glance at Min Woo, then back to Ranath. 'Was that really on your request?'

'That's correct,' Ranath says.

'We're going to incur late fees if we—'

'I understand.' Ranath swipes her hand to remove the status

data, leaving only the inventory numbers. 'Walk me through it. What do we have that's construction grade—or can be retrofitted for construction?'

Sandip shakes his head. 'Construction assemblers are too specialised to be retrofitted. Material-processing bots, maybe, but even those would take more time to retrofit than it does to build new ones.'

Ranath stifles a sigh. She expected as much, but it was worth asking. 'Construction grade, then.'

On the projection, the inventory numbers transform into five towers of tiny bricks. One of the towers turns white, the other four remain orange.

'We have about five thousand in stock at the moment, give or take.' Sandip points to the single white tower. 'One thousand of the new generation drones. The Harmony contract, ready to ship.'

Right. The biggest contract they've signed in years, and the first for the much-improved mark-four machines. The profit they'll make on this deal will cover the miners' fees for a year, or more.

Sandip moves his finger to the first of the orange towers, half of which turns red as he points. 'Five hundred units for the general reserve.'

Ranath nods. This is the stock the Yun Ju Council pays them to maintain, an emergency supply in case of major damage to any of the member stations.

'Then the two thousand earmarked for the 'mining project'...' Sandip trails off, his tone suggesting he'd like an explanation of why they need that many.

Ranath hasn't clued him in on Ark yet; she still needs to make up her mind if she's going to trust him. He might be better equipped to help them if he knows what's at stake—or he might prove a traitor and she'll have another problem on her hands. For now, though, she's got bigger worries than Sandip's confusion. On the display, three and a half of the five towers are now red. Only fifteen hundred drones remain unassigned—half of what she needs for Li Qiang.

'Any other commitments?' Min Woo asks.

'Yes, four hundred units for various ongoing contracts. So that leaves over a thousand in surplus. Do you have a new deal in mind?'

Ranath sniffs. 'If you can call it that...'

Sandip raises an eyebrow, but she cuts off his unspoken question. 'What's our daily output?'

Sandip rubs the back of his neck. 'Construction assemblers are the most complex to produce. We get ten units per day from a dedicated cube, but at the moment we only have one running at full capacity. The other two are at half speed while we convert to the new generation.'

Damn. They used to make fifty per day, that was the number stuck in Ranath's mind. But those were the old drones, and four cubes running at full capacity.

'I thought we had more cubes?' Min Woo asks. At least she's not the only one confused, even though that's not exactly reassuring.

'We do, plenty more, but they make other types of assemblers—agro service, repair and maintenance, you name it.'

'So, twenty per day?'

'Yes, at the moment. We'll go up to thirty within a month and then forty once the new cube comes online.'

Too late. Ranath stares at the projection, the numbers swirling in her mind. They've got eleven hundred spares; they could maybe push that to fourteen hundred if she can stall Qiang for two weeks. Still less than a half of what he wants. The only way she can meet the obligation is if she gives him her own stock, the drones reserved for Ark. She'd be left with only six hundred units, but she could replenish her stock as soon as the other cubes come online. Except all her instincts tell her she won't get that time, that something or someone will make it impossible. Will Qiang keep his side of the deal once the assemblers are his? And even if he does, there's no guarantee how Richardson will react. Whatever Qiang has on the man may not be enough to restrain him. Richardson will lash out, at Qiang and at her, and if he really has proof of her links to Destiny, that will be the end of Renewal and of Ark right there.

Her gaze returns to the red and orange towers on the display table. Decision time. She's not going to give away the Yun Ju reserve, nor the repair drones—they are needed for safety. She doesn't want people killed; besides, that's one way of turning everyone against her. That leaves only one option. Still slightly short of the agreed numbers, but with the new generation drones, Li Qiang will get all the promised efficiency.

'Ester?' Ranath calls into the air ahead, knowing that her assistant would be listening in on the meeting. 'Cancel the deal with Harmony.'

The others' eyes drill into her, Min Woo anxious and Sandip bewildered.

Ester's reply comes in hesitant. 'What reason should I give?'

'No reason.'

They will pay the cancelation fees but offer no explanation, no apology. Let the others wonder what has happened and reach the inevitable conclusion that Ranath's hand was forced, that she had no choice. Just about when Li Qiang gets his delivery.

A small smile plays on her lips. This is going to stir things up quite a bit. And if she's lucky, it will take a while before she's in the firing range. Maybe just long enough to set her own plans into motion.

She checks the time: early evening by Yun Ju's coordinated clocks. The accountants won't check their messages till the morning. Then they will take a while to confirm the information and pass the news up the ranks. And young Zhu Fujikawa will need a moment to consult with her mothers before deciding on the course of action in the face of such a flagrant violation of their agreement.

'That will be all, everyone,' Ranath says, turning towards her private rooms. 'Go and get some rest. I'll see you all back here tomorrow morning—and call in the Ark leads, too. And have Tarkovsky on call.'

She doesn't expect to sleep much, but, as if to rebut her, moments after the light goes off in her bedroom, she falls into colourful dreams. She's back in that small apartment on Tian Gong, bedecked with a collection of rugs and prints her mother had collected. Ranath doesn't remember the details, just the smell of them, warm and somehow dusty even though the cleaning bots had combed through them. Her grandmother's cat was still with them, an ancient creature that spent its last years sprawled on Grandma's empty bed, purring loudly, as if the old woman was about to return for his overdue pets.

Her mother is there, too, curled up watching that same vid, the colours reflected on her face. Sometimes she cries, and then she calls to Ranath and they hug. Ranath never asks about the reason for the tears, her mother's tight grip on her shoulder telling her she wouldn't get the answer.

She wakes up to the soft purring of that long-dead cat drifting away into memory. Will they have cats on Ark? Of course they will. Pets, and animals, and orchards. Not at first, of course, but one day. And it really doesn't matter if she lives long enough to see it.

Sandip and Min Woo are just arriving as Ranath enters the office. Ester, Joe Chang, and Pauline Cart, the two Ark project engineers, stand around a side table laid out with a light breakfast. Ranath nods gratefully to Ester. The woman is always so thoughtful.

Min Woo makes the introductions, skirting around Chang's and Cart's job descriptions, but Sandip is too focused on the fruit plate to notice the omission.

'Any news?' Ranath asks as she refills her coffee.

'Nothing so far,' Ester says. 'It appears they've got some holiday they celebrate on Xin Ju today, so we may not hear from anyone at Harmony before tomorrow.'

'Huh!' Ranath grins. Good luck for once. An omen? She turns to the Ark engineers. 'Time is exactly what we need. Have you been briefed?'

Cart nods. 'We got the key points. We've just been talking about the next steps.'

'We should start with about five hundred assemblers,' Chang says. 'That's enough to help the miners get their base done quickly and with enough noise to conceal the work going on on the lead shell.'

Sandip pauses with a piece of fruit halfway to his mouth. 'The lead shell?'

Dead silence follows as everyone but Sandip stares at Ranath. She really has to figure out what to tell him before the poor man's brain short-circuits. Or before his nescience gets them in trouble. The truth would take too long to explain, but he needs to know something. 'We're building an agro platform there. A new type.'

Sandip's eyes widen, questions forming on his lips, but she cuts them off before he wastes everyone's time. 'Later, Sandip. It's a highly sensitive project, as you can appreciate, so we've kept it under wraps as much as we can.'

The man nods. 'Well, that makes several things clearer already. If I may, which is our real purpose—the mining or the 'platform'?'

He's catching on fast. No surprise there, she only hires the best. 'It's... complicated.'

Sandip nods again, as if to allow that more information will be forthcoming. 'And the Harmony contract? Where does that fit in?'

'Nowhere, really. We're being blackmailed.'

The silence that follows this statement is so complete Ranath can hear Ester swallow her coffee.

'We are to deliver three thousand assemblers to the Sunrise Group, or...' Ranath hesitates. Everyone here probably knows the rumours about Renewal's origins, but saying anything aloud is as good as a confirmation. 'Let's just say that the repercussions are not something I'm willing to entertain. And we don't have enough machines for both them and Harmony, so—'

The distinctive, high-pitched ping in her ear cuts her off. The Caretakers' summons. The second time inside a week. Ranath winces, then clears her throat to cover it up. The yellow icon flashes urgently on her wrist band. That the Caretakers would risk another contact so soon could only mean bad news. And just when she thought luck had given her some breathing time.

She presses the icon on her wrist band for three seconds—a hold message, the agreed sign that she can't accept the call. The others are staring at her, Min Woo's brows scrunching with worry.

Ranath clears her throat again. 'Well, we don't have enough machines for both of them. And giving up ours is out of the question. The project... It's a matter of our long-term survival. How long till the lead shell is... fit for use?'

'We have a foothold,' Cart says. 'For the rest, it's a matter of how many machines we get.'

The high-pitched sound rings in her ear again. It's the same ping as before, the same pitch and the same volume, yet it sounds more urgent now, more persistent. Ranath's hand trembles as she slides it over her wrist band, concealing the flashing icon—not fast enough to avoid Min Woo's questioning glance. A cold wave sweeps over her—apprehension that quickly turns into anger. The Caretakers have chosen to disregard her hold message. They whistle her in like a minion—while she's the one doing her utmost to fulfil the mission they have pledged themselves to.

Whatever they've got to tell her, she's sure she won't like it.

'Have the miners departed yet?' she asks.

'The first wave only,' Min Woo says.

Ranath hesitates. The ownership deeds have finally come through. The moon is hers now, but she still needs Renewal's resources to finish the construction. Only then can she start bringing the people—and once enough of them are settled, they will invoke the Habitat Ownership Act the same way the stations once did. Nothing is secure until then. Richardson may sway the Council to freeze her assets. The Caretakers may decide she's become enough of a liability to justify the risk of using their proxy powers to remove her.

If she waits too long, she may lose everything. But if her hasty actions draw too much attention, she may end up causing the very problem she fears.

The ping in her ear returns—and this time it's definitely louder, the vibration drilling into her brain. Ranath grits her teeth in frustration and pain. She could tell her system to mute it, but who knows what the Caretakers would do then? She touches the flashing icon, and the countdown clock starts running down her three minutes. And maybe this meeting is just what she needs to decide the course of action.

She turns to Min Woo. 'I'm afraid I have to leave you for a moment.'

The others pause, their brows rising in surprise and worry. She called them for an urgent meeting; they must realise that only an emergency would make her leave.

Their curiosity presses against her, but Ranath ignores it. She can't tell them the truth, and there's no point in lying. 'Please continue without me. I hope I won't be long.'

Min Woo nods, trying not to show his worry. 'Of course.'

Twenty seconds remain on the countdown clock as Ranath enters the meditation room and locks the doors. She positions herself in the middle of the floor, her head high, her fists clenched tightly at her sides. There was a time when she looked up to those people, the shadowy figures that contacted her only hours after her father's second—and last—message had arrived. When she learned that she would never see him return home from Bethesda, but that she could, under their guidance, continue his mission.

She was living in the backwaters of Tian Gong station back then, running a small business away from the scrutiny of the big factions, heeding her late mother's warning to always hide her identity. But the whispers had reached her even there, rumours of changes, of powerful players disappearing, vanishing into cold-sleep or returning to Earth. Destiny was going into hiding. By then she'd learned who they were: a secret society within the Yun Ju's elite, connected in the belief that they alone could save humanity from annihilation. The Bethesda experiment was a risk they'd known could backfire, and they'd put plans in place to mitigate the fallout: hide, cover their tracks, and wait for a chance to try again after the dust had settled. Appoint care-takers to safeguard Destiny's assets until the time was right for another try. Ranath was still in tears, mourning the father she'd never met, trying to figure out what it meant for her future— when the offer arrived. *Do you want to continue your father's mission?* She did, she so much did. That was her chance to vindicate him, to prove him right, to get closer to him even when the man himself was gone forever.

To save humanity and make her mark on the future.

She accepted the offer—and that very day she became Zhu Ranath, the head of Renewal, a brand-new yet surprisingly wealthy corporation run from a tiny office on the outside ring of Tian Gong station. She's come a long way since then.

The seconds run down to zero. The air seems to shimmer as the image coalesces on her lenses. The Caretakers appear before her: two, three, then more, their projected figures identical and interchangeable. They make her think of shadows—if, in some inverted world, shadows could be made of light. More figures still appear behind them, five or ten, the distant shapes undefined as the photons of their projections merge into a glowing aura. They stand in a semicircle in front of her, like a tribunal.

Ranath's stomach tightens, but she holds herself firm. She's never seen that many of them, not even on that first day.

One figure steps out of the group. 'Greetings, Caretaker.'

The figure bows lightly, and all the others mirror the gesture. The ritual used to have weight; it made her feel she was part of something bigger than her one existence. Now it feels cultish and pretentious, like the rest of their interactions. Still, she's got to play her part.

She returns the bow. 'Greetings, Caretakers. Why the urgent call? I dearly hope nothing precipitous has happened?'

'We are here to prevent it from happening,' the forward figure says. 'You can start by telling us why you have cancelled the Harmony contract.'

Ranath winces. She expected they'd find out and that they wouldn't like it—but she didn't expect them to react so soon, even before Harmony's own zhus. 'News travels fast, I see.'

'As fast as we need it to.' The lead figure takes another step towards her. 'Your actions are endangering our future. Do I need to remind you that Renewal doesn't belong to you?'

'I haven't forgotten that.'

'Haven't you? You are risking our assets and reputation for your private ambitions. Your job was to safeguard Renewal's capital, not to squander—'

'I've managed to grow it substantially, too. More than tripled, actually.'

'No one denies that, Ranath.' The figure shifts its weight, its shoulders rising in a frustrated breath. 'You've been everything we've hoped for—until now. The Saturn acquisitions make no business sense. And now you've cancelled a profitable contract to preserve your folly.'

Ranath hesitates. How much do they know? They intercepted her message to Harmony, but can they access Renewal's protected data? Do they know her stock levels, her production output? What else?

'The blackmail left me no choice,' she says, studying the glowing faces for reactions, expecting outrage and gasps of shock.

She gets snorts and huffs of impatience. They know about Li Qiang's extortion. They know *everything*.

'You have enough stock to meet both requests. And yet you chose to cancel the important deal and protect the stock you've built up for your 'habitat'. We rejected that project years ago. Why are you still wasting resources on it?'

Ranath doesn't answer. Back when they first rejected her proposal, she believed she could change their mind. That they were simply too cautious after what happened on Bethesda, too stuck in the paradigm of fixing the problems on Earth to dare examine other possibilities. But maybe it wasn't just caution. The Caretakers have spent decades making themselves feel good with proclamations and rituals, believing themselves humanity's saviours just waiting for the right time. Never needing to put that belief to the test with any action. They've grown complacent, fat on Renewal's profits, satisfied in their make-believe. They were never going to accept her plan—any plan that threatened their comfortable lie.

'Hopefully, we're not too late to revert the damage,' the lead figure continues as if her silence was another thing to be ignored. 'You must contact Harmony immediately. Offer apologies and deliver their order in time. Do we have your agreement?'

There can be only one answer: 'No.'

The figure draws back as if stricken. Its lips twist with rebuke. 'How dare you refuse? Have you forgotten your pledge?'

'Not a word of it. You, however—'

'Have you forsaken the mission your father gave his life to? Turned your back on his sacrifice?'

Ranath tenses, anger swelling inside her like a tsunami. 'Never. And don't talk to me about sacrifice. You know nothing about it. His, or my mother's.'

She was nine when she saw her father's face for the first time, when her mother explained who he was and why he'd left them. Much later, she understood the full depth of his sacrifice: leaving his young wife for a mission he believed was humanity's best chance, not knowing if he'd ever return. Realising that if he failed, he'd be the face of the Bethesda disaster, condemned by all. Her mother hoped to wait for him in a cold-sleep pod—but a rare health condition made it impossible. Once she realised she wouldn't live long enough to see him return, she used his frozen seed to bear the child they'd both wanted.

Ranath looks away, the memory making her quiver—but they turn with her, projected on her lenses, the entire tribunal of ghostly caretakers staring her down wherever she turns.

Ranath glares back at them. 'I've worked twenty years to make Renewal a powerful player, to make Destiny ready to act. I am ready, and I am acting. What have *you* done?'

The lead figure lifts its arm in an appeasing gesture—but it's too late. She will have it all out now, right here.

'You've done nothing but talk. You want me to follow your orders—I don't even know who you are. You are ghosts, hiding behind empty promises. You want me to listen—then stand next to me. Show your trust. Reveal yourselves.'

Silence.

'Reveal yourselves!'

'You should know we can't do it,' the lead figure says. 'We're not hiding from you, Ranath. Or, not only from you.'

This gives her pause. She hasn't considered this angle—but it makes sense, now that she thinks of it. Only full anonymity can ensure their safety. They're hiding from each other.

But it's not only safety—it's power. Destiny had members in all the factions. They are still there; that's how they found out about Harmony and Li Qiang's blackmail. They could be anyone, insiders from Liberty and Sunrise, maybe even people from her inner circle. Working behind their boss's backs, building their own shadowy kingdoms.

The thought chills her. Maybe they aren't just complacent or conservative. Maybe that, too, is a pretence while their true goal has shifted. With the power they wield, they can become a shadow government running all of the Yun Ju like a puppet show. And all the Caretakers have ever cared for are their own interests.

They are not Destiny, not anymore. Only she remains.

She drops her head, the enormity of the challenge over-whelming her for a moment. She is alone again, with the ghost of her father to guide her in her mission. She draws in a slow breath, letting her muscles relax. She's ready. She has always been.

She takes them all in, the spectral tribunal ready to pass judgement. Not anymore. The judges have become the accused. 'You have one last chance. If you are Destiny, if you honour your pledge, then reveal yourselves now.'

'Are you threatening us?' a different voice asks.

Ranath doesn't answer. Her gaze slides from one glowing face to the next. She can wait them out. She's used to games, and she's done being played.

'You should know that we can destroy you.'

'I know you will try.' Ranath holds their glares as she taps her fingers to cut the connection.

The figures in front of her vanish, melting into the air even as their brows scrunch into frowns and their mouths open in protest.

Ranath closes her eyes. She's on the piste again, facing her opponents through the mesh of her fencing mask. Make a plan. Never lose sight of the enemy's blade. Be ready to defend—and to strike.

First things first: she needs to know who she can trust. Anybody could be a Caretaker, even those now in her office. She accesses her system and checks the recording of the other four finishing breakfast as they point to charts and figures on the projection table. She zooms in on the faces of her two aides: Ester and Min Woo, both animated and engaged. No hint of distraction, no unexpected narrowing of the eyes or twitching of the lips that could betray someone listening in on another meeting. There's no guarantee, ever, but her gut says that at least those two can be trusted.

She wiggles her fingers to send a voice message, one for each of her aides. 'Min Woo, get the miners to take all our assemblers. Tell Cart and Cheng to go full speed with the construction and prepare for the settlers. Ester, I have a need for your special talents. Find out who on the station has been in encrypted comms during the last hour. Report to me only.'

The confirmation pings arrive almost immediately. Good.

She was right thinking this meeting would tell her what to do. The time for caution is over. She needs to act and hope she hasn't left it too late. Destiny—Ranath—is going to war.

SIXTEEN

JASON

Jason paces across the fake-wood floor of his living room, to the wall with its faded pictures then back to the drinks cabinet, the empty bottle of Otto's whisky rocking with each turn. The morning Sun hits the window blinds, their shadows like steel bars over the floor. It makes him think of that lion Aunt Nathalie took him to see in the Feidi zoo, apparently the last of the species. His father was dead by then, his mother dying, but all Jason remembers is the scruffy animal pacing across its enclosure, its gaze empty and confused. He's become that lion now, his world snatched from under his feet, the curtain pulled from his eyes. All his life, all the sacrifices, the compromises, and the humiliations—it's all been for the cause. He thought he was helping humanity survive—instead, he's been a rag puppet played by those who found him useful for their own goals.

He rubs his eyes, though they are dry now, have been, the whole long night. The recollection of the Bangladeshi protesters makes him turn back towards the bottle, but it's empty, the whisky used up to numb his mind and his feelings. Too many of them to even remember: skinny children, angry farmers, desperate families. He thought he was fighting for their future.

Instead, he brought them the phage. He thought his politics could save them, his elaborate maps of loyalties and conflicts, his scheming and his sacrifices. He thought he was their guardian angel—instead, he sowed death.

It ends here; it must, even if the future is only a blur in his fevered mind. His first instinct was right, though: they can no longer exist as 'us' and 'them'. The Yun Ju must be destroyed—politically, economically, whatever it might take. The thought makes him shiver. Can he even do it? Does he have the strength the task will require? Or have his bones grown too soft after the decades of bending?

He pushes the doubt away, reaching for the burning fury that sustained him as he stumbled back from Khalil's apartment, as he drank and paced and plotted through the night. His guilt won't help anybody now. His anger will guide him through what he must do.

A chime makes him wince, the sharp sound sending a spike of pain through his temples. He stops, frowning for several seconds before realising it's the building's entrance system. Someone's requesting access.

Jason makes his way to the hallway, his movements slow now that his pacing rhythm has been broken. He pauses with his hand on the door, staring at Khalil's name on the identifier, unsure if he can face the man again, if he can face anyone ever again. But there's a job to be done.

Jason pulls the door open, then steps aside, as if he himself might give Khalil the phage.

Khalil nods a greeting, his eyes bloodshot and rimmed by dark, puffy circles. Not likely he got any sleep, either. He wrinkles his nose. 'Vodka?'

Jason huffs. 'Nope. Whisky. Scotch, too. All gone now, I'm afraid.'

'Probably for the better,' Khalil says. 'How about coffee?'

Jason nods and shuffles to the kitchen. The gift wrap still

sits on the counter, the *Happy birthday!* message blinking in neon colours. Khalil's brow rises at the sight. He seems about to ask, but Jason sweeps the package away to the trash and turns his back on him, busy with the coffee.

Neither speaks while the coffee machine makes its gurgling noises. This, too, is a luxury blend, from the plantations maintained to keep the plants in the biosphere. Limited supply, reserved for the wealthy and the influential. And the Yun Ju, of course. They get at least half of the harvest, maybe more.

'Are you all right?'

Jason winces. He's drifted away, his thoughts a jumbled mess. 'Yes, yes, of course.' He stops, shakes his head. 'I mean, no. I'm very fucking not all right.'

Khalil's hand lands on his shoulder. 'Take a seat. I'll get the coffee.'

Jason nods. He slides on the chair and closes his eyes. He needs to be strong now, stronger than ever. Stronger even than when his wife left, and then his daughter. He can't let his guilt get in the way.

He looks up again when Khalil places a steaming mug in front of him. 'Thanks.'

'We've done some more digging.' Khalil slumps into the seat opposite. 'Sandy says you're right, the correlation between the phage outbreaks and the blimp's route is too large to be coincidental.'

Jason snorts. Dozens of bitter comments push to his lips, but he swallows them down with the coffee. He can't reverse the past. He *must* change the future.

'Tell me about the Watch,' he says, meeting Khalil's gaze fully for the first time this morning. 'How long have they—you— been going?'

'Over a century, in one form or another. Started when the last of the billionaires moved up to the Yun Ju. We knew then that it would become an 'us' and 'them' situation. And those never end well.' Khalil pauses to pour milk into his coffee. Soya, of course, the easiest to grow, especially the modified seeds they get from the Yun Ju. 'But it really became 'the Watch' just before the Bethesda mission. They'd had enough information to suspect that something seriously bad had happened in the colony. They sent two people on the rescue mission. One was killed, I think, but the other managed to get your aunt to help him.'

Jason cocks his head. The message from Bethesda didn't say who did what, but he always believed Aunt Nathalie was the one to defeat the Guardian and unravel the conspiracy. Or maybe he just wanted to believe it, because a moment of consideration would make it obvious that she couldn't have done it on her own. But he wanted her to be a hero—if only so he could believe it was in his blood.

He hides his face in his coffee, embarrassed, but Khalil doesn't seem to notice.

'They never made it public, of course. Zhang Min insisted on keeping his part hidden so nobody could trace him to the rest of the organisation. But I saw his messages. Anyway, they figured out that wouldn't be the end of it—either Destiny would come back or somebody else would step in to fill their place. The Yun Ju is too dependent on us not to want to control us.'

Jason snorts. 'I thought I was controlling them.'

Khalil shrugs. 'You were, to an extent. Without the Alliance—'

'Spare me. I know what I did, even if it's too late to change anything.'

'I mean it, though. You've kept us from the brink for two decades. God knows what would have happened if you hadn't negotiated the trade deal.'

'No phage spreading blimps?'

'Stop feeling sorry for yourself, Jason. You can only move forward if you look at facts.'

Damn. He *was* feeling sorry for himself, centring his own pain and guilt. 'You're right.'

Khalil waves his arm. 'It's important because many in the Watch think the Alliance is the root of all evil. That it's run on bribes and only to benefit the Yun Ju. I used to think that, too, before I saw what we actually do.'

Khalil pauses, apparently confused by his use of the word 'we' with reference to the Alliance. Then his face hardens again. 'We, all of us, we can only move forward when we face the facts. Without the Alliance, the fertile regions would trade with the orbit directly, and the climate-affected regions would by now be wastelands. We could have had war. And that's a fact.'

Jason nods slowly. 'Yes. I believe that. The first ten years of the Alliance made all the difference. But somehow, it's not working anymore. What's changed?'

'We got too successful. Too close to independence. They couldn't tolerate that.'

Jason drums his fingers on the table. His foot is tapping nervously so he makes an effort to still both his hands and his feet. Khalil's assessment fits with his own: the plan he'd put in place had worked, the global food supply had been stabilising, till about eight years ago, when the phage returned with a vengeance.

'Who's doing it? Is it a coordinated action from all of the Yun Ju or a single faction?'

Khalil puts his mug down and leans back. 'We don't know. Richardson must know; he is probably coordinating it, since he's our main contact. It's hard to imagine the rest of the Yun Ju would know nothing—but we have no proof. They could as easily be too self-absorbed to even notice.'

'Destiny?'

'Destiny has been lying low ever since Bethesda. They may still be out there, but our guess is that they're either plotting something even bigger or got so comfortable in their hidey-holes that they've given up their messianic ambitions.'

'What's your plan, then?' Jason asks. 'You must have had a plan when you infiltrated the Alliance. What did you—'

Ha pauses at Khalil's empty chuckle. 'We wanted to expose you. Show the world proof that you've been selling us to the Yun Ju.'

'Well, you've got it now. You can expose me for spreading the phage. Is this what you're going to do?'

Khalil's gaze is probing. 'Would you allow it?'

'You'd have my full cooperation.' Jason shrugs. 'For what good that would do.'

'You don't think it will?'

'No. I've considered it, believe me. Run through every scenario with each swig of my whisky. Wondering if an open trial or a suicide note would be more effective. But neither would make a difference. The world already hates me. They'd make me the scapegoat, throw in an expendable, low-level official, and that would be the end of it. Just like what happened with Destiny and the Mind-Link.'

Khalil puffs out air. 'I agree. And so do Sandy and most of the others. No, I don't think that's the way.'

'What do they propose?'

Khalil doesn't answer. He glances at his wrist pad, taps in a quick command. 'Nothing's been decided as yet.'

Jason raises his brow in a silent question.

'We can get a secure line out of Otto's place now. We're ready to talk, if you are.'

Now Khalil's gaze turns into a question. Jason hesitates. How much can he trust the Watch? They don't trust him at all. Still, without them, or at least without Khalil, he'd soon be going on another phage-spreading mission. They have good reasons to doubt him—and he won't get far without allies.

He nods. 'I'm ready.'

. . .

By the time Jason arrives, after a hasty shower and a change of clothes, another large screen has appeared in Otto's abandoned living room, most likely wheeled over from Khalil's apartment. Two chairs face the monitors, a kitchen stool between them now serving as a refreshments table with a jug of water, two glasses and an empty coffee cup. Seven greyed-out avatars watch him from across the room, Sandy's face the only unconcealed image in an inset over the projection. They start with cautious questions, a rehashing of Jason's earlier exchange with Khalil. Feeling each other out and then concluding that, while they can't entirely trust each other, they can't afford not to try. Even that decision is not unanimous, but Jason will take what he can get. As long as they agree on the objectives.

'What conclusions have you reached?' one of the figures asks, the tone making it sound like a test.

Jason strolls to the kitchen stool and pours himself a glass of water. His hands are oddly still, even as everything inside him is shaking.

He examines the absent faces, stopping at Sandy. 'You were right in what you said yesterday. They don't want us dead. They want us on our knees: too sick, poor, and vulnerable to put up a fight. Each time we get more comfortable, they find a way to squash us down. Nothing will ever change as long as they are up there, unaffected by what's happening to the rest of us.'

'Are you suggesting destroying the stations?'

'That's not what I mea—' Jason starts, but the words die on his lips. Because yes, that's exactly what he means. He's already tried politics, and trade, and every trick he could think of—yet with every passing decade the Yun Ju has only grown more distant, Earth reduced to a resource to be exploited and pilfered. More politicking won't change that. They have to force the orbitals to return, and they won't come willingly.

Not as long as their sky palaces remain untouched.

They have to destroy the stations.

Jason trembles. He brings the glass to his lips, trying to drink but unable to swallow, the magnitude of his conclusion overpowering his senses. He watches himself as if from the outside, realising this is the only possible course of action, knowing in his bones that this is what he must do even as he can't comprehend how, or who the person who could contemplate such things even is. Jason the warrior. Jason the destroyer. Ludicrous. He is Jason the politician, the courtier, and the manipulator. He's got nothing in common with the person who could possibly do it. Except for their purpose. Their resolve. Their understanding that everything else has failed and they are left with no other means to protect those they swore to keep safe. And so the politician must become the insurrectionist.

He puts the glass down on the windowsill. 'Yes. We have to destroy the stations.'

'There are thousands of people there,' Khalil says.

'I'm not suggesting murder. Or collective punishment. Not everyone there is responsible.' He breaks off before he mentions his own daughter. Do they know? Probably. It doesn't matter. 'I don't want to kill anyone. But we have to destroy the stations, so they have no choice but to come back.'

'Do you think that will fix it?' a female voice asks. This time the tone makes him think this is a question they've asked before, again and again. They know the answer, but need him to say it anyway.

'I don't know if we can fix it once they are here. I do know things will only get worse if they don't. These ivory towers have to come down. Unless you have another solution?'

Silence, then a gruff voice from the figure on the right. 'And how are you planning to do it?'

You, not *we*. Not yet.

'I thought you'd have some suggestions. Don't tell me you haven't considered it.'

Another silence. Probably still wondering how much they can say, if he's trying to bait and expose them.

The female voice breaks the stalemate. 'It's harder than you'd think. The elevators are the best-protected structures on Earth.'

'The elevators are out of the question anyway,' another figure says. 'The risk is too big of the cable whiplash hitting the ground.'

'We don't actually have any orbit-capable weapons, do we?' Sandy asks.

'No. I wish there was truth to that rumour, but the Yun Ju made sure they were all destroyed. At least as far as I know, which...' Jason shrugs. He didn't know the truth about his own aircraft so he's probably not a reliable source on anything.

'That's the intel we have, too,' the gruff voice agrees. 'Anyway, even if we damage one station, they'll just regroup and relocate. They'll hibernate in one of those old ships and send out assemblers to build them five new stations instead.'

Jason bites his lip. Good point. But there has to be a way, something they haven't yet considered. They just need to find it. 'Do you have any people up there?'

Another silence. Khalil glances away, his lips twitching.

'I know you don't trust me; I can understand that. So don't give me details. But I'm not an engineer, and this requires insider knowledge. We've got to find a vulnerability, and one that's within our means to exploit.'

'We have... sympathisers,' the gruff voice says. 'But no real "spies", if that's what you mean.'

'And not for the lack of trying,' Sandy says. 'You may have noticed, the Yun Ju are rather selective in who they let up there. Mostly those without attachments on the ground.'

The words sting, but Jason forces his thoughts away from his daughter.

'You don't spy on paradise,' the gruff voice continues. 'The few people we manage to recruit stop returning our calls within months.'

'We do have engineers, though,' another grey avatar says, one that hasn't spoken before. 'And access to old blueprints, from when the first stations were built. Nothing on the new ones, though. We might find a way to damage or destroy a minor outpost, but they'll just fix it or build a new one.'

'And there's no way we could avoid bloodshed,' the female voice says. 'It's not like we can go there and give them a warning.'

'That's the problem, really.' The gruff voice pauses. Khalil said that the Watch didn't have a single leader, but that person speaks like they carry more weight than the rest.

'What is?'

'If such a vulnerability even exists, we won't find it from here. And nobody in the Yun Ju is going to help us destroy their slice of heaven.'

'Well then, I might have found a way to make myself useful.' Jason smiles, for the first time in days. 'I'm going to do something you can't. I'm going to have a tour of Liberty.'

'And they'll just let you up there?' Sandy asks.

'Why not? Nevil Richardson has invited me before. Now is a perfect time to pay him a visit.'

The small passenger plane makes a wide circle around the Sun-baked peak of Kilimanjaro, avoiding the proximity of the elevator shaft anchored ten miles south. The craft's piloting AI follows the wind, ensuring the jet's wake won't disturb the diamond-silk cables. Or maybe just avoiding getting shot at by the elevator's defences—either way, Jason gets a good view of the Feidi down below: the old centre, where the Two Horsemen bar once stood, the Mdega street market, the remnants of the business district, its once shining towers now covered in red dust. Out to the west, the desert is reclaiming the former Chinese quarter, its pristine gardens and green lawns abandoned when the Chinese government gave up on the enclave. It's still formally part of China, as the visa in Jason's pa-pian can confirm, but they've lost interest in financing it after the stations moved to private hands.

The aircraft rolls into the final approach just before Jason can see the Feidi University. This was Aunt Nathalie's farewell gift to him: a full scholarship, including, most importantly, the entry visa. The education that would ensure his future. It did, too: got him the degree in sustainability that led to the job with the Alliance. He met Maia there, and they got married at the university's small chapel. Annalie was born not far from here, in the same hospital where his mother and baby sister had once died.

Jason pulls his gaze away from the window, from the memories. He blinks, his eyes moist, his emotions still too raw for the landscape now below him. Singapore or the Atlantic elevators would have been a better choice—but they are much better protected than the Feidi, and he is here looking for weak spots and opportunities. The Watch engineers have supplied him with a list of questions and a thorough briefing on what they called 'the areas of highest potential.' He probably understood half of what they meant; in any case, he's resolved to make copious notes and hopes they can make sense of what he sees in the Yun Ju.

They land on the outskirts of the old industrial zone, the very place where the Sky Sharks once shot his father and the other protesters demanding that the Yun Ju return their share of medicines. Things have come a full circle, it seems. Except this time the ending will be different.

The other passengers are mostly low-ranking zhu-yuan returning from whatever business their orbital bosses conduct on Earth. Only agriculture and some higher technology require the Alliance's license, and the Yun Ju make sure they have their fingers—and profits—in everything else. Spreading their proprietary technology, too, Jason realises. Just in case Earth got the idea of doing anything themselves. His anger returns, hot and bitter. Good, he will need it to guide him.

The door opens, letting in two figures in slick, silver suits, their visors drawn, their faces invisible. Jason shivers. It's not the first time he's seen the Sharks, but not here, so close to where his father's blood soaked the red dust. The zhu-yuan pay the Sharks no attention, fussing with their belongings as they prepare to exit the craft. The other two grounders, a woman with coiffured crimson hair and a person in long yellow robes reminiscent of a monk, exchange uneasy glances. They've all had their passes checked before boarding, but only the Sharks and the elevator's security systems can actually let them inside.

The first of the zhu-yuan makes their way towards the Sharks, but the silver suited figure raises their arm. 'Please wait your turn.'

The zhu-yuan frowns, glancing at the other staffers, then, sceptically, at the three grounders. Jason stifles a snort. It won't occur to them that any of the Earthlings might get preferential treatment. But then, he's not getting it because of who he is but because of who has issued his invitation.

The Shark makes their way towards him, the chip reader in their hand. Jason forces his gaze away from the nozzles of the weapons at their sides, the bulky tasers moulded into the suit arms. He presents his wrist, and the machine chirps in confirmation.

'Please follow me, Mr Nevsky,' the Shark says. 'Mr Richardson has reserved a personal cabin for you.'

And just like that, all eyes are on him, surprised, worried, and scornful in equal measure. Jason didn't expect anonymity, that would have been too much to hope for—but it seems Richardson wants to make a statement of his visit. To show how well connected he is? How good a hold he has on Jason and the Alliance? That, and probably another dozen goals and schemes the Liberty's boss is currently playing. Jason puts on a satisfied face and follows the Shark out of the aircraft. He will play his part, too. He will play it excellently. Right up to the end.

Yet another Shark team checks his chip as he exits the elevator to board the transit shuttle, as if he could have somehow transmuted into a different person in the hours it took to reach Liberty's orbit. The Sharks are polite, firm, and armed to the teeth, which effectively dampens Jason's willingness to put up an argument. If storming the station had ever been on the agenda, the very sight of the Sharks would put an end to it. Whatever they are going to end up doing will need to involve brains, not force.

'Thank you,' the lead Shark says as the implant reader chirps again. 'You are now authorised to enter all visitor areas.'

Visitor areas. Jason hasn't exactly expected they'd let him near any vital systems, but until now, sneaking around to locate those hasn't been out of the question. So naive of him; he should have realised they'd have him tagged and monitored at all times.

He floats down the connecting tube, awkward and self-aware in zero-g, his mood turning sour. The shuttle was one of the points the Watch engineers mentioned as a potential vulnerability, but all he can see are rubbery walls and the nozzles of the Sharks' weapons still only a few steps away. Will he even recognise a weak spot if he walks into one? He has no technical knowledge. He could be sitting on a ticking bomb and wondering if he's hearing crickets.

The third cordon of Sky Sharks greets him on arrival,

though this time they keep their distance, relying on their instruments to warn them of any danger. After all, he could bring them the plague. Or the phage. Wouldn't that be a case of cosmic karma?

The thought brings a joyless chuckle that Jason manages to turn into a grin as Nevil Richardson strides into the arrivals hall. He's taller and broader than his projection, thick muscles tensing under his shirt, his white hair bouncing with his steps. Everything about him is restless movement, his eyes darting, his fingers beating an impatient rhythm. The man is like energy incarnate, like a pressurised container about to burst.

'Jason! You're finally here! I thought I'd never persuade you to visit.' Richardson squeezes his hand in a firm grip. He smells of something citrusy and bright. He glances at the carry case trailing behind Jason. 'That's all your luggage? Never mind, we'll get you suited up for the reception.'

'The reception?'

Richardson doesn't answer for a moment, his eyes on one of the five people in his entourage. A young, slender person nods in acknowledgement.

'In your honour, of course. It's not often that we get such esteemed visitors.' Richardson leans over him conspiratorially. 'And honestly, we'd jump on any excuse for a party...'

He chortles and pats Jason on the shoulder. 'Come. A tour first, or a snack? Are you hungry?'

Jason's stomach tightens at the mention of food. He's too nervous and tired to eat, and Richardson's cologne gives him nausea. 'A tour, if you don't mind. I can't wait to see your little kingdom.'

Richardson guffaws again. 'Smaller than yours, but not that little!'

Jason joins him in the laugh. Is that how the man sees it—Earth as Jason's kingdom—or is he trying to make him feel important? The answer to that depends on how much

Richardson knows about the phage, Volkov's tricks, or the disinformation-spreading scientists.

They travel up from the docking port on the outside ring to the middle level. The elevator door opens onto a promenade that runs the length of the ring, with protective bulkheads so perfectly integrated into the design they might as well be part of the decor. Jason came ready to be impressed—Richardson is just the man to put on a show—but the sight exceeds his wildest dreams. He expected to feel claustrophobic, expected to sense the pull of vacuum from just beyond the walls, to dread the restless pounding of radiation on the station's hull. Instead, the walls are distant enough to make him feel he is walking down a city street, an illusion maintained with clever use of holograms and lighting. The ceiling glows with a perfect imitation of daylight; the air smells of spring and budding flowers.

'The proper, big stations have at least four rings,' Richardson's saying, ostensibly unaware of Jason's awe. 'The premiere league, Yu Huan and us, we both have five. Xin Ju and Yun Shi have four, just about what you'd call a station. New Hope...' His nose crinkles with disgust. 'Well, they are hardly a player. Not that the woman lacks aspirations...'

He casts Jason a sideways glance and he nods, too distracted by the view.

'It's a matter of safety, you see,' Richardson continues. 'Here, we don't get any trace radiation. Nothing at all. And we can make some creative use of the space...'

He trails off as they enter a garden—a park really—with walkways snaking among blooming cherry and almond trees, fragrant orange blossom that Jason now realises is the scent he smelled down the promenade. A narrow stream rushes under an arched bridge, cascading down a stone waterfall before disappearing into the distance. The park seems impossibly large, stretching out for miles, the illusion perfect even though Jason knows the far end must be a projection. He looks up: they are inside an atrium, two floors high, with the upper level encircling the space with a viewing platform.

Jason gasps. He doesn't care that Richardson can see his admiration, the man's chest pumped so wide he's about to burst. This is a miracle, a place Jason wouldn't have believed to exist, a paradise of light and beauty. And there's something else, something he noticed without even realising: the faces of the people they passed along the way. Satisfied, content, at ease. Comfortable at the deep level that comes only when your life is secure and your future hopeful. He looks around, at the people watching them from the upper level, at the children playing chase over the arched bridge. He hasn't seen that many smiles since his wedding day. Genuine smiles, too, not those fake ones he keeps in the jar by the door.

Another, painful gasp escapes his lips. This is what Earth should feel like—but it was all stolen from them, is being stolen from them by the phage and the disinformation. Maybe by Richardson himself.

Jason forces a delighted grin onto his lips. His hands may be shaking, but Richardson is not the kind of person to notice, not when all he expects is praise. 'Well, what can I say? You've smashed all my expectations. No wonder they are all queueing to join you here.'

'Of course they are.' Richardson resumes his amble down the path lined with sweet smelling bushes. 'Though, do you have anyone particular in mind?'

'Oh, a scientist I met in the elevator. A new hire for the Xin Ju station. And she's not the only one, I hear. I've already had some of our science bodies complain about the "brain drain".' Out of the corner of his eye, Jason studies Richardson's reaction. He must pace his questions, so his host won't grow suspicious.

'Ha! It's a free world! When we have an opening, and they want to come, it's their choice. Don't blame us!' Richardson chuckles, but then his smirk turns sour. 'Though that's not the case for Eyre and her "Academy". She's been poaching your people for years. Some say she stores them in cryo-pods, in case she needs them later.'

Jason manages not to flinch at the mention of the Academy. Does Richardson know about Annalie? Probably not, or he wouldn't be so cavalier with the comment.

A silence follows, Jason scrambling for something to say while his mind reels from the reminder that his daughter is so close, cruising above Earth in another artificial paradise, maybe even walking through a garden just like this one. Is she happy there? Free from him, free from her memories and her night-mares? What would she say if he told her he'd come here to try to destroy her dreams?

It wouldn't stop him, of course. Just like Maia couldn't stop him when she told him he was being used. He should have listened, then. Should he listen now?

Richardson's talking again, and Jason forces his attention to the man's booming words.

'Anyone else you met on your journey? Anyone interesting, I mean.'

Jason nods, grateful for the change of subject. 'A man dressed like a monk who spent the entire trip instructing people to seek enlightenment. As you may guess, he wasn't the most popular passenger.'

Richardson laughs. 'Another of the cultists going up to the heavens.'

'The cultists?'

'There's a bunch of them renting a place at Tian Gong. The Sun Seers, or something like that. No idea how they manage to pay. My guess is they're running sweepstakes across the planet for one loser per year to win their lucky spot.' Richardson laughs again. 'Tian Gong's barely got two rings. And they're sitting in a pretty high orbit, higher than us, even. If anything goes wrong... But then, they are in a hurry to meet their makers, so I guess it fits them just fine!'

Jason sniffs. He remembers hearing about them now, a reclusive group no one knows much about. Maybe something the Watch would find useful? He makes a mental note to follow up, but right now, there's another religious leader he needs to handle. 'Speaking of cultists... Patriarch Volkov is the one on my mind. He and his president brother.'

Richardson stiffens, his steps falling out of rhythm. He glances over his shoulder at the five staffers following two steps behind, like ladies in waiting. Ready to assist—or protect, though Jason can't imagine what danger he could possibly pose after all the scans.

'Any news about the orbital side of their trade?' he asks.

'It's tricky... You say it's fruit, right?'

Jason nods. A white petal drifts down to land on his shoulder, the scent of orange blossom overpowering even Richardson's cologne. A feeling of déjà vu overcomes him, and for a moment he's back in the Siberian Archipelago, strolling through the presidential garden with Alexy Volkov again. It's almost like the two spaces follow the same design. It could be a coincidence or a side effect of the similarity of location—one an atrium, the other a courtyard, limiting the choice of plantings—either way, he can't un-see it now, the two palaces blending in his mind. The two men, too, Richardson and Volkov, so similar in their ambitions.

He has no doubt now these two are in cahoots. But that swindle is only a minor trespassing, insignificant compared to the phage or the disinformation campaigns like the one Hike ran against the red rice. That is what he must stop, now, even before they find a way to destroy the orbitals for good.

'Very tricky,' Richardson repeats, nodding thoughtfully. 'Fruit is always in high demand. The trade must be quite lucrative...'

The man wants to pay him off to keep quiet about his trade with Volkov. Jason has got no experience in accepting bribes, but he's given enough of them to know the works. This is the part when they feel each other out to decide if the moral standards are low enough to suggest an inducement. He hated himself every time he did it—but he did it anyway because corruption was a better choice than riots or hunger. And if this is how he can get Richardson to trust him, then it's an opportunity he can't miss. Who knows what else Liberty's boss might divulge once he believes he's got Jason on his payroll?

Jason keeps his expression neutral. 'I'm sure it is. Volkov certainly looks like he doesn't need to worry about retirement...'

Richardson's frown turns into a grin. Message received. He waves his arm in a sweeping gesture. 'Wouldn't this be a great place to retire?'

Jason returns his smile. This is a risk, though. Richardson could spill more information if he sees Jason as one of his own, a future citizen of the Yun Ju—but Jason still needs the appearance of power that comes from his position in the Alliance. Without it, he's useless to anyone here.

'A perfect place to retire,' he says, watching Richardson's smile grow wider. 'In a few years. After I've settled my affairs. And found us a suitable replacement.'

The *us* in this sentence is perfectly ambiguous—and they both know it.

'I'm glad we have an understanding.' Richardson nods, confirming the deal. The details will still have to be negotiated, likely through aides or impersonal messages so the main players don't get tarnished by such trivia. But then the money will appear in Jason's account while the two of them never mention the matter again.

They resume the walk, admiring a water feature while Jason considers his next question—when Richardson stops abruptly.

He turns to his entourage, his face paling in shock or anger. 'She's done what?'

He glares at one of his staffers, the lanky young person maintaining eye contact while their chin twitches ever so slightly. Subvocalising. They must all be wired, at least externally, like Khalil.

Richardson's jaw is working, his fists tight as he turns back to Jason. 'My apologies. I'm afraid I have to leave you now—one of my fellow zhus has got herself into a bit of a mess. Laina and Paul will show you around. And I will see you tonight at the reception.'

He storms away, three of his staffers scurrying behind him.

SEVENTEEN

LIZ

The workshop seems crowded with all ten of them there, the three teams gathered on the opposite sides of the triangular display table. Not an even spread, though: the other two teams have four people each, while Liz has only Essa on her side—and he's not even part of her team, only helping her untangle the current Shield algorithms.

They've been working for several days now, and most nights as well, sometimes taking turns napping in the watch room, a tight space with several narrow beds reserved for the active Shield team when a solar event was forecasted. Essa has kept the teams separate, insisting it would prevent them getting stuck in the same ruts that derailed their previous attempts. But that meant the other teams had four people dismantling her algorithms and comparing them to the current models; she was alone, trying to understand the behemoth of that model with only Essa to drop an occasional hint. She had to admit he was right, though, because it kept her mind fresh, and each time the three groups compared their results, there was something new to learn for each of them. And each time, they celebrated those discoveries with cheers and coffee-cup toasts, delighting in the progress they were making. It took Liz a moment to realise that they were not competing, that this was not like the Academy, or even here, with the other graduates. They were a team, and it really didn't matter who was right as long as they were making things better together.

Liz rubs her eye, suddenly emotional. It's such a relief to be here, surrounded by the expectant faces as they watch the graphs materialising on the display. This is what she's always wanted: to be a scientist, an explorer of knowledge, free to focus on her work instead of her family, her tainted name. Maybe do something useful, something that could save actual lives, not like what her father... She pushes the thought away. She won't let him spoil this moment.

'You all right there?' Essa's voice says in her ear, the man as watchful as ever.

She gives him a grateful smile. 'I'm fine. This has been amazing.'

'Ha! The fun is only starting. Look.'

Liz focuses on the display, the three forecasts lined up to show their differences and the similarities. Each graph comprises multicoloured lines for every aspect of solar activity, from magnetic fields to the radiation spectra, the characteristics of the flares and the magnitudes of the CMEs, every prediction derived from a separate, equally complex algorithm.

'Okay, Essa, stop torturing us.' Sal, the thin-faced leader of team B, produces an exasperated sigh. 'You're enjoying it too much!'

Essa sends them a dancing stick figure icon in response. But then another graph appears in the middle of the display table: the actual data. The room falls silent as they all lean in, comparing the reality to their predictions. Gradually, the voices return, increasingly agitated.

'Oooh, that's looking good.'

'Still off with the magnitude here.'

'Yeah, but if we took their prediction for the timing, the path would line up with the magnetic field. That will get you the magnitude.'

Liz says nothing, her eyes tracing line after line. Not perfect, but the closest she's been, especially in the effects on the radiation belts, her focus area.

She glances at Essa. The dancing stick figure returns to her field of vision, this time holding a golden trophy. Judging by the absence of any reaction from the others, he's only sent it to her.

The others are still dissecting the graphs, pointing and zooming in on the misbehaving sections, when the sound of footsteps makes her turn. Lars leans against the doorframe, his arms folded. Next to him stand five figures in the red uniforms of the Shield, the people who put the theory into practice, studying live solar data to manage the mag-field generators. Too soon or too late, and the station could suffer terrible damage. They're still using the current model, but by now everyone must have heard about Essa's team's progress.

'Thank you for coming,' Essa says through the room's speakers. 'Despite the late hour.'

Liz swallows, apprehension fighting with pride in her chest. She's done well, by her own standards. But has she done well enough?

Lars nods at Essa. 'Let's have it.'

Essa swivels his chair back to the display table. 'As a reminder: the model depends on complex interactions of all the measured outputs. It's like a braid made of braids. Except it's a wrong analogy, because braiding makes a rope stronger. Here, it's the opposite: the weakest link reduces the overall accuracy exponentially. In our current model, the rebound effect on the Van Allen radiation belts has been the main problem, but the new algorithm is proving much more reliable.'

Liz tries to look indifferent as Lars's eyes shift from Essa to her. She makes herself look all cool and professional, no matter how loudly she's screaming inside. *Hell, yes!*

'We're testing each strand separately,' Essa continues, 'and there's still work to do, but we have enough data now to recommend incorporating the new algorithms into the working model, at least in parallel.'

Lars nods thoughtfully. One of the Shield team crosses their arms. *Ag Sima (they), Shield Operations leader*, appears on Liz's lenses as she focuses on the person. So handy.

'Your work is less than a week old,' Ag says. 'We'd require a lot more testing before replacing a proven model with a prototype.'

'I'm not suggesting a replacement,' Essa says. 'But our results—'

'Show me,' Lars interrupts.

Essa doesn't answer, but the screens at the back of the room come to life with an array of graphs and result tables. Lars and the Shield team move towards it, past the display table and the other researchers.

Liz squints, examining the graphs over the heads of the Shield people. Most of it is her model, she's certain, but there are additions and alterations she hasn't seen from any of the others. Essa must have been working in parallel, combining the most accurate elements of their forecasts.

'The last fifteen level four solar events,' Essa says. 'Actual data versus predictions from the current and the new model.'

The fact that he doesn't offer another comment means that the numbers are clear enough to speak for themselves.

'That's still only fifteen events,' Ag says, but their tone has lost its combative edge. 'And you're off on proton energies. Below the accuracy of the current model.'

'As I said, the work is ongoing,' Essa says.

Lars turns to face them. 'Ag is right that we can't rush anything. Fifteen events are not statistically significant—but this is looking too good to be ignored, especially since we're talking about the highest impact events. Good job, everyone.'

He gives the researchers an appreciative nod, pausing as his eyes meet Liz. He nods again, just for her, and Liz seems to grow another five centimetres. She bites her lip to stop herself from grinning. Cool and professional, remember?

'Essa, get those proton energies corrected out as soon as possible. Ag, import the new model into a parallel system and start running them both. Until the new model is verified, the current model remains the standard.' Lars waits for Ag to acknowledge his words, then adds, 'Not a bad way to end the week, eh?'

Judging by the volume of voices, everyone is in agreement. Ag and the rest of the Shield team nod and smile now that the pressure of decision has passed. They follow Lars out of the room, and then it's time for the scientists' handshakes and congratulations. Liz joins in the throng of hugs and back-pats, feeling more alive than ever. She's floating, proud of her work, proud of her team, delighted to finally belong somewhere where the others respect and maybe even actually like her. Essa joins in with a new selection of dancing stick figure icons—he must have designed those just for the occasion—and she wishes she'd thought of making one herself, just to thank him.

But then it's time to leave for the day, the researchers trickling out through the open door, away to join their families and friends. Liz remains by the display table, suddenly wondering if the graduates are out for the evening, exploring the local eateries or maybe even venturing up to splurge on a night out in the inner ring, like when Ranath gave them the free pass. From the ruckus they made on their return, they must have had a great time.

'Going or staying?' Essa asks in her ear.

She looks up to see him watching her from the other side of

the room, where his own workstation looks like a cocoon of screens.

Liz shrugs. Essa must have figured out by now she's got no friends to run to. 'And you? Have you got family? I mean, if you don't mind saying.'

'I don't. I don't mind saying, I mean. I've got a partner, yes, but Sam's a workaholic.'

Liz laughs. 'Worse than you?'

'Way worse. Works in a sealed bio-lab, too, so I don't see them for weeks at a time.'

'I'm sorry.'

'Nah. We like it this way. Anyway, I'm staying. Will have another crack at those protons. They won't let me sleep.'

'Want help?'

Essa considers the question. 'I've got an idea I want to try first. Why don't you run another simulation in the meantime?'

Liz nods. 'Send me the data.'

She retreats to her own desk on the other side of the room, starting by removing the coffee cups that have somehow managed to breed in her absence. She deposits them in the recycler and picks up a tisane, a herbal blend popular on the station. The taste is growing on her, a hint of sweetness and lemon zest, just enough to keep her refreshed. When she returns, Mr Sunshine has taken over her chair, but he settles for her lap and some pets. This may not be the worst way to spend the evening.

By the time she processes the data, the cat is asleep, snoring loudly. On this occasion, Essa has included the actual outcomes so she can verify the projections herself. The results check out beautifully against the actuals, three more scenarios towards Ag's 'statistically significant' sample.

Liz stretches. 'Done here. How's your progress?'

No answer comes, so she follows up by sending a message to Essa's system. *You alive there?*

The reply is a stick man drowning under an avalanche of

numbers. 'Almost there. If I'm not finished in ten minutes, come dig me out.'

'How about we both take a break and get some food?'

No answer, of course. He's lost to his work again. Okay, she will give him the ten minutes, and then she's getting a snack. And maybe some out-of-the-roster treats for Mr Sunshine.

She changes the display to her other setup, the one she's been testing on live solar data. Simulations are fine, but if she were to catch a real discrepancy between the models—

Liz sits up, Mr Sunshine sliding off her lap with a disapproving meow. She checks the dates, then the screen configuration. It's correct, her program running as intended.

Showing a high-level solar event within the next hour.

'Essa...'

No answer. She rushes across the room to Essa's station. His eyes are closed when she approaches, his eyeballs twitching under the eyelids. His screens flash with equations he must be running on his lenses.

'Essa!'

His eyes pop open.

'Whoa, you scared me. I'm...' He trails off, reading something in her expression. 'What is it?'

'A level three, at least. Enough for a big rebound effect.'

'What? Wait, how?'

'I've been feeding live data into our model. Hoping to catch some discrepancy we could use. And I just checked the output.'

Silence follows. Essa closes his eyes, and the forecast from her screen appears on the main display. An instant later, another forecast emerges next to it—the same time stamps but with the maxima not exceeding level two and offset by fifteen minutes. No trace of rebound.

'The current model,' Essa says, his simulated voice breathless. 'Fuck.'

'Fuck,' Liz repeats. 'Will they even see our forecast?'

'Not unless we tell them. But they'll still base the response on the current model. They will have to preserve the power...' Essa trails off again. This time he stays quiet for over a minute, and Liz has to stop herself from calling for his attention. 'Lars's on the way to Ranath's office. He'll meet you there. Go!'

Liz starts to move, but stops after three steps. He's the one who should be going, not her. He knows the model inside out, knows all their systems. 'Why aren't you—'

'Someone needs to feed the sensor data to the model. It's not integrated yet, so it all has to be done manually. And I'm the fastest. Go!'

Liz nods and starts to run.

She has no idea how to get to Ranath's office, but her lenses point the way to the same elevator they took with Jacques the other day. She barely notices the greenery now, her eyes on her feet as she tries to outrun her questions. Is the model correct? She's sure it is. But could the data be wrong somehow, the inputs faulty...? Or is the station about to be hit? And which station? Not all of them will be in the path of the storm. Some will be out of its cone, others shielded behind the cover of Earth. How precise is the model's timing? The stations move so fast, minutes will make all the difference.

The arrows stop before she runs out of questions. She is in front of a white door, covered with geometric designs etched into the surface. Liz glances around, but there's no trace of Lars. Should she wait? Knock? How do you announce yourself to Zhu Ranath?

The door slides open before she can figure out the answer. Someone is moving towards her, a slim Asian man about her age, dressed in a navy jacket with gold trim, a deep frown scrunching his brows. *Min Woo Lee (he), Renewal Corporation,* pops up on her lenses.

He waves his arm, his tone impatient. 'Come on in.'

Liz follows him inside a large office, about the size of Essa's workshop. The floor here is the same strange 'marble' as in the reception hall: white with grey veins, and yet soft and warm under her feet. To the right, the entire curved wall is a projection surface, now idle. Halfway along its length, four chairs surround a massive table, it, too, looking like it's made of stone. Two workstations sit against the opposite wall, one occupied by a plump, olive-skinned woman with black hair braided around the crown of her head. *Ester Ashen (she), Renewal Corporation,* according to Liz's lenses. There's more furniture deeper inside, chairs and tables and something that looks like an antique wooden desk, but Liz's attention snaps to the side door she hasn't so far noticed. Ranath storms inside, her hair glistening with moisture, her hands fastening the cuffs of her black jacket. Her gaze seems to glide over Liz to her two assistants.

'How serious is it?'

'Not very, if we are to trust our current model,' Ester Ashen says. 'But that's apparently under debate.'

'Where's Lars?'

'On his way. He was... otherwise engaged,' Min Woo says.

Ranath rolls her eyes, then focuses on Liz. 'Explain.'

Liz shrinks under her gaze, the black pupils making her think of weapon sensors zeroing in on a target. An absurd association; Liz has never seen a weapon, let alone a targeting system. And Ranath is just a woman, flesh and blood like the rest of them, if with a hell of a lot more money.

'We have developed a new model based on... on new developments. A new algorithm. We've been testing...' Liz pauses. Ranath's brow is tightening with impatience; in a moment she will cut her off. Rightly, too. Liz is taking too long, fumbling like a schoolgirl. She can do better.

She shakes her head, steeling her nerves. 'Okay, the details can wait. The thing is, we have a new model. It's still in testing, but so far it's proving highly accurate in forecasting high-level events. It is predicting one now, but the Shield team's response is still based on the old model.'

Ranath nods. 'I assume there's a reason why we can't handle both eventualities?'

'They are very close together,' Liz starts as the door opens and Lars rushes inside. He's changed clothes since their earlier meeting; tight red trousers and a flowing pink shirt make it look like he's run out of a party or a date.

'Too close together,' Lars says. 'If the new model is correct, then we'll need all our defence systems on full power. But if it's wrong, we'll have run our banks dry by the time the other front hits. It's a level two, the edge of a storm front we can easily deflect, but only if we have the power.'

'I see.' Ranath looks away for a moment, her eyes glazing over and her chin trembling like someone subvocalising a message. Then her gaze returns to Lars. 'Your recommendation?'

Lars grimaces. 'The new model is good, but it's too untested. We still have... about forty minutes. I'd like to put all the systems in high readiness and monitor the data until either of the forecasts firms up.'

Liz nods. This makes sense. The models are so complex, with dozens of factors influencing each other in recursive loops, each based on probabilities inferred from the current readings. The closer they get to the actual event, the more reliable the data, and the forecast. And they only need moments to power up the mag-generators. Except... what if they need to evacuate?

She's opening her mouth to ask the question when the other woman, Ester, leans from behind the workstation. 'We have a preview. From Essa Nguyen.'

'Put it through,' Ranath says.

'I must go back to the lab, work this with Ag and the team.'

Lars juts his head towards Liz. 'Elizabeth can give you the details.'

Ranath nods, and he rushes out before Liz can suggest that she should go with him since this is about her model—but no, it's not 'her' model, just parts of it. Besides, Essa is there, and Lars is more likely to listen to Essa than to her. Maybe it's better if she stays here, with the person who will make the final call.

The air above the supposedly stone table shimmers, then solidifies into a hologram of Earth, its Sun-facing side bright blue and the nightside obscured by darkness. Tiny icons of the stations encircle the planet like beads gliding along coloured threads. They follow their orbital paths, in an out of the Sun-facing danger zone, their speeds dictated by their position.

Min Woo points to a blue arc moving in from the edge of the projection. 'Is that the storm?'

'Yes. The Shield team has been tracking it for a couple of days.' Liz traces the arc as it approaches the stations, expanding even as its trajectory bends away from them. 'It follows the lines of the magnetic field between Earth and the Sun—so we'll only get the edge of it as it passes.'

'If you've been tracking it for days, then why are the two models so different?' Ranath asks, her eyes not leaving the holo.

'Because the current forecast doesn't account for interaction with the Van Allen belt. Usually, it doesn't impact the model, but we're at solar maximum and the belt's already been rattled...' Liz trails off. How to explain this without drowning them in physics they don't understand? 'Essa, can you make it interactive?'

'Done,' Essa says over the room's speakers. 'It will track your hand.'

Liz touches the clock icon to roll it back. The projection zooms out, and the storm retreats far beyond the purple bands of the Van Allen radiation belts. She traces the lines of the belts with her finger. 'Charged particles from the solar wind caught in Earth's magnetic field. Normally, they just sit there, and we sit here, in between the two belts, in what we call the 'safe zone.' But each time a storm passes, they get rattled. Recently, it has happened enough times to put the whole belt on edge. And now we have yet another storm front ramming right into it.'

On the projection, the blue arc of the storm enters the outer belt. Liz holds her breath as shockwaves ripple down its simulated band. Its edge breaks, the solid line replaced by frayed outlines of filaments shooting out, into the safe zone and the stations' orbits. Next to her Min Woo gasps. Even Ranath looks pale, her knuckles white on the edge of the table.

'One more thing,' Liz says. 'With the worst-case scenario, the ejected particles will be relativistic. We won't have the time to react.'

'How bad can it get?' Ester asks, now also at the table.

'The power surges could rip out most of the outer ring,' Essa's voice says. 'Our magnetic field can deflect it, but only at full power—and provided it's fully deployed before the surge hits.'

Ranath nods. 'Show me our position.'

'The best I can get you is a ten-minute window,' Essa says.

The projection zooms in again. The belt and the storm front vanish, leaving only the planet and the faint circles marking the stations' orbits. Not just the stations—there are also storage depots, agro platforms, and an array of smaller outposts, some of them inhabited. Sections of the circles light up in red to mark the paths they will travel over that ten-minute window.

Liz leans over the table, into the warm, ozone smell of the projection. She's vaguely aware of the others leaning in with her, their breaths mixing as they all peer into the image. There's Yu Huan and Xin Ju, safe on the nightside, shielded by the planet. Yun Shi is heading into the nightside. And on the other side of the planet, Liberty and New Hope move the other way, out of the protective shadow into the Sun-facing danger zone.

Ranath gestures at the image, zooming in on their position. New Hope's trajectory is split almost half and half between the shadow and the exposed zone. Liberty seems even closer to the dayside, but they're higher and slower so both stations might cross the line at a similar time. The projection rotates. Names pop up above the icons: growth and production facilities that Liz has never heard of. The An Ju station, with the mothballed colony ships still in the docks. How many crew stationed there? Another swipe of Ranath's fingers, and the projection zooms in on Tian Gong, right at the zenith of the oncoming blast zone.

'Damn,' Min Woo swears.

'We have to warn them,' Liz says.

'And tell them what?' Ranath spins towards her. 'That we have an untested model that even we haven't adopted yet? A model that requires them to use up all their power before the real storm hits? And what if you're wrong?'

'We can send them the model, so they can decide...' Liz stops. There's not enough time to discuss the model, not when they can't even agree within their own team.

'We're running the numbers, but for now the two models overlap,' Lars says from an inset in the holo.

Liz glances at the projection. Of course they overlap—they will, until the shockwave hits the outer belt. And then, if the energy is high enough, they will have only seconds.

'We must inform Tian Gong.' Liz turns to face Ranath, but the woman pays her no attention.

'They don't have the power reserves we have,' Min Woo answers instead. 'They will use all they have and then they'll be defenceless.'

'For what it's worth, I've sent my counterparts a message,' Lars says.

Ranath pushes away from the table, her mouth scrunched in a bitter grimace. 'I hope you made it clear it's an untested model. Because they will come for our skins otherwise, whether the storm hits or not.'

Liz stares. Why would anybody blame them for offering a warning? What is she missing? She glances at Min Woo then at Ester, but the woman is back at the workstation and Min Woo is busy with a handheld pad.

'I made it very clear,' Lars says. 'Anyway, so far, they're all "thanks but no thanks". Liberty hasn't even bothered to answer. Apparently, my counterpart is at the Nevsky reception.'

Liz manages not to wince, holding perfectly still as she swallows a gasp. Nobody looks at her, but from the way the other three tense she can tell they know who she is.

'The Nevsky reception?' she hears herself say, her lips forming the words before her brain can stop them.

'Mr Alliance himself, apparently visiting,' Lars answers. 'And they're having a party in his honour.'

Her father is here. Visiting Liberty. Why? Who cares? Just more of his games, more of his machinations. Is he in danger? Does she care? Yes, she does. More than for the people on Tian Gong? She knows nobody on Tian Gong. She hates him, but not enough to wish him harm.

She swallows, lightheaded and nauseous. Ranath and Min Woo turn back to the projection, and Liz makes herself turn as well, her movements jerky as if she is operating a puppet. The image has zoomed in again: the two stations almost level now, New Hope pulling ahead, into the danger zone with Liberty only moments behind.

Should she send her father a message? How? Would he even listen?

'Time?' Ranath asks.

'Five minutes,' Lars says. 'Decision time.'

EIGHTEEN

RANATH

Five minutes.

It takes ninety seconds to spool up the generators to full power.

Ranath leans over the projection. New Hope is pulling ahead of Liberty; if the surge does come, they will get the full hit while Liberty might be spared. Damn. She shifts the image again. Some automated production sites, four growth platforms, all from Liberty. They will make a heck of a mess if they get blown up. She rotates the image further, her heart speeding up as Tian Gong comes into view, her old home, now right in the path of the blast. About a thousand people there: the cultists and Nebu Owande's co-op. Including the home base of the Sky Sharks.

'We've got to warn the others.' Liz is talking again, pale and stiff.

Is she thinking about Tian Gong? Or her father? Does she hate him enough to want him dead? Doubtful. She might just try to warn him.

Ester, restrict her comms for internal only. And let me know if she tries to contact anyone outside.

Her nails bite into the balls of her hands. Still there. The station, or its husk?

'They powered their generators just seconds before impact,' Lars says. 'Was it you?'

Ranath lets out a breath. Liz's head shoots up, the woman's eyes measuring her in a new light. It almost makes her laugh. She's not a murderer. She'd save all the people she could, as long as it didn't threaten her plans. Because the endgame is bigger than anyone here's paltry existence, including her own.

'We've got the sensors,' Ester says as the projection table comes to life.

Ranath rushes back to the table. Red icons blink everywhere she looks. The factories and the growth platforms are gone, their former positions marked by expanding blotches of the debris zones. Liberty's damaged, but they're not calling for help, so it can't be that bad. Pity.

She zooms in on Tian Gong. The glow of the alert icons obscures the details—but no loss of integrity. The station's holding, even if parts of it appear critical.

'Tian Gong is evacuating all non-essential personnel. Requesting assistance,' Feng says. 'Casualties at Xin Ju—seems they got the tail end of the surge. Liberty says they are coping but may require central resources. The Shark emergency teams are attending.'

'Ester, send a general message: New Hope is offering shelter to all those in need, for however long it may be required. And send a personal note to major—colonel—whatever the Sharks' leader calls herself: "We will make sure your families are safe with us, so you can continue to attend to your duties without worry. All medical care will be provided".'

Ester nods, a glint of understanding in her eye.

Ranath continues, 'Feng, send all the shuttles you have to Tian Gong. Bring everyone here. Especially the Sharks—we really need to give them peace of mind.'

Feng's reply comes back hesitant. 'There's over a thousand people there. I'll need more resources to prepare the space for them. Maybe convert the reception area—'

'I'll put another team on that,' Ranath says, glancing at Ester. 'Besides, I don't think we'll get more than half of them to join us.'

'The cultists?' Min Woo asks.

'I don't think they are coming.' Ranath puckers her lips, her fingers drumming against the edge of the table. With both Richardson and the Caretakers after her now, she'll have to start moving the settlers to Ark very soon. She'll need a ship for that, and she won't get a better opportunity. 'Min Woo, get one of the colony ships here as soon as possible. We may need extra space, even if we have to put some people in cryo-sleep.'

Min Woo holds her gaze. Ranath could be more open without the Nevsky girl listening over her shoulder, but she can't send her away, not just yet.

'Will the ships have survived?' Liz says, just on cue.

'They've been unpowered and mothballed for just such eventualities. They should be fine, or at least one of them. That's all we need.'

Min Woo's already talking to someone, his lips moving as he heads to join Ester at the desks. Ranath returns her gaze to the projection. Numbers have appeared next to the stations, red for the dead, blue for the injured or missing. She grits her teeth. New Hope has lost two people, probably when the generator blew up. Fifteen wounded. She may have never met them, but those are her people, the citizens she needed to protect. Still, it could have been worse. Much worse. She checks the numbers for Tian Gong. Eighty-five dead, but the numbers keep climbing as she looks. Nineteen at Xin Ju; they've been lucky. Only blue figures at Liberty, though. Those bastards really don't deserve their good fortune.

Ranath points to the symbol. 'Liberty's reporting injuries,

but those will be people in the outer ring or near critical equipment. Nobody at the reception.'

She locks eyes with Liz and waits for her to nod. She's still sickly pale, her gaze dashing between Ranath and the projection in a mix of confusion and something else, something Ranath can't quite define. Like something in her is recalibrating, new understanding setting in, directions shifting.

Time they had an honest chat. Well, mostly honest.

She pings her aides to call if they need her and beckons Liz to follow her to the far side of the office, to her grandmother's wooden desk and the antique horary. Ranath pulls out one of the chairs and points Liz to the other, yet they both remain standing.

Her fingers tap the command for a privacy bubble, and the office sounds fade away, leaving them in stillness disturbed only by Liz's hurried breathing.

'Some things we need to get straight,' Ranath says. 'I know who your father is, and I don't care. I selected you as one of the interns in full knowledge of that fact, because I'm interested only in your work and what you can contribute here. Besides, I know something about... being stuck with a heritage you had no part in earning.'

Liz's eyes widen and Ranath allows herself a sad smile. It really is uncanny how similar their stories are. Except Liz's father is alive, and she *chose* to abandon him.

'Anyway. You are new here, and all the newcomers I've met make the same mistake: assuming the Yun Ju is a monolith and some kind of paradise. We're neither. We have different histories, different beliefs and interests. The balance here is fragile. And the worst part is, everybody suspects everyone else of trying to get ahead by sabotaging the others.'

'But... this doesn't—'

'Make sense?' Ranath laughs. 'We are still human. "Making sense" doesn't factor into much of our behaviour.'

Liz shakes her head, wanting to protest, but Ranath lifts her hand. 'We can debate this when we have the time. But I need you to understand what you saw here today. See, Renewal is a new faction, and we have recently made some significant progress, partly thanks to bright young people like yourself. But the old players, they don't like it. Particularly because...' Ranath pauses, hesitating. It's an act but not entirely so, a truth but not a confession. Still, her voice shakes ever so slightly. At least it makes it sound genuine. 'Because of who my father was. I don't want to talk about it; let's just say he's done things I'm not proud of. I have to carry that legacy, and they hate me because I've managed to succeed anyway.'

Ranath looks away, steadying her voice. This is pure theatrics, but she needs Liz to believe her—and from the way she's nodding, her eyes bright and tearful, Ranath has hit just the spot.

'There are people out there who want to destroy me,' she says softly. 'They are just waiting for the right tool. And this storm, it was such a tool. If we'd issued an official warning and the surge hadn't come, they'd accuse us of sabotage. That would have been the end of us. Of course, I didn't want anyone to get hurt. So I've contacted people privately. It was still a risk, but, as you said, we couldn't just "do nothing".'

'It was a brave thing to do. You saved Tian Gong,' Liz says with such compassion that Ranath has to summon all her restraint not to lash out. Next thing Liz will be patting her on the back.

Ranath leans in, making her face earnest. 'Now, I need you to promise me something. You can't talk to anybody about what I've told you. Not even about my message to Tian Gong. *Nobody* may know. I have reasons to suspect... that not everybody on the station has our full loyalty. And if the message spreads, it may reach those who will use it against us. Can I trust you?'

Liz straightens. 'Yes. Yes, of course.'

She nods repeatedly, her expression eager, but the confusion hasn't left her eyes, like a veil waiting to be pulled.

Ranath puts a hand on her shoulder. 'Thank you. And thank you for saving us all. Quite a few people owe you their lives tonight. I won't forget that.'

She drops the privacy bubble and leads Liz out, back into the open space of the office. *Ester?*

Yes?

Reinstate her comms but put a tracker on her. I want to know if she contacts anyone outside the station.

NINETEEN

JASON

It starts just as Richardson is introducing Jason to Liberty's trade commissioner, the person directly in charge of all the Alliance business. They are at the station's main banquet hall, its walls covered in blue silk embossed with golden lilies. People in exquisite evening clothes cluster on both sides of a thirty-metre-long buffet table. The air smells of flowers, roasted vegetables, or chocolate, depending which way Jason happens to turn his head. The trade commissioner cracks a joke about the Yun Ju's insatiable appetite for fruit when Richardson suddenly turns pale. He storms away before Jason can ask what's happened, managing only a truncated wave at his guest of honour.

The room goes quiet: voices cease first, then the clinking of forks against porcelain plates, then the music from the string quartet in the far corner. Every eye seems to follow Richardson, brows raising, lips parting, but it's all moving too fast for Jason to parse if it's a cry of panic or annoyance.

Someone's running towards Richardson. Their mouths move as if both men are shouting, but no words reach Jason. He gasps as the lamps flicker, the simulated candlelight supplanted by harsh blue emergency lighting. A tremor runs through the floor, as if the station itself took a deep breath. Jason holds still, waiting, scanning the faces around him to gauge the scale of impeding danger. Nervous and agitated, but nobody seems to panic. A good sign, or just lack of information?

The next instant, something hits—or explodes—he can't tell, only echoes reaching them through the layers of the station's rings. The floor quakes, the grating sound drawing cold sweat on his skin. Someone screams, a single cry cutting through the silence. Jason stops breathing, stunned by the sudden vertigo of realisation that this perfect ballroom is but a bubble falling through space, blasted by something powerful enough to send the plates tumbling through the millions of tonnes of steel and fibre.

And then everybody seems to take a collective sigh of relief, the bubble of voices rising into a giddy crescendo. The music returns, shyly at first, then purposeful, as if the musicians are determined to chase away the ghosts of whatever unpleasantness has just transpired.

'Whoa, that was... interesting,' the man next to him says. The trade commissioner, Jason remembers. Bob or Roy or something.

He takes a moment to steady his breath. 'What happened?'

The man stares, frowning, until his eyes widen with realisation. 'But of course! You have no wire. I'm so sorry, that must have been terrifying.'

Jason manages a feeble smile. 'Nothing I'd care to repeat anytime soon.'

'Nor would I, to be honest.'

'All in a day of a space farer,' Richardson booms, approaching from a side entrance. His grin defies the paleness of his cheeks and his stiff movements. Three staffers trail behind him, the lanky person Jason saw earlier and two he hasn't met. Judging by their focused expressions, all three appear to be working, their networked minds sending and receiving messages on their boss' behalf.

'Nothing to be afraid of, my friend. I told you, this is the safest station around, and we're in its most secure area. All we have to worry about are some broken glasses.' Richardson gestures to the banquet table and laughs. 'I did like that set, though!'

Bluster, all bluster. The more Richardson tries, the clearer it is to Jason that something has indeed gone very wrong.

'So, what was it?' he asks again.

'A solar storm. Bigger than I've ever seen.'

Jason stiffens. He thought this was a malfunction, something that only affected Liberty—but a solar storm would hit all of the Yun Ju. Annalie... Is she safe? 'Have the other stations been affected?'

'We're still gathering data...' Richardson waves at his staffers. 'Minor damage on Xin Ju and New Hope, but Tian Gong has taken a hit.'

'Two rings only,' Bob—or Roy—says. 'It's a miracle they've survived at all.'

Richardson nods. 'The station's probably a write-off. They're evacuating.'

Jason's mind is racing. How 'minor' was damage on New Hope? Would they even know to inform him if something happened to his daughter? She should be safe, though—storms are her speciality, she'd have been watching the show from some secure location. They'd keep their monitoring teams safe, wouldn't they?

He forces his attention back to the conversation. Bob is asking about Harmony's destroyed manufactories, and if it's going to impact 'the mess with the assembler deal', whatever that means.

'I want to see her refuse anyone now!' Richardson tuts. His gaze finds Jason and he produces a heavy sigh. 'Unfortunately, we haven't entirely escaped harm. The station's fine, but we've lost five agro platforms. Until we rebuild, I'm afraid we'll have to count on your help even more than usual.'

Jason nods. 'Always happy to assist our orbital cousins. And of course, if you ever wanted, you're always welcome back on terra firma.'

Both men guffaw as if they've just heard the best joke.

Richardson pats Jason's shoulder. 'Thanks for the offer, my friend, but we're not that desperate!'

Jason joins in the laughter, his stomach tight and his fingers curling into fists. Isn't it just hilarious? To think they could walk the ground like mere mortals. He coughs, bile rising up his throat, but he makes it look like a chuckle.

'How about debris?' he asks, trying not to sound too hopeful. 'There must be lots of it after the destruction.'

Richardson shrugs. 'There will be, at first. We've got path-clearing drones out already. They're pretty effective at vaporising anything that gets in our way. But stuff like that either gets flung out of Earth's gravity well or settles into some stable orbit where it won't bother us. More of a problem for the shuttles and the elevators, but they've got their own defences.'

Damn. It seemed such a promising idea.

Bob starts to say something but pauses as Richardson's face drops, his brows scrunching into a scowl. He turns to his entourage, locked in a silent exchange that makes the vein in his neck throb.

When he turns back to Jason, his face is flushed with anger. 'That damn woman... She's evacuating the Sharks to her station.'

'Who?'

'Ranath Eyre. She's moving the Sharks to New Hope.'

Bob hisses with disgust.

Jason glances from one man to the other, realisation dawning. He's not entirely up to speed on Yun Ju's internal politics, but he understands that there's no love lost between the players. The Sharks are their joint security—and the only people in orbit with real fire power. They're supposed to be neutral; that's why they've been stationed on a minor outpost. And now they are on New Hope.

'You believe that will cause problems?'

Richardson folds his arms, the cuff of his azure jacket stained with something red. 'Of all the stations, that's the last place where I'd want to have them. I don't trust that woman. She's playing some nasty games, I tell you. No wonder, really...' He leans closer, his voice hushed, the scent of wine in his breath mixing with his cologne. 'Between friends... you may be aware that she—well, that whole faction—they smell of someone who needed to hide their money very quickly. About twenty years ago.'

Richardson holds his gaze as Jason makes himself nod, his entire body tensing as if paralysed by an electric shock. So, this is where they've been hiding. Renewal is Destiny, the Mind-Link creators. Disguised as a minor faction, lying in wait till everyone forgets what they did. Are they launching a new plan, another devious attempt to take control? Are the Sharks part of it? He shivers at the memory of their guns, so easily turned against anyone their leaders declare the enemy. The guns that killed his father.

And now his daughter is there with them. Is that also some part of Ranath's game?

His chest tightens, his breath rugged. He needs to hurry. Whatever plans they are cooking, he must stop them before it's too late.

Jason doesn't get to see Richardson again till just before his departure two days later. The host and his senior staffers disappeared soon after the reception to deal with the fallout of the storm, and for a moment Jason dared to hope he'd be left to his own devices and get a chance to attempt the questions the Watch engineers have given him. No such luck. Instead, he gets stuck endlessly touring the gardens with whoever happens to be available: a teacher, a botanist, and, on the final morning, the chaplain—a prompt reminder that Liberty is an American station after all. Reverend Nichols at least proves loquacious enough, even if he'd rather bemoan the state of his congregation than offer anything remotely useful for how Jason might go about destroying the Yun Ju.

'I hope the reverend didn't bore you to death,' Richardson says after the chaplain finally deposits Jason at Liberty's zhu's private offices. 'If his sermons are anything to go by, he at least tries to be engaging?'

They meet in the foyer, Richardson's handshake firm but his face betraying a string of sleepless nights. His eyes are blood-shot and rimmed with grey circles, his skin without lustre, and his usually perfect white hair pulled back into a hasty ponytail.

'Not boring at all,' Jason says as he follows the man inside. 'Though we mostly discussed the correlation between solar storms and Sunday service attendance.'

Richardson laughs. 'Got to look at the bright side, eh?'

The office is large and luxuriously decorated in blue and gold. Retractable screens partition the space into sections that feel private and almost cosy, with navy-blue armchairs and computer stations concealed inside gilded cabinets. Richardson leads the way to a low table laid out with refreshments, the most prominent of which is an ornate silver bowl filled with finely cut fruit. A perfect mid-morning snack, and a pointed reminder of how precious fruit is to the stations—and especially to this station. Four chairs surround the table, but for the first time since Jason's arrival, his host's ubiquitous staffers have made themselves scarce.

Richardson stifles a groan as he plonks himself into the

chair. He glances at the food but reaches for the coffee instead. His hand trembles, the cup clinking loudly against the saucer, and he glares at it, annoyed either at his hand or the flimsy porcelain.

'How are the repairs going?' Jason asks. 'If you don't mind me saying, you look like you need some rest.'

Richardson sniffs. He puts his cup down, then picks it up again, his lips puckered. 'The repairs are fine. More than we initially thought, but nothing we can't handle. Still, we got lucky: Tian Gong's barely holding together. If that whole station blew up, the amount of debris might have forced us to evacuate. Just the thought of it!'

Jason's eyes widen. This is it, the plan he needs: enough debris to force a general evacuation, even if it's temporary. Once they are all down on the planet, he'll think of ways to keep them there. Appeal to reason, or destroy the elevators. He'll figure out a way to stop them from returning.

He busies himself filling his bowl, hoping to conceal his excitement. They'll make the Yun Ju uninhabitable. The idea has come up in his talks with the Watch, but they rejected it because it required blowing up an entire station, killing thousands. No one would agree to such bloodshed. But Tian Gong is empty now.

Or is it? Are the cultists still there?

'It's been a wakeup call to everyone, I tell you,' Richardson continues. 'We got all the engineers meeting up to plan reinforcements. I don't want to count on luck next time this happens.'

Jason nods with what he hopes looks like encouragement, not anticipation. Whatever they end up doing, it will have to happen soon, before those reinforcements materialise.

Richardson falls silent again. There's clearly more on his mind than he's letting on. Still, he's invited Jason for this last meeting so there must be something he needs, or he wouldn't bother. Jason refills his coffee and waits.

'The station's going to be fine, as I told you. The agro platforms are a bigger loss. They can't be repaired; we have to construct new ones. For that we need assemblers, and it seems we're now the last in line...' Richardson massages his jaw like someone recovering from a punch. 'I'm not going to bore you with details. The thing is, it will be months before the replacements are ready. And we need to figure out what we do in the meantime.'

'Will you need extra food shipments? I'm sure we can—'

'We're not going to starve. We have enough reserves, and we get the basics through the usual channels.' Richardson pauses, holding his gaze. Getting to the point, the reason Jason is here. 'It's the business side I'm worried about. Not the biggest part of my trade, not by far, but, well, significant enough. I can't leave my customers disappointed, or they'll look for other suppliers, and that would be... unfortunate.'

Right, that's one puzzle solved. He knows now how they were getting Volkov's shipments: up the elevator, then to one of the agro platforms, probably disguised as fertiliser or other biomatter. And then it could be moved around as part of Liberty's own produce. Clever. Except now the platforms are gone, and they are stuck. Richardson's likely discussed the matter with Volkov already and hasn't found a good enough—or fast enough—solution. He needs Jason—and if Jason plays this right, he'll prove himself useful, maybe learn more secrets in return. But Richardson doesn't trust him yet; it's clear in how he avoids naming Volkov or the nature of his business with him, even here in his private office. Everything he's revealed so far is either deniable or unprovable now that the platforms have been destroyed.

Jason hesitates. How should he react? Would he be expected to ask for more money? Or consider this a way to firm up their new alliance? He has a lot of experience in the bribing part, not in being bribed. But he's the new partner in this game, and he has to prove himself first.

He takes a sip of coffee. 'We need to find a way... to arrange the delivery. Humanitarian supply, maybe? Aid following the storm?'

Richardson grimaces. 'That would apply to all the stations affected. And we really can't claim the need...'

True. Jason frowns—but then a new thought makes him shiver, like crossed wires igniting a spark. He takes another slow sip, careful not to appear too excited. 'We could send aid to Tian Gong. If the cultists haven't left...'

'No, most of them are still there.' Richardson leans across the table, a grin pouring onto his face. 'They'd definitely need aid. The station's empty now; it's a matter of time before their food stocks run dry. And their health... There's little left of Tian Gong's shields.'

'I'm sure their brethren on Earth will be happy to send resupplies,' Jason says. 'And if any of our food growers happen to consider a donation, the Alliance will be happy to facilitate.'

'We will help as well, of course. Bring medical personnel, remove surplus... Waste management... We won't get in the way of the repair crews, of course. Whenever they get enough assemblers to start the work...' Richardson taps the table as he confirms each detail, then once again at the end. 'A good plan, Mr Nevsky.'

'Simple and efficient, if I can say so myself.'

They exchange another grin just as one of Richardson's staffers appears in the room.

The woman smiles apologetically. 'Your next visitor is here, Nevil.'

'Oh, I almost forgot.' Richardson lowers his head conspiratorially. 'And good timing, too. Mr Allen, you see, is a refugee from Tian Gong. He chose not to remain on New Hope, so we've offered him shelter—him and whoever else prefers not to stay on that three-ring excuse for a station.'

'Most generous of you.' Jason puts down his coffee and rises.

'Till next time.' Richardson grabs his hand for a hearty shake. 'Do come visit whenever you find the time.'

You are so wrong, Jason thinks as he heads back through the frosted glass doors of the foyer, passing the silver-haired man in a graphite-grey jacket waiting there. *Next time* you *will be visiting me.*

I just need to figure out how to blow up a station.

TWENTY

LIZ

Liz gapes at her new desk. *Her* desk. Her *permanent* desk, even if it's still the same portable workstation she's been using for two weeks. But now, when she focuses on it, her lenses read, *Elizabeth Lake, Shield Analyst*, and her heart thumps with pride. The paperwork came through earlier this morning: full resident status, effective immediately. Formal certificate of her completed internship. Then the job offer, which she accepted so fast she almost gave herself whiplash. She's made it.

'Welcome to the team,' Lars says, patting her shoulder. 'I mean, formally. You deserve it.'

The small crowd of analysts gathered around them cheers. There's Sal, thin-faced and tall; Ariel, with the broad smile under a crown of afro hair; Henry, almost bald and probably too old to still be working; Ennie, broad and muscular, and with the most contagious laugh Liz has ever heard. And Essa, his face expressionless but his eyes so bright they could light up the room. Her friends.

They are in Essa's workshop, the place the same and yet different, if only for the number of colourful objects piled up on *her* desk. There are old-fashioned edible greeting cards, a potted plant (engineered for low light), and the figurine of a knight in golden armour wielding a giant shield, the department's unofficial mascot. She's seen those on other desks, the figure's oversized head mimicking their owner's—and this one has her face, brows scrunched in a frown and lips tightly pursed.

Liz chuckles at the sight. 'Is that how you see me?'

'Have you ever looked into a mirror?' Essa's voice answers, and everyone laughs.

'We made it squishy, too,' Sal says. 'Just in case you need to unload some stress.'

'Just don't throw it,' Henry says. 'The equipment here is rather delicate.'

'Well done,' Ag says, they and three other visitors from the active watch peeking in from the entrance. Ag folds their arms. 'I know that new model wouldn't have progressed so quickly without the rest of the team, but it's fair to say it wouldn't have got there without you. And that's to say, quite a few people owe you their lives. Thank you.'

The room falls silent. Liz wants to say something smart, something about how it was Ag's team who operated the generators and managed their defences and made sure they held through the ordeal... But they all know it, and they don't need her patronising remarks. So she wipes her eyes and looks for a tissue to blow her nose before she will embarrass herself any further.

'All right, then.' Lars waves his arm, sending the others away. 'Back to it. That mountain of new data isn't going to analyse itself. And your protons are still off, Essa. See you all back at dinner!'

They file away, back to the analysts' offices, where Liz will join them once the space is reshuffled to fit another workstation. The room falls quiet again, and it's just her and Essa staring at each other across the room.

'Thank you,' she says.

'The squishy was my idea,' he says proudly. 'Stress-resistant foam. My design, too.'

She picks up the figurine and brings it next to her face. 'Honestly? Couldn't you give me a trace of a smile?'

'It was a life drawing.'

Liz rolls her eyes. She considers a biting response but ends up propping the squishy over her screen, where it can watch her work. She blows out loudly and slumps into the chair, exhausted.

The last two days have been a whirlwind of questions and checks, verifying the model and integrating it into the Shield's systems. The station's crowded with refugees; the medical and the repairs teams rushing through at every hour. She's barely slept the last two nights, and it's not just the work or the commotion. Her nerves are still raw, the memories flash under her eyelids the moment she closes her eyes. How close they came to disaster. How helpless and guilty she felt, unable to alert anyone, not even her father. Ranath's warning about those who wished them harm, the idea that even trying to warn the others could be used to attack them.

She thought she'd left the politics down on Earth—but it seems the Yun Ju is just as full of it, and just as ugly.

'What is it?' Essa asks.

Liz shrugs. 'It's just... not how I imagined it.'

'Your promotion? I thought—'

'No, that's not... I mean, this is totally beyond what I imagined.' She looks at her desk again, at the cards and the toys. 'Better by an order of magnitude.'

'What then?' He pauses, sensing her hesitation. 'Assuming it's something you want to talk about.'

Liz bites her lip. She's promised Ranath not to reveal what she told her—about her father, and about her suspicions. But nothing else that happened that night is a secret, not to Essa and the rest of the Shield team on duty. They kept open comms, heard how Lars sent warning messages to the other stations, and got ignored.

She picks up the squidgy effigy of herself and stares at its furrowed brows. 'I imagined... I thought there'd be more cooperation. Like, we're all up here, in space. When something goes wrong, we only have each other. Even if Earth wants to help, they are too far and too poorly equipped. But it isn't like that.'

Essa takes a moment to answer. 'You're forgetting, you're not dealing with people here. You're dealing with competing corporations. They're always on the defence, always suspecting the others of trying to buy them out, destroy them, sabotage them... It's become part of their nature, like eating or breathing.'

Liz huffs. 'Even when we're trying to save their lives?'

'It *is* their lives. Especially here, with Renewal.'

Is that what Ranath meant when she mentioned her father? The old gossip that Renewal had roots in Destiny? Could that be true? If so, then it's no wonder Ranath wants nothing to do with him. The shame... it must be very much like what Liz feels when someone mentions the Food Alliance, the same pang of guilt at the very sound of her real name. Nevsky. That must be why Ranath never uses her last name. Eyre. Liz is almost tempted to look the man up—but not today. And maybe it's better not to poke that old story, ever. It was so long ago. She'd do better supporting Ranath, helping her build a better future. Liz wouldn't be here without her.

She stretches and picks up one of the greeting cards: from Ariel, with *You are brilliant!* stencilled in neon letters above a picture of an equally bright Sun. How appropriate.

A message icon pops on her lenses. *Quarters allocation.* She blinks it open, gasping as she reads. She's been assigned room 1378C in section three of the middle-ring habitat zone. The rest of the message consists of links to lodging management systems, furnishings rental, and customisation options. There are pictures of the place: a bare room with a foldable screen that can create a separate sleeping area, the whole thing even more basic than the graduate quarters—but it's *hers*, her new home, which she will be able to decorate and improve with the money she'll be earning in her new *permanent* job.

Her shoulders heave. She wipes her eyes again, turning away from Essa, embarrassed. She's waited so long. Tried so hard. It's been worth it.

'Got your room?' Essa says.

'How did you—'

'I just approved it.' A stick figure appears on her lenses and makes an exaggerated bow. 'Not the best area, but you can move after the refugees—'

'Wait. Don't we need all the space for them?'

'Not on this deck; they are just passing through for medical checks. Those who will be staying here for any period of time are headed for the inner ring. Everyone else will move into storage until Tian Gong's safe enough for them to return.'

'Storage?'

'Cryo-pods, either here or on that colony ship that just docked. Standard procedure for emergencies. And free longevity treatment!' Essa laughs. 'Anyway, you're not taking space from anyone, so no need to worry. And if you accept the standard issue furniture, you can move in tonight.'

Liz opens her mouth, but she has too many questions to decide on which one to ask first. Her own place. 'So... the furniture...'

'I'll show you. And if we're lucky, we'll have you set up before dinner.'

Liz's new place consists of walls, a bed, three cabinets, and a mini food processor—and it's already the best home she's ever had. She's pre-ordered a window from her first salary, though she still needs to choose the projections. A cityscape? Too much like her old life. A forest? Probably good for sanity, but no. Maybe just the vista of Earth from low orbit, with sunrises and sunsets and the old nostalgia. Yes, that will be perfect.

She hurries back to the graduate quarters to pick up her things before the celebratory dinner Lars is throwing for her. She checks the time. The others will probably all be there, just back from their duties, but for the first time, she realises with relief that she doesn't care. It's not that they can't damage her prospects anymore—she really just doesn't care what they think, whether they hate her or mock her. It was never about her, always about their perception of what she was or wasn't. It's their mistake, their loss. She's moved on.

The voices quiet as she enters, all heads turning towards her. Liz ignores them, heading to the corridor leading to the bedrooms.

'Look who's here,' Alejandro says.

Liz would roll her eyes, but even that seems too much bother.

'So, how much did your daddy pay for your promotion?'

'Oh, shut up,' someone protests, probably Vithakan, though Liz doesn't turn to look.

'What, you think she really invented that "new model" all by herself? What's the chance of that? They spoon-fed her the solutions so she could take the credit and not have to pretend she's actually working for her promotion.'

'Even if it was true, what's that to the rest of us?'

'You're just going to take it and do nothing?'

'What *can* you do?'

'And that's assuming any of it is true.'

'Hey, Liz, what do you say? Is it true?'

Liz pays them no attention. A small part of her wants to stop and yell that she already told them and they chose not to believe her, so why would she try again? She squashes down the remnants of her anger. She doesn't care. They are not worthy of her rage.

She is halfway down the inner corridor when the sound of quickly approaching footsteps makes her swing around. It's Kene, her face scrunched in something between disgust and worry.

'What do you want?' Liz blurts.

Kene stops, silent, as the arguments from the main room echo in the tight space. 'You don't care about us anymore, do you?'

'No. No, I don't.'

Kene is the first to wheel around, rushing away back to the main room. Liz turns the other way, crossing the last few steps to her bedroom and slams the door behind her. She doesn't—didn't—care, up to that moment. It's different with Kene. They used to be friends—she was the one who brought Liz food when she was exhausted, the one who cheered her on. And then, after the meeting with Ranath, Kene reached out to her, tried to soothe the relations. She deserves better. She at least deserves a question, a conversation.

Liz swings the door open and leans out. 'Ke—'

Down the length of the corridor, Kene's just reaching the outside door, disappearing into the corridor. Liz hesitates—but no, she's not going to chase her. She needs to hurry if she wants to get her things back before dinner. Besides, she can do better. Once her new home is ready, she will invite Kene over for a tisane and a proper chat. They will clear everything out—and maybe they can be friends again.

She nods to herself. Yes, that's a better plan. After all, they have all the time in the world.

TWENTY-ONE
RANATH

Nebu Owande brings the cup to her lips but then lowers it without drinking. A medical patch covers her hand, though she's assured Ranath it's only a scratch she acquired while tripping on her way to the shuttle. Must have been a bad scratch if she still needs the patch two days later, but given the state of her station, Nebu got out just fine. She seems in shock nonetheless, her eyes wide and pupils dilated, her movements jerky and her attention flitting.

'It came so fast,' she repeats. 'I was just talking to the engineers about the storm alert when your message arrived. I knew from the tone of your voice that we had only moments. They didn't want to do it, but I told them to. Luckily, they listened.'

Ranath nods. Nebu is the closest Tian Gong has to a zhu, but the station is managed by a loose conglomerate of her co-op, some minor businesses, and the Sun Seers, the cult renting most of the outer deck. Nebu's co-op is the most influential player in that group, but if her engineers decided to revolt, they could have called for a general meeting, a 'consensus,' or some other nonsense. And now they'd all be dead.

'I'm glad they did.' Ranath reaches for the coffee jug and

fills both of their cups. They sit on the soft antique armchairs in the far corner of her office, away from the sharp lights and the constant flicking of numbers on the projection table that tracks the rescue shuttles moving between their stations. 'I'm curious, though. What made you trust me? We sent warnings to the others, but they assumed we were trying to trick them.'

Nebu produces a nervous chuckle. 'I'm not sure I'd call it "trust"... Trust is difficult when you're a third-rank player. But I couldn't think of anything you might possibly gain from my destruction.'

'That's a... useful way of looking at it.'

She glances up as Min Woo strides towards them. He looks like he hasn't slept for days, his hair ruffled, clothes stained and carrying a distinct whiff of old sweat. Ranath probably looks the same, except she likely smells like a pot of coffee.

'We've processed all the shuttles now,' he says. 'We have seven hundred and thirty-eight refugees on board. If I'm correct, that's about three-quarters of all your inhabitants?'

Nebu sighs. 'Yes. I pleaded with the Sun Seers' prelate but... he thinks it's a sign.'

Min Woo grimaces. 'With all due respect, I'm not sure how many of them are capable of informed consent. We should—'

'We can't just kidnap them.' Ranath rubs her face, exhaustion creeping in. Apparently, the cultists are a new breed of Sun-worshippers, except they don't consider the star a deity but believe that its radiation will lead them to a higher state of consciousness. Instead of enlightenment they get cancer, in many cases so advanced that Ranath doubts if her medics can make a difference. 'We can go back in a couple of days—after we're done with the people already on board. How are they anyway?'

'Coping. We had some injuries, mostly from the escape panic, all treated now. We've assigned quarters to everyone staying on New Hope. Yu Huan and Liberty are taking about a hundred each. Disappointing, but to be expected since we've requisitioned a ship.'

The old colony ships, each containing thousands of cryopods, have been maintained from communal funds precisely for such emergencies. One ship could store all of Tian Gong and New Hope combined, with pods to spare. Of course, some people will prefer to stay awake, but preferences are a luxury for another time.

'*The Covenant* has just arrived,' Min Woo continues. 'It's too big to dock, so we're using shuttles to transfer the refugees. We should have everyone settled or stored by the morning.'

'Excellent. Thank you.' Ranath nods.

Min Woo shifts his weight, glancing between her and Nebu. He clearly has more to tell her but not in company.

Ranath rises with a soft groan. She pushes her shoulders back, stretching her tired muscles. 'I think we all need some rest now. Nebu, I hope your quarters are satisfactory?'

'Oh, they are perfect. I don't know how I can ever thank you...'

Ranath gives her a smile that she hopes doesn't say *I'll think of something*. 'Do you need a guide to take you—'

'No, I'm already connected to your system.' Nebu smooths her crumpled dress as she gets up. She is a head taller than Ranath, willowy, with high cheekbones and charcoal-black skin. Her lips tremble as she stretches them into a lopsided smile. 'I didn't expect kindness, you know? Not from anyone in the Yun Ju. It's all talk about how we're in it together, but in reality... Anyway. I said I couldn't see how you'd benefit from my destruction, and that's true. I also can't see how you'd benefit from helping me—but if there was something... just let me know. I'm fine trading favours with someone who saved my skin.'

Ranath doesn't answer, leading the way towards the exit. Was her warning an act of kindness? Or was it a simple calculation, the measure of the benefit of having the Sharks on her station and a debt of gratitude with Nebu—if she could ever make any use of it? The warning was a risk; if the surge hadn't come, she'd have been accused of sabotage. Not even the Sharks were worth it.

She recalls the moment, her eyes on the icon of Tian Gong station, in full sunlight, right in the path of the storm. Her old home, the place where her mother lived and died. She imagined it ripped by the storm, electric circuits overloading, life-saving machinery bursting into flames. She couldn't let that happen.

So, kindness after all. Kindness with a dose of nostalgia, both of them equally disappointing. These feelings are luxuries, things she can't afford to indulge in with everything that's at stake at the moment. What is Tian Gong compared to Ark? New humanity versus the embers of the old, destined to fail, to burn out into ash maybe even within her own lifetime. She will not let herself repeat this mistake.

She bids Nebu goodnight, then turns to Min Woo the moment the doors close behind her.

'The ship—*The Covenant*, you said? Does it meet our requirements?'

'Yes, in all respects. We're already working on the additional sections. They'll be in separate modules, so can be easily detached.'

'Are our pods ready?'

'Mostly, yes. The bigger problem is removing *The Covenant*'s own cryo-pods so we can install ours. Otherwise, we'd need to defrost the settlers to move them.'

The settlers. The future residents of her new world being readied for transport. Her crop of the most promising graduates, the volunteers hand-picked by her Earth scouts. They have all agreed to wait with her for a better future, even if it took a decade.

'Get everything ready as quickly as you can without anyone noticing. They are all watching us now, don't forget.'

'We're being very careful. There's no way anybody can track us between the refugee shuttles, the supplies, and the maintenance packages shifting back and forth. But, no, I won't forget. They *are* watching us and not even trying to hide it. Liberty's launched a spy satellite masquerading as debris monitoring, except it happens to watch the debris in our orbit, not theirs.'

Ranath snorts. 'Typical. Li Qiang will be watching, too, maybe through the same satellite. Those two are in cahoots more than they'd let on. Anything from Harmony?'

'The most coldly worded question if they could get some of their contracted assemblers now, to fix the previous damage and reinforce Xin Ju's defences.'

'Send them their allocation from the general reserve plus ten per cent from Li Qiang's lot. He's not getting any until the repairs are done and the debris trapped. Blame it on emergency procedures. He's not going to complain; they'd eat him alive if he got his full shipment at this time.'

Ranath strolls to the refreshment cart waiting in the corner. Her stomach grumbles. She reaches for coffee, but honestly, another cup may just be more than her body can take. She picks up a bunch of pink grapes instead (a new, nutrient-fortified design) and forces herself to eat. She's forgetting something, an important question she needs to ask him.

Damn, of course. 'How are the Sharks?'

'Mostly still out there, checking on Tian Gong, helping with debris removal, and so on. I must say, they're better prepared and organised than I expected.'

'The families taken care of?'

'Already stored on *The Covenant*, as per your instructions. There have been some questions, though, so you may want to handle that soon.'

'What questions?'

'Some families requested to stay awake. I think we've handled that well enough, but you might want to have a chat with Major Par. She's just returned, by the way.'

'Fine, call her in. No, wait. Tell her I'll come to see her, if she's not too tired.'

Min Woo's brows rise, but he nods with approval. His fingers twitch and his lips move, and a moment later, he nods. 'She's expecting you.'

Ranath heads to the door just as Ester walks in, a cup of coffee in her hand, her mouth half-opened in a yawn.

'You were supposed to be off,' Ranath says.

'I was. I slept for four hours. Don't I look it?'

Ranath stifles a yawn. Damn, these things are contagious. 'Min Woo, your turn for a break. We have to maintain some levels of sanity here.'

He snorts. 'And you?'

'After I've dealt with the major. Go.'

'I need a minute,' Ester says, waking up her interface.

Ranath hesitates. She doesn't want to keep the major waiting. 'A minute.'

'I was going over the comm logs again—from the time of your recent... meeting.'

The Caretaker meeting. Ranath had never explained her dealings with them, or even mentioned that there was something like the Caretakers, and her aides knew better than to ask. Both Ester and Min Woo must have developed some theory about those annual conferences and about her past, but she hasn't volunteered any explanation. It's not that she doesn't trust them—they have access to all her business affairs, they know everything about Ark, the one project she's given her life to—but her past is too private, too sensitive to let anyone pry.

Ranath leans on the chair. 'Have you found anything new?'

After her last encounter with the Caretakers, she asked

Ester to examine the logs to see if anyone on the station had been in encrypted comms over the duration of that meeting. That wouldn't provide definitive proof—there were too many cheating lovers or rumour circles that used encryption—but it could give her a hint if any Caretakers were hiding on New Hope. It didn't work. By bad luck or by design, her meeting coincided with a couple of security reviews which created too much encrypted comm noise to yield anything useful. Ester promised to keep digging, but with the storm fallout, Ranath hasn't held much hope.

'Not yet,' Ester says. 'But I might. It's complicated, but all encrypted comms have a nexus point with the event organiser. They open the channel, so to speak. So, we have encrypted links going from the participants on each station to that nexus, and sometimes internally within the station if there are local participants. That's why I can't confirm anyone on New Hope.'

Ranath gives her a nod even though she's way too tired to follow. Ester guesses the truth anyway.

'Okay, the short version. We have encrypted links coming to New Hope from those nexus points. These are the other meetings we know about, the security reviews. But there are several lines that don't fit the pattern. I gave up on those initially, because the only way to identify them is from the other side, from where the senders logged in. But if we had access to the local systems, we might find something.'

Ranath stares, forcing her brain to function for just a little longer. How can they access the comm logs of another station? Nobody will let them—

Nebu. Nebu will let them. She's pretty much just said so. 'Tian Gong?'

Ester nods. 'One line, not accounted for by any other meeting.'

Ranath taps the other woman's shoulder. 'Good work. Send Nebu a message.'

.   .   .

Ranath checks the time as the elevator door slides closed. 3.00 a.m., not the usual hour to pay anyone a visit—but nothing has run as usual over the last two days. She pushes her fingers through her hair, glancing at her pale reflection in the polished door, then decides she doesn't care. Besides, a dishevelled look will make her case stronger.

She steps out onto the utilitarian flooring of the middle deck, trying to remember the last time she ventured down here. It's been years. She really should come more often, get to know her people better. Get them to know her. It could help if there's ever a situation to test their loyalty.

The corridors are finally quieting down, only the active-duty wards still crewed. The Sharks are the only refugee group stationed in the middle ring. Nebu and Tian Gong's high-ranking staffers got the guest quarters in the inner section. The banquet hall and two of the roomiest recreational areas have been transformed into makeshift lodgings for the other civilians. The middle ring houses the station's most vital systems so Ranath's not too happy to have strangers here, but if she can't trust the Sharks, then she can't trust anyone. Besides, she's made sure she *can* trust the Sharks.

The arrows on her lenses lead her to the fitness area converted into a dormitory. For now, it's just beds separated with flimsy screens without so much as a noise dampening. Apparently, that doesn't matter as all she can hear is the heavy breathing and occasional snores of people too exhausted to want anything beyond a pillow and a flat surface.

A tall, heavyset woman stands leaning against the entrance. Olive skin, black eyes, dark hair flattened where her helmet pressed it to her forehead. She's wearing glossy grey under-clothes, a vest and leggings made to slide into a space suit.

Her head jerks up as she spots Ranath, like someone dozing off on their feet. 'Zhu Eyre?'

Ranath manages not to grimace. 'Ranath, please. Zhu Ranath, or just Ranath. Major Par?'

'Just Par.'

'Thank you for letting me see you at this hour. I thought it'd be best if we spoke in person.'

Par nods. 'So, what's the bad news?'

'Bad news?'

'Come on. I don't have zhus coming to see me in the middle of the night for good news. Especially the zhus who put all our families on ice.'

'I saved your station. Maybe your lives.'

'That, too.'

Ranath huffs. Par is so refreshingly straightforward. Verbal sparring with someone like Li Qiang has its pleasures, but right now, Par is what Ranath needs. Maybe she won't even have to lie.

'I want you to know how grateful I am for your work.' Ranath walks slowly away from the dormitory door, hoping the woman will follow.

Par groans as she pushes herself off the wall. 'So grateful you don't want my people to hear it?'

Ranath tilts her head as she looks the major up and down. 'I have a feeling we are going to get along. Now, shall we?'

Par nods. They walk in silence for a few steps, just out of earshot. It's up to Par what she shares with her people later, but not until Ranath has said her part.

'I see you like straight talk, so I'll give it to you straight: I had your families put into *The Covenant*'s pods to make sure you didn't leave.' Par swings towards her, but Ranath continues, her voice quiet but unwavering. 'Or rather, to give you an excuse to refuse to leave.'

'What do you mean?'

'The reason you were housed on Tian Gong is because it's a small, neutral station. Now, if I didn't bring you here, where would you go? Yu Huan, or Liberty, or Xin Ju? Whichever it would be, the others would protest. In the end they'd have to split you up among the stations. And then they'd be reluctant to give you up, waiting for the others to do it first. Do you see where this is going?'

Par nods. 'I hate to say it, but you're right.'

'Sometimes I do wish I wasn't. But on this occasion, I'm sure the result would be splitting your group—and that's just the first step in arming the stations. New Hope may not be as neutral as Tian Gong, but we're still the smallest faction. And now you can just refuse any advances by saying you want to stay near your families. I'd be surprised if you haven't had any invitations already...'

Par huffs but doesn't meet her eyes, which is all the confirmation Ranath needs.

'Feel free to share this with your people—I've got no secrets from them, but this needed to be your decision.'

They reach the end of the corridor and turn back towards the dormitory. Par's posture has changed, more relaxed now and more tired.

'Just one more thing, since we're being honest,' Ranath says. 'I don't know what you've been told about me, and I'm not going to waste either of our time trying to prove or disprove anything. But you need to know that not all of my neighbours wish me well. Some wish it were us and not Tian Gong that got damaged. They might use the storm as an opportunity—'

'To attack you? You can't be serious.'

'They won't storm the station or any such nonsense. At least, I hope not...' Ranath manages a chuckle. 'But having you here does make me breathe easier.'

Par produces something between a shrug and a head shake.

'Whatever you say... Our duty is to protect all the stations, so if we see anything suspicious, you can be sure we'll act on it.'

'I know you will.'

They stop by the dormitory door, listening to the cacophony of grunts and snores. Despite the noise, there's peace in the sound. Is that what the sleep of the righteous sounds like? Well, it's pretty damn loud.

Ranath turns to leave. 'Thank you, Major. All of you. You saved a lot of lives today. Sleep well.'

Ranath doesn't sleep well, her night filled with dreams she can only remember the edges of when she wakes up. Something's bothering her, something hiding just outside her grasp, like a premonition. She shrugs it away. If her subconscious has anything to tell her, it should speak clearer.

She emerges into the office with the breakfast drone in tow, not expecting to find anyone there despite the late hour. She ordered everyone to rest, because she needs their minds, not just their bodies. The cleaning bots scurry away as she enters, but the place still smells of sweat and coffee. Fresh coffee.

Ranath peers over the workstation to find Ester still in her chair, a more tired and paler version of the woman she left there six hours before.

'Ester, I told you—' Ranath stops at the sight of her aide's expression.

Ester looks at her hands, her shoulders lifting in a deep sigh. 'I'm sorry. I should have thought about it earlier.'

'What is it? Facts first, guilt later.'

'I sent your request to Nebu, for whenever she woke up. Apparently, she didn't sleep either, so she got back to me right away. She found me an engineer with access to the comms logs. Not the content of the comms but the logs...' Ester shakes her head, hurrying herself along or trying to keep her focus. 'Anyway. I found the person I was looking for. I'm pretty sure he was in your meeting. Too many coincidences for anything else.'

'What's the problem, then?'

Ester looks up to meet her gaze. 'He arrived with the first wave of the refugees. And... and then left on the first transport to Liberty.'

'Fuck.'

'Pretty much. We missed him by a few hours. If I'd thought about the nexus approach—'

Ranath's hands curl into fists. She wants to punch the desk or the screen, but that won't help anyone. 'It's done. You did think about it, so now we know who he is, and we can keep digging.'

Ester nods. She looks devastated, but she will pick herself up. Ranath doesn't hire people who wallow.

'Is that engineer still around? We don't want him sent into storage. Keep him here and his family. And anyone else who might help. We need to find out *everything* about that man, even if we have to go to Tian Gong and dig through his closet. What's his name anyway?'

'Tamir Allen. At least that's his current name. I can't find any record of his birth.'

Ranath's brows rise. He could be one of the originals, one of the first Caretakers or maybe even a member of the old Destiny itself, emerged from cryo-sleep sometime along the way. Someone who could have known her father.

Someone who sent him to his death.

Ranath steadies herself, her mind in turmoil, her emotions piercing her logic as if her heart was a hedgehog wrapped in a paper towel.

Ester moves her hand, and an image appears on the screen: a small group of refugees, families holding their children's hands, tiny luggage drones trailing behind them. Then comes a single, silver-haired man, his skin wrinkled but his posture straight and his body muscular in the tell-tale way cryo-treatment defies ageing. He wears a graphite grey jacket with a metallic sheen, a red shirt peeking from between the lapels. They are walking down a corridor she recognises: one of those leading to the shuttle docks. Here, on New Hope.

Ranath clenches her jaw to keep her chin from trembling in helpless fury. She gestures to the screen, zooming in on the man's face. He glances around as he moves, checking the interior. His eye catches the camera and his lips curl into a smirk. But then he looks away, just another refugee lost in the crowd.

Ranath steps away from the screen. She is all logic now, all action. The Caretakers promised her war, and the storm might have given them opportunities she's not anticipated. She can't allow them the chance to move first. Ready or not, it's time to set things in motion.

'Min Woo, as soon as you're awake, start moving our pods. We must be able to depart at a moment's notice.'

TWENTY-TWO

JASON

Jason reaches the ground in a half-empty elevator, the Yun Ju's attention to its earthly business temporarily diverted in the aftermath of the storm. He spends the trip alone in his cabin, building and demolishing scenarios, and wishing he'd studied engineering instead of sustainability. The latter didn't do him—or anyone—much good. He knows what they have to do: create enough debris to force the stations to evacuate to Earth, even temporarily. How to do it, is another matter entirely.

He catches up on the news as he's waiting to disembark—this time at the Atlantic base, as that elevator was the closest to Liberty at his departure. He hasn't accessed the Alliance systems since he left. His people would contact him with anything urgent, and he didn't want to tempt fate using his passcodes inside the Yun Ju. No encryption is unbreakable, especially with the resources they have.

The news is the usual mix of anti-Alliance protests, political manoeuvring, and the new crop of populists promising to take back control and fix every ailment, if only they get the votes—and the donations. He skips to the agricultural section, and his heart sinks at the images of another failed harvest in southern

Africa, the continent's only fertile region. The details will be in his work files, of course, but he can't resist following the conspiracy trails blaming a new crop disease, apparently engineered by the Alliance to control the population. Oh, the irony. Another report catches his eye: a delay in the delivery of new pollinator drones. These just happen to last only one season, requiring a 'new and improved' batch to be supplied by the Yun Ju, but they are now too busy dealing with the storm fallout to notice that within a week there will be little left for the drones to pollinate.

He wonders why his aides haven't pinged him—this surely is something he could have brought up with Richardson—but then the answer presents itself in the next news bite: the drones aren't actually late, the Yun Ju did all they could, but the storm destroyed the shipment on the way to the elevator. The replacements are being produced with utmost urgency. Jason scoffs. This *could* be true—or it could be another of the occasional cues the orbitals orchestrated to remind the Earthlings how lost they'd be without them.

Not for much longer.

He travels straight to the office, then spends the rest of the day on reports and accounts and everything he desperately doesn't want to be doing. Things must look like 'business as usual,' though, so he grinds his teeth and waits till the evening, when even he would normally break for the day. Tonight, he's going out for dinner: Khalil has invited his boss to a meal he cooked himself. Apparently, Aya will be there, too. An evening out with his team, nothing more. Certainly not an insurrection.

Jason enters the building, the memories of the other night still fresh and raw. He glances towards Otto's apartment, but it seems empty, the door lost in the shadow of a faulty light. Jason knocks on the door at the other end of the corridor, and Khalil lets him in, a strained smile on his lips.

'Welcome back! It's just the three of us, I'm afraid. My partner and kid are with the grandparents.'

Good move. They'd be safer there, if anything were to go wrong.

Khalil beckons Jason to the kitchen, towards the source of the mouth-watering smell. The space is a mirror version of the one in Jason's home, all the apartments on the Alliance Compound sharing the same basic design. Khalil's cabinets are mock wood, though, and the countertops carry additional appliances Jason doesn't recognise. Probably useful for someone who does actual cooking.

Aya leans against the breakfast bar, a tall glass in her hand. She straightens as he enters, her expression pained. 'Hi there. We've been waiting for you to get back.'

'Well, I'm glad to hear that. It did occur to me you'd have declared me lost in the storm and hurried with a replacement.'

They laugh, and for a moment it's like the old days, before he knew the truth. Just he and his team, doing their best to keep humanity from starvation and war.

He glances at Khalil.

'We can talk here. I've put filters on all the systems, nothing gets out unprocessed.'

'I'm with you,' Aya says quickly, before Jason can figure out how to ask what she knows.

They'd agreed that Khalil would broach the matter with her in Jason's absence, then proceed based on her reaction.

'I showed her the maps: the phage and our trips,' Khalil says. 'She figured it out just like you did. We took it from there.'

Good. The three of them work together so closely, it would be impossible to hide things for very long. Besides, Aya is one of the smartest people he knows, and with an engineering background.

Khalil leads them to the table laid out with a dozen plates of delicious-smelling food. It feels out of place now, too domestic and normal, as if they were not about to start a revolution. But even insurrectionists need to eat.

'Wang will be joining us,' Khalil says as the screen to the side of the table lights up. 'Others may be listening in, but Sandy's our official liaison.'

Makes sense. The Watch needs to balance how much they reveal of themselves—in case Jason changes his mind or the connection gets exposed.

Sandy nods a greeting, then focuses on the dishes on the table. 'Takeaway or can you actually cook?'

'Does this look like takeaway?'

Sandy sighs. 'Nope. I was just hoping. I've been stuck with food rations for days. But never mind me. How was your trip?'

'Eventful.' Jason takes a seat opposite Aya, Khalil and Sandy's screen at the other two sides of the square table.

'Do you know who does it?' Aya leans towards him, her hands clasped tight. 'The phage or the rice campaign?'

'No. With the storm, I barely got a chance to talk to anyone important. But whoever does it, I'm sure they all know. They watch each other like hawks, spying on every move. They all know, and they are fine with it.'

'But why?'

'Because they depend on us. And we won't resist them as long as they keep us weak and divided, fighting each other and not them. That's not going to change as long as they are up there and we're down here. They already see us as something of a lower species. You should have seen how they laughed when I suggested they evacuate to Earth.'

'So you still think—' Khalil starts.

'We have to destroy the whole concept of the Yun Ju. They must be as dependent on the welfare of this planet as we are.'

'That's all very nice,' Sandy says. 'But have you found anything we can use to actually make it happen?'

'They've just weathered the worst storm in decades,' Khalil

says. 'There's nothing we can throw at them that could match it. And even if we find something, they'll just evacuate and repair, like they are doing right now. Or wait it out in one of those old ships.'

Jason picks up his fork and examines its teeth. Sharp enough to pierce food, but not skin. A tool suitable to its purpose. He looks at his two aides, then at Sandy. 'You're right, that's exactly what they would do. There's no point attacking the stations. We have to damage their space. Make orbit uninhabitable.'

'What?'

'How?'

'Create enough debris that they won't be able to recapture it quickly. Lots of fragments, big enough to cause damage. Send it on elliptical orbit so it keeps crossing their paths, like a comet trail. They'll be able to clear it eventually, but it will take time— and all the while they will be at risk. They'll have to evacuate.' Jason pauses, waiting for them to digest his words and reach the only conclusion. 'We have to destroy Tian Gong. And we have to do it now, before they finish the repairs and the reinforcements.'

Aya puckers her lips, concentrating. 'It could work... If we create a trail of debris with just the right initial velocity... Especially if we get to hit more platforms and create a cascading—'

'I hate to break the party,' Sandy cuts in, 'but how exactly would we do it? No way we can get explosives past the Sharks. And how would we even get to Tian Gong? It's not like you can score another tour, especially now.'

Jason leans back with a grin. 'Humanitarian aid. And apple delivery, courtesy of our friend in Siberia.'

He lets them stare at him for a moment, enjoying this fleeting triumph. Then he reveals his new arrangement with Richardson, and how they'll be using Tian Gong as Volkov's delivery base.

'Not bad,' Sandy agrees. 'At least it gets you to the station. But we need explosives, not apples. Unless you were planning to shoot the apples into space for your debris…'

'That's where you come in.' Jason glances at Aya, then at Sandy. 'And your engineers. We've narrowed the target to one station—you must be able to find a way to—'

'Wait.' Khalil raises his hand. 'Go back. The humanitarian aid is for the Sun Seers, right? So they are still on Tian Gong? Are you planning to blow up the station with all those people there?'

The icy glare he gives him sends Jason deeper into his chair. Jason glares back. It's the lives of two hundred cultists who chose a slow and painful death against the future of Earth. Against the hungry children who will never get that choice. How can it even compare?

He knows the answer, though. It's murder. It's a line that once crossed can never be un-crossed. And what's the worth of that future if that's how you start to build it?

'Some may be beyond our capacity to move. Too far gone bodily, or mentally. But we'll do everything in our power to save those who can be saved.'

Khalil holds his gaze. 'We must. Or we're not better than they.'

They sit in silence for a moment, staring at the cooling food.

Aya tears a piece of the pita bread and dips it in the bowl of humus. 'Okay, let's get back to the concretes. *How* are we going to blow up the station? Do your people—'

Khalil shakes his head. 'We don't have anybody on Tian Gong, and we certainly don't have anybody with access to explosives. Only the Sharks control those. Well, the miners as well, but they are out of reach. So the answer is "no".'

'Can we make some? There must be things on the station we could use?' Jason asks.

'Probably. But that requires having people there for long

enough to produce explosives without anybody noticing. And even then, I doubt we could manufacture sufficient quantity to blow up the entire station into small enough pieces to make orbit "uninhabitable", as you said.'

Crap. Jason stabs his fork into a piece of cauliflower until it crumbles into mush. 'There must be a way... Another solar storm?'

Aya huffs. 'I hate to disappoint you, but we don't quite control those.'

'But we're at solar maximum. The Sun's flaring so often that we—'

'Those are regular flares, regular storms. Not like whatever that last one was. Dean Abiola and the Science Council are still begging them for data, but they've gone silent, of course.'

Jason catches Khalil's glance, but the man averts his eyes. Jason swallows. His daughter specialised in heliophysics. And she is on New Hope, the station that detected the storm first.

'What?' he asks.

Khalil doesn't meet his gaze. 'A new talent from the Aspire Academy has apparently been instrumental in cracking the science. She's already been promoted and granted residence as reward for her work.'

'A new talent?' Aya frowns, sensing there's more to the message.

'Someone called Elizabeth Lake.'

Jason's heart sinks. She's done it. Saved all those lives. Got herself promoted. Secured the future she's dreamt of. The future he is about to destroy.

Aya is still glancing between Khalil and him, waiting. Khalil must know, but Jason's grateful he lets him decide what to tell her.

'My daughter,' he says, relived that his voice doesn't break. 'She hates me so much she's changed her name twice, and now finally escaped to the Yun Ju.'

'Could she help us?' Aya says.

'Did you hear what I just said?' Jason almost shouts, frustration and hurt getting the better of him. He shakes his head, exhaling loudly. 'I'm sorry. I didn't mean... She hates me, Aya. If you tell her it's me, she will do everything to stop us.'

'What if we didn't tell her it's you? If the Watch—'

'We tried.' Khalil's voice is soft, almost apologetic, and yet his words burn like venom. Like betrayal. *Another* betrayal.

Jason swings to glare at him, and the man shrinks under his gaze.

'My turn to apologise. But there was nothing helpful I could tell you, and I saw no reason to... to broach the subject.'

'The subject being my daughter?'

'Yes. Because I can imagine how much it must hurt. I'm a father, too, Jason.'

Jason opens his mouth, then closes it again. He clasps his hands and lowers his head, his forehead pressed against his knuckles, taking a moment to refocus. 'Okay. Okay. Well, it's all in the open now, so you might as well tell me everything.' He looks up again. 'I want to know. She will always be my daughter.'

Khalil picks up a bowl of roasted vegetables that still smell good even though by now they must be cold and fills their plates. 'We have... a sympathiser among the graduates. Someone we asked to try to get close to your daughter the moment we found out who she was. But then another graduate revealed Elizabeth's identity. It didn't go well—especially since they accused her of gaining her place by nepotism.'

'Damn,' Aya says through the mouthful of food.

Jason produces a mirthless chuckle. Oh, the irony. She's gone to the ends of the world to get away from him only to score even more hate for her efforts. Even if she hadn't despised him before, she surely would now.

'We made a mistake, too, by not telling our person. So, her

reaction was, well, spontaneous, but not the most helpful. She tried to remedy it since, especially after we told her the truth, but the damage is done. Elizabeth has cut herself off. And now that she's got a promotion and a contract, I don't see how we can make her sympathetic to the cause. She seems to have become Ranath's favourite, too.'

Renewal's zhu as the mother she lost too soon. It makes sense. So much sense it hurts to even think about it too long, so Jason shakes his head and changes the subject. 'Something else I've heard: Renewal is Destiny. Or at least it started with their money. And it seems they are planning something new.'

'What?' Aya almost drops her fork.

Khalil grimaces. 'There've been rumours. Nothing concrete, but yes, something's been happening. People we haven't seen for decades coming out of cryo-sleep. Like someone poked a stick in the nest. It could have been the storm, though. We really don't know.' He drums his fingers on the table, annoyed. 'It's next to impossible to get reliable intel.'

'Okay. I'm still trying to digest it all,' Aya says. 'And it's making me dizzy, to say the least. But if there's a chance Destiny is back and cooking something new, then we must hurry. Destroying the Yun Ju will take care of it all, Destiny and the rest of their conniving. And the best plan we have is to blow up Tian Gong. Right?'

Jason nods; Khalil glances at the screen. Sandy's been quiet for so long Jason's managed to forget their remote presence. Sandy appears to have muted the feed, their lips moving in another conversation, but they wave their hand for the three of them to continue.

'So—how?' Aya doesn't look at them as she asks the question, her arms crossed, and her face scrunched as she considers the options.

'We have no explosives,' Khalil says. 'Or maybe a small amount we can create on the spot. Hacking a shuttle and ramming it into the structure—assuming we could even do it—won't produce enough debris. The only source of power is whatever's already on the station.'

'And the Sun,' Jason says. 'Can we get hold of their storm forecast?'

'The regular one is public; we use it as well for our comms satellites. But the new one, the model that predicted the super storm, that's still a secret.'

'Wait.' Aya puts her palms flat on the table and leans towards them. 'We don't need a super storm. A regular storm will do, a level two even, if we keep all the systems powered up and turn off the shields.'

'That would cause massive surges,' Jason says. 'But is it enough to destroy the station?'

'Not an intact one, but Tian Gong's already damaged. And if we channel the surges to the weak spots in the structure...' Aya's voice loses conviction, and she shakes her head. 'It could work—but we'd need to know exactly where those weak spots are. We'd need to have the blueprints.'

Jason glances at Khalil, but his aide is looking at the screen and Sandy's grinning face.

'Well, some of us have been working while you're enjoying your dinner... And as I've just been informed, we may be able to get our hands on those blueprints.'

Aya gasps. 'For real?'

'Tian Gong was one of the first stations, before the New Trade War and the industrial embargoes. The prototypes are not exactly public, but... let's just say we may have a way.'

'We have a plan then,' Jason says. 'Sandy, get your people to talk to Aya. We need proper engineers here. Khalil, you need to locate the Sun Seer leaders. That's official Alliance business, under a humanitarian aid banner. Official, as in, we can talk publicly about it, but let's try not to get too much attention. We don't want anyone asking why we're spending tax money on Yun Ju cultists.'

'I'll get on that,' Khalil says. 'I assume you want to talk to Volkov?'

'Yes, that requires a personal treatment. Expect some additional funds to help with the operation...' He sniffs, amused by the absurdity of letting himself be bribed by the two men he detests, only so he can bring them both down with their own money.

Aya and Khalil exchange glances, neither joining in his amusement.

'One more thing,' Aya says gravely. 'If this plan is to work, the timing will have to be perfect. Rerouting the power, switching off the shield generators—this can't be done much in advance.'

Khalil tenses. 'Someone will have to be there when the storm starts. And they will have very little time to get out.'

'We'll find a way.' Jason gives them a thin smile. 'I'm sure we will.'

TWENTY-THREE

LIZ

Liz's new bed is the most comfortable she's had in years—maybe because it's hers, or at least not something temporary like the Academy dormitory or the graduates' quarters. She took the standard-issue pillows and blankets but splurged on 'silk-touch' sheets. They feel amazing—smooth as, well, silk, cool when she's hot and warm when she wraps them tight around her after a long day's work. She should sleep like a baby. And yet, every night her own stifled scream wakes her up trembling and terrified. It starts with her father: they are back in the apartment in the Alliance compound, and he's watching the news with his fingers curled around the armrest, his face pale and his chin trembling. On the screen, military police drag away protesters spitting his name like curses. She doesn't see them, doesn't need to turn to the screen to know what it shows. It's her father's face that haunts her dreams, his stubborn stare. He hates what he has become, and yet he won't stop, tenacious in his delusion that he is making a difference. Then suddenly he is at a party, lifting his glass as the floor shakes under his feet. His eyes widen and he turns to her, his brows rising with disapproval. Somehow, she's with Ranath then, leaning over the projection table, watching the stations move into the blast zone. Watching *Ranath* move them in and out of the blast zone, her mouth pursed and her gaze frigid as she plays her cosmic chess. And the next instant Liz is alone, a piece of debris floating away from the station, ejected into vacuum, cold and lost forever.

She wakes up clutching her new soft blankets, trying to hold on to—what? Who? She can't tell. Instead, she spends the rest of the night endlessly replaying the events of that night in her feverish mind, looking for the source of her nightmares. It's not the storm itself, she's sure. As much as it was terrifying, the stations have weathered it well. Even Tian Gong. The only casualties came from the blown generators, and these are now being reinforced. The new model has been shared with all the Shield teams, and they now have even more brain power to iron out the missing details. Next time a surge like that comes, they will be ready. When she thinks about a future storm, there's no worry in her chest, no accelerated heartbeat, no sweaty palms—to the contrary, all she feels is anticipation for another opportunity to test her theories.

So, if it's not the storm itself that haunts her, what is it?

She arrives at the workshop armed with two cups of coffee and slumps into the chair. The greeting cards are still there, their bright colours still making her smile. She just needs to get through whatever it is that's bugging her, and get on with it.

'You too?' Essa says from his corner of the workshop.

'I—what?'

'Having nightmares.'

Liz swivels her chair to face him. '*You* are having nightmares?'

Essa responds, facing her from across the room, 'I'm human, if you failed to notice. And it was the scariest experience in my life. But at least I've got Sam to cuddle me to sleep.'

Liz smiles. She's never been a romantic, but the idea of Sam and Essa warms her up from the inside. 'Is Sam staying?'

'Yep. The surge destroyed some testing equipment in their lab, so they're all off till it's fixed. And at the moment, I rather like that.'

'More storms for you, then?'

'Eh, thank you, I'll pass.' Essa pauses, then starts again, his simulated voice softer. 'You could see a medic, you know? You've been through a lot in a short time. You don't get bonus points for toughing it out.'

'I'm not.'

'Well, then I hope you're getting some great sex because you don't look like you've slept much.'

Liz chuckles. 'I wish...'

'Want to talk about it?'

'My sex life?'

'Whatever's keeping you up at night. And given how you're deflecting, you probably should. Though not necessarily with me.'

Liz hesitates. 'I would, except... except I'm not sure it's really the storm.'

'Are you... No, forget it. Tell me more.'

Liz puts her elbows on her knees. What can she tell him without mentioning her father? And is it really about her father? Her guilt about not warning him? Maybe. Or maybe how she really wanted Yun Ju to be different, but it's turned out to be just the same.

She drops her head. 'What if it'd been somebody else who came up with the new model? Would they even warn us?'

No answer comes for a moment, then Essa's hesitant voice. 'Maybe. Not everybody hates us. Some probably find us useful.'

Liz snorts.

'It's the reason our Shield team is so well staffed. Why we have the Academy and people like you. So we don't have to rely on the others.'

She waits another moment, then asks the question that sits

so deep at the back of her mind she hasn't realised it is there. 'Is Renewal really Destiny?'

'Is that what's eating you? Shit, I should have realised when we met, when you gawked at me for having the Mind-Link. See, I grew up here, it's always been part of the story. I've only heard rumours, though, nothing concrete.'

'Do you think it's possible?'

'Yes. Too many coincidences, with Renewal coming into money just at the time when the news from Bethesda broke. All those people disappearing.'

'Disappearing?'

'Moving to Earth or going into storage. Lots of whispers and finger pointing.'

'Then how come they didn't find proof?'

'Because they didn't want to. Too many important people were involved, some faction leaders even. There was talk about Li Qiang's father and the old Fujikawa, from Harmony. It had become something like a social club for the influential. My guess is, they made sure the whole thing got swept under the carpet.'

'I thought they did find some people, back then.'

'Minor players. Scapegoats, or those already dead, like the Guardian. They got all the blame. Anyway, it was a really long time ago, Liz. It's history. They are probably all dead now. It's just something the others use to blame Renewal for anything that goes wrong. I bet you someone out there is trying to figure out how to blame us for the storm...'

Essa chuckles and Liz joins in, her laugh turning wooden as a memory flashes through her mind: Hiroko's words on that first debrief just after their arrival, when she wondered about all the cryo-pods. *There's a whole section with just the pods. Hundreds of them. And most apparently occupied.*

Hundreds of cryo-pods, like those they are using now for

the refugees from Tian Gong. Except those pods were already occupied back then... By whom?

Is that where the old Destiny is hiding? In New Hope's cryo-pods? Why hasn't Ranath done anything about it? Is it because her father was one of them, and she remained loyal despite everything? Questions bubble up like foam on a cresting wave and Liz opens her mouth to ask Essa—but no, that would break her promise to Ranath not to mention her father. Liz will keep her word—and find another way to get to the truth.

'You are probably right,' she says, and turns to her screen. She can feel Essa's gaze on her for another moment, but then he, too, turns back to his work.

Liz works late, the job a soothing refuge for her turbulent mind. But finally, even Essa leaves, and she's alone, the corridor lights shifting to evening orange. She collects another cup of tisane and calls up the station map on her display. It's full of her annotations: the eateries marked in yellow and blue, for those she's already tried and those she found tempting but too pricey; green flags for the places she wants to explore: the park on the opposite side of the ring, and the theatre where the projection connects directly to one's lenses and hearing implants. Fun— but not where she's going to find the cryo-pods.

She shifts the map beyond the recreational areas, to the hospital and the medical labs. Hiroko is a medical engineer; she probably works there now. But she saw the pods during the onboarding week, when they were shown all over the station. The pods could be anywhere.

Liz could just ask the system. It couldn't be such a secret if Hiroko got to see them in the first few days on the station. The pods are not a secret—only who's in them. Still, probing the system directly seems like a bad idea.

Liz leans back and takes a sip of her tea. The cryo-pods have to have their own section, especially if there are so many. Where? The inner ring is unlikely—it's mostly offices, residences, and cultural centres. It's the station's prime real estate, not storage space. The middle ring is a better option: it has the medical facilities and the cryonics lab. Very little storage, though, and mostly for practical use like the cleaning bots. The outer ring seems the best answer: plenty of space and not many visitors. And she recalls hearing that part of the fourth section had extra shielding.

She returns to the map. There it is: the reinforced repository, a large space with no further detail as to what it houses. She zooms in, comparing the floor plans of the outer and the middle ring, and grins. The 'repository' sits exactly below the cryonics lab. There's even an inner elevator connecting the two. Gotcha. Time for an evening stroll.

Only days ago, Liz wouldn't have been able to descend to the outer ring—but she is a resident now, and with the high-level security clearance provided to the Shield team. Now the elevator takes her down with barely a reminder of increased radiation exposure—the very reason for the special cover over the 'repository.' She half expects to find guards or security cordons but reminds herself that there's nothing secret about the presence of the pods. Every station has a cryo-section; it's the identities of the occupants that are confidential, like medical data. She's probably going to learn very little from this escapade, she realises, but she's got to try or let herself be tormented by curiosity over more sleepless nights.

The doors open onto a dim passage, the lights redundant for the drones operating here. The long corridor stretches the entire circumference of the ring. Rubbery tiles clad the floor, probably to provide extra grip for the delivery carts rolling up and down between storage depots. Similar dark material covers the walls, muting all sounds into murmurs. Liz can barely hear her own footsteps. Her throat tingles in the hot, dry air, recirculated by the machinery crammed into every inch of the walls—the support systems that keep the station alive. And yet the space feels separate from the cosy interiors above, as if she's suddenly been transported away from New Hope and into an alien realm.

She walks past the water storage, the precious liquid captured from the Belt asteroids and passing comets. A supply cart swooshes by, swathing her in a cloud of hot, sticky air that makes her cough. More storerooms lay farther down, their contents unmarked. Ahead, a bulkhead door separates the sections. It opens to let through another cart, offering her a glimpse at what lies beyond. Section four seems brighter, the floor tiles a lighter hue. Liz speeds up, her feet thumping a dull, muffled rhythm. She glances around. Every corner of the station is monitored by automated security systems. There will be cameras, temperature and pressure sensors, everything to scan for potential risks. Her presence here would be recorded, but no one is likely to notice unless the system flags it as 'hazard.' Still, best if she doesn't linger too long.

She passes the bulkhead into section four. The sound has a different quality here, the floor harder, as if meant for heavier equipment. Thick metal panels cover the walls, with regularly spaced doors on both sides. Not regular doors, though, more like bulkheads or emergency hatches with small porthole windows. Like those in labs with atmosphere control.

Liz moves closer, tiptoeing now even though the corridor is empty. She stops by the first door, sliding to peek through the small round window—then jumps away as the sensor flashes. No entry. Authorised personnel only.

Liz flattens herself against the wall, breathing heavily. The red-lit message remains on the door panel, but there is no sound or any indication of alarm. It's just the sensor. Of course she wouldn't be allowed to enter the lab. But she can still look.

She returns to the door, her blood thumping in her ears as she leans towards the window. Inside, tall racks hold pill-shaped cryo-pods stacked on long shelves. She tries to count them: twelve per shelf, four shelves per rack—but how many racks? She can see three, but there must be more beyond what she can spy through the tiny window. And that's just this one room.

She sidles twenty metres to the next door, barely daring to breathe as she peers through the window. More racks, the setting identical, except here several shelves are empty and many have gaps as if some pods have been removed. A movement catches her eye, something grey and bulky at the far end of the chamber. She leans closer. Her breath fogs the glass. She wipes it away with slow, careful movements, desperate not to attract attention. The thing at the back of the room rolls closer. It grinds as it rotates towards the racks. Long prongs slide under the nearest pod and lift it out of its cradle on the shelf.

Liz gasps. They are removing the pods. Why?

She covers her mouth with her hand as things click into place. It's Destiny. They are waking them up. Because what else could it be? The refugees are on *The Covenant*, and these pods had been here before the storm. Old residents, now returning.

She leans on the wall, trying to calm her breathing. She was twelve when the message from Bethesda arrived, but the horror is still fresh in her mind. Now it's all back in a flash: the pictures of the empty settlement, the abandoned modules where thousands of colonists had perished, murdered by their neighbours, their families. All because of the Mind-Link implants Destiny had tested on them, implants designed to control human minds. Implants that they'd planned to use on everyone on Earth.

They are back. Why now? Liz can't begin to guess—except that all the commotion with the refugees and the storm is probably the best opportunity they've had to disappear into the crowd. What are they planning? A different version of those implants, or something even worse? There's got to be a reason they are emerging now—and whatever it is, they must be stopped.

Liz turns back, walking gingerly at first, then springing into a run as she crosses the bulkhead back into section three. She has to tell someone. Does Ranath know? Of course she does; it's her station, she knows everything that happens here. A thought makes the back of Liz's neck prickle. Ranath's father was in Destiny. She claimed she disapproved of him, but did she? It could have been a lie. Ranath could be covering up while she was secretly setting the scene for Destiny's return.

Liz bites her lip. Ranath is Destiny. The betrayal tastes like blood on her lip. She doesn't want to believe that her mentor has lied to her. And—Ranath knows who she is. Is this why she's invited Liz here? For some idea of revenge on Liz's father and her great-aunt for bringing Destiny down?

No, this is insanity. She has no idea of Ranath's intentions. And really, this is not about Ranath. The only thing that matters is that Destiny is back and that they need to be stopped before they set their plans in motion.

Who else can she tell? Her father, of course, but that's out of the question. She'd have to reveal her location. He'd never leave her alone, never let her stay in the Yun Ju. She'd lose everything she's worked for. There must be another way.

The elevator door opens, and Liz steps into the cool interior, away from the dry, scratchy heat of the outer ring. She leans on the wall, letting its chill seep into her. She could talk to Essa. She trusts him, but... he was too dismissive about Destiny when they talked. He'll think she's panicking, acting out her nightmares. What she saw won't be enough to persuade him. Or anyone, really. She needs hard proof. The names of those woken up would be a good start. There must be a record—

An empty chuckle rocks her frame. Alejandro could help her. He's the security expert, that's how he discovered her name. Hiroko might have access to the medical files. The other graduates could have useful advice—except she can't talk to them, not anymore. They've burned the bridges with her, and she with them. Too late for trying to mend anything, even if they didn't insist on hating her.

Her thoughts return to Essa. But even if he believed her, what could he do? Inform Ranath? That's one way of ending both of their careers very quickly. Message the Yun Ju Council? They never wanted Destiny found in the first place. They'd make sure it stayed hidden now. No, she needs someone outside the Yun Ju. Someone with power and influence on Earth. That leaves only one person.

Liz's heart sinks. No. She's not going to talk to her father. Not after everything she's done to get away from him. Besides, what could he do? He can't bribe Destiny away. She's spent her childhood listening to his talks about saving the world, but what has he really accomplished? Earth was still on the brink of starvation, and the politicians still played their games. Instead of saving the world, he's ruined his family and his life. She ran away to claim her future for herself. She has it now: a job, friends, prospects. If she raises the alarm, she'll lose it all.

Liz shivers, the chill of the elevator seeping into her bones. Maybe she should stay quiet. Forget she saw anything. Keep her head down, do her job, enjoy her life. She's saved plenty of lives already with her solar models. She should take care of herself now.

The door opens and she steps out onto the familiar ground of the middle ring. Her new home. Her dream home.

Damn it. Destiny is waking up. She can't let them take control again, not after what they did on Bethesda. And the one thing she knows about her father is that he won't quit. Even if he fails to stop them, he might make enough noise to send them back into hiding. He's the only one with a chance. She must call him.

How? She must find a secure connection, something beyond the filters she can install on her home system. Her workshop computer would do—the Shield has encrypted messaging built into the comms, a relic of the New Cold War, when both the Americans and the Chinese were obsessed with espionage. She could send the message from her own desk, but there's no telling when Essa will walk in on her, day or night. Except—except Essa is overdue for his medical check, delayed by the storm. He'll have to go soon, tomorrow or the day after. Can she wait that long? A part of her wonders if the delay might offer her another solution, anything but calling her father. But no, there's no other way. The moment Essa leaves for his check, she must be ready.

TWENTY-FOUR

RANATH

Ranath wakes up to a missive from Nevil Richardson, requesting a conversation 'sooner rather than later.' She wants to stall or even ignore him entirely—it's not like she doesn't have enough on her plate already—but the tone of the message makes her reconsider. Richardson could never be called a gentle-man, but this level of directness is unusual even for him.

She picks up a tisane (the medi-bot decided she was over-caffeinated, so she's supposed to quit for a week) and heads to the far end of the office, her personal space with its own privacy filter. Min Woo and Ester will listen in, of course, but there she can cut their link off with merely a blink. She has no idea what makes her think she might need that option, but she is too under-caffeinated to dwell on it. (She might send that medi-bot for maintenance. Just for a week.)

The holo-emitter on her antique desk doesn't have the reso-lution of the projection table so when Richardson appears, he, too, looks hazy and pixelated, like an antique. His smirk, though, is gamma-ray sharp.

'Hello, Eyre. Hope you're having a great morning!'

Ranath leans back in her plush armchair. If the use of her

last name is his attempt to rattle her, he needs to try a lot harder. 'Most excellent, Nevil. And you? Heard you lost some platforms? I'm sorry.'

She ends with a grin that makes him snort, then nod in appreciation. It does make things easier that they don't have to pretend to have each other's best interests at heart.

'That is the reason for my call, actually,' he says. 'One of the reasons, at least. I need to rebuild the platforms, and get some small repairs done on Liberty's hull. I need assemblers. The new generation ones, those you were saving for Li Qiang.'

Ranath takes a sip of the tea. Interesting. Not entirely surprising that he knows about the new generation drones, the news might have slipped out in a conversation with Qiang or Harmony. But that he knows about her deal with Qiang—his blackmail, to be correct—is unexpected. Li Qiang wouldn't have revealed his plans, and the shipments are on hold till the emergency repairs are completed. That leaves only one way Richardson could have learned about Qiang's order: from the Caretakers. That man, Allen, must have made contact. Could have been someone else, too, but that's the simplest option. Allen rushed to Liberty for a reason. Now he's working with them, feeding them the information they need to squash her. No wonder Richardson sounds so cocksure.

'You've received your share of drones from the general reserve, I trust?'

Richardson tuts. 'Let's not insult each other, if you will? I need triple the number if I'm going to be done in time.'

'In time for what?'

'In time for another storm. We're still at solar maximum as you may remember. Even low-level storms will delay construction. I'm sure your brilliant science team will agree.'

Ranath searches for an undertone in those words, something that would betray that he knows the identity of that 'brilliant science team,' but he sounds merely irritated and a bit envious. Richardson is not a good enough actor to pull this off, which means he doesn't know she has Nevsky's daughter on her station—even just after the man's visit. *Very* interesting.

'I will need Li Qiang's agreement to cancel his order. It does precede yours.'

'You have qualms about cancelling orders now?'

'Let's just say I don't want to make it a habit.'

'I'm afraid I have to insist. I'm sure you'll find a way to explain it to Yu Huan. They haven't suffered any damage in the storm. Nor have they shown any interest in helping those who have. I will be sending humanitarian aid to Tian Gong, by the way.' Richardson lowers his head, scowling accusingly. 'I know you got some residents out—mostly those with means to pay or those you find useful, like the Sharks. I'm going to help those you left behind.'

Ranath reaches for her cup to hide her frown. What's this about? Richardson wants to help the cultists? He's about as likely to turn into a philanthropist as she is to grow angel wings. There's something on Tian Gong he—or the Caretakers—want. What?

'We have offered assistance to anyone who would accept it,' she says.

'I'm told some people there are beyond the ability to choose for themselves. At least our friends from the Alliance think so, and I'm happy to assist. Have they reached out to you as well?'

Ranath puts down her cup. Now he's just mocking her. 'What are you getting the Alliance to do for you, Nevil?'

Richardson laughs. 'Now, I would never! I think they have a soft spot for the cultists, that's all. Or the Sun Seers have more influence on Earth than we realised. Either way, it never hurts to score some brownie points with the Alliance.'

Ranath sniffs. He's lying, for sure, but this seems as much as she's going to get from him for now. 'I'm always happy to help, of course. Just let me know what you need.'

'I need assemblers. And some of the Sharks you have stashed on New Hope. Send them to help with the cultists, and we will shift them over from there. Nobody else needs to know.'

Right. He knows she will never let him have all the Sharks, so he'll try to do it in stages. 'They will need to be consulted—'

Richardson raises his hand. His face grows cold as he leans towards her, the corners of his lips turning down in a bitter grimace. 'This is not a negotiation, Eyre. I've got all I need to shut you down for good. Especially now, after a certain visitor... a *very old* visitor, shall I say, has provided hard data. You will continue only for as long as I find you useful. Don't disappoint me.'

Damn. She expected the Caretaker to do exactly that, but the confirmation jolts her all the same.

Richardson holds her gaze for a moment, and then his expression breaks, a satisfied smile replacing the scowl as if even he couldn't sustain the moustache-twirling villain game for too long. There's too much kid-who-stole-all-the-toys in his enjoyment of his victory, the pleasure of winning superseding all purpose of the game.

And the game isn't over for as long as they are playing.

Ranath drops her head, defeated. The humiliation stings, but that's just another emotion she must spurn. Richardson loves winning so much he'll be back for more, like an addict searching for his dopamine hit. That might just buy her enough time to figure out the Caretakers' next move. Let him play with her like a cat tormenting a mouse. As long as the game continues, the mouse might find the right spot to bite.

'I will inform Zhu Qiang about the change of plans,' she says feebly. 'You will have the shipment in two days.'

'One day. Don't stall, Ranath. I'm not an idiot.'

'One has to try...' Her smile is so pathetic that anyone but Richardson would see through it—but he's too drunk on his triumph to even want to.

He laughs and nods his goodbye, his expression almost friendly. Oh, they can be friends now when he has her where he wants her. Ranath grits her teeth and keeps her smile on until his image blinks out. She glares at the space where his face used to be, her fingers coiled into fists as she fights the scream rising in her throat. It's not over. Far from it. She lost a bout, but the match is only starting.

Ester and Min Woo are both in the office as she drops the privacy bubble and strides to join them. They've heard everything, their faces apprehensive, worried even.

'What do you think—' Ester starts, but Ranath cuts her off.

'Later. Min Woo, the pods?'

'We've moved half of them. I have to limit how much machinery I'm sending back and forth.'

'Find a way to speed it up. A minor incident in the dock could do the trick; something needing a swarm of repair drones. You figure it out. And start moving the bio containers and everything else. I want the ship ready to depart in forty-eight hours.'

Min Woo's mouth drops open. 'You realise...'

'I do. Ark's not ready. But we—they—can wait it out on the ship, and if we leave it too late, none of us are going anywhere.'

Min Woo bobs his head, his expression not entirely convinced.

'Also, I need to talk to Li Qiang. Let him know it's urgent.'

'I will. One more thing: Elizabeth Lake visited the cryo-section last night. She seemed distressed afterwards.'

'Distressed?'

'Well, she abandoned the area at a run.'

Damn. 'What did she see?'

'Nothing much. Could have noticed some pods being moved but I don't know why that would alarm her.'

Ranath gives an exasperated sigh. That's the last thing she wants to worry about now. 'Who knows? Do we still have a tracker on her comms?'

'Yes,' Ester says. 'She's made no transmissions outside the station.'

'Keep monitoring her. And maybe seal the pod section?' Ranath shakes her head, changing her mind. 'No, that would raise suspicions. Just keep watching it, Min Woo.'

Min Woo departs with a nod, and Ranath turns to Ester. 'Anything about that Tian Gong man?'

Ester grimaces. 'Still looking. There's surprisingly little digital trace of him—no birth certificate, no school records. He was well off, but there's no business registered to his name other than a couple of trust funds managed through a syndicate.'

Ranath nods. A Caretaker, for sure. And those 'trust funds' must be his share of Renewal's revenue. The money they are so afraid of losing. 'Anything else?'

'Not yet, but I may have something soon. Nebu's engineer has given me a name of a Tian Gong's systems manager who he thinks has some information—but they're already in storage on *The Covenant*. I'm getting them out, but it'll take a few hours.'

'Good. Keep asking around, maybe you can find more connections.' Ranath hesitates. She'd like to have a look around at the man's home, but that would require breaking his privacy seals. Easy to do, harder to explain—to Nebu or anyone else. Allen would get pinged as well. Too much risk for the chance he's left behind anything useful. The option is still on the table, but not right now.

'Li Qiang is expecting you,' Min Woo says in her ear.

'Thank you. Let me just grab some coffee.' To hell with the medi-bot. She needs her brain fuelled.

Ranath abandons her tisane cup and replaces it with fresh brew, swallowing a large gulp with a relieved sigh. Oh, the small victories.

This time she takes the call in the main office, the projection programmed to leave her aides out of sight. She signals the system and Li Qiang appears before her, his smile as perfect as his clothes, though the shadows under his eyes suggest he hasn't been sleeping well, either.

'Ranath! A pleasure to see you, as always. I hope nothing unpleasant has necessitated this urgent call?'

Ranath huffs. 'How long have you got?'

'That bad?' Qiang's concern looks almost genuine, but the way his eyes drill into her suggests he has a hint of what's coming. 'Do tell.'

'I'm afraid I have bad news. Richardson wants your assemblers—and he hasn't left me any space to refuse.'

'On what grounds? He got his share of the general reserve, as far as I understand?'

'He has, of course. He claims he needs more.' Ranath shrugs. 'He probably does, but that's not the point. The point is, he knows about your order, and he wants a chunk of it. And he's made it clear that he won't take no for an answer.'

Qiang scowls. 'How did he know about my order?'

'Not from me, if that's what you're implying.' She holds his gaze, and for a moment they are back on the fencing piste, facing each other through the mesh of their masks. She can't tell him how Richardson got the news—the Caretakers are the most likely source, but it's not something she can mention. 'It's not so hard to guess, anyway. That I've cancelled Harmony's contract is public knowledge. So, it's either you or Endeavour, and if I were Richardson, I know who I'd suspect.'

Qiang reaches for his drink, a tall glass filled with light blue liquid. 'The timing of the storm was rather unfortunate.'

Ranath doesn't comment. They both know that Qiang's plan relied on securing the assemblers before anyone noticed. The supply is limited; all the others could do would be to place their orders and wait while he went on with his construction. The storm put the plan on hold—but until Richardson's demand, it appeared to be only a temporary delay. She waits for Qiang to continue, to renew his claim to hold Richardson back as he promised. But his former certainty is gone, replaced by a troubled frown. She thought she'd enjoy seeing him stumble, but today it only gives her more reason to worry.

'Whatever you had on him isn't working, is it?'

Qiang sips slowly, his brows scrunched in thought. 'He... he's made a move I didn't expect.'

'What move?'

Qiang puckers his lips. He's probably considering how much he can tell her without weakening his position, but this time she's ahead.

'Let's save each other some time, Zhu Li. We both know Nevsky's been to Liberty. And now they're launching joint humanitarian aid for the Sun Seers.' She pauses to watch Qiang's eyes widen with surprise. 'So let me offer you a theory: whatever you had on him had to do with the Alliance. And now he's cut a new deal with them, so your hook no longer catches. Am I correct?'

Qiang shakes his glass, making the ice cubes jingle. He examines them, each cube containing something pink or red, like frozen fruit. 'I haven't exhausted my options yet.'

Ranath keeps her face still. This is as close as she's ever been to seeing Qiang admit defeat. Only a pity it's Richardson who's beaten him, not her.

'See, I don't really care who gets the assemblers,' she says slowly. 'I'd prefer it to be you—for the sake of our friendship. But I have to protect myself first. I have to know what Richardson's planning, and you can choose to help me or watch him put your assemblers to his use.'

Qiang smiles thinly. 'Do you think you can stop him?'

Ranath considers her answer. She's not sure if she can protect herself, especially if the Caretakers are working with Richardson now. Perversely, that might buy her a little time. Richardson wants to attack Renewal by linking it to Destiny— and that's the last thing the Caretakers want. Renewal is the source of their income. They will be looking for something that can destroy her personally, without damaging Renewal. Somehow Tian Gong fits into that plan, but she has no clue how. Maybe she can't stop Richardson, but all she needs is more time to push Ark past the point when they have a foothold and enough settlers to invoke the Habitat Ownership Act.

'I hope *we* can stop him, Zhu Li. Oh, don't get me wrong. I don't want *you* to win, but I don't want you to lose either. I rather like what we have now.'

'I can see why.' Qiang finishes his drink. His shoulders relax as he pulls in a deep breath. Good, he's made up his mind; for now, keeping the status quo works for both of them. 'What do you want to know?'

'How were you planning to control him? And how does the Alliance come into it?'

Qiang jingles the remaining ice cubes in his glass. 'Fruit.'

'What?'

'Our dear friend has a significant side business smuggling fruit from the planet. Over the Alliance allowances, for his personal trade.'

Ranath scowls. 'I know he's had, shall we say, extra supplies. And I can see that could ruffle some feathers on the planet—but is that enough of a business to—'

'I think you underestimate the scale of his profits. You may start with checking with your own purchasers. Planet-sourced fruit is expensive, the more expensive the harder it is to grow. It's become something of a status symbol, too, though such details might escape your attention, dear Ranath.' Qiang gives her a smile one might offer an adorably clueless child. 'You'd understand if I showed you the bills for my last reception. I've obviously failed to impress you, but my fruit plates were the talk of the town...'

'You are right. I have underestimated the profitability of his business.' Ranath taps her fingers on her thigh, thinking. 'I assume you figured out how to ruin it for him?'

'Yes. I identified his source and his supply chain. All in a nice package, ready to deliver to the Alliance if he stopped cooperating.'

'And then Nevsky shows up here...'

'And departs with a spring in his step and new plans for "humanitarian aid to the Sun Seers." Honestly, who do they think they are fooling? Though I guess, there's nobody left to fool.'

'He paid off Nevsky?'

'I admit, I was surprised as well. That old man held off for a long time. I guess everybody has a price. And he's probably getting ready to retire, building himself a nest egg...'

Following in his daughter's footsteps, Ranath thinks but doesn't say. It makes sense. He'd want to be close to his daughter, maybe hope to rebuild the relationship before he's too old. Delay his old age, even, with some cryo-treatment. It makes sense—and yet... Qiang is right, Nevsky's never accepted a bribe—at least not one she's heard of. That's why Richardson had to use all the nasty tricks to manipulate the Alliance. Ranath knows enough to decide she'd rather not delve into the unpleasant details. Something had to make Nevsky turn, something bigger than the payoff he could have easily obtained before. It could be his daughter, or his age. Or it could be something else entirely.

'I assume you have proof?' she asks.

'As good as. Richardson processed his shipments on one of the destroyed platforms. He needs a replacement—and now Nevsky is there, just in time for the storm. My guess is they'd been talking about scaling up, and the storm gives them the perfect excuse.' Qiang waves his arm. 'But that part is only a guess. The "humanitarian aid" announcement is a fact. I don't think you're buying either Richardson or Nevsky being so concerned about the cultists...'

Ranath shakes her head. 'No, that was the first thing that got my attention. So, they will ship the fruit to Tian Gong, and Richardson picks it up from there.'

'Exactly.'

They sit in silence for a moment, lost in thought. Ranath calls for another coffee, and Qiang refills his glass from a silver pitcher jingling with the frozen fruit. (Was he trying to impress her in this call? Or just savouring the luxury?)

'I'm afraid that's all I've got,' Qiang says. 'I'm... looking for opportunities, of course, but at the moment you have more scope for action. You have Nebu, and access to Tian Gong. And the Sharks, of course. Let's not forget the Sharks.'

Qiang's smile turns bitter. Almost too bitter—unlike Richardson, Qiang is an excellent actor. He might have another layer of game in mind, but that's a worry for later.

'I may pay the cultists a visit,' she says. 'Wouldn't want to miss an opportunity to show my charitable side.'

Qiang almost chokes on a piece of fruit. Ranath is considering a biting response when a message from Ester appears on her lenses, marked urgent.

Elizabeth Lake has placed an encrypted call to her father.

Listen and record, Ranath sends quickly. *Do not interfere.*

'Do keep me apprised of further developments,' she says to Qiang. 'And I shall do the same.'

'I'm sure you will,' Qiang says, still smiling. 'After all, I wouldn't want to lose my best fencing partner.'

'Nor would I,' Ranath says, realising she actually means it. How quaint.

They disconnect, and the smile dies on her lips. She doesn't have enough to stop the Caretakers, but she has what she needs to get Richardson's attention. At least it's a start.

And now dear Liz might just help her to figure out what Jason Nevsky is up to.

TWENTY-FIVE
JASON

Alexy Volkov grins as he lifts a glass. 'I knew there was hope for you yet, Stepanovitch. I can't tell you how happy it makes me to see you come back to the fold.'

Jason keeps grinning in return, his knuckles white on the edge of his seat—luckily out of sight of the projection. Ever since they started talking as partners, after Richardson sent the man a message that Jason Stepanovitch Nevsky could now be trusted, every conversation has made him hate Volkov more. The man is the essence of everything Jason despises: a narcissist with an ego that could power a city, fortified with unshakeable conviction that he's the chosen one, placed there by God himself to fulfil his mission. At least Richardson doesn't pretend to be saving anyone.

'Now you need to brush up on the language of your fatherland,' Volkov continues. 'English is so ugly. Not the language of the future.'

Jason tilts his head, surprised. 'So, you're not—'

'Not going up to the Yun Ju, no. Why would I? I have everything here, and without the storms or the radiation. Nothing can beat good Russian soil. That's where we're meant to be, Stepanovitch.'

Jason nods. He does agree with the sentiment—apart from the Russian part. 'We are the creatures of Earth.'

'Exactly.' Volkov grins again, then shifts in the way that signals the end of the meeting. The *audience*, rather, but Jason doesn't care for such details anymore. 'My people will be in touch very soon.'

'I'll be waiting—' Jason starts, but the image has already blinked away. Another petty statement. *Well, fuck you, too.*

He leaves the room in a sour mood, then reminds himself that he's accomplished exactly what he set out to achieve. His part of the plan was pretty much done, with the first shipment of Volkov's fruit already on the way to the Feidi elevator, cleared with Alliance export permits. Hooray.

He grabs a glass of water—the most suitable drink for this celebration—and joins Aya in the main room of Khalil's apartment.

He steps into an animated conversation: Aya on one side of a portable holo projector, four Watch engineers on the other. The engineers are still only silhouettes, colour coded for ease of reference, their voices filtered. They've all agreed preserving anonymity was the best option—they had no time to fully establish trust, and even if, *anyone* could be compromised. Especially someone with their daughter in the Yun Ju, as most of them hinted but never said openly. Jason encouraged the idea—the Watch had to remain undetected so they could keep going no matter what happened to him or his plan.

'The main power conduits are triple-shielded,' the blue engineer says. 'With mechanical surge protectors. Nothing we can hack remotely short of rewiring the whole station.'

They are all leaning over the marked-up holo of Tian Gong's schematics. To Jason, it's a tangle of lines of different widths and textures, from the dark, solid bands of the base frame to the almost translucent greys of the superstructure. The power cables pulsate in orange and red; these are the main arteries supplying the station's vital systems. He doesn't understand much of it, despite Aya's best efforts. Whether it's because technology has never been his forte or because the scale of the task now seems overwhelming, he can't tell. The engineers have been at it for hours now, with nothing resembling an actual action plan.

'How about here?' Aya points to a blurry section of the schematics. 'This relay was damaged when their generator blew up in the storm, and it's a secondary system so probably lower priority for the repairs.'

'But it doesn't—' Red starts, but Yellow cuts them off.

'Wait, I've just got the report...'

A loud ping in Jason's earpiece drowns Yellow's voice. A private message icon blinks on his wrist band. Jason glares at it in annoyance and surprise—not many people have his personal code—but then his eyes pop wide open. It's Annalie. His daughter is calling him. His muscles tense in instinctive reaction. Is she in danger? Has something happened? Another storm, or something worse? He turns on his heel and rushes back to the comms station in the other room.

It takes forever for his private system to link to the screen, but then she's there, Annalie, staring at him across the digital space. She's got older—of course—the last traces of the rebellious teenager replaced by the hardened features of a determined woman. How long has it been since they've last talked? Seven years? Ten? Too long. Much, much too long.

'Is everything—' he starts, but she's speaking at the same time.

'Don't try to trace this.' Annalie pauses, then starts again, speaking faster, as if expecting a rebuttal. 'I'll explain. But please don't. It's important.'

'I'm not. And I won't, I promise.'

Annalie nods. She licks her lips, and suddenly all he can see is his little girl running back from school to tell him about the great new thing she'd learned. But no, that's just wishful thinking. She is a woman now, with a life that did not include him anymore.

Jason makes an effort to pull his gaze away from her face to examine her surroundings. It's an office, but too generic and uncluttered to be real. An auto-generated filter, and a basic one. 'Are you safe?'

'Yes. That's not about me. I've got to tell you something. Something you must know. But...' She trails off, glancing around as if to check she's alone.

Something secret—something she doesn't want anyone to hear but important enough to force her to contact him after all the effort to hide her identity. If it's not personal, then it must be something related to New Hope or Renewal, because that's who she's hiding the message from.

'This is an encrypted link,' she says. 'But nothing is unbreakable if they happen to be looking. I don't know why they would, though. They know... Anyway, is it secure on your end?'

Jason nods. 'Very much so.'

'Okay. I'll be brief. Two things you need to know: first, Renewal, on New Hope, is most likely the successor of Destiny.' Annalie pauses, too briefly for Jason to ask how she knows or to mention that he's reached the same conclusion. 'Second, there are hundreds of cryo-pods on the station. And they've begun waking up the occupants.'

Jason gasps. He was right. Destiny is rising. He can't be sure what it will be—or if it will be anything at all—but the risk is too big to be ignored. He must hurry, must destroy the Yun Ju before they regain their foothold.

Annalie's watching him, waiting for his reaction. He can't tell her anything. An encrypted link won't help them against

Destiny. They are probably tracking every word, every mention of their name triggering some alarms. They will hear about this conversation. Is Annalie at risk? His chest tightens at the thought—but whatever damage her message could have caused them has already happened. Attacking her now would only confirm their presence. For the moment, she's safe. He must keep her that way.

'I don't think you need to worry, darling,' he says in a tone he hopes sounds flippant. 'I understand you're anxious, we both remember Aunt Natalie's message. But it's been so long... If they were going to come back, they'd have done it a decade ago.'

Annalie flinches. Her lip curls with such disappointment and hate it sends an icy spike down his back. She must have risked a lot to bring him the message, must have agonised for days before calling him—only to have him dismiss her. Jason holds her gaze, willing his eyes to speak, to make her understand he's only playing a part. For her sake and everyone else's. He clenches his jaw to stop his chin from trembling. He must let her know, somehow.

'I'm sure you saw something odd or suspicious, and your mind just went to the worst thing you could imagine.' He forces a chuckle. 'Remember how your mother was terrified of spiders? Any piece of dust in the corner and she'd be screaming it was a black widow!'

He leans forward, watching her reaction. Annalie is still scowling, but her forehead scrunches with confusion. Her mother was an entomologist, but she specialised in arachnids. They used to have a pet tarantula when Annalie was little. She must remember that.

Finally, her eyes widen. 'Yes... Yes, I remember... You think I'm wrong? That it's not... them?'

'I'm sure there's another explanation. But don't you worry, darling, if I see any trace of those bastards, I will squash them like bugs.'

She's nodding now, maybe remembering how her mother gently evicted any insects that would invade their home. Whatever it is, Annalie's eyes are bright again—still confused, but without the bitterness from only moments before.

'Thank you for calling, though,' he adds, his tone turning serious. 'I missed you.'

Annalie blinks, then looks away. This one call won't begin to repair things between them, but it's the first time he's heard from her in a decade. He must take what little consolation he can from the fact that despite everything she chose to call him.

'I've got to go,' she says after a moment's silence.

'Of course. Congratulations, though. You've done some stellar work with the storm algorithm. If you can forgive the pun.'

Annalie freezes. 'How do you know?'

'It's your speciality, isn't it? I knew you'd do great.'

'So, all this time...'

'You are my daughter. I had to make sure you were safe.'

They look at each other for another moment, emotions playing on Annalie's face that he can read as clearly as when she was a child: confusion, reluctance, hope. It's anger that wins in the end, though. Her face hardens again, and her brows tighten.

'I've got to go,' she says, and cuts the link before he can manage another word.

Jason stares at the empty screen. He should be wondering about Destiny and their plans, but all he can think about is how much he wants to hug his daughter again, even if it was to be the last time.

'Got a moment?' Khalil asks from behind the door.

'Come in, I'm just done.' Jason swivels his chair towards the door. He frowns at the sight of Khalil's troubled face. 'Bad news?'

Khalil closes the door behind him, cutting off the hubbub of the engineers' voices, which seem to have risen an octave. He leans against the wall, deflated. 'Pretty much, yes. I did manage to speak to Sunlit Prelate Smith, which is the highest level here on Earth. The top boss is *Enlit* Prelate Levine, by the way, up in Tian Gong.'

'Enlit?'

'Yep. Enlightenment's been done, you see. Anyway, no chance to talk to Levine, and Smith was... Unhelpful doesn't cover it. She accused me of religious intolerance, of trying to sabotage the church, jealousy for knowledge I couldn't dream to attain, and a few other things. She refused to acknowledge that the people on Tian Gong might be in trouble—though they would gratefully accept any financial or material aid, of course.'

'Damn. Anybody else in the organisation who could be more forthcoming?'

Khalil shakes his head. 'That's the worst part. I never liked calling them "cultists" because... well, their views do seem extreme, but the word's been used to discredit minority religions for centuries, so I just don't like it.'

'You have a point there.'

'Except now I've met them—and the Sun Seers *are* a cult, in the worst definition of the word. Militaristic and manipulative, and apparently in full control of all the aspects of their people's lives. I couldn't find a single record of anyone ever leaving the sect.'

'Which means there may be people on Tian Gong who want to leave but can't?'

'That's what I think, yes.'

Jason chews the inside of his cheek, considering. This could be good news, or very bad news. If enough of the cultists want to leave, he might be in a position to help them stage a rebellion. But if there's too few of those, or if they have already been incapacitated, then he might be unable to remove them. Which means giving up the plan, or blowing them up together with the station. Fuck.

'There was that man with me in the elevator on the way up,' he says. 'I don't have his name. But he's new there, so maybe... I don't know, but it's worth a try.'

'At this point, anything is worth a try.' Khalil nods. 'I can get his name from the passenger manifest.'

'Shit!' Aya's voice cries from the other room, angry or disappointed.

Khalil and Jason exchange a wary glance. What now?

The colour-coded engineers are gone when they return to the main room, the grey schematics of the station replaced with something resembling a thousand-legged spider.

'What happened?' Jason asks.

'For a moment I thought we had a way in. A really good way in.'

'And?'

Aya pulls in a chair and slumps into it with a groan. 'Tian Gong is one of the early stations, from when they still worried about potential debris impact on Earth. So they gave it a nifty self-destruct system to blow it to smithereens—or just to small enough pieces to burn out in the atmosphere.'

'Let me guess,' Khalil says. 'They've disabled it.'

'Not that we can tell, which makes it even more irritating. I'm not sure the current occupiers even remember it's there. Anyway, they've slapped on several layers of access codes, which we might possibly be able to crack but not before they automatically rotate to a different configuration. And that's not even what kills this idea dead. Even if it's still there, and we had the codes, the debris pattern is useless to us.'

Aya gestures at the thousand-legged spider. 'It just flies out in every direction. We need something we can channel into an elliptical orbit, one that will regularly cut across the paths of the stations. Self-destruct won't do that. And, if you want to kill this dead idea's corpse, at the time we'd need to activate, it would either obliterate the nearest station, or the elevator cable, or both.'

Khalil grunts. 'Well, that's as dead as dead goes. What are the other options?'

'Wait,' Jason cuts in. 'You said "time to activate." Have you figured out a window?'

'We got the forecast. Ninety per cent chance of a decent size storm when Tian Gong is in a perfect place to get the brunt of it. Except it hits in two days and all we have is a draft of an idea for a plan.' Aya glowers at the thousand-legged spider, her expression even more disheartening than her words.

'That means you have two more days,' Jason says. 'And you can keep on working while I'm in the elevator. I'll need—'

'I should be the one going,' Khalil interrupts. 'The media are already in a frenzy about your last visit. And the aid to the cultists.'

'That's why it has to be me. I'm disposable. They can't hate me any more than they do. You two might consider petitioning for my dismissal when I'm too far for them to stop me.'

Jason forces a chuckle, but neither of them cracks a smile.

Aya is still looking at the display, her face pale.

'What?'

'We might get something in time. But...'

'But?'

'The only other plan—an idea for a plan...' Aya puffs up her cheeks and blows out slowly. 'The only way to pull it off is to set things up from inside. And whoever does it may not have enough time to escape.'

'Fuck.' Khalil punches his palm with his fist.

Jason walks to the window. Just like Otto's place, it overlooks the playground with the rusting seesaws where Maia and Annalie used to play while he worried about Destiny and saving the world. He swore to his aunt he'd never give up. It seems the time has come to make good on his promise.

'We can't let this chance slip,' he says calmly. 'We may not get another storm before they complete the repairs. Aya, inform your team. We have only one shot at this.'

'But...' Khalil starts, but trails off without finishing.

'You know it makes sense. You two need to continue, and so must the Watch. This isn't over, far from it. The real challenge will come once we get them down here. It will be up to you to lead the change.'

Aya stands up stiffly, the display lighting up again. 'We'll find a solution. We have two more days.'

Jason nods. 'I leave tonight. Just one thing—Khalil, can your "sympathiser" get a secure message to my daughter?'

'It can be arranged.'

'Good. Let's hurry.'

TWENTY-SIX

LIZ

Liz slinks back inside her quarters. Her heart pounds so loudly she can't hear her own footsteps, but somehow, she's managed to leave the office and reach the home without any trouble. She's still shaking, expecting every noise to turn into station security knocking at her door. Will it be the Sharks? She shivers at the recollection of their silver guns. Not the Sharks, please, not the Sharks.

She called her father from her own desk, just as she'd planned. Essa took a day off for his medical, and probably to enjoy Sam's company before they returned to their lab. She waited till the evening anyway, long enough for the other analysts to leave but not so long that her presence would seem suspicious. Nobody walked in on her, and she managed to call and even stay for a few minutes afterwards, pretending to work till her nerves finally gave up on her.

She leans against the door, waiting, but the corridor outside is quiet. Has she got away with it? The encryption would be easy to break from within the station—it's their own code, after all—but it'd require someone knowing there was something for them to decrypt in the first place. As it is, the record will probably linger in some comms buffer, gathering digital dust until it is superseded by newer data. Every second that passed without the Sharks knocking on her door suggested that no one has paid her message any attention. Especially since she called a private number, not anyone important, like the head of the Food Alliance.

Liz chuckles, finally letting her muscles relax. A drink would do her good, but she hasn't bought any yet, and it's too late to venture out in search of a bar. Instead, she grabs a chocolate snack and plops herself into the newly delivered recliner—a modern design that meshes nicely with the rest of the scant decor. Her apartment is still mostly bare, but Liz has put up some personal touches: the blue velvet recliner and the fake 3D panorama of Earth on the main wall.

Suddenly, her mood bursts, the relief replaced with a new tension in her shoulders. Seeing her father again stirred up too many feelings, too many painful memories. Too many good ones, too, but she doesn't want to dwell on those. The whole conversation was odd, though. The way he reacted to the news, the way he talked about her mother to make her realise he was putting on an act... Why, though? He said the link was safe on his side. Did he think she was being monitored? He should have trusted her to do her own research. But that would only be typical for him to assume he knew better.

Liz huffs with annoyance as she peels the chocolate bar open. Her father knows where she is—has known all along. She thought she'd escaped his hounds, but they'd followed her through all the years at the Academy. This should make her angry—except that he's never tried to interfere, never tried to stop her. She was so sure he'd use his powers to keep her on Earth if he only knew. She was wrong. What else has she missed?

A knock at the door makes her stiffen. Her heart resumes its pounding, her hands curling tight around the chocolate bar.

They've found her. Destiny, or the Sharks, or Ranath. They've heard her conversation and they—

Another knock, a fast tap-tap-tap of a small hand. The Sharks wouldn't be knocking. Ranath would summon her or have her delivered. It has to be someone else.

Trembling, Liz tiptoes to the door. Oh hell, whoever it is, they've either found her or they haven't. She focuses on the door mechanism and her lenses signal it to open.

It's Kene, her arm raised, about to knock again.

Liz lets out a loud breath. 'Oh, thank god…'

Kene's brows rise. 'Who were you expecting?'

'Nobody.'

'I see.'

They stand on opposite sides of the entrance for an awkward moment before Liz's heart calms down enough to let her think. 'I'm sorry. Come on in. Please.'

She gestures for Kene to enter, her hand covered in chocolate from the bar she squished. Kene doesn't seem to notice. She steps inside, glancing around at the decor.

'Nice. Is this how the locals live?' Her voice brims with snark.

'You'll get your own place soon,' Liz says, then grimaces at how patronising it sounds. 'I mean, I'm sure you'll be one of the… Crap.'

Kene sniffs.

'Why are you here?'

'I have something for you.' Kene pulls a small box from her pocket and retrieves a foldable visor, like those some still use for games. Nowhere near as good as what Liz's lenses and the audio implant can deliver.

Liz stares. Is that a gift? A peace offering? She puts on a smile. 'That's very thoughtful—'

'It's not a present.' Kene cuts her off with a glare. 'You think I'm here to buy your approval? I'm not Alejandro.'

'Then why are you here? Because if it's any more of his nonsense, then you'd better leave.'

Kene bites her lip. 'You're not making it easy, you know?'

'What do you—'

'You could have just talked to me.'

'I tried.'

'That first night, yes. And true, I didn't listen. But I reached out later, more than once, and you shut me out each time.'

'I guess we both fucked up, then.'

'Probably. Only worse than you think.'

'What do you mean?'

Kene cocks her head at the visor in her hand. 'You should watch it.'

'But—'

'Just watch it. I'll wait; I need this thing back.'

Liz reaches out for the gadget, first with her chocolate-smeared hand, then with the other. She catches Kene's questioning glance. 'Chocolate. Wait, I'll just...'

She hurries to the bathroom and puts her hand under the cleaner. It spouts a puff of pressurised droplets, and the remnants of her chocolate bar vanish into the collector. When she comes back to the room, Kene is stretched out on the recliner, her eyes closed. The visor sits on the coffee table, waiting.

Liz picks it up, curious and apprehensive. Too many disturbing events have happened in recent days, too many discoveries she'd prefer not to have made. Somehow, this will be another one, she is sure. For a moment, she wants to give the visor back, forget about the pods and Destiny, and go back to the good old days when all she had to worry about was Alejandro revealing her identity. But there's no going back.

She slides the visor on. The mechanism clicks as it connects to her own system, and the opening titles of *The Warriors of Azkend* start playing. It takes about ten seconds before the game starts to fade, replaced pixel by pixel by another image. And then she's looking at her father's face again, his clothes and surroundings just as she's seen them earlier today. He must have recorded this message soon after—and sent it to Kene? Through a secret visor? How was that—

'Hello, Annalie.' Her father's voice cuts through her speculations. 'Elizabeth, if you prefer. My apologies for cutting you off in our conversation. I'm glad you understood my meaning, though. Not the cleverest trick with giving your mum arachnophobia, but it's all I had at the moment. I'm probably not cut out to be a spy...'

He smiles weakly, but his brows are scrunched, and his entire body bunched up and tense. 'You are right, I believe: Renewal is linked to Destiny, and they are coming back. I have no idea about their plans as yet, but given who we are talking about, I doubt it's anything good. Now, this is important: I don't know what measures you took to encrypt your message, but unless this is another area of your expertise, I suggest you assume they've heard it. They will probably track any mention of the name, or just track you, because they must know who you are. Don't take lack of reaction as evidence, they may simply want to see your next move.'

Liz shivers. He might be right. She hopes he's wrong, wants to tell him how he's been wrong about so many things, but the man she's hearing from now is so unlike the despondent figure she remembers of her father. Something has changed—in him, or maybe in her as well. She can't tell what, it's nothing more than a feeling yet, but it's as present as the air she breathes.

'So, that's the first reason for this message. Stay safe, Anna— Elizabeth. Don't contact me again; if there's anything urgent, talk to the person who delivered this recording. Now, the second part is harder. I can't say much, other than that I'm not going to let Destiny try their tricks on us again. Until your call, I wouldn't have thought of asking for your help, but I can imagine

how hard it was to reach out, given your feelings towards me.'
Father pauses, his chin trembling as he forces a self-deprecating
smile. This is costing *him* just as much, she realises. 'But first
you have to know some ugly facts. Then you can make up your
mind.

'You know how people have always accused me of selling
them out for bribes? Turns out they were underestimating the
damage I helped cause. All without my knowledge, though.
And all orchestrated by the collective efforts of the Yun Ju.'

Liz listens with growing horror as her father recounts the
story of his phage-spraying blimp-jet, the disinformation
campaigns turning the populace against the very food needed to
keep them from starvation, the brain-drain, the technology
embargoes, the plans to keep Earth dependent at any cost, even
if it means famine and death. All run from and master-minded
by the Yun Ju.

Liz touches the visor to pause the message. She's breathing
hard, her hands shaking and moist with sweat. Can this possibly
be true? Yes, it can. As much as she wants to believe no human
being would do that to another, she knows enough of history to
realise that they would, and they did. The countless wars fought
for the personal ambitions of deluded leaders. The indifference
of the rich to the suffering of the poor, equally true for individuals and nations—especially when those who suffered were
nameless and far away. The climate and resource-destroying
actions of entire generations when everyone already knew how
close they were to the brink. Destiny, wanting to impose their
rule by manipulating people's minds. Nothing has changed
since then—*they* haven't changed, they were still the same
selfish humans playing the same selfish games. Even right here,
on the stations.

What about her father, though? Could he be complicit,
despite his denial? He wouldn't be telling her, then. And
anyway, she can't believe he'd ever do anything like that.

Despite everything, she's always known that he is a believer, that he thinks he's doing what he must to save the world from famine. It's not why she hates him. She hates him because he's sunk to using the same tools as the dictators he's enabled. Bribes and exploitation, anything to keep his precious Alliance going. Even as she kept trying to tell him that people were dying, from hunger or at the hands of the corrupt governments he paid to keep in power. She trembles at the memory of the day when she first confronted him. She was fifteen or sixteen, a printout of a report in her hand, a journalistic expose on his actions. He'd been her hero until that day; he was saving the world, and she couldn't have been prouder. She was sure he'd set everything straight, prove to her that the accusations were wrong—but he just stood there, pale and numb while she screamed louder and louder, desperate for him to deny them. Her mother led her away eventually, disillusioned and sobbing. Liz left for college soon after. She grew to despise him even more then, not just for his actions but for the way his name wrecked her own life, his shadow following her everywhere she went. The pain is still with her, even now. The shame and the humiliation each time anyone spoke her name. Maybe even more so because she realised it was her father's twisted way of trying to do the right thing. He wasn't even corrupt, just deluded.

Liz shakes her head, pulling herself back to the present, back to the message. If this is what the Yun Ju is doing now, how much worse will it get with Destiny back in charge? Her arm feels heavy as she touches the visor to resume the recording. Now she understands the change she saw on her father's face: the pain and disappointment, the crushing disillusion not unlike what she'd felt on the day of their argument. But there's also the same stubborn resolve that somehow, he must solve all the world's problems just by himself.

'I am working on a plan—that's all I can tell you at the moment. If it works, we'll put an end to both problems: the Yun

Ju and Destiny. I...' He grimaces, looking for the right words. 'You are in a unique position to help us, but it will cost you. The Yun Ju... it won't be the same afterwards. Your future won't be as you imagined. But the stakes couldn't be higher. You know that, or you wouldn't have called me. The future of humanity is in our hands.'

He sucks in a deep breath, as if stopping himself from saying too much. His lips quiver in an attempt at a smile that doesn't quite make it. 'If you decide to help, pass the message to the person who contacted you. If not, then I beg you not to reveal their identity to anyone. I hope... I hope things will turn out well. For you, and for all of us.'

The message cuts off abruptly on the intake of his breath as if there was more he decided to edit out before sending. More compromising details, or promises, or warnings. Liz leans against the wall, then slides to the floor, her thoughts in turmoil. What's going on? A Yun Ju plot, Destiny coming back, her father's secret plan to put an end to it all? And how does Kene fit into it? Is her father a master conspirator now, running some secret cabal? That doesn't even begin to make sense. And yet, there is his message, and there is Kene still asleep on the recliner. And the weight of a decision on Liz's shoulders.

She removes the visor, her hand dropping heavily to the floor. The noise is enough to make Kene stir. She turns, scanning the room till her gaze finds Liz.

'Finished?'

'Yes. Have you... have you seen it?'

Kene shakes her head. She pulls herself up from the recliner and stretches. 'It's one view only. It's all gone now, erased.'

Liz stares. This *is* a conspiracy. And Kene and her father are in on it. 'Do you know at all what it's about?'

'Not this... aspect of it. But I know some things.' Kene shrugs, but the gesture is forced and her gaze flitting. She probably still hates Liz and resents having to come here.

Liz scrambles to her feet. 'Do you... still believe what Alejandro said?'

'Nope. I figured it didn't make sense soon after. Would have told you, if you'd let me.'

'I'm sorry.'

Kene shrugs again. She puts out her hand for the visor. 'I need it back.'

It's surprisingly painful for Liz to give up the gadget, even if it's nothing more than *The Warriors of Azkend* now. It is still the only proof that she hasn't imagined this whole thing. She sighs as she hands over the visor and watches Kene slide it back into her pocket.

Liz has so many questions—but Kene's taken a big risk coming to see her. It's not fair to ask her to incriminate herself more, not before Liz confirms her commitment to the 'cause,' whatever it is. And that's not something she can do, at least not yet. There are too many unknowns, too many things she doesn't understand.

Kene looks up at her then, expectation in her wide black eyes. She wants an answer. She might not know what Father has asked of Liz, but she's clearly expecting a message.

'I... I need to think. About everything.'

Kene's lip curls. Liz can almost hear the *I told you so* she's going to pass back to her father or whoever else she's working with.

'Let's get together soon, though,' Liz adds quickly. 'For a coffee or...'

She trails off at Kene's loud snort. 'Sure. Let's grab a coffee one day. You can show me around.'

Kene turns on her heel and leaves without another look at Liz. The door closes on her with such finality, it feels like a slap. Well, to hell with Kene. What does she know? She hasn't lived her life knowing her father was an enabler to the most despicable dictators and tyrants. Having to hide—

Liz shakes her head. No, she's just feeling sorry for herself, and it's time she stopped. Kene's life could have been even worse, for all she knew. And this isn't about either of them. It's bigger and more important than anything in their own little lives.

She drops down on the recliner, still warm from Kene's body, and closes her eyes.

What kind of help would her father want? He said the Yun Ju wouldn't be the same afterwards. That includes New Hope and Renewal. And her job here. So, whatever he's planning will either be impossible to keep secret and will get her fired, or... Crap, she's still thinking too small. Renewal is Destiny. If things go well, there will not be Renewal anymore.

The others here may move to other stations—Essa, Lars, Ag, the others on the Shield team. Not the graduates, they don't have full residency. And certainly not she, even if she somehow managed to conceal her involvement. She's still her father's daughter.

She sits up. That's the problem, though—she is still his daughter, and he is still the same stubborn man, stuck in the same old ways. After twenty years, where has it got him? Spraying the phage on the people he swore to protect. What's the chance this time his plans will turn out better?

Shit. Liz rubs her eyes with her fists, wet with frustration and anger—at her father for being what he is, and at herself for getting so stuck in her pain she snapped at anyone who tried to touch it. She shouldn't have shut Kene out. Hell, she shouldn't have shut her father out, she should have kept trying to convince him to change his ways, to see the truth. Instead, she's made it all about her. And now Destiny are back and there's no one who can stop them.

She winces at the ping of a private message. Her eyes focus on the clock on her lenses. Somehow, it's seven thirty in the morning already, the lights in her quarters brightening to day mode. She opens her messages and gasps.

It's from Ranath.

Good morning, Elizabeth. Do join me for breakfast.

The projection table in Ranath's office is back to looking like something made of grey stone. Now it's set up with an exquisite breakfast of yoghurt, fruit, and pastries laid out on porcelain platters. A serving bot hovers nearby with a selection of cold and hot drinks. There are only two settings, though, and two tall grey chairs.

Liz looks around, confused, when Ranath appears from the far end of the room, the privacy bubble dissolving behind her.

'Good morning, Liz. Thank you for coming so quickly. I'm rather hungry!'

Liz nods, biting her lip before she mentions that she didn't think she had a choice.

Ranath gestures to the chairs. 'Please, don't look so worried. It's just a chat. And I think we're overdue for some time together.'

Liz takes the place she indicates. She accepts the tisane the drone offers and makes herself take a sip while Ranath selects the fruit to mix in her yogurt. The drone fills her cup with coffee, and she wrinkles her nose in disappointment.

'Decaffeinated. I had my medi-bot decommissioned, but it seems to have passed its notes to the house systems. They are getting too clever for my liking.' Ranath gestures to Liz's empty plate. 'No food?'

'Maybe later.'

Ranath takes a spoonful of her yoghurt. She seems relaxed, but there's something edgy in her movements, her voice slightly higher and her gestures too wide, as if she has to work hard to create that appearance. She looks tired, too, her lips downturned whenever she forgets to make herself smile. Destiny must be keeping her busy.

'We really should have talked earlier,' Ranath says. 'I should have made the time, especially after what you've done for us with your storm forecast. And to congratulate you on your promotion. Now it just looks like I've summoned you to talk about... I guess you know what.'

'Why don't you tell me?' Liz says. She's not going to reveal anything Ranath doesn't already know, so she might as well try to find out how much that is.

Ranath smiles, and this time it seems genuine if a bit patronising, like a master player approving of their apprentice's move. 'Why did you go to the cryo-section? We monitor that area, you know. I wouldn't have made anything of it, except for how you reacted. You looked... upset?'

'Who's in the pods?'

'You know the identities are confidential. We've had a lot of new arrivals, though, with all the Tian Gong refugees.'

'They would be going into storage, though. Here or on the ship. That's not what I saw.'

'What did you see?'

Liz hides her face in her cup, gathering her thoughts. She can keep pretending ignorance, but that won't work long against Ranath. And if she knows about Liz's visit to the cryo-section, her father was probably correct assuming their conversation would have been recorded. She gains nothing by lying to Ranath—and if there's the slightest chance that her mentor isn't part of Destiny, then she might be much better placed than her father to fight them.

Liz swallows, her voice hoarse. 'I saw pods being moved. Presumably to be revived. And I know this station has links to Destiny, so I drew my conclusions.'

She expects Ranath to laugh or mock her suspicions away, but she only nods, as if she's found a solution to a puzzle.

Then her face turns stone serious. 'Your observations were correct—but not your conclusions. We're not waking anyone up. And the pods you saw have nothing to do with Destiny.'

Liz hesitates. These are just words, and as much as she wants them to be the truth, Ranath has all the reasons to lie. Time to try something from Ranath's own playbook: a question hard enough to make her mask crack. 'Was your father in Destiny?'

Ranath's lips quiver. She returns to her yoghurt, her cheeks just a shade paler.

'He was, wasn't he?'

'My father is very much dead. I barely knew him.'

Liz pulls in a breath, the cup in her hands shaking so badly small drops of tisane sprinkle on her arms. She's simultaneously surprised by her courage and dismayed by how effectively she is burning bridges with the very person who holds her future in her hand. But she's crossed that line now, and for once she won't be thinking only about her own life. She must know. 'Are you in Destiny?'

This time Ranath gives her a small smile. 'I was.'

'Was?'

'Destiny is dead. A closed chapter. They lost their teeth and their minds.'

Ranath holds her gaze, her expression open, the smile still on her lips, something between triumph and regret, like one might feel for a fallen enemy. This is exactly what Liz hoped to hear, what she'd have prayed to hear if she knew how to pray.

Too exactly. She got what she came here for, served on a porcelain platter with a topping of honey and yoghurt. A perfect lie, cooked up just for her.

Ranath sees right through her, of course. 'I can't prove my claims about Destiny, if that's what you're wondering. But I can answer your question about why we're moving the pods. And that will also explain why I'm telling you anything at all.'

She seems to waver, measuring Liz with an appraising glance as if trying to assess her worth. Then she bobs her head, decision made. A new expression pours over her face: excitement, exhilaration so genuine it's contagious. Ranath jumps to her feet, her fingers tapping up commands against her thigh. Five small drones approach an instant later, then a bigger one, which unfolds itself into a flat surface. Within moments, their breakfast is transferred onto that new table, the arrangement equally elegant even if a bit more crowded. The stone table becomes a projection surface again, glowing as it fires up the emitters.

Ranath turns to her with a toothy grin. 'This, my dear Elizabeth, is Ark.'

The projection consolidates above the table: an asteroid or a very small moon, round but too irregular to be a planet or anything artificial. It rotates slowly, revealing several darkened spots, mostly at the equator. Ranath makes a slicing move with her hand, and the rock splits, the top half of the projection vanishing. The cross section reveals layers of concentric circles surrounding an inner cavity about a fifth of the rock's diameter. There, the circular arrangement breaks into criss-crossing lines or membranes. Liz leans closer, and at the same time Ranath zooms in on a section of the rock. Liz gasps. The concentric circles—these are decks, like the rings of the station. Several are coloured green, with an inscribed legend marking them as agro zones. One, close to the central cavity, is blue, apparently filled entirely with water. The top layers are machines and storage, secured under a thick layer of protective rock. In between sit— Liz tries to count but gives up as her eyes slide from one exciting detail to the next—at least seven habitat decks, complete with parks and gardens and even just open space for humans and animals to roam. The legend doesn't give the scale, but just the number of habitable decks tells her that the rock must be huge, a level of magnitude larger than the biggest station.

Liz steps back from the projection, her mouth dry as she tries to find the right question. 'Does this exist? Is it real?'

'Not in this form—not yet at least. This is what it will look like once it's done. But it's very real.'

'Where is it? When will it be done? Who's going to—'

Ranath raises her arms to stop the deluge. 'It's a small moon of Saturn. It won't be completed for decades, but it doesn't need to be finished to be habitable. It just needs enough to support the settlers. When it's completed, it will be fully self-sustaining.'

'Wait. You said Saturn?'

Ranath grins again. 'Yes. Far enough, I hope.'

Liz keeps staring. Ranath's been so proud of what she's built with Renewal. Can she really be planning to abandon it? Why?

'I think you need to do a bit more explaining,' she ends up saying.

'I'm pretty sure you can figure it out for yourself. Have you been checking the news?'

'Which news?'

'Either. Both. Any. It's either bad or horrible. Earth is eating itself alive. The north is hoarding the food, and the south is already on the brink. It's a matter of years before the whole thing implodes. And before some rogue nation learns how to build rockets again. Because they blame us for everything, as if the Yun Ju poisoned their crop.'

Does she know about the phage? Liz shivers at the possibility. If Ranath knows, if she did nothing to stop it, then she's as guilty as the others.

Ranath grimaces. 'There are rumours—I don't know how true they are—that some in the Yun Ju have been... less than helpful. I did try to intervene, several times, but the Council believes it's the only way to keep us safe. That Earth still has weapons, or will have, if we let them. Most in the Yun Ju believe it's a matter of self-preservation. We depend on the planet too much to pull our finger off the trigger, so to speak.'

'Do you believe that?'

'I think they are both beyond redemption. I think the Council is right that Yun Ju will not survive if the planet gets stronger. So, they will both escalate to more and more despicable actions, each trying to suffocate the other one. And the same will happen on Earth between the food-growing and the manufacturing nations, between those who have and those who need. There will be wars, deaths in the billions, then reckoning and reconciliation, like after the scarcity wars, followed by a few decades of peace and cooperation before the cycle starts again, with a new crop of villains and victims.'

Ranath turns to the projection, her cheeks flushed and beads of sweat on her forehead. Liz hasn't considered her capable of such emotion. Liz is trembling, too, as if standing at the edge of something momentous, an understanding that will change everything.

'They will never change,' Ranath says. 'They've had hundreds of chances over the millennia, and it always comes back to the same.'

'What then?' Liz asks, her voice breaking.

'We let them be. Let them sort out their problems because we can't change anything. We start again. On our Saturn base at first, and then—who knows? Space is big.'

Liz follows her gaze to the projection. The image zooms in, focusing on one of the decks. An icon blinks on her lenses, requesting access. She blinks in confirmation, and suddenly she is there, standing in an open field surrounded by distant trees. A stream rolls by, cascading over a rocky outcrop into a pond, or a lake. A fish jumps, spraying a rainbow of droplets. Farther out, a rowing boat rocks as two people push off a small pier. She turns back to the field, watching couples and families walk or run, dogs chasing balls, birds flapping across the sky—not sky: a white surface, bright but not blinding, with the perfect light quality of a sunny day. But what really takes her breath away is the space: there's no visible edge to it, but what she can see is kilometres across, with bluish outlines of what looks like a city in the far distance.

This is a world. Not a planet, not Earth, but close enough to be as good as. If they can really build this, if they can move there and start again...

Liz sways, breathless. This is it, the answer. Ranath's right. They can't fix Earth or the Yun Ju. They can patch holes, darn, and repair, but the fabric is too thin to save. It will fray again until it unravels itself into war and chaos. That's why her father has failed, despite all his good intensions. That's why Yun Ju has failed, still tied down to the planet and its heritage. This world was spent, finished. And thanks to Ranath, they had the chance to start anew.

Liz meets Ranath's gaze, mirror smiles pouring onto their faces.

'I think I'll have some breakfast,' Liz says. 'And a lot more questions.'

TWENTY-SEVEN

RANATH

Ranath spends the next thirty minutes answering Liz's questions about Ark. She shouldn't waste so much time, except she's actually enjoying it, finally talking to someone as enthralled by the idea as she is. It was a risk revealing Ark to her, but with Nevsky and Richardson now in cahoots, she needs someone with a chance to dig out what Nevsky is up to. It seems she made the right call: Liz just gets it, exactly as Ranath has hoped. They have both tried to make things work in the world they've inherited, both have lost their fathers to the cause, even if Liz's loss is only symbolic. Ranath's sure the pain is the same—or maybe worse. At least her father could never disappoint her. For a moment she wonders if she'd ever feel that kinship if she had a daughter. In this case, maybe it's better to choose one's family?

Liz stuffs her mouth with a honey-glazed pastry. 'So, how many people do you want to start with? And where will they come from? You said the best of the best...'

'Sounds familiar, doesn't it?'

'The Academy, yes. But—'

Ranath smirks. 'Have you ever met anyone who wasn't selected to stay on the Yun Ju?'

Liz tilts her head, confused. 'Actually—'

'Oh, they are there. Those too selfish or obnoxious to keep. Like your dear friend Alejandro.' Liz huffs loudly, and Ranath continues, 'The truth is, we keep those whose contribution is needed right now, like you. And we keep those good enough. But those truly exceptional, they get a choice. If they agree, they go into the pods till we're ready.'

Liz's mouth drops open. 'So, you—'

'I've been collecting the best humanity has to offer for a decade now. Scientists, engineers, artists, philosophers. Both Academies are my main source, but I have scouts searching for outstanding individuals. Gifted children from deprived backgrounds or conflict areas. No, I don't steal them!' She laughs at the minute tightening of Liz's brows. 'They get a stipend to go to school, enough to sustain their family, if they have any. When they are old enough, we have a chat. If they agree, their future is secure, and their family taken care of. I haven't met any yet who didn't think they got a dream deal.'

'Is that who's in the pods?'

'Exactly.'

'And if you're not waking them up, that means you're moving them, right?'

'To the ship, *The Covenant*.' Ranath sighs. 'That's the bad news. I think—no, I know—that other players in the Yun Ju are mounting an attack on me. Yes, it's linked to the Destiny rumours. I could explain, but it's not the best use of our time. The thing is, they don't care about Destiny. They just want to bring me down for their financial gain. If they're successful, I'll lose Renewal, and the funding I need to finish Ark.'

Liz freezes with the cup halfway to her lips, horrified. 'What?'

'I haven't lost yet; I'm still fighting. But I have to consider the worst-case scenario. And that means being ready to send everything and everyone ahead to Ark.'

'But—you said it wasn't ready?'

'It isn't. We have a small base, though, and the miners are getting it operational. It's not optimal, we'll be losing time by working on the habitat before finishing the main structure, but we have no choice. We can keep people in cold-sleep for decades, but most of the tech we used to send fauna and flora to the colonies either no longer functions or has been removed from the ships. Anyway. It's complicated, but we have enough for them to start, even if it's not how I imagined. Once they are there, they will declare independence and I will cede the ownership to them. That way nobody can touch them, no matter what happens to Renewal or me.'

'Wait, what do you mean "them"? You're coming, too, right?'

Ranath sighs again. 'I've always hoped to be able to join eventually, but my mission is to provide resources: money, assemblers, bio-matter, anything they'll need to make Ark fully autonomous. That's still the plan, but... Well, let's not talk about the worst-case scenarios until we have to.'

Liz is ready with another question, probably about her own place in Ranath's plans, but both Min Woo and Ester have already pinged her that they need to talk to her, and a text message from Richardson has just popped into her mail. This conversation has been exceedingly useful, though—Liz has embraced the idea with more zeal than Ranath dared to hope for. Understandable, on second thoughts: the woman has spent her life escaping her legacy only to have it catch up with her once again. Ark offers the final escape, for both of them.

'I've got to return to my duties,' Ranath says, reaching for the last helping of pickled pears. 'But... there's one more thing.'

'Yes?'

'I'm not going to lie, and you've probably figured it out

already: I've heard your conversation with your father. You made a valiant effort to hide it, but... Well, you should probably stick to solar storms.' She gives Liz her most motherly smile, and the other woman chuckles self-consciously. 'We know your father is planning something—we knew before your conversation, so don't worry about revealing that. He's made several uncharacteristic moves recently, like accepting a large bribe from Liberty for additional supply of fruit, something he's never done before. I know, because tracking the Alliance is a big part of my survival strategy. Your father is one of those misguided souls who keep trying to fix the world, not realising it's beyond his—beyond anyone's—ability to fix.'

Liz tries to keep her face neutral, but there's no trace of denial in her posture. Ranath's guessed right that attacking her father directly would be a bad move. Liz might think she hates him, but he's still her father.

'And now he's sending "humanitarian aid" to Tian Gong's cultists,' Ranath continues. 'Something that will probably get him fired, if the media reaction is anything to go by. So yes, it makes me think he's got a "plan". One that will probably fail, but not before it makes a huge mess.'

Liz doesn't say anything. She's unsettled, though, so at least part of what Ranath's said is news to her.

'I have no idea what he's planning, and no interest in it, really, unless it affects us in any way. But the timing is unfortunate. It could help us—or it could expose us in the worst possible way. It could destroy our one chance for Ark.' Ranath glances at the projection still hovering above the table, then leans across the remains of their breakfast and puts her hand on the young woman's arm. 'I don't wish him any harm, Liz. I might even not do anything to stop him. But I must know his intentions—and you are the only person who can help me.'

'I don't know what he's planning,' Liz blurts out. 'I have no idea.'

'I believe you. But you might be able to find out.'

'How? It's not like he's just going to tell me.'

Ranath nods. 'This is, indeed, a quandary. But I might think of a way if I knew you were willing to help me.'

Liz bites her lip for a moment. Her eyes shoot to the projection of Ark, and something in her face breaks. 'I think you are right. Earth is broken, and the Yun Ju... No, Ark's the best—the only—way forward. I will do what I can to make it work.'

Min Woo and Ester are in her office the moment the door closes behind Elizabeth.

'The first shipment has reached Liberty,' Min Woo says, snatching a pastry from the retreating drones. 'The second batch will leave in a couple of hours, when they are closest to that manufacturing cube.'

Ranath blinks on her mail files and retrieves Richardson's message. It's only two lines confirming he's received the assemblers and that he 'looks forward to fruitful collaboration.' No complaints and no gloating, which makes it sound like he means it. She is being useful, and as long as she stays that way, he may leave her alone to focus on his actual rival: Li Qiang. That would be good news, except for how the Caretakers are going to react to this change. They want to use Richardson to destroy her, not work with her. If she's lucky, that will make them turn against Richardson—but she doesn't believe in luck. More likely, they will search for a new tool with which to hit her. Li Qiang? The Fujikawas, still furious at her for cancelling Harmony's assembler deal? Any of them would oblige. The Caretakers won't let go until they get rid of her and reclaim their money. She really is running out of time.

'How are we doing with the pods?'

'People are already in place; we're moving the bio-containers now. Also, Tarkovsky's confirmed that the latest batch of assemblers have arrived. He didn't sound too surprised at the numbers, so I think he's figured out what they are really doing there.'

'Have a chat with him, Min Woo. See how much it would cost to keep them quiet. Or threaten to fire them, whichever you find more effective—as long as you don't actually fire them, because we do need them.'

'I've already hinted at something along those lines. I'm also preparing the next batch of our assemblers for transfer to *The Covenant*, but it's getting tricky. We now have three spy satellites circling our production cubes, so it's next to impossible to hide any movement. Incidentally, one of the satellites happened to encounter a random piece of debris, but they've replaced it so quickly I didn't bother with the rest.'

Ranath chuckles. 'Good on you for trying, though. At least we keep them busy. Now, route all future shipments through here, including those going to Liberty or Tian Gong. It won't fool them entirely, but will make tracking the numbers more difficult.'

Min Woo taps something on his wrist band, then nods. 'One more thing: the Alliance is sending their first "humanitarian aid"—and Nevsky is coming along. Just him and three minor employees I've never heard of.'

'This *is* odd...' Ranath leans on the chair by Min Woo's usual workstation, her face scrunched in thought. 'Is he going on to Liberty?'

'He's requested transport to Tian Gong, that's all we know.'

'He's been trying to contact the Sun Seers, too,' Ester says from behind her screen. 'A chain of unencrypted messages about the health risks to those remaining on the station, asking for a meeting, and so on. As far as I can see, he got one reply inviting him to join them.'

Ranath slides into the chair, thinking. Nevsky wouldn't be delivering the aid in person—unless his presence was key to his plan, not just his shipments. It's possible that he will transfer to another station once he leaves Tian Gong. Maybe that's it: he just hopes to get fired and stay on Liberty. No, Richardson wouldn't allow it so soon; he needs Nevsky to manage his fruit business at least until the new agro platforms are ready. Whatever Nevsky is planning must be connected to Tian Gong itself.

'Did he contact any other Tian Gong residents? Or Nebu?' Ranath asks.

Ester taps something on her screen, then wrinkles her nose with disapproval. 'He did contact Nebu, actually. I wonder why it wasn't flagged... Oh, it's just a copy of the message he sent to the "Enlit Prelate Levine" asking for "consideration of his followers' wellbeing." He's really persistent about trying to save them.'

Ranath's head shoots up. 'Or just getting them out of the station.'

The three of them exchange glances.

'That could well be the case,' Min Woo says.

'But why?' Ester asks.

Ranath sucks her teeth. What are the options? He could be trying to take over the station—but to what purpose? Nobody's going to let him keep it, and she's got all the Sharks.

'What does he really want?' she asks aloud. 'He's spent his life manoeuvring and cutting deals for the Alliance. Suddenly, he jumps ship and starts working for Richardson—which I don't believe for a second.'

'Speaking of which,' Ester says, 'his actual ship, the blimp-jet he got from the Council, has been grounded for weeks. It's never been down for that long.'

Has Nevsky figured something out? Ranath's not sure how the Council or Liberty or whoever were using the blimp-jet they've gifted the Alliance, but that gift had to have some thick strings attached. And if Nevsky has finally caught up to how he's been used...

What would she do in his shoes? That level of betrayal is hard to imagine, but oh, she'd find a quick way to send the perpetrators to oblivion. She's not a murderer, but anyone has their limits. Even Nevsky. And—

She jumps to her feet. That's it. Nevsky is very much not a cold-blooded killer. That's why he wants the cultists to leave. Because he wants to destroy Tian Gong.

Ranath starts to pace, ideas taking shape in her mind. Why would he target Tian Gong? It would make sense if the Sharks were still there—they protect the elevators and the stations. Destroying them would leave the entire Yun Ju open to attack. And even someone wanting to spare the cultists could consider the Sharks a valid military target. Not to mention that sixty years ago the Sharks shot his own father.

She shakes her head. No, he must know that the Sharks have left Tian Gong; it's been talked about all over the Yun Ju after the storm, just when he was here. Still, the idea has wedged itself in her mind. Nevsky may have planned to attack the Sharks, because without them, the Yun Ju is vulnerable. Because that's what he really wants: to destroy the Yun Ju.

Ranath stops. That would explain his abrupt change, that sudden 'cooperation' he's struck with Richardson. It gives Nevsky a pretext to travel to Tian Gong. But what's the endgame? Tian Gong is just one station. Even if he managed to weaken it beyond repair, it will do nothing against the rest of the Yun Ju. Unless he's bringing some kind of contagion...

'Min Woo, Ester, find out who the other three coming with him are—specifically, their specialities. They might be virologists or engineers or, who knows, explosives experts.'

'What are you thinking?'

'I think he's trying to attack Tian Gong. Possibly the rest of the Yun Ju. I don't know how, though. Those three others might give us a clue.'

'On it,' Min Woo says, and turns to leave.

'Wait. Are Nebu's maintenance teams on the station?'

'Day time only. They take turns to limit radiation exposure until the generators are back online.'

Ranath nods. 'I'm going to ask Major Par to join them. Mr Nevsky will need some help unloading his wares, won't he?'

TWENTY-EIGHT

JASON

Jason checks his messages, probably for the tenth time since he boarded the elevator that morning. Still nothing beyond the Enlit Prelate's invitation to join 'the selected.' Apparently, the honour befalls all those who've spent any time in orbit and thus received their dose of radiation, though the prelate doesn't put it in quite those terms.

Three engineers have joined him, the three Watch specialists who've worked with Aya on the outlines of their plan, now officially employed with the Alliance. They work quietly in the corner of the cabin, finalising the details. It's not an easy task when their communication is reduced to code words and shortcuts, and all their electronics shielded so that the elevator's systems—and whoever is monitoring them—wouldn't get access. Judging from their expressions and half-hearted nods, they are making slow progress. Hopefully, not too slow. They have already passed the middle of their ascent.

Out of desperation—or boredom—he resends his message to William Avery, the monk Jason met on the elevator on his trip to Liberty. The icon changes from *sent* to *received* to *acknowledged.* Jason frowns. Either this is new, or he's failed to notice the *acknowledged* part before, too impatient for replies. But this *is* a reply. If Avery had no intention of talking to Jason, he could just ignore the message, not acknowledge it. Khalil suggested that the Sun Seers communications may be restricted by the church elders. This could be Avery's way of getting around them. Jason could be misreading it, but he loses nothing by following the hunch. He dictates another message, confirming the docking arrangements and asking for help with unloading the provisions. That should make a good excuse if Avery is caught sneaking away to meet him—if that's indeed what the man wants.

Jason sighs. He's checked his other device, too, the secure one Khalil has procured from the Watch. It's to be used for the most confidential messages—like one telling him that Annalie—Liz—has offered her help. No such news yet, and as much as he'd like to believe, it's probably not coming. He knows that she watched his recording the same night he sent it. He didn't expect an immediate response—or at least, he didn't admit that even to himself—but by now she's had time to consider her options. She could have asked for proof of what he'd told her, could have requested details of his plan. Anything would be better than this deafening silence. What's stopping her? She realises the danger Destiny poses or she wouldn't have called him first. Did she just hope to deliver the news and have him deal with it? Or... He drops his head. It has to be the other thing, his confession about his part in spreading the phage and enabling the Yun Ju. No wonder she's disgusted. He's failed everyone. He failed her mother and failed her, and all his efforts only made things worse.

He winces as his wrist band buzzes with a message. Not the secret device, just his regular mail, but the message is marked as encrypted and without a sender ID. He touches the icon. He's wearing contacts now, on Khalil's insistence: a fully external device that he can extract at a moment's notice. His skin still crawls at the thought of them, but the practicality is undeniable.

His vision blurs, and a text message in English appears hovering in the air in front of him:

For your attention, a selection of files you will find interesting. This is a fragment of the cache in my possession. I believe you can put it to good use.

Jason reads the text again, but there's nothing more. No signature, either. Another icon appears below, inviting him to view the attached documents. He reaches out to unroll the attachment but stops at the last moment. This could be a way to put a tracker on his system, maybe even on his new contacts, external or not. The elevator's comms node would be easy enough to hack; that's why the engineers are so careful. Whatever the secret message is, it can wait till they reach the station and deploy the signal jammers.

The shuttle door opens onto a dim corridor, lit only with fluorescent emergency strips in the walls. They've docked at the cargo port in Tian Gong's axis, apparently a standard procedure for stations in a state of emergency. The lack of centrifugal 'gravity' will certainly help with unloading the provisions. Cargo drones should be waiting for them here, but Jason's not sure what they will actually find. Tian Gong is not entirely abandoned; apart from the Sun Seers, there are maintenance crews working to repair the damage. They still shuttle back and forth to New Hope, though, avoiding radiation damage for these last few days before the shield generators come back online.

Jason floats into the transit bay, scanning the area for drones or even a loading cart they could use. The door on the far side opens. Jason peers into the murk, hoping to see Avery arriving to help—and to talk. But the sight of the silver figures entering the bay makes him stop. Sky Sharks, their visors closed, their skin suits like silver bullets. He shivers as they approach, his own gaunt figure reflecting in their helmets, floating helplessly like a moth frozen in resin.

The lead Shark opens their visor. A female face, with short hair and space black eyes. 'Mr Nevsky?'

He nods, his throat too dry for speech.

'We're here to help you unload. And take your stuff down to the Sun Seers' deck, if they let us.' The woman glides towards him, a small smile cracking her lips. 'They've not been exactly welcoming, but we can always try. I'm Par, by the way. Major Par, or just Par, whichever you prefer.'

'Jason.' He turns to the three engineers lingering by the airlock. He'd rather not introduce them, so it's fortunate that Par hasn't introduced any of her people. 'We've got help! That should speed things up.'

Even from the distance, he can see the engineers' postures relaxing.

Par chuckles. 'We do tend to have this effect on grounders...'

And for a good reason, Jason wants to add, but this would be a very bad time to bring up his father's death. He puts on a smile instead—and makes a mental note to remember that Par is unpleasantly observant.

The woman signals to her people, and they follow the engineers back to the shuttle, four bulky cargo drones floating behind them.

'I was hoping some of the Seers would come as well,' he says. 'Have you been in touch with them?'

'Nobody is in touch with them, Mr Nev— Jason. Or rather, *they* are not in touch with anybody.'

'How do you handle deliveries? I mean, they've received provisions before, haven't they?'

Par sighs. 'Some. I won't lie, Jason; I'd rather not expose my people to radiation to feed those who choose to stay here and die slowly. It's not fair on those who do want to live.'

'That's why I'm here, actually. To figure out if they've made that choice or have been forced to.'

'They are all adults. Nobody on the inside has weapons. I can't see—'

'You haven't dealt much with cults, have you?'

Par shrugs. 'Not my area of expertise, no.'

'The whole point, the thing that makes a cult a cult and not a religion, is in the way they manipulate and control their—'

Jason breaks off as Par spins around. Her visor slides down and a snub-nozzled gun appears in her hand, out of nowhere. In the corners of Jason's vision, two other Sharks appear back in the bay, sliding along the walls.

They've seen something. Someone. The person Jason was hoping to see.

'Avery?' he calls, praying this school of Sharks is less trigger-happy than the one that killed his father. 'William? Is it you?'

'Yeah! We've come to help unload.'

Par raises her visor, but the weapon is still in her hand. 'You know this person?'

'I do. He's not dangerous. You said yourself, they don't have weapons.'

Par nods, and her gun seems to vanish into the life support pack on her back. 'You're right. Total overreaction. I just don't like people slinking in on me.'

Jason gives her an understanding smile, as if anything in his life experience could make him relate to her statement. Still, she may have just betrayed something about her intentions: even the Sharks shouldn't be so jumpy, especially here, on their home station, and when they're the only ones carrying guns. Not unless they expect trouble. It's not a coincidence then that they've showed up to greet him. Somebody has sent them. Not Richardson—Jason's cargo contains only the aid package, a last-minute change of heart with which both Volkov and Richardson reluctantly agreed. For this first delivery, the risk is too big that someone would want to check the contents. It seems he's been right. The Sharks may be trying to examine his cargo, or even worse—his actions. That's going to make his job way more difficult.

But that's something to worry about later. Jason turns towards the source of the voice, a pile of crates stowed at the opposite end of the bay. 'It's okay, William. Thank you for coming. We can use some help.'

Three figures emerge into the light, Avery and two others following a few metres behind. Their movements laboured, they propel themselves by the handholds mounted into the ceiling. Jason keeps a smile plastered to his face, his lips tight to stop himself from gasping. Avery still looks almost like the man he met on his way to the Yun Ju, though his face has acquired a haggard edge, with shadows and angles where there used to be dimples. The pair behind him are another story: gaunt, almost skeletal, with bald patches of missing hair, their yellow robes stained with something that makes Jason think of oozing wounds.

Par gasps, but shuts her mouth as Jason shoots her a quick glance.

'Thank you for coming,' he repeats. 'We brought food and medical supplies.'

'We are fine,' Avery says.

The three Seers glance from Jason to Par to the other Sharks still lingering by the airlock.

'Of course you are.'

'We came to help,' Avery repeats. 'All three of us.'

Par raises an eyebrow, but Jason gives her a minute head shake. *Stay out of it.* She sniffs but doesn't comment, her expression expectant.

'Why don't we get started, then?' Jason points to the airlock. 'The crates are still in the shuttle.'

When the Seers start to move, Jason glides towards Avery

and puts his hand on the man's shoulder. The others pause, but Jason waves his arm to urge them on. They seem to understand because they continue towards the shuttle, leaving the two of them alone, with Par watching from some distance away.

Jason rotates to bring himself face to face with Avery. The man's shoulders tremble under his touch. Avery is a giant of a man, but now he seems feather-light, and not just because of the absence of gravity. Jason pulls himself closer. The man's panting breath hits his face, hot and sour.

Jason taps his wrist band: three, then two, then three taps again to activate the signal jammer. His earbuds buzz with low level static, then cut off.

Avery winces. 'What's that?'

'A comms jammer. They can't hear us now.'

'They can't?'

'No. How are you, William?'

'But they…' Avery trails off, his head tilting from side to side, his brows wrinkled in expectation. Then his eyes widen. 'There's this high-pitched noise they send when they disapprove. It's like cutting your skull in half. But it's not here now.'

'They can't hear you.'

'You are right.' It takes another moment for Avery to continue. 'They're not letting anyone leave. The doors are locked, only the Elders have the codes. The comms are blocked, too. It all goes through the Elders. And…'

Jason waits. Avery shivers again, but then nods, as if pulling himself together.

'Nobody has seen the Elders in weeks. Even before the storm. They're all shut away in the inner rooms. We're not allowed to talk about them, either. Most of the others are too far gone to notice anymore. But a few of us still have our senses.'

'Do you want to leave?'

Avery's muscles tense. He pulls in a heavy breath, but ends up shaking his head. 'I can't. They'll punish the others if we don't return. We only got out because you asked for help. But we have to be back in forty minutes, or they'll punish everyone. Us, too, when we're away from your jammer.'

Jason wants to swear. This is worse than he expected. How could this kind of abuse ever be allowed to happen? But then, the Elders paid good rent, all from the donations of their Earth-bound brethren. It's happened before, will happen again. Nothing new under the Sun. He sniffs at the damn pun. Well, this is one case of abuse he can be sure to end very soon.

He squeezes Avery's shoulder. 'Go back and don't say anything. Do what they expect you to do. I'll get you all out very soon. That's a promise.'

Avery meets his gaze, the big man's eyes moist and expectant. He nods once, then pushes himself away, towards his comrades approaching with a cargo drone stacked high with crates.

Jason waits till he's out of earshot, then turns to Par, floating a few metres away, her arms crossed, her head bobbing with an approving nod. She's heard most of the conversation; the jammer blocks transmissions, not ears.

'I've got a job for you, Major Par,' he says. 'If you'll oblige?'

'Officially, I'd need clearance from Zhu Nebu Owande. But... since those people don't have full residency, only a tenancy agreement... I think they might fall under your jurisdiction?'

'Totally.'

'The station will sue you for loss of rental income...'

'Let them,' Jason says, and a grin spills out on Par's face.

TWENTY-NINE
LIZ

Liz lies in her recliner watching the Earth news play on her lenses. Food crisis in south Africa, escalating riots in Singapore, a threat of civil war in Brazil. The Alliance is on the brink of collapse, again, accused of food hoarding and mismanagement. The planet is eating itself alive, just as Ranath said. There really is no hope for them here. Will Ark be any better? They are still the same human beings, even if brilliant. And the thing human beings do best is mess things up for each other. Still, those selected for Ark are the smartest and the most talented—if they can't learn from past mistakes, nobody will. Liz isn't entirely convinced that Ark will prove to be the paradise Ranath hopes for, but it's an experiment that must be given a chance. The possibility that it *might* work is too important to lose.

She winces as the image shifts to display her father's haggard figure arriving at the Feidi's private airstrip on his way to the elevator. It's drone footage and taken from some distance, the projection grainy and breaking up as other news-hungry fliers bustle for the best angle. The announcer's voice booms in her ears, their words reinforced by the red letters flashing as they speak: 'Jason Nevsky's new swindle exposed: precious food resources rerouted from the needy to benefit the Yun Ju cultists.' Liz mutes the broadcast as the announcer questions how much Nevsky's clique got paid for stealing food from starving children.

She sits up, focusing on her father. He's lost weight, his jacket hanging loosely on his hunched shoulders. He races across the tarmac in long, unsteady steps, three others hurrying behind him, their collars raised to obscure their faces. A caption jeers the hypocrisy of using personal transport while the Alliance's super-ecological blimp-jet sits unused. The phage-spraying blimp, Liz wants to tell them, but she can't, and he won't. What is his plan? Why is he coming to Tian Gong? It's not the cultists, Ranath is right about that. What, then?

She could ask him. Tell him that she wants to help and hope for enough details to guess his intentions. But that would be a lie—and as much as she still resents him, the idea of offering help only to spy on him makes her cringe. Is Ark worth it? Maybe—but if they start by building the foundations on lies and deceit, there's not much hope for a second chance.

Her father reaches the transit cab, but then he stops and turns to face the drones. He's looking right at the camera, right at... her. His lips move, and Liz scrambles to unmute. By the time she's done, only a thin smile remains on his lips, and then the cab's door closes behind him. Liz rewinds the transmission, but there's no sound, the drones too far to catch his words. She tries to read his lips, but the image is too grainy even for the broadcasters now speculating about his message.

Liz slumps back, deflated and slightly baffled by the sense of loss his missing words have left her with. It doesn't matter. It's nothing she hasn't heard before. And if she really wanted to hear from him, she should go to Kene.

She disconnects the news drip and lies still for a moment, but her body's too tense for repose. Things have slipped her by, too many of them—her father with his plans, Ranath with hers.

All while Liz spent her days obsessing that no one knew who she was. And now her future is about to be shaped by others, once again. Not just her future. Everyone's.

Ranath is right that Ark is the better choice—and that her father's schemes may get in their way at the most critical moment.

What kind of help could he want from her? She has no power here, let alone on Tian Gong. If he thinks she has some influence on Ranath, then he's never met her. Liz might have a better chance with tectonic plates. What, then? She has no access to any critical systems, even within the Shield. She can analyse the data and prepare the forecasts but not act on them.

It has to be it, though—the one thing that she can do but Kene can't. She frowns, trying to recall the latest projections. She's taken a couple of days off, formally to settle in and deal with her nightmares, something Essa very much encouraged. There was a CME in the forecast, but nothing beyond the ordinary. Things could have changed, though.

She checks the time as she hurries down to the lab. Approaching seven in the evening. There will still be people there—there are always people there—but Essa might be gone. She'd prefer not to see him today, not to have to answer questions about how she is, and what she's been up to. Not to have to wonder if someone in his condition will have a place on Ark.

No such luck. Essa is at his desk, his gaunt figure lit by the cold light of his screens. They retreat from him like the petals of an opening flower as he swivels his chair towards her. A dancing stick figure appears on her lenses.

'Look who's back! Got bored without me?'

Liz forces a smile. He looks so pale. His mind is brilliant, but not his body. She's never asked Ranath about her definition of 'brilliance'—but if it doesn't include people like Essa, is that really the best of humanity?

She pushes the worry away. Ranath is too smart not to see that.

'Well, there are just so many strolls up and down the park you can take, you know... Though I've considered getting a dog.'

'I'm not sure Mr Sunshine would approve.'

Liz looks around, but the cat's nowhere to be seen. Probably doing his evening rounds. 'What have I missed? Got any exciting storms for me?'

'A couple, one still in probability, the other already on the way, but they're both meagre level twos, I'm afraid.'

Liz chuckles. 'On the other hand, I may have had enough excitement for a decade. I can do with boring.'

She crosses the space to her desk, the greeting cards still neatly arranged behind her squeezy effigy. Her screen lights up, sensing her presence. All the recent forecasts are there, arranged by time stamp and probability score. The two Essa's mentioned are highlighted in red, as either confirmed or above the probability threshold that necessitated action. Liz opens the first one. Due in thirty-four hours, at the higher end of level two, but still nothing to worry about. The unshielded platforms will need to power down and deploy surge protectors; the stations will barely notice. She calls up the map with the simulation of the storm's trajectory. The purple arc stretches towards Earth following the lines of the magnetic field. The image zooms in as the storm front hits the Yun Ju. And there, right in the path of the surge, sits the blue icon of Tian Gong.

Liz studies the image, her heartbeat accelerating. This can't be a coincidence—her father coming to Tian Gong right at this moment. His plan must involve the storm. How?

She leans back, trying to make her tone casual. 'Are Tian Gong's shields working? They'll be getting the full hit.'

'Yeah, I've checked with them. They've lost a couple of generators, but one's back online and the others are getting replaced. They'll be ready in time.'

Liz nods, but the uneasy feeling has settled in her stomach. Somehow, her father's plan involves the storm. He wanted her help—was it with the forecast? She has too little information to speculate about his intentions, but this is the kind of news Ranath might want to hear. And it's a chance to confirm that she's right about Essa. Liz sends a text message asking for a meeting and receives an invitation a moment later.

Ranath examines the projection, her eyes narrowed in total focus. Liz waits at the other side of the table in an eerie repetition of the other night, the night of 'her' storm. The memory makes her queasy, even though this time the storm line on the display is an unremarkable level two. She tries to follow Ranath's gaze, shifting from the storm to the icon for Tian Gong station, then to the icon for Liberty, some distance ahead of Tian Gong. Liberty will catch only the faint edge of the storm, a minor risk even without shields. A couple of their growth platforms might catch it, too, but even they shouldn't be affected. All the other stations are safely out of the danger zone. New Hope won't even catch a glimpse of it, safe behind the planet.

Ranath rewinds the clock, watching the stations move. If she has any clues about Liz's father's plans, she isn't letting on. And for the moment, Liz has something else on her mind.

'I've checked with Essa. He says that Tian Gong's generators will be back online by the time the storm hits.'

'That's what I've been told. Assuming they don't catch any delays.' Ranath doesn't look at her as she speaks, her eyes tracing the lines of the storm's impact.

Liz glances behind her as Ester leaves the room. This is as good a time as she's going to get. She licks her lips. 'Will someone like Essa... Will he be invited to join Ark?'

Ranath rewinds the clock again, frowning as she stares at the slowly changing figures. 'His condition... Is it hereditary?'

'Er... I don't think he's planning to have children.'

'Not everybody will—but everybody will have to contribute their genetic material, especially at the beginning. We have limited numbers so need every person to create a strong enough genetic pool.'

There's no hesitation in Ranath's voice, no regret. She moves the lines on the display with the focus of a chess master setting up a gambit. It's how she looked on the night of the storm, coldly analysing who will be hit and how it affects their station. That's Ranath's job, Liz reminds herself, and somehow that makes her think of her father. He did his job, too. At least he didn't look like he enjoyed the game.

She winces as Ranath's hand lands on her shoulder. She steps in front of Liz, her black eyes large with worry.

'I'm so sorry. I can be so insensitive.' Ranath cracks an apologetic smile. 'I've trained myself to abide by logic alone. I needed it to survive. But it makes me stupid, too, sometimes. Not realising the hurt I'm causing. Essa—he's a friend of yours?'

'He is.'

Ranath sighs. 'I'm not going to lie and tell you we can take everybody we like. We could, if we had the time to expand slowly, like I planned. But...' She juts her head at the projection. 'But people keep interfering, and now we have to rush with a plan that's far from perfect. We *must* ensure a strong gene pool, or we may as well not bother. I know you understand that.'

Liz nods. Of course she understands. Ranath is right. But being right doesn't make it feel any less wrong. Because Essa *is* brilliant. And he *is* a friend. How many more brilliant people will they leave behind? Or maybe not just brilliant but friendly and fun?

'It's all about choices,' Ranath says. 'It's not about us, or what we find pleasant. It's about the future of humanity. If we compromise now, we will end up like Earth.'

Right again. The point of Ark is to give them a fresh start.

But they must make it work, with the right infrastructure, the right biosphere, the right gene pool. The exclusion feels wrong on some fundamental level, but really, with such a small pool every choice matters, will matter for generations.

It's only logical, isn't it? Then why does everything inside her cry otherwise?

Ranath gives her another smile. 'We can make a few exceptions, though. I'm sure one extra person won't be a problem.'

She squeezes Liz's shoulder, her eyes already wandering back to the projection.

She stays with Ranath for another moment, or until it seems okay to leave without making it look like she's running away. Her mind is battling its own storm wave, emotions and logic twisting around each other like the bubbling lines of magnetic field on the solar surface. Ranath is right, Liz knows that. And Ark is their best chance. Except it all sounds wrong, too, and she can't tell if it's the omission of Essa or the fact that Ranath suddenly sounds very much like her father. Sacrificing everything to save humanity—she's heard that before, too many times. All it ever did was destroy her family while humanity remained unsaved.

She makes it back to the middle ring, then hesitates over whether she should go back to her quarters or to the labs. Neither seems like a good option. She needs to talk to someone, needs to ask questions and get honest answers. Essa would give her those, if she could mention anything to him. Could she? Would Ranath know? She might, and then who knows what would happen to Essa? He might find himself in a pod till Ranath found it safe to release him. Bad idea.

Liz turns and before admitting the fact to herself, she is heading to the graduate quarters. She can talk to Kene. At least

Kene knows that... that there is something to know, even if they can't share the details out in the open.

The old pain returns as she approaches the door, the babble of voices spilling out from behind it like back in those first days. She sucks in a deep breath and enters.

All eyes turn to her, the conversation cut in mid-word. Liz keeps her head high, scanning the faces for Kene. Her eyes meet Alejandro's. His lips curl into a smirk, but for once he doesn't say anything.

Liz crosses the common room into the corridor leading to the bedrooms. She sends a ping as she walks, something she should have done earlier. What if Kene isn't even there?

Can we talk?

She stops outside Kene's bedroom, waiting.

The door cracks open. Kene's black eyes take her in, then the door opens. 'Come in.'

'Thank you.'

Kene stops a couple of steps into the room, her arms crossed.

Liz glances behind her, at the walls, the floor, trying to figure out what to say. 'What do you know? About my father's plans?'

'I don't know what you are talking about.'

Damn. Of course, she thinks Liz will betray her. 'I'm not going to tell anyone. I just need to know.'

Kene sighs. 'Honestly, I don't know. Why don't you ask him yourself?'

Fuck. Liz leans against the wall, her shirt clinging to her back. She doesn't want to see her father. Doesn't want to remember all their previous conversations. But he is either going to help or hinder the Ark project, and she must know. And then she will decide which of the two options she prefers.

'I think you are right,' she says, and turns to leave.

THIRTY
RANATH

Ranath rewinds the projection once again. The way Tian Gong and Liberty are positioned against the oncoming storm front—it's just too perfect to miss for anyone watching. She is sure now that's what Nevsky is planning: blow up Tian Gong in such a way that the debris will destroy Liberty, and use the storm as his cover. They must do it now, too, before the repairs are completed or the storm cover story won't work. That's why he hurried back so soon after his previous visit. It doesn't explain why he'd come in person, but maybe he's the kind of manager who doesn't trust his people to do things properly. Or maybe he's kept the whole thing hidden from everyone but the three engineers. That would make sense, if he wants to avoid liability. Now they can all leave the station just before the storm and claim ignorance.

She's pretty sure she knows how he'll do it, too: that the old stations had a self-destruct setting is not exactly a secret. Yu Huan had it, too, but Ranath's sure Li Qiang's father got rid of it ages ago. They could do it because Sunrise owns that station—Tian Gong is still under lease from the Chinese government. Nebu manages it, but she's not even a zhu, just the largest rent-payer. The self-destruct system has been a thorn in the side of all the previous occupants, but all they could do was slap on another layer of access restrictions.

The projection pauses, the clock indicating the exact moment when an explosion on Tian Gong would have the most impact on Liberty. Ranath saves the image and the data in her personal file. What she still doesn't know is if Nevsky wants to annihilate Liberty or merely to damage it. All he needs to do is time the explosion a bit sooner or later, and Liberty will survive, if bruised.

She shuts down the projection. Liz is no longer there, she realises, departed while Ranath was still figuring out the details. Unusual lapse of concentration for her, especially after the earlier gaffe. Ranath should have guessed Liz had feelings for that Essa person, should have given her a placating answer. They could take an extra settler or two, even with imperfect genes. She'd gladly include Essa, if it made Liz happy.

Ranath rubs her face. She needs to rest, the exhaustion is making her blunder. And the biggest decision is yet ahead of her—because she still needs to figure out what she's going to do about Nevsky's plan.

She could warn Liberty and play the hero—except she can't prove anything, and Nevsky is now Richardson's ally. And if he's just trying to damage Liberty, that would be the perfect distraction for her to move all the remaining assets to *The Covenant* and launch it towards Ark while everyone's sensors are scanning for debris. By the time they realised what she'd done, the ship would be halfway there. By the time the Caretakers could start legal procedures, she'd have transferred the moon's ownership to Ark residents.

On the other hand, if Nevsky's trying to destroy Liberty... There are five thousand people there. Some would survive, but not many. Could she live with herself if she said nothing? Is even Ark worth it?

Probably. Ark is the future of all humanity, the best chance they have to renew themselves. What are five thousand lives compared to that?

Still. It's five thousand people. She wouldn't blink if it was just Richardson or Allen, the Caretaker. But the others are innocent. She'd much rather not carry that burden.

'We've got a confirmation that the three people with Nevsky are engineers,' Ester says from her desk. 'Very recently hired, too. Like, just before boarding the elevator.'

'As I thought. They will get money and promotions, and if they want to stay employed, they won't go around boasting about having blown up a station.'

'Do you still think they're trying to destroy Tian Gong?'

Ranath nods. 'Yes. Though I'm not sure what they are trying to achieve.'

She turns away from her aide. She hates lying to her own people. Lying to Richardson or Qiang is part of the game; they both expect it. But not Ester or Min Woo. But if she tells them it's about Liberty, then they might feel responsible. They might even want to do something about it, something she might not approve. Besides, she's not exactly lying. She doesn't know Nevsky's endgame.

A message pops up on her lenses. From Liz, a request for permission to transfer to Tian Gong. She wants to talk to her father and ask about his plans.

Ranath considers her answer. A part of her doesn't want to let Liz go, strangely protective and even... jealous? Ranath wants to laugh. But there's no denying it, she's developed some motherly feelings for the young woman. Maybe because she sees so much of herself in her that it's become important that Liz approves of her, even likes her back. And if she can't make her believe in Ark, then...

Ranath pushes the thought away. Ridiculous. She knows what's right and what she must do. Liz can't hurt her plans, even if she reveals them to her father. Nevsky is not a danger to Ark, the Caretakers are. And if Liz can find anything about his plans, that could make Ranath's task so much easier.

Of course you may go, she sends, straining to make her voice warm. *Whatever you can find out would be a huge help. But also, you don't need my permission. You are a full resident now; you are free to go anywhere you want.*

She turns to Ester. 'Elizabeth is going to Tian Gong. Can we plant something on her that would get past Nevsky's jammers?'

Ester scrunches her face, considering. 'I could plant something on her wire... It's highly illegal, though.'

Ranath shrugs. 'No more than what Nevsky's doing there. We need to know.'

Ester nods. 'Then I'll get it done.'

Ranath turns towards her private rooms. Maybe she can catch some sleep; that would probably do her good before she makes any hasty decisions. Too many things hang in the balance, too many questions still unanswered.

'Er, there's one more thing,' Ester says. 'I've got some news, though I can't quite make sense of it.'

'What is it about?'

'That man we were tracking, Tamir Allen. The one who rushed off to Liberty.'

The Caretaker. Ranath's breath catches, and she clears her throat. 'What about him?'

'I got to chat with those Tian Gong's systems managers we've defrosted. Apparently, Allen has recently retrieved an encrypted data package that was buried within the station's main programming. I mean, that's about the last place you should "store" data, that's why it got their attention. Allen had all the passwords, too, not something he should be able to have.'

'Do they know what it was?'

'Old comms packages. No idea about the actual content.'

Ranath starts to frown, but then the realisation slams her like a blow to the stomach. Her throat constricts as she sucks in a desperate gasp.

Old comms packages. Messages. Letters.

'How old?' she manages to ask.

'Between fifty-five and twenty years ago.' Ester glances at her uneasily. 'They speculated if it could have something to do with Bethesda, but the timing's off. Too late for the colonists, and too early for when the news came. It could have been messages from a family member, but there's no record of any crew with links to Tian Gong. And family messages wouldn't be encrypted and buried like some pirate treasure.'

Ester shrugs, her gaze probing. Ranath looks away. This is too much, even for her.

It's *her* messages. Her mother's probably, too. The love letters to the husband she knew she'd never see again, recorded in the depth of the night when she thought Ranath was asleep. Ranath's letters, the diary of her childish accomplishments to make her father proud. Her drawings. The picture of her first crush.

Her proclamations of how she understood and supported everything he stood for.

She thought she'd destroyed all records, erased all traces. That the pad locked in her bedroom was the only copy of her father's messages. Maybe it was—but someone had preserved the outgoing messages and hidden them away for decades.

She walks away, leaving Ester to stare after her with raised brows. That's how they are going to destroy her. The Caretakers will use the messages to attack her personally, to link *her* to Destiny without implicating the corporation she runs. If they succeed, she will be removed, and Renewal will get a new zhu, someone the Caretakers will be able to control.

There will be an investigation, of course, but whatever it proves doesn't matter. By the time they declare her innocent of her father's 'sins,' she will have lost Renewal, lost access to its funds, to the assemblers, to the whole support system she has created for Ark. The Caretakers may not even stop there—her plans might be revealed, the settlers awakened and shamed out of participating.

It will be the end of Ark. The end of her.

Have they already shared it with anyone? Does Richardson know? Li Qiang?

She returns to the antique desk in the far section of her office and engages the privacy bubble. She's shaking, her knees soft and her breath ragged. Her messages. All her letters. Dragged into public, inspected and questioned. Her teenage worries, her tears, her plans. Her very soul bared to the masses. She can already feel their gazes, their eyes narrowing with cruel curiosity as she stands there, naked and exposed.

She won't let that happen. She will sooner destroy them all than let them peek at her pain. Richardson and the Caretaker are a good place to start.

She glances back towards the projection table, now idle. The record of what it showed is safe on her personal system. She knows exactly when the self-destruct needs to be activated to destroy Liberty.

Jason Nevsky might do it for her. If not, she will have to do it herself.

THIRTY-ONE

JASON

Major Par makes short work of the Sun Seers base. It seems all she needed was the clearance Jason gave her. He stays with the Sharks as they force their way past two bulkhead doors and multiple threatening messages to arrive in a vast chamber, made to look even bigger by its mirrored walls. More mirrors form triangular pillars scattered over the entire space, all angled towards the curved window in the space-facing wall. On dayside, the light would be blinding. Jason can't imagine how anyone could preserve their sight after more than a few hours here. Even starlight provides sufficient illumination to see the stooped figures squatting by the walls or lying prone on the cold floor. Some turn to watch the Sharks, no emotion registering on their haggard faces. Others clutch their heads in their hands, cowering in pain. Several don't move at all.

Jason gasps, then covers his mouth at the stench of rot and sweat.

Par doesn't say anything, but her dismay is clear on her face. The Sharks disperse to check the rest of the space.

'They found the Elders,' Par says a minute later, and heads towards the inner chambers.

Jason wants to follow, if only to punch each and every one of them, but he needs to focus on his main purpose here. They have twenty-two hours left till the storm hits. One of his engineers is gone already, peeled off the group as they marched towards the Seers' base. He nods to the other two, and they are gone the moment Par steps out of sight. They will use their jammers as soon as they get to their targets. That won't hide their location, but if anyone's watching they'll only see grey blotches of lost signal.

A loud groan ripples through the Seers—but it sounds like relief, not pain.

'It's gone,' Avery says, emerging from the darkness. 'The noise in my head, it's gone.'

He turns in the direction where Par went, his eyes wide and hesitant. A ragged breath shakes his frame, but then he straightens, his jaw set. He starts to move, and this time Jason follows. They find Par in a chamber hidden behind reinforced doors. The room is well lit, the decor comfortable if not luxurious. The biggest difference is the smell—the stench of the main hall replaced by the flowery scent of cool, purified air. Seven people in long yellow robes sit at a round table with a honey-coloured, glowing top like the surface of the sun. Around them, side tables are stacked high with food and emergency supplies, most in unopened boxes.

Avery clenches his fists, but Par steps between him and the Elders.

'We've disabled all their emitters,' she says to Jason. 'They can't control these people anymore.'

'Thank you. Now we need to ask everyone if they want to be evacuated.' Avery snorts, but Jason ignores him. 'Do you have any medical personnel?'

Par nods. 'I've got a couple of field medics.'

'Have them see to the injured. If they judge anyone unable

to give informed consent, evacuate them anyway. Will New Hope accept the refugees?'

'I believe so, yes.' Par tips her head towards the Elders. 'What do you want to do with them?'

'Keep them under lock. If they give you any trouble, tell them you will release them into the care of their parishioners.'

Par and Avery share a grin that Jason doesn't quite like—but the woman is too professional to let her feelings dictate justice here, no matter how deserved. He steps away, leaving the Sharks to their work. This has turned out better than he expected: the cultists are on the way to be evacuated, and the Sharks will be busy for hours. He can only hope his engineers will find their task equally painless. They seemed to have produced a plan they were happy with—or at least not unhappy with—while still on the elevator. He's dying to ask them for details, but they haven't had the chance to talk in private since leaving the surface. He must be patient and trust them to do their jobs. His task is to give them space to do it. They have twenty-two—twenty-one and a half—hours left.

Jason stays with the Sharks for another two hours, until he's sure his departure won't look suspicious. So far all but a couple of the Seers have agreed to leave, but it will take till the morning to transport them all out to New Hope. Perfect.

He retreats to the place they selected for their camp: one of the duty rooms for the nightshift technicians. It's on the inner ring, better shielded from radiation, but right next to the elevator linking the two decks and not too far from the station's ops room, in case they needed access to the central computers. The space has got some chairs and a cot they can use to catch a few hours' rest, though Jason doesn't think there's much chance for that.

He starts by attaching the signal jammers to the walls just as the engineers have showed him. Now they'll be able to talk, whenever any of them gets a moment to update him. He'd much rather go to check on them himself, but that's just asking for trouble. He should stick to the plan and wait—and hope the option they've come up with doesn't involve him setting things off manually.

The thought makes him pause. He sits down on the cot and closes his eyes. Will he have the strength to do it? He must. But there are so many things he wants to do still, so many words to say. It's not his time to go yet.

He shakes his head. What will come, will come. He must be ready. And he should start by writing a letter to his daughter in case he never gets to say all those words.

He pulls out a flat screen from his bag, then remembers the odd message he got in the elevator. Opening it there was too risky, but if it does contain a tracker, the jammers should take care of it. He syncs his wrist band with the screen and calls up his mail. The anonymous message appears first, just as he saw it before:

For your attention, a selection of files you will find interesting. This is a fragment of the cache in my possession. I believe you can put it to good use.

He touches the attachment icon, and it unrolls into an old-style video message. The info-stamp blinks into view, and Jason gasps.

Video message
From: undisclosed, Tian Gong station, Earth
To: Passenger 37, rescue ship The Samaritan
Sent: 4 December 2354
Received: unknown
Play message

He recognises the format. He's seen it a thousand times on

the dispatches Aunt Nathalie sent from Bethesda. Except this message was sent from here, from Tian Gong station. He checks the date again. It must be a mistake. Or an odd coincidence, because this was sent nine days before Aunt Nathalie's message arrived. Nobody knew yet what had happened on Bethesda. Who sent this? And who was the 'Passenger 37'? *The Samaritan* carried thirty-six crew. But then there were the others: the Guardian and his Sharks. Could 'Passenger 37' have been... the Guardian?

Jason wipes his forehead, his fingers sticky with sweat. Destiny. They would have been communicating with the Guardian. Sending instructions for how to proceed. He punches the play icon, and steels himself for the sight.

A woman appears on the screen: young, maybe thirty, long black hair falling over her face, her lips cracked and her shoulders heaving in silent sobs. Tears roll down her cheeks. She rubs them away with rough, impatient movements.

Her chin trembles as she starts to speak. 'Dad? Please, tell me it's not true? I know you won't get this in years, but... I hope you are still out there, back in the cryo-pod, on your way back. It's been three days since your message... I keep hoping you're just too busy, or maybe you are wounded and recovering... That I will hear from you any minute now. But I'm losing hope.'

The woman throws her hair back and looks straight at the camera. Jason winces. He knows that face, he's seen it in the news often enough. Ranath Eyre, the Zhu of Renewal. The Guardian's daughter.

The daughter of Destiny's spy on Bethesda, the man who died to protect their secret, to prevent the warning being sent to Earth. And now she's here, running Renewal, waking up Destiny's agents.

And she has *his* daughter.

He stares at the young woman's face, her pain solidifying into determination as she wipes her eyes once again. She bites her lip, holding herself tight. Her gaze drills into him, her dark eyes brighter with every word.

'I won't give up, Father. I will continue what you started. Your name won't be forgotten. Your mission will continue, in me. I will let them all know what you died for. They won't forget your sacrifice. I love you, Dad!'

The video winks out, leaving five new attachment icons. Jason checks them one by one: all videos, all addressed to Passenger 37. Three from Ranath and two from an older woman with similar facial features, dated decades earlier. He listens to one recording, the accounting of how she decided to carry the child they'd hoped to have. Ranath's mother, he realises.

Jason shuts down the screen, his head spinning. Who sent him the files? Why him? Because they want to stop her, and they need his help. Could the messages be fake? Anything could be faked, but why bother if a simple DNA test could disprove it? Ranath's birth certificate would have her parents' DNA record. No, this is real, he knows it in his bones. He rubs his face, forcing himself to focus, but his thoughts keep returning to his own daughter. Is she safe? Does Ranath plan to use her against him? How?

He winces as the door opens.

Jose, the engineer he used to refer to as 'Blue', slides inside. 'You all right?'

'Yes. Yes, I'm fine.' Jason puts the screen away. No reason to burden the engineers with information they can't do anything about. 'Didn't expect you yet. How's your progress?'

Jose glances around. 'Have you—'

'I've put up all the jammers as you told me.'

'Good. I'm going back in a moment, but needed to brief you. We've got a plan, and it's going to work, but it's more compli-cated than we thought. They've made big changes from what we had in the specs. We can still do it, but it's going to take all the remaining time. You've got to keep the Sharks busy, or we're toast.'

'Have they seen you?'

'I don't think so. We keep moving, starting in one place, then on to the next just in case anyone notices the signal outage. But once they're done with the Seers, they may get curious, and we don't have time to play hide and seek.'

'Leave it with me,' Jason says. He's got no idea what he'll do, but he'll think of something. 'And... your plan, will it—'

'If we get everything done as we want to, we will all get out of here in time. Just keep the Sharks away.' Jose gives him a reassuring nod and slides out of the room.

Jason blows out a relieved breath. Despite all the bad news, it's good to hear he's not about to die just yet.

The message ping buzzes in his ear. For a moment he stands frozen, wondering if he's messed up the jammers—but no, they are supposed to block the station's systems, not their personal comms. He can still send and receive messages.

He glances at the ident flashing on his wrist band. Major Par.

'Can I help you, Major?'

'There's someone here to see you. Elizabeth Lake, just arrived from New Hope. Do you—'

'Yes.' Jason pauses, swallowing air as he tries not to shout. His heart rams against his chest bone. 'Yes. I'd like to see her.'

THIRTY-TWO

LIZ

Liz travels with the Sharks heading back to Tian Gong after they've delivered the first group of cultists to New Hope, those in need of urgent medical care. She watched from a distance as the doctors received them, and the medics' faces told her she probably shouldn't try to come closer. Why anyone would inflict it on themselves was beyond her understanding. The Sharks seem to share the sentiment as that's all they talk about during their transfer. Liz sits at the far end of the small passenger space, still too wary of their silver uniforms and hidden guns to strike up a conversation. She listens, though, to the descriptions of the mirrored chamber, so bright in daylight that even their visors struggled with the load. Of the Elders, cosy in their well-shielded and well-stocked rooms. Of the implants all cultists received on arrival, which would emit head-splitting noise at the most minor sign of disobedience. Of 'that Nevsky guy' and how he tricked them and took responsibility for busting them out. She stops listening then, not quite ready for the note of approval in their voices. They don't know the real Nevsky the way she does.

They take the elevator down from the cargo dock, the

centrifugal 'gravity' asserting itself as they approach the rings. The cabin stops at the inner deck, just for her. The Sharks will continue down to the cultists' base in the outer ring. Liz steps out, her eyes adjusting to the dim lighting in the empty hall. She looks around, her heart thumping as if she's due for an exam, one for which she's failed to prepare.

'Elizabeth!'

She shivers at the sound of his voice, then chides herself for her reaction. She's not a wounded teenager anymore. She is a Yun Ju citizen, a respected expert, a woman with her own life.

Her father stops a few steps away. He's trying to smile, but it comes out crooked. His fists clench and unclench until he pushes them into his pockets.

'Nice to see you again.' His voice breaks and he clears his throat. 'I'm glad you came.'

Liz purses her lips. She doesn't want him to think she's decided to help. She hasn't decided anything yet, other than that she wasn't going to lie to him, or to Ranath. If she can't trust the person she will ally herself with, then it's not the kind of alliance she wants for herself.

'Is there a place where we could... talk?'

'Yes. I've commandeered a small room. It's not much, but it's... er... comfortable.'

They walk in silence down several corridors before entering a tiny space that looks like a smaller version of the watch rooms for night-shift Shield technicians. Certainly not 'comfortable,' but she hopes her father has installed a privacy filter to prevent the station's systems from spying on them.

Father closes the door. 'Did you get wired?'

'External only. I can switch it off at any time,' she says defensively, again reverting into child mode in his presence. Damn.

But he only nods. 'I've got contacts. Can you imagine?'

Liz stares. Wired contact lenses are barely more invasive

than a wearable screen, but for her father even that's a huge step. She knows no one more strongly opposed to any kind of brain-tech, though this is nothing like the Bethesda's Mind-Link he fears, nothing even like the Mind-Link Essa uses today.

'Long story,' Father says, answering her unspoken question. 'Anyway, that little 'pop' you've heard, that's the signal jammers. This room is safe; no one can hear us here.'

Liz hasn't heard any 'pop,' but then, she was too busy thinking about what exactly she was going to tell him now that they were here.

He points to one of the chairs and plants himself on the cot opposite. They look at each other in silence, probably both wondering where to start.

'Have you heard my message?' Father says. 'The one I sent through the sympathiser?'

'She's a "sympathiser"? Of what?'

'Have you listened to it?'

'I have. Is it true? The phage, the manipulation?'

'It is. Every word I said in that message is the truth, to the best of my knowledge.'

Liz nods slowly. She never doubted it, not really, but it helps to have the confirmation. 'What are you planning to do?'

Father hesitates. He glances at his hands, then back at her. 'Have you come to help me or to spy on me?'

Now it's her turn to look away. 'I'm not sure yet. Maybe both.'

Father snorts. 'Well, at least you are honest.'

'So... how are we going to do it? Because I don't know if I can support you unless I know what you are planning, and you won't tell me what you're planning until I promise to support you.'

'Fair assessment,' Father says. 'How about this: what would you do in my place?'

'I don't know.' Liz rises and moves to lean against the wall, putting as much distance between her and his troubled face as the small room allows. 'You don't exactly make the choices I would. Because I wouldn't have teamed up with dictators. I wouldn't have sold my soul to keep my place in the Alliance.'

Father flinches, his eyes wide. 'Is that why you think I did it? To keep my job?'

Liz shrugs. It's the wrong time for this conversation, but once the door has opened, all the words she suppressed for a decade bubble out of her mouth like from a pressurised container. 'I know what you're going to say—how it was the only way, how you did everything to save humanity. You may have even believed that. But what you actually did? How many lives did that cost? How much suffering? And here we are, after two decades of the Alliance, still teetering on the brink of war and hunger, exactly like when you started. All your struggles, all your work, and we're still nowhere. So I don't know how I can trust your plans this time, because you may have the best intentions, but what will come out of them in the end? Even more pain?'

She watches as his lips turn into a thin, downturned line, and then he drops his head into his hands, his shoulders trembling. Liz looks away, her anger spent, replaced by remorse—for him, for herself, for everything that could have been. She doesn't want to hurt him; she's no longer sure if he even deserves it. But she has a decision to make, and she must know it's a good one.

'We haven't fallen,' her father whispers.

'What?'

He looks up at her, as pale as ash. 'You said we're still teetering on the brink. We haven't fallen. That's what I've been working for, all those years.'

Liz leans forward, her lips parting as the gears in her head shift to a new perspective. She hasn't thought about it that way.

'And if not for the Yun Ju, not for the phage—we could have

done better. But instead of helping, they do everything to sabotage us. They need us down so they can stay up. They need servants so they can be the masters. And I'm done playing their game.'

Liz sinks back into the chair. Maybe she was wrong thinking he failed at his mission. Especially with all the crap the Yun Ju threw his way. Maybe just keeping everything from falling apart was a Herculean achievement.

And she's underestimated him all her life.

'So what are you going to do about it?' she asks.

He takes a long moment to answer. There's something ominous in the way he looks at his hands, examining his fingers as if they belong to someone else. As if wondering what they are capable of doing. 'Destiny is back. I don't know what they—'

'They're not.' Liz shakes her head. 'I mean, I was wrong about the pods. It's not Destiny.'

'How do you know?'

Liz hesitates. *Because Ranath told me* doesn't sound like a good enough answer, not unless she tells him what she knows about Ark. 'Because I know who is in those pods. And it's not Destiny.'

'Have you seen them? Talked to them? Or are you just taking Eyre's word for it?'

'Ranath's.' Liz corrects automatically—then continues before he can comment, 'Why can't you trust me? I know what I'm saying. I have evidence, even if I can't share it with you. I didn't go behind your back, and I won't go behind hers.'

'Fair enough.' Father's tone gains an icy edge. 'As long as you know who you're aligning yourself with. Do you know who her father was?'

'What does it matter? He is dead and she's no more responsible for his actions than I am for yours.'

Father's brows arch. 'You know, then? You know she is the Guardian's daughter?'

'What?!' Liz's mouth falls open and she can't make herself close it as she glares at him in wide-eyed dismay.

'She pledged herself to his mission, too.'

'How do you know?'

He reaches for a flat screen laying on the edge of the cot. Liz waits, licking her dry lips with impatience. He beckons her to join him, and she sits next to him on the narrow cot.

A woman's face appears on the screen: dark hair, face wet with tears she tries to wipe away. 'Dad? Please, tell me it's not true? I know you won't get this in years, but... I hope you are still out there, back in the cryo-pod, on your way back. It's been three days since your message...'

Liz scowls at the screen long after the image has vanished. Ranath admitted her father was in Destiny. She also said she wasn't proud of what he'd done. This message didn't look like that was true. Did she lie or—

'Ranath Eyre is the Guardian's daughter, sworn to continue Destiny's mission,' her father says. 'Did she tell you that?'

'I've lied to plenty of people about who my father was.'

'I believe that. But then, you haven't sent me any messages promising to continue my mission.'

'She could have changed her mind.' Liz tips her head to the screen. 'That was a long time ago.'

'She could have, yes. Do you think she has?'

Liz doesn't answer. Nothing is straight with Ranath, nothing certain—only games and strategies and tactics. Having the Guardian for a father would do that to you, probably. Liz should know, she has played her share of the games. Changed her name, twice, pretended she was someone else to get away from his shadow. Still, that's not the question here—the real question is Ark. And Liz's choice.

'How did you get those recordings?' she asks.

'Someone sent them to me. A rival, I guess. It's a whole set of messages, from Ranath, and from her mother. I've got no doubt they are genuine.'

He picks up the screen, opening another recording, when a message icon blinks on Liz's wrist band.

'I've got to talk to you right now,' Ranath says in her ear, her voice breathless. 'I know what your father is trying to do, and it's not pretty.'

Liz glances at her father. He's peering at her wrist band, his face scrunching as he tries to decipher the icon.

'Er, I need a moment.'

'It's from Ranath, isn't it?'

'Well...' Damn, she promised herself she wouldn't lie. 'I'll be a moment.'

Her father shakes his head. 'I never trusted those wires.'

'What do you—' Liz starts but he speaks over her, his voice hard and projecting.

'Why don't you end the charade, Ranath? You've been listening to everything we've said. Why don't we have a conversation?'

Liz swings to face him. 'But you said there was a jamming filter here.'

'There is. But your wire uses different relays—and someone's hacked it.'

Liz shakes her head. *Ranath wouldn't do that*, she wants to say, but the truth is, she knows better. Ranath *would* do that.

She stands up. 'He's right. Can we all just talk?'

Her vision blurs, and suddenly Ranath stands in front of her, as real as if she is with them in the tiny room.

She turns to Liz, her expression pained and almost shy. 'I'm sorry, Elizabeth. I really am. But too much is at stake to leave it to chance. I had to know.'

'You could have asked,' Liz says.

'I have. You refused to help me, didn't even tell me you'd

been in touch with your father. How could I trust that this time would be different?'

'I didn't lie to you.'

'You didn't tell me the truth.'

'I couldn't just go behind my father's back!'

'So you're a faithful daughter now?'

'Are you?'

Ranath winces—and so does Liz, surprised by her own outburst. They stare at each other over the digital space, only the low buzz of the room's air circulators breaking the silence.

'My father gave his life for what he believed was right,' Ranath says eventually, her tone deliberate, each syllable projected with unwavering conviction. 'I do not agree with or follow Destiny's plan—though it might have been more effective than what your father is trying to do. I chose a different path, and I trusted you enough to share it. And you've betrayed me.'

'I didn't betray you. I came here to talk to my father and ask about—'

'His plan? I can tell you what it is: he's going to blow up Tian Gong to destroy Liberty. Murder the five thousand people living there. That's what *your* father is trying to do.'

Liz flinches. Impossible. She looks at her father, waiting for his denial, but he just sits there staring questioningly at her. He's not linked to the conversation, she realises, Ranath is projecting for her alone. She opens her mouth to ask him, but Ranath continues, her voice booming in Liz's ear.

'I showed you Ark. I showed you the future. That's where we belong. There's nothing here, on Earth or in the Yun Ju, that can compare. You know that.' Ranath seems to draw nearer, so close now that their hands could touch. She smiles, her eyes radiant again like when she showed her Ark for the first time. 'This is our chance, Liz. You've seen it. Think of the art we will make, the science we can discover. We can become what we are meant to be. It's not too late. I'm sorry I lied to you. I hate myself every time I'm forced to lie, but it's self-defence. You know now who I am; you can imagine what my life's been like. And I have to protect Ark, no matter what it costs me. It's never been about me, never will be.'

Ranath drops her head. When she looks up, her face has hardened again. 'There's nothing left for us here—just the same war, pain, and hate. The last spasms of a dying civilisation. It's up to us if humanity will emerge from it renewed, or if it will burn out to nothing. But time is running out. My enemies have made their move, and we have only moments left. You've earned your place on Ark, and I want you at my side as we usher in this new world. But you must leave now. No more talk, no more questions. Come, Liz. Let's do it together.'

Ranath reaches out her hand, her projected fingers sliding through Liz's arm. The air shimmers, the background unrolling to the panorama of that endless green meadow with a lake and boats and laughing children. The future, hers for the taking.

Liz steps away, blinking the projection away. Ranath's still there, the most vulnerable she's ever been, the most hopeful. Another hand touches Liz's shoulder—her father, his face worn and tired, his lips cracked from biting. He starts to speak, but she shakes her head. 'Wait.'

Why is she even hesitating? Ranath's right: Ark is the future. It may not be as perfect as Ranath hopes, not with the way she makes her selection, but it's still the best chance they have. Essa will be just fine, and so will everyone else who didn't make Ranath's cut, living their lives as they always have, not even realising that a splinter of humanity has sailed away. She should go. This is what she's wanted her entire life, a new start, free from the burdens of the past.

'We must go, Liz,' Ranath repeats. 'Before it's too late.'

Liz glances from Ranath back to her father, the man she blamed for everything and the woman who promised her a new world.

'Are you planning to destroy Tian Gong?' she asks.

He seems to shiver, but then blinks a slow, silent confirmation, for her only.

'Does your plan require killing everyone on Liberty?'

'What? God, no!'

Liz smiles—not at the news but at the realisation that she has no doubt that he's telling the truth. He would never betray her, no matter what it cost him. And that's the difference—the trust she can give so easily because he's never deceived her, not even when he could have placated her with easy lies. How can that compare to Ranath's lies? What world will the woman build if that's how she starts?

'He's lying,' Ranath says.

'I trust him.'

'You choose him over Ark?'

'No. I choose him over you. I choose him, and Essa, and truth.'

Ranath gasps. She takes a step back, her body tensing in shock. She pulls in a long breath through her nostrils, her teeth clenched. Her voice cracks with ice. 'Have it your way, then.'

She holds Liz's gaze for another instant, and then the connection flicks out. And somehow Liz knows this is far from over.

THIRTY-THREE

RANATH

Ranath glares at the empty space where Liz stood only seconds ago. Her words cut through her, repeated in unending echo in Ranath's mind. *I choose him over you.* The betrayal so complete and so unexpected, Ranath struggles to breathe, her chest constricted, her lungs refusing to draw air.

I choose him over you.

She leans on her old desk, her head down. Why does this hurt so much? Why does she care? That woman is nothing to her. Just someone who reminded Ranath of how she used to be, someone she could imagine her daughter would be like. But Liz is not her daughter. Her approval means nothing. Just a waste of time and resources. That's what you get for letting yourself feel. Ranath's not going to make that mistake again.

She straightens, taking in her private corner of the office for the last time. It's time to go. Time to start the future.

She drops the privacy filter. Ester and Min Woo wait by the workstations, their expressions uncertain. She's made a mistake by letting them listen in to Nevsky's conversation with his daughter. She thought he'd confirm his plans for Liberty—instead, he revealed her identity to her aides. Ranath cut their link before they could see the recording, before they could gawk at her tears and offer her their pity. But they know now, and she has to deal with that and with what comes next.

She walks leisurely to the middle of the office, stopping next to the grey display table. 'In case you're wondering, yes, it's true. I am the daughter of the man known as the Guardian. Eyre was my mother's name. Now, before you start wondering: I am not Destiny. The people who are trying to stop me are. Like that man you've been tracking, Ester. They want to stop Ark. I won't let them. Will you help me?'

Ester nods. 'Of course.'

'We don't choose our parents,' Min Woo adds.

Ranath manages not to snap, though it's becoming surprisingly difficult. She is a hornet trapped inside a glass jar, her emotions too raw for her containment. Just one more day. A few more hours.

'Thank you. To be honest, it's a relief not to have to hide anymore.' She turns around and activates the projection. The data updates with the recent storm forecast, the line of its progress shifting closer. *A few more hours.*

Ranath stifles a sigh. She really does hate lying, but there's just no other way. Her aides may have pledged their loyalty, but if Liz's betrayal has taught her anything, it's not to rely on others to see things through. They tend to lose sight of the end goal the moment unpleasant decisions need to be made—that part requires strength few seem to possess. And there will be no rest for as long as the Caretakers can threaten her. As for Liz and Nevsky, damn them to hell. They shouldn't have watched those files.

She runs the projection, pointing to the storm line and the stations. 'This is what Nevsky is after: he's using Tian Gong to destroy Liberty, and he'll blame the storm for the carnage.'

Ester and Min Woo gasp in horror. Just as she expected.

'Can we stop him?' Min Woo asks.

'We can do something better. If we change the timing on the self-destruct, we can make sure the debris will miss Liberty. It will still create a mighty mess, though, which is just the distraction we need to get away.'

'You mean...?'

'We are leaving. Departing for Ark in seven hours.' Ranath grins, watching their shock turn to excitement. 'Min Woo, prepare the ship for departure. Use all the resources we have, secrecy be damned.'

'What about the refugees? And the Shark families we have on board?'

'We will drop their modules once we're a sufficient distance away. The Sharks can tow them back with their shuttles. It'll keep them busy.'

Ester nods. 'That's a clever move.'

'Well, thank you.' Ranath chuckles, and for a moment she feels like her old self again.

'Is Tian Gong empty?' Min Woo asks, trepidation sneaking into his voice.

'It will be, by the time we activate. One thing we can thank Nevsky for.'

He's still watching the projection, his skin a shade paler. Ranath hasn't expected him to be so weak—but then, they've never before blown up a station.

'Go, get everything ready,' she says with quiet confidence. 'We must leave on time, if we are to save Liberty.'

Min Woo nods, his focus returning.

'Ester, go with him. I'm sure he can use a hand.'

'But—'

'I know what to do. I'm not entirely helpless without you, you know? Besides, I don't want either of you anywhere near. If anything goes wrong, nobody's going to believe we were trying to save them. They will turn on me, because of who I am. I don't want you implicated. So, go, and don't come back here. Everything that happens now is on me.'

Her aides nod gratefully, and, at least in Min Woo's case, somewhat relieved. They hurry out, leaving Ranath alone with the projection. She walks to Ester's abandoned workstation, considering her actions. She's lied again: she has no idea how to access Tian Gong's systems. But her aides have become liabilities; Ester has seen too much, it would be too easy for her to check the timings and figure out that Ranath's plan doesn't involve saving Liberty. Just the opposite.

What now? Nebu's given them the codes to use for repairs and to deal with the cultists, so that's not an issue. Tian Gong's engineers could easily do it, except they are unlikely to agree to blowing up their own station. She needs someone trained in security, someone who won't ask too many questions. Someone with ambition and something to gain. Someone like Liz's old nemesis, Alejandro.

She grins as she puts in a call, voice only. 'This is Zhu Ranath. I'm short of people and have an urgent job. You come recommended. If you can manage it, you have your promotion, and your residency.'

The man at the other end of the line stutters, 'Of... of course! What—?'

'Come to my office. Now.'

It takes Alejandro two hours to locate the self-destruct commands in Tian Gong's systems, then another hour to break through the layers of encryption and access codes.

At first, Ranath watches him work, wondering if the task is really so difficult or if the standard for the graduates has dropped, but then she notices how his hands shake each time she draws near, missing keystrokes and mangling lines. He is making progress, though, and he hasn't as much as batted an eye when she told him they needed to access the self-destruct to prevent Nevsky from using it.

Ranath summons the remains of her patience and puts a hand on his shoulder. 'You are doing great. Don't worry, you've got the promotion in the bag already.'

His shoulder bunches under her hand, a grin pouring onto his face. 'Thank you, ma'am.'

Oh, deluded soul. But that's the thing with bullies: they cower before real strength. Ranath walks away, her back to him as if she trusted him fully, while the office cameras watch his every keystroke. The trick works, though, because in the next thirty minutes, he's through.

'I'm in,' he says, then frowns. 'Doesn't seem like they've touched it. The last access was—'

'Perfect.' Ranath crosses the room to stand at Alejandro's side. 'That means we're in time. They were leaving it to the last moment, exactly so no one will notice. Now we can make sure they won't be able to access it anymore. May I?'

Alejandro jumps to his feet. 'Of course.'

Ranath could have summoned another chair, but she wants the screen to herself. She adjusts the display so he can see it standing next to her. Her finger traces the lines of code. It's far from her speciality, but she's been around long enough to know the basics. 'I change the access passwords here, correct?'

'Yes, but there are multiple layers—'

'Yes, you said. But as I've told you, they will keep it till the last moment, assuming they have the right codes. A few changes are all we need. Now, if you excuse me—and I think you have a message you need to attend to.'

Ranath signals her system to forward the residency package she's prepared. It's a formality, but she's added a few forms he needs to complete, just to keep him busy.

Alejandro's face brightens like a full moon as the message

appears on his wrist band. 'Thank you, Zhu Ranath. Thank you!'

'Thank *you*. Now, I would strongly recommend you don't mention what you did here to anyone. You have your residency, but I'm holding off on the promotion till this blows over.' She sniffs at the unintended pun. 'Don't make me change my mind.'

'I won't! No way!'

'Good. I'll be in touch if I need you again. So maybe don't celebrate too hard?'

Alejandro grins, then finally gets the hint that it's time to leave. He squeezes in another dozen *thank yous* before he reaches the exit, then finally the door closes behind him.

Ranath returns to the screen. A single command installs a newly generated set of access codes over the self-destruct system. She reloads and updates, and then opens the self-destruct settings again. A new icon appears, red and ominous: ACTIVATION PROCEDURE. Ranath's hand trembles as she touches the glowing letters. Can she do it? Can she live with herself if she does?

Can she live with herself if she doesn't?

None of it is her fault. Nevsky is finishing what the Caretakers have started. They could have just let her have Ark, except they were too greedy. How long before Earth obliterates the Yun Ju anyway? How many wars will they fight before the inevitable ending? Time to move on. In a few hundred years, only historians will concern themselves with the matters of this humanity.

The icon changes under her touch. She selects the timer and types in the hour, minute, and second she memorised from the forecast.

START TIMER?

Another deep breath, another reminder to keep her focus on the things that really matter.

START NOW.

The clock comes to life, the digits flashing each second of the running countdown. Four hours, thirty-three minutes, and fifteen seconds to go.

Ranath closes the system. One more thing to do: a voice message, to be sent an hour from now. That should give them enough time.

'This is Zhu Ranath to Major Par. Unfortunately, my worst fears have come to pass. My project, even my life may be in danger. This gives me no choice but to leave the Yun Ju. *The Covenant* is departing now. Before we go full burn, we will detach the modules housing your families and the refugees. They will be left safe with marker beacons and enough power to allow you to tow them back to the station of your choosing. Please, do not delay. You must set off immediately in order to reach them in time.'

All done now. Four hours left. She looks around at her office, her grandmother's antique desk, the old horary, her collection of knickknacks. There are more in her private rooms, trinkets and gifts she has accumulated over her lifetime. She should pack some of them, if just as memories. But does she want to remember?

She strolls through her quarters, passing the shelves of accreted goods. Nothing here is worth keeping. This is a new start, a brand-new humanity, reborn from the flames. A new start for her, too, even if it won't be what she expected. Ranath picks up the pad with the recording of her father's message and leaves, locking the door behind her. Let it all burn.

THIRTY-FOUR

JASON

'Are you sure this will do it?' Jason asks as Annalie powers down her wired lenses and emitter.

She blinks and wrinkles her nose as she tries to focus on something that's not there. 'It's all gone. Switched off now, just as the technician said. I'm glad I opted for external...'

They share a look, the words left unspoken. Jason should feel vindicated, but he's just relieved that she's safe, and that they can finally really talk. They rush through explanations, his motives and her knowledge of Ranath's plans, that bizarre idea of Ark and the fear of attack from Earth. He would laugh if he had the time, but it's more important to make Annalie recognize why the Yun Ju has to be destroyed, why they have to force them to return to Earth and build their future together. He hopes she understands—she doesn't say much, just listens, nodding or frowning when things connect in her mind.

They pause when Jose, the engineer, appears in the door. He slides inside, then freezes at the sight of her.

'It's okay,' Jason says quickly. 'She's... she's part of the team.'

Jose's brows rise higher, but he doesn't comment. He wipes his forehead, his hair slick with sweat and his eyes bloodshot.

'We're done with seven sections. Taking a break now, before we lose track of what we're doing.'

'Do you need food? Anything—'

'No, we have our rations. And it's probably best we don't move too much. The Sharks have been keeping busy, but that's not going to last much longer.'

True. Jason checks the time—over four hours since they started removing the cultists. Another six hours left on his timer. 'Are we on track?'

'Yes. If we don't get any surprises, we'll finish with a healthy margin.' Jose bobs his head, but his expression remains troubled.

'What is it?'

'Something's odd with the central systems. We've seen circuits coming online that shouldn't have power.'

Jason turns to Annalie, and she nods. Ranath. 'Is she trying to stop us?'

'I don't know what she's doing.' Annalie bites her lip. She looks at the engineer. 'What kind of circuits?'

Jose glances at Jason, hesitant.

'It's all right, tell her.'

'The superstructure integrity mechanism.' Jose takes a breath, searching for words to explain. 'The station's construction is modular; it's a chain of separate sections held together by a lattice superstructure. That's how they used to build before we had assemblers. It also helps when they need to refit or replace something—they can disconnect a fragment of the ring or even remove it entirely without damaging the rest. The systems we saw activating, they keep everything together.'

'Could that be due to the current repairs?' Jason asks.

'No, that damage is too superficial. Mostly the outer surface and the generators.'

'So, if Ranath is trying to stop us, how would she—' Jason shakes his head. 'Why not just send the Sharks? Arrest us, contain us, that would be way easier.'

'I don't know if she's trying to stop us. I do know she'll try to use us. The question is, how can we be most useful?' Annalie leans on the chair, her gaze lost in thought. 'Ranath wanted to know if your plan would help or hinder her own. She knows your plan now. If it hindered her, she'd have stopped us already. So it will probably help, maybe by creating a distraction so the others have something else on their hands.'

She glances at Jason, and he nods. 'Makes sense. But then, why is she doing anything at all? Why not just let us proceed?'

Annalie's eyes widen. 'Because she wants to do it differently. She wants to do what you wouldn't.'

Of course. Richardson is Ranath's biggest enemy. 'She claimed I wanted to destroy Liberty—that's what she wants to do. She wants to destroy them and blame me for it.'

Annalie is shaking her head as if she can't believe his statement but can't find arguments to refute it.

Jose gasps. He puts his hand to his chest, pale as a ghost. 'The self-destruct. This is exactly what it would look like after someone's started the timer.'

They stare at each other for a frozen instant, then Jason jumps to his feet. They have to stop it. How? If they try to access the station's computer, the Sharks will notice. Or Ranath will notice and make the Sharks stop them. But the alternative is sitting on this bomb and waiting till she decides when it goes off. 'Assuming she wants to destroy Liberty—when would she time it?'

Jose closes his eyes, concentrating. 'Off the top of my head, three hours from now.'

'Call the others. We've got to stop her, Sharks or no Sharks.'

'They're on their way. Come.'

Jose leads the way to the station's ops room, a short way down the corridor from Jason's base. Rings of concentric consoles fill the entire space, facing outward to the full-length screens in the walls. The screens are blank now, but the consoles light up at Jason's touch, displaying status data for the myriads of Tian Gong's systems. Shit, where to even start?

Jose circles the room, checking the stations one by one.

'Is anyone on duty here?' Annalie asks.

'No, it's all automated,' Jose says. 'The critical systems have been mirrored to New Hope so they can monitor everything from there.'

'Could they have seen what you saw?'

'It's not something they'd have included. They are trying to repair the station, not blow it up.'

'But a self-destruct system? How is it possible no one would—'

'Because it wouldn't have crossed their minds they might need it. Or maybe they did see it, but she locked them up or paid them off.' Jose huffs, exasperated. 'Now, are we going to debate this or are we going to try and stop it?'

Annalie lifts her hands in an apology.

'What do you want us to do?' Jason asks.

'Check all the consoles for any icon with a timer or anything that looks like self-destruct or structural disassembly. We don't have the access codes to the main system, so our only chance is to find a back door.'

Jason waves to Annalie. 'Take the outside ring, I'll take the middle.'

They shuffle in silence, leaning over each screen. The other two engineers arrive to join the search, the five of them lurching forward like the hands of an ancient clock.

Jason is almost level with Jose when the man stops.

'Got it!'

Jason swings to look—then gasps at the sight of the orange letters flashing in the corner of the screen. 2:54:12. Less than three hours.

Jose is already typing a command, opening a menu and another. The other two engineers rush towards him. Jason steps away. He can't help them; he can only get in their way. He closes his eyes, trying to remember the projection Aya showed him—the thousand-legged spider that would take out Liberty, maybe also the elevator cable. Which? The Feidi or Singapore? How much destruction will it cause?

He heaves, cold sweat pouring down his back. How could anyone do that? Sow death on such scale? He peers over Jose's shoulder, hoping the timer was an illusion, a wrongly set clock, a mistake... No, it's still there, the digits rolling down, inexorable. 2:53:34. 2:53:33. 2:53:32.

Where is Annalie? Jason swivels to find her moored outside the circle of consoles, her face pale, her fingers clasped around the edge of a chair. She couldn't have seen the timer from there.

Jason crosses the room towards her. 'What is it?'

'I didn't believe she would do it. I still can't.' Annalie blinks, her eyes moist. She pulls in a breath, steadying herself, then lifts her arm to indicate her wrist band. 'I've checked my messages. Kene's been trying to reach me... Ranath summoned one of the graduates, a security expert, for a "special assignment." He wouldn't say what it was, but he's just returned with his residency certificate.'

Jason nods. 'Her own people might have refused. Or she hid it even from them.'

'That's not all. I tried to send a message back, but nothing's going through. I'm cut off.'

Fuck. Jason taps his wrist band, not trusting his contacts anymore. He selects the Alliance headquarters, an urgent call. The screen flashes orange. Local comms only. No outside access.

He's beginning to turn to the engineers when a voice rings in his ear.

'This is Par. We have an emergency we need to attend to. We will be leaving Tian Gong in a few minutes, and I'm not sure when we'll be back.'

'What's the emergency?'

'*The Covenant* is departing. We've got to retrieve the modules it'll dump before they run out of power.' Par stops, her voice hard with anger. 'They've got all our families there, and the refugees.'

So that's Ranath's plan. Annalie was right, she wants to use Tian Gong as a distraction. Jason glances at the engineers, their postures and nervous movements a clear sign that they haven't made any progress. No, Ranath's too clever; she'd have blocked all pathways. They won't get through, not in the time they have. The only chance is to try something she hasn't anticipated. Jason doesn't know what, but a heavy feeling settles in his chest.

'Your cargo shuttle's still in the dock,' Par continues, 'so you can use it to get to the elevator.'

'Are you going back to New Hope?'

'We'll stop there to drop off the last of the cultists.'

'Have you got them all?'

'All but five stubborn...' Par cuts off as if she muted the mike for the epithet.

'Okay, listen: tell them we need to sanitise the space or whatever you want, but take them all with you. On my authority.'

'My pleasure.'

'Also, Elizabeth Lake needs to return to New Hope.'

Next to him, Annalie shakes her head.

'Fine, but she must be at the section three dock in five minutes. We won't wait.'

'Understood.'

Annalie keeps shaking her head, her eyes wide, as if she, too, knows something she can't put into words.

'We found the timer,' he says. 'Two hours and fifty minutes.'

'Can they—'

'We'll do what we can. But you have to go back—try to talk

sense to Ranath or find that graduate who set this up and get them to undo it. Or at least send out a warning.'

She nods but doesn't move. 'Come with me. You're not an engineer, you won't—'

'You know I can't.'

'Why?'

'Go, Elizabeth. You have less than five minutes.'

They stare at each other for another moment. Jason has no control over his arms as they reach out and she falls into them. His daughter. His little girl.

'I'm sorry, Dad.'

'I'm sorry, too. But this is all I've dreamed of for years. I love you so much.' He plants a kiss at the top of her head, the scent of her skin unchanged from when he held her as a child.

'Annalie,' she whispers. 'My name is Anna Nathalie.' She looks up into his eyes and smiles. 'I'll see you soon. I've got so much to tell you!'

He pushes her away, propelling her towards the exit. 'I can't wait to hear it.'

And then she's gone, disappearing behind the door, only the heat of her embrace still warming his heart. It's enough.

THIRTY-FIVE
ANNA NATHALIE

Annalie sprints the length of the corridor leading to section three. She hopes she's running in the right direction; the floor here has no colourful stripes or any other signs to guide her. She needs her lenses—and if Ranath's still listening, then maybe it's a chance to talk to her.

Her finger bounces as she tries to locate the tiny emitter button, and she has to stop and wait the full five seconds before the familiar icons rematerialize on her lenses. Good, at least she's going the right way.

She focuses on the comms symbol, her voice shaky. 'Ranath? Please, we've got to talk. Ranath?'

No answer, not even a ping confirming that the message has gone through. No way to tell if Ranath's ignoring her, or if the signal is blocked just like the rest of the comms.

Annalie speeds up, panting as she falls inside the elevator and requests the dock. Thirty seconds left. When she bursts out of the doors on the outer ring, the Sharks are ushering the last of the yellow-robed cultists into the airlock, their gestures edgy and impatient. The silver uniforms still make her shiver, and she's not sure if she can trust anyone here, but she needs their help, at least with the comms.

Annalie pushes to the front of the line, past the medics and the scruffy figures of the cultists, to the tall woman who seems to be giving the orders. *Major Par (she), Sky Sharks Commander*, appears on her lenses. So helpful again, when the tech is not spying on her.

'Are the shuttle comms working?' she asks as she follows the woman inside.

Par looks at her as if she's lost her mind. 'Why wouldn't they?'

Annalie opens her mouth—but it's too much to try to explain, even if she was sure she could trust the Sharks.

'Later,' is all she manages to say.

She slides into the first available seat and closes her eyes as she sub-vocalises. *Ranath? Please respond. You can't let all those people die. We'll find another way. I'll do all I can, I swear.*

No answer, but this time the icon on her lenses confirms that the message has been transmitted.

Annalie tries again, then sends more pleading messages to Ester and Min Woo.

'If you're trying Ranath, don't bother,' Par says. 'Apparently she's disappeared.'

'*The Covenant?*'

Par shrugs as if to say, how am I to know? But even on *The Covenant*, Ranath should receive the message. Unless she's in cold-sleep. Anyway, it doesn't matter why she's out of reach— the fact is Ranath's not going to help them.

What now? Annalie bites her lip, struggling for focus as the shuttle pulls out of the dock at maximal acceleration. The Sharks really *are* in a hurry.

She looks at Par, and the woman returns her gaze with the same frustration and anger. 'What do you need?'

'Let me use your comms,' Annalie says. 'I... I don't trust my wire.'

Par's eyes widen again, but then she makes a sound that's something between a snort and a curse. She reaches to the wall and pulls out a screen attached to a flexible arm. She angles it towards Annalie but not so much that she can't see it herself, her brow lifting in a question.

Annalie nods. She needs all the allies now—it's just her word against the power of Ranath's lies. Somehow, she has to persuade the others to help her, persuade them that Tian Gong is in danger and that Ranath—and not her father—is responsible.

She starts with Nebu Owande, but the woman won't even take her call until Annalie introduces herself as Anna Nathalie Nevsky. Owande listens, her face growing increasingly confused—but not alarmed, not in the least.

'I'm sure there's an explanation,' Owande says with a cold smile. 'I'll be sure to ask Ranath. But you may start by telling me why Jason Nevsky is accessing my station's systems. My engineers are going to block him—'

'No! Please, listen. Tell your engineers to check the self-destruct settings. They can see for themselves. Maybe they can disable it, though I'm sure Ranath has anticipated—'

Nebu Owande waves her hand dismissively. Annalie gasps, her throat tight as she searches for words that may persuade her, when Par leans over from her seat.

'This is Major Par of the Sky Sharks. I strongly advise you to listen, Zhu Owande. I believe Ms Nevsky's telling the truth. Ranath's out of reach. *The Covenant* is departing, and as I understand, it's taking most of your people with it.'

Owande freezes. Her lips move without sound as she subvocalises, and then her eyes grow wide and her chest heaves in panicked gasps.

'I don't know what's going on,' she says eventually. 'But it doesn't look good.'

'Please contact your engineers, whoever's left,' Annalie says. 'Get New Hope's people to help. We have to be able to stop it.'

'How much time do we have?'

'Two and a half hours.'

Owande's mouth falls open. She nods curtly and disconnects.

Annalie pulls in a deep breath. Owande's engineers will fix it, surely. If she has any left.

She sends another message telling Kene to find Alejandro, only to hear that he, too, has disappeared.

'Keep searching,' she sends. That's all she can do.

'I'll give you three of my people,' Par says. 'They are good, but I don't know if anyone is good enough to break through Ranath's encryption in two hours.'

'Is she gone already? Can you catch up with *The Covenant* and—'

'No chance. We have the fastest shuttles, but they're no match for a real ship. They're still in the dock, but their engines are powered.'

'Shit. It's just us, then.'

'It's just you. I'm off getting my kids back before another fucking zhu decides to play chess with them.'

THIRTY-SIX
RANATH

The station is a mess—it was bad enough with the refugees, but at least they didn't stink. Now the Sun Seers are everywhere, hobbling down the corridors with dazed faces, their fetid robes mouldy brown rather than yellow. Ranath hurries past the grim crowd, down the arrivals passage and towards the shuttle that will ferry her to *The Covenant*. She'd stupidly given the Sharks the use of her private dock, so now she has to wade through their latest delivery. At least this bunch consists of those most able-bodied, though she's not sure she can say the same about their minds.

She passes a pile of discarded robes, the smell making her gag. A fitting farewell to this rotten world. Nothing like that could ever happen on Ark. Not long now. The inner door slides open, and she's only metres from the airlock and the shuttle waiting to take her away forever.

'You going to the elevator?' a rasping voice calls behind her.

Ranath spins to face a trio of cultists, and they shrink under her gaze. She considers informing them she doesn't give rides to humanity's detritus but decides they are not worth her breath.

They chose to come to Tian Gong and get themselves locked up in the radiation trap. It's a wonder they even understand English.'

The door seals behind her, finally cutting off the putrid smell.

'We're ready to go,' Min Woo says in her ear.

'Almost there.'

She's entering the airlock when her wrist band flashes the hateful icon. The Caretakers. Ranath laughs. Too late. They can't stop her now, no one can.

Except—they will try, and who knows what they'll come up with? Nothing is secure till she—till the settlers—reach Ark.

The icon flashes again. There's no sound, though, no high-pitched summons piercing her eardrum. Ranath hesitates. The icon looks different, too, somehow smaller, though she can't be sure. She touches the symbol, but instead of the three-minute countdown, the comms link lights up on her lenses. A single figure appears before her, an old man with grey hair and Asian features, his square head and stubborn gaze somehow familiar.

'Hello, Ranath. What a mighty mess you've made.' The man's chest heaves as he draws a long, tired breath. 'I told them years ago they had to watch you more closely, but who listens to old men?'

Ranath pauses. She wants to ask his name and why he'd reveal his face now, when they all refused her before—but she has to play it smart. There's a reason behind everything the Caretakers do, and she can't let them distract her with their tricks.

'What do you want?'

'Personally, I'd like to spend some time with my family, now that I get to see them again. But the others insisted I call you because they think I have a chance to fix what they've broken.' The man sighs, the lapels of his white-and-gold jacket crinkling with the motion of his wide chest. Where has she seen him before? 'See, your father was my friend back in the old days. A brilliant man. So devoted. Such a pity...'

Ranath presses her lips tight. She won't let them manipulate her. She waits another moment, her eyes locked with the man's.

Finally, he cracks a reluctant smile. 'You won't win, you know? We—they—however you want to call it—know too much. About your past, your deals, and the mess you're making with Tian Gong. Whatever you're trying to accomplish, they will stop you. A few weeks back, you could have negotiated. Now they are too angry with you to let you get away. They will sue you till you've got nothing—and no one—left. They will turn you into a symbol the same way they did with your father.

'That's really why I'm calling you now. I feel like I owe it to him, for the sake of that old friendship. Your life as you knew it is over—but I hear you're a capable player. I'm sure you can save yourself. Maybe even come back, one day. I'm told you owe my son a rematch. He really does like his fencing.'

The man nods, and before she can try to answer he's gone, the last pixels of his image vanishing from Ranath's lenses. She recognises him now, of course, from old images and the contours of his son's face. Li Wei, Li Qiang's father—he was—is—Destiny. Did Qiang know? Did he fake his ignorance back when they fenced, and he told her Richardson claimed to have found proof? Did Qiang give him that proof?

Ranath leans against the wall. She trembles, hot and cold waves sweeping up her flesh. Focus. The old man had been gone for years, she never knew if he was dead or in cold-sleep. She knows now. Destiny brought him back, and he can't be the only one. They are waking up the old guard, regrouping, getting ready for the final strike.

'Ranath?' Min Woo calls again. 'Where are you? Is everything all right?'

Ranath closes her eyes. She's so close. Everything she's dreamed of, all those years. Her Ark, so close she can almost smell its wide-open fields.

Li Wei is right—they won't let her get away. When the dust of Tian Gong has settled, someone will point their finger at her. Nevsky or his daughter, if either of them gets out alive, the Sharks, maybe even Nebu. It doesn't matter if they prove her guilty—they will come looking for her on Ark, barge in with their dirty feet and petty concerns. Contaminate the seed before it has the chance to take root.

She won't let them. It was never about her. Whatever happens to her, she won't let them destroy Ark.

'Ranath?' Ester's voice is tinged with panic.

'Change of plans.' Ranath swallows before she can say the next sentence. 'I'm not going with you.'

Even from this distance, Ranath can feel the walls vibrate as the great ship fires up its main engines. She lets herself revel in the sound and in the knowledge that nobody can catch up with them now, that all they need is to reach Ark and invoke the Habitat Ownership Act.

Ranath switches on her pad, the best encrypted gadget in the solar system, and probably the most expensive. Three new messages: one, an automated report on *The Covenant*'s progress, steadily accelerating after it's dumped the passenger modules for the Sharks to pick up. The second is the answer from Sunlit Prelate Smith, now in control of the church and much in need of donations to reform and repair her flock. Smith is only too eager to accept Ranath—and her generous membership fee— into the fold. Ranath, or rather, Katarina Soto, is one of them for now, the new identity gradually erasing her old self in global databases, one DNA record replaced by another. A trick she set up when she took over Renewal, just in case its past ever came back to haunt her.

The last message is the confirmation of the legal filing: the transfer of ownership of Ark to The Ark Collective, Inc. She draws a relieved breath. It's done. No one can touch them now. What they will do with Ark in the future is up to them.

She will still help, of course, as much as her new position will allow. This was always the backup plan—a backup to the backup, really. If things had gone as she'd planned, she'd still be the zhu of Renewal, watching over Ark from a distance. Joining them was the second option, a dream come true, except that they still needed help she could only provide from the outside. In the end, she must settle for the least favourite alternative. She's become a liability, a wanted fugitive. Her very presence could destroy them. Now she can keep Ark pure.

Ester and Min Woo will cooperate; she's told them to release any information the investigators will demand. They played no part in Tian Gong's demise. The one person who did will happily corroborate their account, reporting how she tricked him into helping. She is the villain in this story now, and she's fine with that. She can carry the burden. After all, it was never about her. Not in the least.

Ranath smiles, calm in the knowledge that she's done the right thing, protected what's most precious. Now it's only the small matter of getting herself out of here.

She returns to the corridor and the three cultists still waiting there.

'I've changed my mind,' Ranath—Katarina, she'd better get used to her new name—says. 'I can take you to the elevator. Get more of your comrades; I've got space.'

A moment later there's twenty of them there, jostling and gesticulating. Katarina picks up a discarded robe, holding her breath as she ties it around her. She motions them on, and they file behind her into her pristine private shuttle. By the time the airlock closes, she is but another yellow-robed figure, a pilgrim returning home from their desperate ordeal. The church has doctors and therapists waiting for them on the ground. The prelate has arranged private transport from the elevator to their main campus —or wherever else their new benefactor might choose to go. As long as her donations keep coming, they won't ask questions.

THIRTY-SEVEN

ANNA NATHALIE

Ranath is gone by the time they reach New Hope, only the blue-tinged glow of *The Covenant*'s engines still visible against the starry sky. Annalie keeps sending messages on repeat, but they all remain unanswered. She can't tell if Ranath's chosen to ignore them or if she's already cut the links to everything she's left behind.

Nebu Owande pings her just as the shuttle docks at the far end of New Hope's Axis. It departs again the moment Annalie and the three Shark security experts seal the doors behind them, rushing to the passenger modules *The Covenant* dropped in its wake.

'We're cut off.' Owande sounds broken, her words coming in spasmodic bursts. 'We can get deep enough... to see that the self-destruct is on. Nothing beyond that. We can just sit here and stare at the timer. She stole my crew. Dumped them in the modules.'

'Listen,' Annalie tries to interrupt, but Owande doesn't seem to hear her.

'Nobody here knows what's happened. Nobody to ask—'

'Listen! Tell your people to restore Tian Gong's comms.

And get everybody to Essa Nguyen's workshop. I'll be there in five minutes.'

Owande mutters a confirmation, but Annalie is already punching Essa's name in her contact menu.

'Liz! You're back!'

'What do you know?'

'Not much. Ranath and *The Covenant* are gone. And I'm guessing we're in some kind of trouble.'

'You're guessing right. Listen, call all the security and engineers you can find. We're trying to stop Tian Gong from self-destructing and taking Liberty with it.'

Essa's silent for a moment. 'Do they know?'

'I don't think so.'

'Then you might want to start by calling Zhu Richardson.'

Annalie nods, though Essa can't see it. The truth is, she's still hoping they can avert the disaster and the investigation that will come with it. Everyone will blame her father, of course; it won't matter that he never targeted Liberty. Ranath will weasel out of it somehow, Annalie is sure. Oh, the other zhus will hate her for it; their power games will continue, but Yun Ju justice is only meant for the insignificant and the inconvenient. And for outsiders, like her father. Still, time is running out, and every minute she clings to her hope is a minute less Liberty will have to evacuate.

The elevator door opens onto the familiar ground of New Hope's middle deck. Kene, Vithakan, and a few other graduates wait outside, Alejandro, pale and hunched, locked between them.

'She said your father was going to destroy Liberty. We were trying to stop it!' he blurts the moment she steps outside.

For all his stupidity, Annalie can't even blame him. She trusted Ranath, too, once. And believed the worst of her father. 'Can you undo it?'

'I can't do anything! She locked me out. I can't even open the doors.'

That's something Ranath would do. Still, he did it once, he might remember something useful. 'Come with us. If you're willing to help.'

'Oh, yes, he is,' Vithakan says gravely, his certainty reinforced by the three Sharks now beside him.

Annalie's wrist band beeps. Two hours left. She turns towards the Shield section and starts to run.

By the time they reach it, Essa's workshop has transformed into an ops centre. Mobile workstations have been rolled in, Tian Gong's and New Hope's engineers and security techs already at work. Lars catches her eye from the corner the Shield team have commandeered.

'Report to that man, he'll tell you where he needs help.' Annalie points the Sharks towards Lars, then turns to Alejandro. Anger and resentment still bubble through her veins, but it's not a time for grudges. 'Go with them. Do what you can—you're the only one who's already dug through that system.'

Alejandro pulls in a breath but ends up with just a nod. His eyes are moist and determined, though, so she knows he will give it all he has. He may be an asshole, but he's not a killer. Unlike Ranath.

What next? Essa's words ring in her ears—they've got to warn Liberty. She can't postpone, whatever it may mean for her father. The risk is too high. Richardson's not likely to take her message, though. She needs—

Annalie searches the room till her gaze rests on a tall Black woman in a flowing silver dress, standing by the wall with a confused expression as if she can't quite believe what's happening.

Annalie crosses the room towards her. 'Zhu Owande?'

'Yes.'

'I'm... Anna Nathalie Nevsky.' The name still catches in her throat, but she pushes on. 'We need to inform Liberty. They won't listen to me, but they will—'

'Do you really think—'

Annalie glances at the grim faces and hunched backs of the security techs. Not a sign of hope on any of them. 'Yes. They must evacuate.'

Spoken out loud, the words make the gears in her mind grind to a halt. Five thousand people. They are not prepared for total evacuation, never planned for anything at this scale. They thought they'd just go into the pods and wait out any emergency. Not this time.

Annalie swallows, her throat dry. 'The Sharks are gone. We can send them our shuttles, but I don't know how many...'

She doesn't finish. From the way Owande's eyes widen, she knows the woman has understood.

Owande straightens, new purpose in her face. 'I run a logistics co-op. This is exactly what we do.' She turns away, her lips moving as she subvocalises a command. 'Zhu Richardson, I have some bad news.'

What next? Annalie checks the time. One hour fifty. Fuck. Her eyes meet Essa's across the space now packed with bodies stooped over a variety of screens, pads, and projections.

We need a visual, she sends, walking towards him. *Tian Gong and whoever's near, and the estimated blast radius.*

'I was just getting those blast details—they don't keep them in the user manual... Okay, coming up now.'

The main screen at the back of the room brightens with a flat image: Tian Gong at its centre, surrounded by concentric rings of red, orange, and yellow. Liberty is there, a fat donut just at the edge of the red zone. Five of its remaining agro growth platforms trail behind it in orange and yellow. The same projection as what Ranath watched the other day, rewinding over and over. Looking for the exact time needed for the worst impact.

Damn, how could Annalie have missed it then? Too late for regrets. Only the future matters.

Something else catches her eye and she gasps: the elevator cable, the silky thread stretching all the way down to Singapore. It's on the edge of the yellow zone, almost out of danger—but one unlucky chunk of debris is all it might take.

The room falls perfectly still. The others must have noticed as well.

'Where are the Sharks?' someone asks. 'They've got to deploy the net!'

'They're gone. She took their families.'

'But this is the elevator! Do you know how many people—'

The voices are rising, arguments and ideas, desperation turning into accusations and attacks. She can't let it end like this.

'Stop it!' Annalie yells, and the room falls quiet. 'Get back to work. We must be able to crack that code. And we need the comms back to Tian Gong *now*.'

The faces around her are twisted by worry or disbelief, but they return to work and the voices settle into their previous level, if more breathless now and higher pitched.

Annalie looks at Essa. He has rolled next to her, his chair raised to standing position, his eyes fixed on the projection.

'We can still do it,' she whispers, but he doesn't answer.

THIRTY-EIGHT

JASON

Leaning against the far wall, Jason watches the engineers. Their nervous movements and terse, reedy voices tell him everything he needs to know. They can't get into the system, and they won't, not in time. Ninety minutes left. Thirty minutes, at least, to reach the shuttle and the elevator. Not the Singapore one, the Feidi or the Atlantic, just in case. The only chance to get out alive.

He closes his eyes, remembering the image Aya showed him: the elevator cable just at the edge of the blast zone, Liberty rushing into it. Five thousand people who don't give a damn about him or the fate of anyone on Earth. Who knows how many casualties on the ground, if the cable snaps?

Only minutes could save them. The stations move so fast, if they could delay the timer by twenty minutes, both the elevator and Liberty would be safe. Twenty minutes' difference. Twenty minutes later—or sooner.

Jason returns to the engineers, steadying his breath as the implications tighten his chest. 'Leave this. We're going back to the original plan.'

The engineers look up, heads shaking, mouths twisting in refusal.

'What's the point?' Jose asks. 'The station will be gone by then.'

'Not if we set it up to go off earlier.'

They stop, frowns turning into nods of understanding.

'We can do it,' Red says, the voice familiar from when they toiled over Aya's models.

'Fifteen minutes will be enough,' Yellow says. 'Twenty, to be sure.'

'No, we can't.' Jose rises from where he's been kneeling by the guts of a console. 'We timed everything for when the storm hits. We need the surge to set it off. Without it—'

He breaks off, his eyes locked with Jason.

'Fuck,' Red says.

'We can set it off manually,' Jason says slowly, desperate to keep his voice from shaking. 'That's always been an option.'

The engineers exchange glances. They know they can make it work—but they do not dare to ask the question.

'I will do it,' Jason says. He forces a chuckle. 'Just tell me which button to press so I don't mess up.'

Jose seems to want to protest, but it's a formality, something they all feel must be argued only for no other solution to be found. They have no time for that.

'Go. Make sure it works. You have less than an hour to get out safely.'

The engineers depart, each with a sheepish nod as if ashamed to want to live. Only Jose lingers in the door, an offer forming on his lips before Jason chases it away.

'Go. But promise me... Talk to Khalil. Tell him to look after my daughter.'

'I'll make sure he does.'

The door slides closed, and Jason is alone again, for the last time in his life.

THIRTY-NINE

ANNA NATHALIE

The main screen in Essa's workshop shows the live view of Tian Gong super-imposed on its expected position and the radius of the blast.

'They're leaving,' someone calls, pointing to the spark of a departing shuttle.

Another voice swears. 'Damn cowards. They still had time.'

'We keep working.' Lars's voice rises above the disgruntled noises. 'It's not over till it's over.'

Annalie traces the departing shuttle. Heading to the elevator, and back to Earth. Her breath catches in her throat. She knows—not sure yet what or how, but she *knows*.

She turns to Essa. 'Can you show me something? Privately. I want to see the blast range depending on Tian Gong's position.'

Nothing happens, as he works with his mind and his systems, then a projection appears on her lenses. Tian Gong, exploding at different points along its route.

'Ranath picked the best moment,' Essa says.

'She did.'

Their eyes lock for a moment. The answer worms its way

into her mind, but Annalie shakes it away. She looks over her shoulder, calling into the room. 'Do we have the comms?'

'What's the use—' a female voice starts, but another cry cuts her off.

'We have a connection! Someone's still there.'

A view of the Tian Gong's ops room appears in the inset on the main screen. Her father's there, alone, leaning on a console with a single flashing light.

He looks up, his eyes searching the room for cameras, then finding one. 'We're still locked out from the self-destruct systems. There's too little time left, so we've given up on that option.'

Annalie steps forward, meeting her father's eyes. 'We're no better here. And... we've just realised the blast might destroy the elevator cable.'

Father nods, unsurprised. 'We can't let it happen.'

He holds her gaze. There's no escaping the answer, and they both know it. Everything depends on the timing of the explosion, with Liberty and the elevator sliding into and out of the blast zone. He can't delay it past the timer—but he can make it come sooner.

'Is there... a manual over-ride?' Annalie asks, her throat dry. *Why have the others left already?* is really what she wants to know but the question won't pass her lips.

'Nothing I can access,' Father says. 'But... there's another option.'

The image freezes, and Dad appears on her lenses in a private link. 'We're going back to the original plan. We were going to use the storm, but we can overload the generators with —never mind the details. We can destroy the station while it's still in a safe position. If we're lucky, we might even get some of the debris field we wanted.'

'That's good, right?' she asks weakly.

'Yes. Yes, it's good.'

'Dad?'

He smiles, his eyes sad.

'You've got another shuttle, right?'

'We can't automate it. Someone has to set it off.'

'Dad!'

He blinks, and his face is back on the main screen for everyone to see. 'I will blow up the station in the next twenty minutes. It won't be a perfect explosion, and the self-destruct might still affect some segments, so pass the message to Liberty to hold the evacuation shuttles and get everyone deep inside the station. That's the best I can do.'

Annalie's shoulders heave, but nobody else seems to realise the implications, their voices rising in triumph.

'There will be a lot of finger-pointing after this event,' Dad continues, 'so let me leave you with this message: my goal was never to destroy Liberty or any other stations. If it were, I wouldn't be sacrificing myself now trying to save them. I can get five thousand lives for the price of my single one, and for me, that's a good deal. But I did come here with a purpose: I want you all to come back to the people you have abandoned. They are your kin. You tell yourselves you're about to be over-run, attacked, destroyed by the hungry masses outside your walls. They are only desperate because of what *you* have done to them. Ask the Council about the phage. About the disinformation campaigns. About seeding unrest and civil wars. Pretending you don't know doesn't absolve you from responsibility.'

Father pauses to glance at his wrist band. 'I've said all I have to say. The rest is up to you. Now, I want a few more words with... with Elizabeth.'

She can barely see him when her father's face returns to her lenses, blurred by the tears streaming down her cheeks.

'I'm sorry, honey. I thought we'd have more time.'

'You don't have to do that,' she says, and doesn't believe it.

'I got to hug you, though. I felt like I had a daughter back.'

'You do! I'm sorry. I should have talked to you earlier. I was so damn selfish!'

'Hush. You made the right choice when it mattered. You made me proud.'

'Dad...'

He wipes away a tear, his lips trembling as he tries to look strong for her. 'I've got to go now. I love you, baby girl.'

'I love you, too, Dad. I'm sorry. Dad? Dad?!'

But his face is gone from her lenses and from her world. There's only silence, and the sound of her sobs. She looks at the screen, at Tian Gong's ring sparkling like a lonely jewel against encroaching darkness—until it isn't, replaced by a cloud of fiery debris swelling in perfect silence.

Annalie hides her face in her hands. She doesn't listen to the buzz of distant voices, tentative at first, then rising in uneasy celebration. Her father is gone. True to his word, always fighting for a better future. At least she managed to tell him she was sorry. No, she's making it about herself again. He's dead. Gone forever. No words will ever make it better.

FORTY

ANNA NATHALIE

The man on the screen has a tired, narrow face, messy black hair, and eyes as bloodshot as Annalie's. He keeps his hands clasped, and she's sure they'd be shaking if he released them. Somehow his pain makes her feel better, comforts her with the knowledge that her father was respected and will be missed.

She listens as he tells her about the Watch, about their mission and her father's part. Khalil even makes her laugh when he reveals that his task was to expose Jason Nevsky's corruption.

'I'm sorry. I underestimated him.'

'Everyone did. But at least you weren't his child.' Annalie wipes her cheeks, her tears returning unbidden.

Khalil opens his mouth, but she doesn't want reassurance. Lies won't help anyone. She cracks a broken smile, an attempt to show that she's all right, or at least not willing to admit otherwise.

'What's going to happen now—to you? To the Alliance?'

'The official line is that your father acted alone. It fits all the parties, both here and in the Yun Ju. The media's already in a frenzy trying to decide if he's a hero or a villain.' Khalil shrugs. 'There's no proof of anyone else's involvement—other than the engineers, but we got them out before anyone here knew what was happening. The Alliance will probably survive. They're still needed, for all their faults. Especially if Aya gets the top job.'

'Who?'

'Your father's aide. Honest and committed, just like he was.'

Annalie pulls in a deep breath, the air catching in her chest in a silent sob. 'Shouldn't you... Shouldn't the Watch try to, I don't know, take over? Speak out, tell people the truth?'

Khalil shakes his head. 'We will speak out through our usual channels and share any information we have. But we must never take an official role. We are the Watch—we can't fulfil our mission from the inside. Still, I'm here if you ever need advice, or any help at all.'

'Thank you,' she says because it seems like the right thing to say. 'And thank you for... for being his friend.'

Kene waits outside her bedroom, far enough from the door Annalie can be sure her conversation was private.

'Thank you,' she says.

Kene's lips quiver in a smile that doesn't quite make it. She squeezes Annalie's arm, then follows her down the narrow corridor of the graduate quarters back to the common room. Voices hush as she appears, but it's a different kind of silence now: compassionate and respectful. Alejandro's still missing, Annalie realises, grilled by station security for his involvement. They will release him soon, she's sure. He was stupid, but he couldn't have known what Ranath had planned. She wouldn't have told him.

There's still no trace of the woman herself, though, other than *The Covenant*'s captain's confirmation that Ranath never came onboard. All they found was a voice message, time-stamped after the ship's departure, assuming full responsibility for her actions against Tian Gong. The other zhus are already speculating about where she might have gone and with whose help. Who benefits and who loses? Annalie can't make herself care. She'd punch the woman's face if she ever saw her again, but the only interest she deserves now is from law enforcement.

The elevator Annalie once took to that first meeting with Ranath carries her up to the inner ring. They've relocated the command centre back to the zhu's office, the space bigger and better equipped for their needs. It was Owande who suggested the move, too pragmatic and unfazed by the ghost of the former occupants, the idea seconded by Ag, desperate to bring the Shield team back to normal operations.

The great room seems untouched, as if its previous inhabitants only stepped outside for a moment. The scent of Ranath's perfume still swirls in the air, permeates her abandoned furnishings. The antique desk remains on the far side of the room, the horary still spinning, the chair facing them in a wordless challenge.

Annalie plops herself down next to Essa at what used to be Ester's workstation. Owande has commandeered the projection table, now tracking the debris and coordinating the Yun Ju's 'all-drones-on-deck' emergency response. Now in her element, Tian Gong's zhu has turned into the embodiment of stoic efficiency. Richardson's red face keeps shouting from an inset in the projection, but Owande remains unfazed. The other zhus look more cool-headed but no less angry. They check in periodically, while their own people analyse the risk to their stations.

There's a lot of debris.

Annalie stares at the projection, wondering which of the myriad red dots is her father's shattered corpse. Probably too soft to count as risk, even frozen. Pity. She'd like it to ram into Richardson's foaming face.

'The Sharks are back,' Essa says as a flotilla of white arrowheads appears at the edge of the display.

Owande zooms in on the Sharks' craft and the dark outlines of *The Covenant*'s modules they tow.

'Good to hear, Par,' she says into the intercom. 'We've set up docking stations with power sources, so you can leave the modules here and—'

Owande breaks off. Annalie can't hear Par's reply, but she can guess the major won't be happy to leave her family in the care of another zhu, even if it's her old Tian Gong boss.

'Fine,' Owande says. 'Leave some of your people to oversee. And yes, New Hope is forecasted to remain safe for at least the next three days.'

Half of the Shield team are modelling the debris now, the fraction that has settled into elliptical orbit, like what her father intended. There's enough of it to pose persistent risk to the Yun Ju, but not enough to become overwhelming. Enough to make the zhus consider setting temporary bases on Earth, but not enough to make it unavoidable.

'What are you going to do now?' Essa asks.

'No idea.'

'New Hope will be looking for a new zhu...'

Annalie laughs. 'You applying?'

'Hell, no. But I hear they don't want Renewal in charge again.'

'Don't they own it?'

'Habitat Ownership Act has been invoked. Renewal will collect rent, but they won't run the station. Anyway, that's what Lars is saying. He's been quite involved.'

'He'd make a good zhu.'

'Maybe.'

They drift into silence. Annalie is trying very hard not to think about anything, but her gaze keeps returning to the debris field in Owande's projection. They've instructed the drones to search for human remains, but...

'I'll go back for a while,' she says. 'Meet the people my

father worked with. Figure out what's best. Clear out his apartment...'

Her voice breaks. Once, she swore she'd never go back to that place. Now she'd do anything to find him there.

'I wish I'd met him,' Essa says.

'Yeah.' Annalie pulls in a breath before it turns into another sob. 'What are you going to do?'

'I'm staying here. The infrastructure is perfect for my connections. I don't know of any place on Earth where I could live a normal life.'

Of course. There's no one solution to the problems, no single answer. But then, her father's plan was never about the Yun Ju as a place—it was about the concept of Yun Ju vs Earth, the exploiters and the exploited, the insiders and the outsiders. They can move all of the Yun Ju to Earth and never change anything. Or they can remain in orbit but start working like partners. That's what her father wanted, and that's her task now, her own mission.

Annalie's eyes brighten. 'It shouldn't be here or there, you know? We shouldn't have to choose.'

'Break down the walls?' Essa asks. 'Seize the means of production?'

A stick figure carrying a red flag appears on her lenses, but she has no idea what it means.

'We need open access: for people, for ideas, for technology. No more embargoes. And no more manipulation. We should be here to make sure the Yun Ju never tries their tricks again. And they have to be part of the same supply flow as the rest of us, the same restrictions.'

'How are you going to do it?' Essa asks.

'No idea. But you are going to help me.'

This time fireworks erupt on her lenses. 'I may be tempted to accept this new position.'

'Good. Because I wasn't asking.' Annalie grins. 'Come.

Kene's getting the graduates together. I've invited Ag and the team, too. There may be snacks and drinks involved, and I've ordered a meal for you.'

'I know. Sam told me. And by the way, your party is now in the banquet hall. And everyone's invited. Lars's treat.'

'Oh, that smells like the launch of an election campaign.'

'As long as there's free drinks...'

'I didn't know you drank.'

'Only when Sam is around.'

'Does it mean I will finally get to meet Sam? I was wondering if you might be having an imaginary friend...'

'Oh, Sam is very real, I can assure you.'

They leave the office, Owande and the Sharks winding down for the day. The worst of the debris has been cleared out for now. More is still out there, tracing its own orbit until it crosses their paths again in a few days.

Kene, Vithakan, and Hiroko meet them in the corridor, and then Sal, Henry, and Ennie from the Shield team join along the way. They smile when they see her, and she smiles back. They are her friends, and they know her true name, and they know her.

There's so much work to be done.

Her father is dead, and she can't change it. She can't change the past. But the future? Oh, she is so looking forward to the future.

A LETTER FROM THE AUTHOR

Dear Reader,

Thank you for reading *Inversions*. I hope you enjoyed Jason, Ranath and Annalie's journeys. If you want to join other readers in hearing all about my new releases and bonus content, you can sign up for my Storm newsletter.

www.stormpublishing.co/mv-melcer

Or sign up at mvmelcer.com/newsletter

If you liked this book and could spare a moment to leave a review that would be hugely appreciated. It doesn't have to be much—even a few words can help other readers discover my books for the first time. Thank you so much!

I wrote *Inversions* to examine what happens after the story ends, after the hero fights their battle and rides into the sunset. In *Refractions*, Nathalie didn't quite "ride into the sunset"—but she made a choice, a decision that would affect those left behind on Earth. While she was sure her decision was right, she also knew she wouldn't have to live with its consequences (at least until she returned to Earth). *Inversions* is that story, the tale of consequences and the effect on those who took no part in making the decision. Of course, things don't turn out as we hoped or expected, the happy end is not really happy, or at least not for everyone. Other people now make their choices—Jason, following in Nathalie's footsteps, Ranath, dreaming up a brave new world, and Anna Nathalie, struggling to define her future separate from her legacy. And as they fight their battles, they make decisions that will affect those around them, and those who come after, again and again. I believe it is an apt conclusion in our turbulent times. In the end, that's all any of us can do— make the best choice, knowing that it will matter, sometimes to those we will never meet.

Whatever your choice, I hope you choose well.

Thank you again for being part of this journey. I hope you stay in touch!

M V Melcer

bsky.app/profile/mvmelcer.com

APPENDIX

Summary of book one: *Refractions*

After two centuries of turmoil over climate change, plague, and scarcity wars, Earth has emerged bruised. The New Cold War keeps borders closed while the rich elites oversee the masses from the luxury of their orbital habitats. Meanwhile, human settlers have reached the distant planet Bethesda in an attempt to establish the first human colony in another solar system.

Nathalie Hart is determined to save her family. But as she tries to stop life-saving medicine from being smuggled into orbit, the protests she instigates end in riots and more deaths. Traumatised and desperate to escape her guilt, Nathalie joins an international rescue mission to Bethesda, which has mysteriously stopped communicating.

Halfway through their journey, the crew is pulled out of cryo-sleep to discover sabotage that has killed the captain. Political manoeuvring throws Nathalie—the only neutral crew member—into the command spot. The international teams are sharply divided, and it appears that something—or someone—on the ship is spurring them on.

On Bethesda, they find the remnants of a thriving settlement—but all the five thousand colonists are dead, murdered as they turned on each other in something akin to madness. Autopsies reveal that the colonists had an experimental version of Mind-Link, a brain-computer interface, designed to alter the minds of the users.

This discovery wakes up a secret—and well-armed—secondary crew hidden in a concealed cryo-chamber. Their leader, the Guardian, takes over command. Nathalie realises that everything that went wrong on their mission did so by design—from the sabotage, to the animosities among the crew, to her own position as the unwilling commander—everything was set up so they would fail to reveal Bethesda's experiment.

When Nathalie manages to unite the crew to oppose the Guardian, he reveals the reasons behind his mission: with resources depleted, Earth is teetering on the brink of war and famine. Destiny, a secretive faction among the orbital elites, created the mind control device to guide humanity towards what they consider to be a more sustainable existence.

Nathalie believes that the Guardian's predictions are correct, and that Earth may indeed be heading for disaster. She thinks about the only surviving member of her family, her nephew Jason, and what it might mean for his future. But she realises that even if Destiny's intentions were good, the mind-controlling device would give them too much power. No one should be allowed to steer others' thoughts and beliefs.

The Guardian dies as he attempts to destroy the ship to prevent her from sending a message back to Earth—but Nathalie sends her warning, not knowing if she has just plunged humanity into an even worse fate.

ACKNOWLEDGEMENTS

A novel has many midwifes, and I am very grateful to all those who helped this baby enter the world, either by direct involvement or indirect support.

My big thanks go to the Elementals, my wonderful critique group, beta readers, and cheerleaders: Laurence Brothers, L D Colter, M. E. Garber, S. L. Harrison, Sandy Parsons, and Lettie Prell. Thank you for sticking with me on this journey and all your advice and encouragement. And for catching all those plot holes!

To Adam Jackson, a friend and a story doctor extraordinaire, for the many late night calls where you patiently got me unstuck by consistently asking all those pesky questions... Your advice and encouragement has meant a lot.

Thank you to the entire team at Storm Publishing for bring this novel to the readers. Thank you to Kathryn Taussig, my editor, and to Alex, Anna, Elke, Naomi, Oliver, and all the others behind the scenes. To Phillip Dannels for the great covers for both books.

Big thanks to the team at Jabberwocky Literary Agency and especially to my agent, Lisa Rodgers, for her insightful comments, her advice, and her encouragement. These are truly appreciated.

To Robert T.L. Chang, who developed the original Mandarin vocabulary used in the world of *Refractions*, and who proved once again that I should not try to translate anything myself. Thank you for coming to the rescue!

To David DeGraff, for science advice—though I strategically didn't ask about the big issues (like the solar storms) and I take full responsibility for any bad science in the novel.

To the folks from the Menagerie, for cheering me on.

To Dave Macarthur, for helping to preserve my sanity during the launch of *Refractions*.

To Mary and Emma Maree again, for letting me cry on your shoulders.

This book is dedicated to my husband, Jan. I could have never done this without your support and encouragement over the years. Thank you for being my friend and my companion, my problem-fixer and my wellness manager. Thank you for your patience on all those lonely days when I wouldn't leave my office. Thank you for being my cheerleader through the high and the low. I know I can always trust you to have my back. Without you, I would never be able to do it.

Thank you.

9 781805 083689